# HIDDEN NATURE

## Also by Nora Roberts

# Series

Irish Born Trilogy
*Born in Fire* • *Born in Ice* • *Born in Shame*

Dream Trilogy
*Daring to Dream* • *Holding the Dream* • *Finding the Dream*

Chesapeake Bay Saga
*Sea Swept* • *Rising Tides* • *Inner Harbor* • *Chesapeake Blue*

Gallaghers of Ardmore Trilogy
*Jewels of the Sun* • *Tears of the Moon* • *Heart of the Sea*

Three Sisters Island Trilogy
*Dance Upon the Air* • *Heaven and Earth* • *Face the Fire*

Key Trilogy
*Key of Light* • *Key of Knowledge* • *Key of Valor*

In the Garden Trilogy
*Blue Dahlia* • *Black Rose* • *Red Lily*

Circle Trilogy
*Morrigan's Cross* • *Dance of the Gods* • *Valley of Silence*

Sign of Seven Trilogy
*Blood Brothers* • *The Hollow* • *The Pagan Stone*

Bride Quartet
*Vision in White* • *Bed of Roses* • *Savor the Moment* • *Happy Ever After*

The Inn Boonsboro Trilogy
*The Next Always* • *The Last Boyfriend* • *The Perfect Hope*

The Cousins O'Dwyer Trilogy
*Dark Witch* • *Shadow Spell* • *Blood Magick*

The Guardians Trilogy
*Stars of Fortune* • *Bay of Sighs* • *Island of Glass*

Chronicles of The One
*Year One* • *Of Blood and Bone* • *The Rise of Magicks*

The Dragon Heart Legacy
*The Awakening* • *The Becoming* • *The Choice*

The Lost Bride Trilogy
*Inheritance* • *The Mirror*

# eBooks by Nora Roberts

### Cordina's Royal Family
*Affaire Royale* • *Command Performance* • *The Playboy Prince* •
*Cordina's Crown Jewel*

### The Donovan Legacy
*Captivated* • *Entranced* • *Charmed* • *Enchanted*

### The O'Hurleys
*The Last Honest Woman* • *Dance to the Piper* • *Skin Deep* • *Without a Trace*

### Night Tales
*Night Shift* • *Night Shadow* • *Nightshade* • *Night Smoke* • *Night Shield*

### The MacGregors
*The Winning Hand* • *The Perfect Neighbor* • *All the Possibilities* • *One Man's Art* • *Tempting Fate* • *Playing the Odds* • *The MacGregor Brides* • *The MacGregor Grooms* • *Rebellion/In from the Cold* • *For Now, Forever*

### The Calhouns
*Suzanna's Surrender* • *Megan's Mate* • *Courting Catherine* •
*A Man for Amanda* • *For the Love of Lilah*

### Irish Legacy
*Irish Rose* • *Irish Rebel* • *Irish Thoroughbred*


### Jack's Stories
*Best Laid Plans* • *Loving Jack* • *Lawless*


*Summer Love* • *Boundary Lines* • *Dual Image* • *First Impressions* • *The Law Is a Lady* • *Local Hero* • *This Magic Moment* • *The Name of the Game* • *Partners* • *Temptation* • *The Welcoming* • *Opposites Attract* • *Time Was* • *Times Change* • *Gabriel's Angel* • *Holiday Wishes* • *The Heart's Victory* • *The Right Path* • *Rules of the Game* • *Search for Love* • *Blithe Images* • *From This Day* • *Song of the West* • *Island of Flowers* • *Her Mother's Keeper* • *Untamed* • *Sullivan's Woman* • *Less of a Stranger* • *Reflections* • *Dance of Dreams* • *Storm Warning* • *Once More with Feeling* • *Endings and Beginnings* • *A Matter of Choice* • *One Summer* • *Summer Desserts* • *Lessons Learned* • *The Art of Deception* • *Second Nature* • *Treasures Lost, Treasures Found*

# Anthologies

*From the Heart* • *A Little Magic* • *A Little Fate*

*Moon Shadows*
(with Jill Gregory, Ruth Ryan Langan, and Marianne Willman)

The Once Upon Series
(with Jill Gregory, Ruth Ryan Langan, and Marianne Willman)
*Once Upon a Castle* • *Once Upon a Star* • *Once Upon a Dream* •
*Once Upon a Rose* • *Once Upon a Kiss* • *Once Upon a Midnight*

*Silent Night*
(with Susan Plunkett, Dee Holmes, and Claire Cross)

*Out of This World*
(with Laurell K. Hamilton, Susan Krinard, and Maggie Shayne)

*Bump in the Night*
(with Mary Blayney, Ruth Ryan Langan, and Mary Kay McComas)

*Dead of Night*
(with Mary Blayney, Ruth Ryan Langan, and Mary Kay McComas)

*Three in Death*
*Suite 606*
(with Mary Blayney, Ruth Ryan Langan, and Mary Kay McComas)

*In Death*
*The Lost*
(with Patricia Gaffney, Ruth Ryan Langan, and Mary Blayney)

*The Other Side*
(with Mary Blayney, Patricia Gaffney, Ruth Ryan Langan,
and Mary Kay McComas)

*Time of Death*
*The Unquiet*
(with Mary Blayney, Patricia Gaffney, Ruth Ryan Langan,
and Mary Kay McComas)

*Mirror, Mirror*
(with Mary Blayney, Elaine Fox, Mary Kay McComas, and R. C. Ryan)

*Down the Rabbit Hole*
(with Mary Blayney, Elaine Fox, Mary Kay McComas, and R. C. Ryan)

ALSO AVAILABLE . . .
*The Official Nora Roberts Companion*
(edited by Denise Little and Laura Hayden)

# HIDDEN NATURE

# NORA ROBERTS

ST. MARTIN'S PRESS
NEW YORK

First published in the United States by St. Martin's Press, an imprint of St. Martin's Publishing Group

HIDDEN NATURE. Copyright © 2025 by Nora Roberts. All rights reserved. Printed in the United States of America. For information, address St. Martin's Publishing Group, 120 Broadway, New York, NY 10271.

www.stmartins.com

Endpaper: sky © Piotr Kloska/Shutterstock

The Library of Congress Cataloging-in-Publication Data is available upon request.

ISBN 978-1-250-37085-3 (hardcover)
ISBN 978-1-250-37086-0 (ebook)

Our books may be purchased in bulk for promotional, educational, or business use. Please contact your local bookseller or the Macmillan Corporate and Premium Sales Department at 1-800-221-7945, extension 5442, or by email at MacmillanSpecialMarkets@macmillan.com.

First Edition: 2025

This edition was printed by Bertelsmann Printing Group.

10  9  8  7  6  5  4  3  2  1

To Bruce and Jason,
my own Mr. Fix-Its

# PART ONE

# DEATH

Now cracks a noble heart. Good night, sweet prince,
And flights of angels sing thee to thy rest!
—William Shakespeare

# CHAPTER ONE

The day Sloan Cooper died began before dawn and ended shortly before midnight. As a corporal in the Natural Resources Police, she'd helped take down a trio of men who spent most of the fall harassing, robbing, and assaulting hikers on the trails in the Western Maryland mountains.

The three men, two brothers and their father, deemed the public lands their property, as sovereign citizens, and all who crossed their borders trespassers.

Now, after a three-day operation during which she'd personally disarmed the father, one John aka Red Bowson, all three were in custody. Sloan figured they'd have a nice long stay in a federal prison to consider the error of their ways.

So satisfying.

Plus, she wanted that third chevron, wanted the rank of sergeant, and this bust could push that through.

Since she'd won the toss, she manned the wheel on the drive back to the Special Ops Division while her partner checked in with his wife.

Joel Warren, a beanpole of a man with deep brown skin and close-cropped curls under his felt Stetson, had a deceptively lazy manner that masked a sharp mind and enough energy to power a small city.

They'd trained together, and both had aimed for the Criminal Investigative Bureau. He, born and raised in DC, and she, from a small town in those western mountains, had found their rhythm early on.

Their partnership of nearly five years worked despite—or maybe because of—their opposing personalities. He: easygoing, do the job, and go home. And she: intense, driven, and buttoned-down.

As she drove, she listened with half an ear as he told his bride they were on their way home.

He downplayed the three brutal days, didn't mention the fact they'd been fired on or the black eye Sloan had earned during the takedown.

Not just to spare Sari the darker details, Sloan knew. Because, for Joel, that was then. This was now.

She had to admire how he compartmentalized.

When he finished, he rearranged his endless legs.

"Not supposed to tell you yet."

"Tell me what? Since you're going to."

"Told my mama, and Sari told her folks. Supposed to wait a couple-three more weeks, but—"

She was a trained investigator, and she knew Joel like she knew a brother, if she'd had one. "You're kidding! Sari's pregnant?"

His brown eyes twinkled as he pointed at her.

"See, I didn't tell you. You concluded, and you're right, sis. I knocked Sari's fine ass up. Nine weeks gone."

"Holy shit, Joel!" Delight had her pumping her fist in the air before she punched his shoulder. "You're going to be a daddy."

"Already feel like one. Weird, right, but I do. Mama says it's a girl, and you know Mama ain't never wrong."

"Mama Dee ain't never wrong. But you're all good if it's a boy?"

"I'm all good."

"How's Sari?"

"She puked every morning for about a month running, but that's passed. Halle-freaking-lujah. She says how she can't wait to get fat. We've got a lot to be thankful for when Turkey Day rolls around in a couple weeks."

He looked at her with a shining grin. "You're gonna be an auntie, sis."

"Auntie Sloan will always have cookies. I'm so happy for you, Joel. Oh, man, I'm so happy for both of you. You'll be great at it."

"How about you and Matias? Ever think about taking that next step?"

"As in moving in together?"

She hadn't thought to check in with the man she'd been seeing for most of a year as Joel had with Sari. Then again, Matias wouldn't expect it—and wouldn't have appreciated a check-in after ten at night.

"Not sure," she concluded. "Mostly no, but not sure. And I know what you're thinking." She ticked a look in his direction. "*Not sure* means just *no*. But it really means *not sure* and *not yet*. We're fine like we are."

"Mm-hmm."

She only rolled her eyes, as she knew that sound. It meant, in his opinion, she was fooling herself.

Maybe so, but she liked her life just as it was.

But he said, "I need a Dr Pepper."

"You always need a Dr Pepper."

"Dr Pepper gives me my sparkle."

"So you say, but fine. I have to pee anyway. And we might as well gas up while we're at it."

Another mile either way would've changed everything, but she cut quickly to the right and took the next exit.

She drove half a mile, winding through the almost middle of nowhere to a quick stop. She pulled up to the pumps.

"You gas it up. I'll buy the expectant daddy his drink of choice. Daddy," she repeated. "Holy shit, Joel!"

She got out of the truck, an athletic woman with her blond hair secured in a bun under her Stetson. Her eyes (the left sporting a shiner), large, almond-shaped, and deeply green, dominated a face of strong cheekbones, a slim nose, and a long, sharply defined mouth.

Like Joel's easy manner, people often mistook those large, fairylike eyes for soft. She could bench-press a hundred and fifty—thirty over her own weight—send a speed bag singing, and run a mile in six minutes flat.

She'd spent her childhood hiking the trails in the Alleghenies, swimming or boating on the lake in the summer, skiing, snowshoeing in the winter. The outdoors had honed her physique and her mindset. Her ambitions and chosen career made, to her thinking, the best of them.

She stepped into the little mart thinking about emptying her bladder, then finishing the second half of the drive home, where she'd take a long, hot shower and sleep in her own bed.

Even as the door shut behind her, she knew something was wrong.

The stance of the man with his back to her—white, brown hair, six feet, a hundred and sixty—and the wide eyes that read fear in the counterman facing her, had her resting a hand on her weapon.

It happened fast.

It took an eternity.

The man spun, and the weapon already in his hand fired.

The first shot grazed across her forehead, a sharp, shocking sting that gave her an instant to draw.

But the second struck her chest, threw her back and down with pain beyond comprehension.

She saw the man running by her—mid-thirties, brown eyes, little scar on the right cheek—as her breath wheezed, as the shocking pain spread.

She tried to raise her weapon, but the world grayed. She tried to shout a warning to Joel, but could barely draw breath.

The shooter—black Adidas low-tops, gray trench, jeans frayed at the bottom—began to fade out of her mind.

Dimly, she heard another shot, then one more.

Then Joel was beside her, pressing down on her chest so the pain screamed in her head. "Sloan, Sloan! You look at me. You fucking stay with me. Officer down, Officer down. Need immediate medical assistance."

She stared at his face—she knew that face—as his words fell away and into a void.

Then his face was close, so close it blocked everything else, and his eyes—dark as two new moons—were fierce.

"You stay with me. Help's coming. I'm here, right here."

"Hurts."

"I know, sis, I know. You use that, use that hurt and stay with me. I'm with you. Don't you go anywhere. Stay here, stay with me."

Pain obliterated time and space. She drowned in it, and went under. When she surfaced, the pain came with her. Screaming like the sirens. Faces she didn't know snapped out words she couldn't understand.

Cold, bitter cold covered her, but didn't numb the wild, unrelenting pain.

But she heard Joel—somewhere as the world sped by.

"You're strong. You're fucking tough, and you're gonna fight. You hear me? You hear me, Sloan?"

Everything was white. Everyone shouted, but the voices bounced off her ears and away. Lights, too many lights hurting her eyes, so she closed them.

Then it was Joel again, gripping her hand, his eyes fierce. "I'm right here. I'll be right here. You fight, goddamn it, Sloan. Don't you give up."

Then it all went away. The pain, the lights, the voices. It all went to black.

When the light came back, it came soft, gauzy. She felt free in that light as she floated. As she looked down at the woman on the table. So pale, so still. So much blood.

All those people around her. They'd cut the poor thing open, she thought, before she realized, with a kind of mild interest, she was the poor thing.

*It's me down there.*

Someone shouted *Clear!* and the paddles made her body jerk. Floating, she sighed. They were working so hard, and she—*I*—looked tired of it. So tired of it.

*You can let her go*, she thought. *Let me go.*

The paddles hit again, and she ignored them.

She could see so much from where she floated. Joel, pacing, pacing, a phone at his ear. She could even hear him.

"She's still in surgery. Her family's on their way. I'll call you when she's out."

She watched him swipe tears away, and that touched her. She wanted to tell him she was fine, peaceful in this soft, pretty light. But there was blood on his shirt, and his eyes were shattered.

"We're not going to lose her, Sari. We're not. She's going to fight. She won't give up. She's not finished yet. Sari, she's not giving up."

*All right, all right, damn it.*

Once again, she looked down at herself. She thought of Joel and a baby coming. She thought of her parents, her sister.

The next time the paddles struck, she let them take her back to the black.

When she woke, the pain was there, but dulled, as if smothered under a warm blanket. The air had a sting to it, one she recognized as hospital even before she registered the beep of machines.

The light, dim but harsh, pressed against her eyelids and made her long for just a moment of the soft and gauzy.

"She's waking up, Joel. Sloan? Baby, it's Mom. Open your eyes now, sweetie. Sloan, my baby, open your eyes."

She blinked. It took such effort and, since everything blurred, didn't seem worth it. She started to close her eyes again.

"Come on now. Give my hand a squeeze and open your eyes. There you are."

She felt her mother's lips press to the back of her hand, her palm, her fingers.

"There's my girl."

"Hospital," she managed. Her throat felt sandpapered, her tongue as thick and dry as a plank.

"That's right, and you're going to be fine. Just fine."

And it came rushing back. The mini-mart, the man at the counter. The explosion of pain.

"Shot!" She tried to push up, barely managed to move her head. "Joel."

"Right here, sis."

She saw them now as her vision cleared. Her mother, ghost pale, blue eyes shadowed and red-rimmed, and her partner, looking worn to the bone.

"How bad?"

"Not bad enough to stop you." He bent down, kissed the top of her mother's head as he closed a hand around Sloan's. "I'll get the doctor."

"Everything's going to be fine now." Elsie Cooper kissed her daughter's hand again. Tears, two warm raindrops, spilled on Sloan's knuckles. "Your dad and Drea are close by. We've been taking shifts."

"How long? How long?"

"You've been sleeping awhile, and healing. This is day three. They put you in a coma at first so you could just sleep. And here you are waking up. Baby? You feel this button?" She guided Sloan's hand. "If it hurts, you can press this button for medicine."

"Okay. I feel . . . mushy."

A tear slid down Elsie's cheek as she smiled. "I bet you do. Here's the nurse. This is Angie. She's been really good to you. To all of us."

"Glad to see you awake."

The nurse wore her gray-streaked black hair in a bob and had red flowers over the pale blue of her scrubs. Sloan judged her at about forty, and felt a trickle of relief when she noted the woman's brown eyes smiled along with her lips.

"Dr. Vincenti will come in shortly. Elsie, Joel, why don't you give me a few minutes to look after Sloan?"

"We'll be right outside," Elsie promised her.

"How bad?" Sloan asked the minute the door shut. "How bad am I hurt?"

Angie checked the IVs, the monitors, then Sloan's pulse by hand.

"Joel said you'd want it straight, so I'll tell you it was bad. And now it's better. You're going to make a full recovery, and you'll have to stop yourself from pushing that. Dr. Vincenti and the surgical team? You don't get much better."

"I died."

"You're very much alive." Angie held a cup with a straw to Sloan's lips. "Sip some water."

Because the thirst raged, Sloan obeyed. "On the operating table, I died. They had to bring me back."

Angie set the cup aside, then took Sloan's hand. "You had an experience?"

"Did I? They zapped me, didn't they? My heart stopped and they zapped me. I think three times."

"The bullet missed the heart, but we'll say the surgery was tricky.

Vincenti's very, very good. You're young, healthy, and strong. And putting those factors aside, we can say, it wasn't your time."

"Three times."

"Yes. And here you are, alive, awake, aware. Your vitals are good. You're stable. If I'm a judge—and I am—we'll move your condition up to good within the next twenty-four. Now, if you're not too tired, and it's okay if you are, the rest of your family wants to see you."

"Yes, please."

"Family makes a difference, too."

Gently, Angie eased Sloan up and turned the pillow to the cool side.

"People who love you make a difference. And you're loved. The call button's right here if you need me. Dr. Vincenti's on his way."

Her father and sister came in. Her father, silver threads starting to gleam in his brown hair and trim beard, his green eyes sheened with tears, leaned over, pressed his rough, unshaven cheek to hers.

She felt him trembling, pulling in air to stop tears.

"I'm okay, Dad. They said I'm okay."

"Scared the crap out of me, Sloan. Give me just a minute."

While she did, she looked over his shoulder at her sister. Drea, face splotchy from recent weeping, her usual lustrous brown hair dull and yanked back in a careless tail, swiped at eyes as blue as their mother's.

She took Sloan's hand, smiled. Said, "Whew."

"Sums it up."

Dean Cooper lifted his head, then cupped Sloan's face in hands as rough as his stubble. "Try not to do that again."

"Okay, Dad."

In a lifelong habit, he kissed her forehead, her cheeks, her lips. "I know you're tired, and rest is what you need. But know we're here."

"I do." She worked to clear the clouds from her brain. "Who's minding the business?"

"We got it covered. Don't you worry."

"Plenty of people in Heron's Rest were pulling for you," Drea added. "And plenty of them pitched in to help keep things going."

"And Joel? He's our hero. You're both heroes."

She felt herself starting to fade, struggled to stay awake. "Did we get him? White male, mid-thirties, brown and brown . . . Did we get him?"

But she dropped off and didn't hear the answer.

When pain slapped her awake again, Joel sat by the bed reading the worn paperback copy of Stephen King's *It* he always kept in his go bag.

Sloan remembered asking him why he kept that particular book packed. He'd told her it reminded him, when he was away from home, that whatever they dealt with couldn't be as bad as Pennywise.

To test his theory, she'd read it herself and could only agree.

"Came close this time," she mumbled.

He looked up, then set the book aside. "Hey there."

"Did we get him?"

"Hit the button. You're hurting."

She shook her head and immediately wondered how the movement could spread more pain. "I want to stay awake. The shooter."

"I heard the shots—two shots. He ran out, fired at me. Missed. I returned fire and winged him. Got his plate number, the make and model of the beater he jumped into, but I couldn't pursue. You were on the floor, bleeding."

"Something off—counterman terrified. I had my hand on my weapon, but he swung around, fired. Twice?"

"Twice."

"I didn't even draw my weapon."

"Yeah, you did, sis. It was in your hand when I got to you. I called for an ambulance and relayed the plates, vehicle, and suspect description. They had him by the time they were loading you in the ambulance.

"Push the button and I'll tell you the rest."

She pushed it, and the pain backed off a few inches.

"Okay, responders spotted the car, driving erratically, and no shit, since I caught him just under the armpit. He lost control of the beater, sideswiped a tree—beater lost that battle. And the dumb shit came out firing. DOS."

"Anyone else hurt?"

"No."

"The civilian, counter guy."

"He's fine. He was shaken up, may have pissed his pants. But he grabbed a T-shirt from the rack so I could use it to put pressure on the chest wound."

"He shot twice. It's not real clear, but . . ." Confused, she lifted a hand to the right side of her forehead, felt the bandage.

"Yeah, no penetration. You got about ten stitches on that one."

Head shot, she thought. The sting of a thousand angry wasps. "Could've been worse."

"Could've been."

"Mom, Dad, Drea. They were here, right?"

"Yeah."

"It's blurry."

"They said that would happen for a while. Don't worry about it. They were here the whole time. I talked them into going home, seeing as they came with the clothes on their backs and not much else. They'll be back in the morning."

"When can I get out of here? Shouldn't I talk to the doctor?"

"You did talk to the doctor."

"When?"

"This afternoon. You've been in and out. They've run a bunch of tests, and you're doing pretty good. They're probably going to get you up tomorrow, get you to walk a little."

"When can I get out?" She wanted to whine, and came very close. "It smells like sick people in here."

As she'd said exactly that the last time she'd surfaced, he just smiled. "You are a sick person, sis. They've gotta monitor for infection and shit like that. And they've got to get you up and around a little. Look, the bullet clipped the—give me a second."

He closed his eyes. "Manubrium. Yeah, that, and a rib. So they picked bone fragments out. You got a busted rib and a hole in your chest. Not to mention the gash in your hard head. So sit back and relax. It's going to be a few days."

"I really want to talk to the doctor. Can you just get the doctor?"

"Sloan, it's past two in the morning. Give the guy a break."

"Two? In the morning? What the hell are you doing here? Go home." Agitated now, she managed to push up a few inches, then just dropped back. "Sari's pregnant. She's pregnant, right? I didn't just dream that?"

"She's knocked up good, Auntie Sloan. She peeked in on you yesterday. Everybody in CIB has come in. And every damn one gave blood. You lost a hell of a lot."

Because they wanted to tremble, he rubbed his hands on his thighs. "You're all full up now. You had both sets of grandparents check in, and your uncle, your cousins, Captain Hamm, and a whole bunch."

"I don't remember any of it. Everything's so goddamn mixed-up and vague. Except . . . I died on the table. The operating table."

"They brought you back."

"Yeah. Three times they had to zap me. I was floating."

But if everything else blurred, that remained clear as polished glass.

"I watched them." She spoke slowly as she remembered every detail. "I saw you, pacing the hallway, blood on your shirt. My blood. In some hallway, talking on the phone. Crying a little. You said my family was coming, and you'd call when I was out. I was in surgery, and you'd call when I got out."

He rubbed the hand he held in his. "Are you stringing me along?"

"It's all so clear, Joel. How can that be so absolutely clear, and everything else not? I was going to let go. I felt so light, and it would've been so easy to just let go. But you were crying a little, and I remembered you'd told me I had to fight. Not to give up, but fight. So I did."

He got up, walked to the window. Nudging the curtains open a little, he stared through the gap into the dark.

"I was talking to Sari. She was scared, crying, and wanted to come. I had to talk her down, talk her into waiting until I said to come. She loves you."

"I know. I love her."

He took another moment before he came back to sit again. "I guess that makes you a miracle, sis."

"I don't feel like a miracle. I got a tube sticking in me."

"For drainage, they said. They'll take it out before much longer."

"They've got me hooked up to all this—this stuff."

"IVs for fluid, catheter deal to catch them when you pee them out."

"It's demoralizing," she decided. "Plus, it freaking hurts. Everywhere. Why are you grinning at me?"

"You're getting better. Bitchy's better."

"Great. Help me break out of this place. C'mon, get me out of here. I'm starving."

He sat up straight. "You're hungry?"

"Hungry is wanting a bag of chips. I said I'm starving."

"I'll get you something."

When he rushed out, Sloan gave in, pushed the button again.

She drifted off, but just under the surface. She broke through again when Joel came back with a little plastic bowl and a spoon.

"They said to start off with this."

"What is it?"

"Beef broth."

"That sounds disgusting." And to the woman who had, only days before, bench pressed one-fifty, the spoonful of broth felt like a ten-pound weight. "It is disgusting," she said, and ate another spoonful.

She managed four sips before she wore out. "Sorry, that's it." She could feel herself drifting, going under again. "Go home, Joel."

Instead, he set the bowl aside, then rubbed his knuckles over her cheek before he sat down. He picked up his book, stretched out his legs, and read.

The next time she woke, the open curtains let sunshine pour in. Her sister sat beside her, hair loose and shining around her shoulders as she worked a crossword puzzle on her tablet.

Sloan said, "Oh, man."

Drea glanced up, shot out a big, bright smile. "It's good to see you, too."

"How long was I out this time?"

"It's just after nine on this sunny November morning. I kicked Joel out—which wasn't easy. Mom and Dad will be in this afternoon. Want some breakfast?"

"Maybe. I want out of here, Drea."

"Who wouldn't? I hear you're taking the first steps toward that— literally—this morning. Let me see about getting you some food."

When her sister went out, Sloan managed to find the controls and brought the back of the bed up a couple more inches. And took her first good look around.

A lot of flowers. That was nice—she'd be grateful. She'd be more grateful if she and the flowers had been in her apartment, but she'd be grateful.

She had beige walls, no surprise there, a lot of machines, a couple of chairs, a door she assumed led to a bathroom. Through the window she could see some buildings, some trees, a parking lot.

For the first time it occurred to her she didn't know where she was.

"Where the hell am I?" she demanded when Drea came back in.

"Hagerstown. Closest hospital, and they've been great. Angie's bringing you breakfast, and news! The doctor will be in to take out the catheter. You're going to take a walk."

"Outside?"

"No." In the professionally cheerful voice she used with clients and customers, Drea continued, "We do have a wide variety of indoor activities lined up for your entertainment and amusement."

"Kiss my ass."

Ignoring that, Drea rolled right along.

"Physical therapy. Whee! Blood tests, urine tests. Such fun! We also have a book of crosswords, just for you."

"You're the crossword addict."

Drea, in her tend-to-you way, eased Sloan up, smoothed and plumped her pillow. "And I'm assured they're an excellent way to exercise your brain. We also have my spare tablet. You can stream movies, TV, whatever."

Reality, and the dread that ran with it, leaked into hope.

"Jesus, Drea, how long am I going to be stuck here?"

"A few more days anyway, but ask the doctor. He's adorable, by the way."

"Are you hitting on my doctor?"

"I would, but he's wearing a wedding ring." She turned as Angie came in with a tray.

"How are you feeling this morning?"

"Better. Like it's time to go home."

"Let's see how you handle breakfast."

"Not beef broth."

"No. We've got scrambled eggs, applesauce, yogurt."

"Coffee?"

"A smoothie for now. We'll check with the doctor on the coffee. He's making his rounds, so he'll be in shortly."

"You said that before, I think, and Joel said I talked to him, the doctor. I don't remember."

"You're on some excellent drugs. After you see the doctor, we're going to get you up. We're going to want you to take short walks several times a day. A therapist will be in later to show you some breathing exercises."

"Can I take a shower?"

"Soon. We're going to keep you busy for the rest of your stay. If discharge is the motivation, use it. You'll get there faster. And food helps."

She gave Sloan's hand a pat, and left.

Sloan managed a few bites of egg, then leaned back. "It feels like I'm starving, then I start to eat. It's exhausting. Nothing tastes right."

"Try the smoothie." Drea held the straw to Sloan's lips.

After a taste, she shook her head. "I want some damn coffee, I want this thing out of me so I can pee like a normal person. I want to get the fuck out of this place, and I want . . ."

She stopped, pressed her hands to her face, mortified tears burned in her eyes.

"Jesus Christ, listen to me! I'm a bratty ten-year-old. I'm alive, and I could be, maybe should be, dead, and all I can do is whine.

"I'm sorry. I'm sorry, I just feel so bitchy."

"Hey, some son of a bitch shot my sister. I'm feeling pretty bitchy, too."

On a calmer breath, Sloan dropped her hands. "I'm top bitch. You can be assistant bitch."

"Figures. Assistant bitch says try to eat a little more."

"Okay."

She tried more eggs, took a spoonful of yogurt.

"Sorry, honestly, that's it."

With a nod, Drea angled the tray away.

"Shit, does Matias know?"

Back turned, Drea fussed with a flower arrangement. "He came to see you the day after your surgery."

"Do I have my phone? I should probably call him, or at least text him."

With fire in her eyes, Drea spun back. "They let him in to see you. Mom and Dad insisted. He stayed about three minutes, and that's probably overestimating. He hasn't been back since."

"Oh." Her brain tried to process it. "All right."

"Is it? Is it all right?"

"No, of course it isn't. Not even close to all right. I'll deal with it."

"If you don't boot that selfish asshole to the curb, I swear, I'll wait until you're back in shape— No, you're stronger than me, and meaner. I'll wait until you're on your feet, barely, then I'll kick your ass."

In the face of her sister's fury, some of the bitchiness in Sloan dropped away.

"You still couldn't take me. I won't have to boot him, Drea. He's booted himself. And I'm either too tired to care, or I just don't. Would you mind getting that food out of here? Even the smell's not hitting right."

"Sure."

As Drea reached for it, Sloan took her hand. "I love you, even though you think you're the pretty one."

"I love you. Trust me, right now I am unquestionably the pretty one."

"That bad?"

"Avoid mirrors for another couple days. I'll be back."

After Drea went out, Sloan glanced toward the bathroom. Now she absolutely had to look at a mirror, but couldn't figure out how.

As she calculated, Dr. Vincenti breezed in.

Drea had it right there. Adorable.

# CHAPTER TWO

Vincenti had an easy manner with a layer of charm. She tried not to think how his adorable—obviously skilled—hands had been inside her chest cavity.

He checked her chart, then her wounds.

He had black hair, perfectly styled in a brush back, heavy-lidded deep brown eyes in a face tanned golden, and a voice she thought hit both soft and lyrical.

"Thank you for saving my life."

"Your partner began that very important job. He made the most out of those five platinum minutes. Applying pressure, talking to you, keeping you focused."

"You had to bring me back."

"We did, and here you are. And healing well. I'm going to remove your catheter, and Angie here will go with you for a short walk. You're not yet to get out of bed on your own."

He pointed at her. "I see in your eyes what your family told me. Therefore, I will be direct. A fall will set back your process, cause complications. So you'll be smart, and call for the nurse when you want or need to get up."

"When can I go home?"

His smile only bumped up the charm ratio.

"You know, it should hurt my feelings no one wants to stay in our fine facility."

"Maybe because it's full of sick people?"

"And we work to get them well enough to leave. We'll see where we are in twenty-four hours. You had a major trauma, and major surgery."

She tried a smile of her own. "But you're a highly skilled surgeon, and I'm young, strong, and healthy."

"I am highly skilled, and you're young, strong, healthy. But you won't bounce back in a matter of days. You will come back, with time, effort, patience, and persistence."

"It seems like being stuck in bed just makes me tired and weaker."

"Today, you'll get up, move a little. Several times. You'll start physical therapy, and we can decrease the pain medication. Soft foods for another day or two, then we'll see."

He changed her dressing himself, and when he moved to take out the catheter, she just stared at the ceiling.

Whatever sound she made brought a smile to his face. "That's a relief, right?"

"A big one. I . . . I had to pee. A Dr Pepper for Joel, and he'd gas up the truck. I went in to pee and get drinks. That's why I went into the mini-mart. I remember that now."

"You may have some blank spots. Nothing to worry about."

She lifted a hand to her forehead. "It could've been worse."

Now he didn't smile. "It often is. I'll check in on you later."

"We're going to get you up slowly," Angie told her. "You're going to feel light-headed, and you want to wait for that to pass. Your gown crosses in the front for access, so your butt's covered."

"Good to know."

It took longer than she imagined just to get on her feet, and to discover her feet didn't feel connected to the legs that felt like overcooked spaghetti.

But she made it to the door, dragging the IV pole, then a few steps beyond into the hall, where Drea waited with a wheelchair.

"I'm backup."

The bitchiness rushed back. "I don't want that. I don't need that."

But in the end, she did need it, and had to bite down on the anger that streamed up from her gut.

"You're frustrated," Angie said, "but you're wrong. You walked for just over two minutes. This afternoon, you'll walk again. And this evening, again."

"You may be top bitch," Drea said as she pushed the wheelchair, "but you're no quitter."

Damn right. So for the next three, endless days, she walked. Two minutes, three, then five at a time. She did the prescribed breathing exercises every hour of the day and whenever she woke at night.

She didn't bring up the nightmares that woke her. They were her business, and she determined they'd fade away. Reliving the moment the shooter had turned, had fired, struck her as normal.

And she'd get through it. She had a goal, and that was discharge.

When that day came, it brought joy, then shock and a low-simmering anger.

She sat in one of the chairs—a relief, and progress. Vincenti sat in the other.

"Your healing's progressing very well. Your appetite isn't."

"Could it possibly be hospital food?"

"You think I don't know they brought you in your grandmother's chicken soup—very tasty, by the way—a cheeseburger and fries from McDonald's, pulled pork and roasted potatoes your mother made. She's sent the recipe to my wife, at my request. I'm a lousy cook."

"Nothing gets by you."

"It didn't get by me you barely ate any of it. You've lost eleven pounds since you were admitted. This isn't unusual, but it's something we need to correct."

"I'll work on it."

"When we do our follow-up in two weeks, I'd like to see at least three pounds gained."

"Two weeks? But—"

"Follow-up," he interrupted. "I'm discharging you in the morning." He held up a hand. "There are conditions."

"I'll meet them."

"You can't live alone. We can reevaluate that in two weeks. Your apartment is on the third floor, no elevator. That won't do for now. Your parents assure me you can live with them at home until you're fully recovered."

"I'm stationed in Stevensville, and my family lives in Heron's Rest. That's almost four hours' distance."

"You'll remain on medical leave, Sloan. You need another thirty days. And you're not to drive until after I see you again. The breathing exercises are important. Continue those. Continue walking. No strenuous exercises, no lifting anything over five pounds. Angie will show you again how to apply clean dressings, and you'll monitor your chest wound for any signs of redness or swelling. Any sign, Sloan, you contact me."

Reading her face, he sat back. "Those are the conditions, and I'll have your word on them."

"Fine." Just two weeks, she thought, and not here. Two weeks with family, in her childhood home. How could she complain?

"Now, a strong suggestion. You're having some nightmares."

She opened her mouth, but she valued truth. So she shrugged. "It's not unusual. I looked it up."

"If you did, then you'd have also read to tell your doctor, which you didn't. We'll let that go. It would also have said, no doubt, there are treatments available."

"I don't need a shrink."

His wonderfully patient eyes held hers.

"So says most everyone who could use some therapy. You were shot, and you were clinically dead for over two minutes. You've had physical, emotional, and mental trauma. My impression of you is while you're stubborn enough to resist getting help, you're smart enough to know when you need it. So think about it."

"All right, I will think about it. I want to get back to my life. I want to get back to work. I didn't die, so I want to live."

"Good attitude. Meet the conditions, consider the suggestion. Go live. I do good work, so don't screw it up."

She'd talked herself into believing it all not so bad, when her captain came in and made it worse.

After he left, she sat, brooding, until Joel came in. He took one look, gave her one of sympathy.

"Captain lowered the boom?"

"Not only thirty more days' medical leave, but another two after that of desk duty. Then I have to get cleared by a medical doctor and the department shrink for active. What the fuck, Joel."

"I'm sorry, sis, sincerely, but I can't disagree with any of that. Getting out of here's the next step. You've got to take the one after that, then the one after that."

"I can't even go back to my own place. How would you feel if you had to go back and live in your childhood bedroom?"

"As long as Sari's with me, I'd be fine with that. My mama's a damn fine cook. In fact, she sent you her chicken and dumplings. They're going to warm it up for you."

People cared, she reminded herself. They helped.

Brooding, bitching, whining didn't.

"I appreciate that."

"Sis, you gotta eat better than you have been. You know that."

"I do, I swear. It's . . . Knowing and doing aren't always the same. I get hungry, then almost as soon as I start to eat, I'm just not. Maybe if I could move again. I mean really move. I need something else to think about. I need work, and I'm doing crossword puzzles and watching Netflix."

"Some pretty good shit on there."

She shoved a hand at her hair, and tried not to remember she'd needed help to wash it.

"I'm tired of myself, Joel, and that's the truth. Tired of being inside my own head. Tired of not being able to walk ten minutes without feeling like I've run a couple miles. Tired of being poked and prodded. I annoy the crap out of myself."

"Good thing I'm a more tolerant type." He sat, then pulled a picture out of his pocket. "Want to see my baby girl?"

"What? Jesus, give it!" After snatching the ultrasound photo, she stared, turned it the other way. "Where is she?"

"They had to show me, too, but I got it now." Leaning over, he traced.

"Okay, one more time." Then she nodded, grinned, and meant it. "I see her! Wow. And she's beautiful."

She handed it back.

"I'm getting her a pink stuffed animal. I'll know what kind when I see it. Thanks for sharing something happy."

"Happy's the best thing to share."

"I've got one, and it turns out it qualifies. Matias sent me a breakup text."

"Fucker."

"No, really, more of a weak coward. No, wait. A weak, cowardly fucker. He said, basically, he couldn't handle it. Seeing me in the hospital that way made him realize we just weren't meant to be. Then he asked that I send back the things he had at my place. And he was sending any of my stuff to my parents' address, since he didn't know when I'd get back. He topped it off by wishing me all the best."

"And how's that happy?"

"I'd planned to see him after I got out of here, tell him we were done, since he was too much of a selfish asshole to spend more than two minutes with me when I was hurt. He saved me the trouble."

"Give me a list, sis."

"Joel, I can handle it."

"Nope. Give me a list of that asshole's stuff, and I'll get it to him. I'll go over with your sister or whoever's getting what you want to pack up for the couple weeks in Heron's Rest."

"I can get all that. They don't have to—"

"Can't drive yet, right?"

Annoyed with herself again, she heaved out a sigh.

"No."

"So why have somebody haul you over there, take the time to get what you need, spend even five minutes on the jerk, when you can get the hell out of here and go home with your family?

"Sometimes you have to let people take care of you, sis."

"Everyone has been, and I swear under the whining, I really appreciate it."

"You're going to have to appreciate it a little while longer. Give me a list."

"It's not that much, really. He's got some clothes in the bedroom closet, and in the top left drawer of the dresser. He's got a quart of oat milk and some tofu in the fridge. The milk's probably gone over by now. I didn't think of it before."

"So I'll dump it. What else?"

As she ran down the list, it occurred to her how completely he'd kept his things—what there were of them—separated from hers. Why hadn't she noticed that before?

Didn't matter now, she decided. Chapter closed.

"How about what you want? I can pass it on to your folks."

"It's a longer list."

"I got the time."

When she finished, she walked Joel to the elevator, then did a circuit of the floor. Maybe she moved slow, but she could celebrate the fact that she moved, and without any real pain.

Discomfort, fatigue, she could handle. Would handle, she promised herself, and made a second promise.

Stop whining.


She slept poorly her last night in the hospital as the dreams dogged her.

When she crossed from the gas pumps to the mini-mart, the wind began to kick and moan. Leaves, shredded from trees, skittered and scraped across the pavement. The lights of the mart glared, almost burned her eyes. Through the glass she could see nothing but that violent light.

When she opened the door, the hinges shrieked, and the air inside went thick and hot.

When she saw, through that hard light, the man with his back to her, her heart began to thump, bringing pain to her chest. Breath, thin and weak, began to whistle through her throat as she laid a hand on her weapon.

Her mind screamed: *Run!*

But he turned. He had no face, just a skeletal mask inside a black hood. When he swung out, and the scythe he carried struck her chest, she reared up in bed, gasping.

She pressed her hands to her galloping heart, felt blood pouring through her fingers.

But when she looked down, panicked, her hands were dry. Trembling, but dry.

Struggling to breathe through it, she lay back down. For a moment, she saw herself floating above, as she had when her heart had stopped beating.

Her own voice sounded in her head.

*Sometimes, dying's easier than living.*

Maybe, she thought. Maybe. But she'd live. The dreams would pass, and she'd live.


Her whole family arrived at noon, with her father leading the way.

"You're all checked out, bags are in the car. Ready to get out of this joint?"

"More than."

Her sister, once again, pushed a wheelchair.

"I can walk. They want me to walk."

"This is the way out. Hospital policy."

No whining, she reminded herself. And settled into the wheelchair.

They stopped by the nurse's station to say goodbye, and say thanks.

"You've come a long way in a short time," Angie told her. "The mark of a good patient."

Sloan let out a laugh. "A good patient? Me?"

"Yes, actually a very good patient. You followed instructions, even when you didn't want to. Now keep doing that."

"We'll make sure she does," her mother said. "We'll never be able to thank you enough, you and everyone, for taking such good care of our girl."

"It's what we do. You've got a real nice family, Sloan. That's going to help you the rest of the way."

Drea wheeled her into the elevator. Not for another X-ray, another test, but to go home.

Outside, she drew in the chilly air like perfume.

"No hospital smell! Just air, cold fall air!"

Getting to her feet, she did a happy dance in her head. Drea wheeled the chair back in while her father went to get the car. Her mother stood, an arm around her.

"I could walk to the car."

"It's cold, baby. Indulge us a little this first day. I know you have to push some, and I promise we won't let you slack off. But we've all been waiting for this day, too. You're coming home."

"If I promise not to push harder than I can handle, you have to promise back you won't let work slide, you won't worry and hover."

"There isn't a parent in the world who can promise not to worry and mean it. But we're going to try really hard not to hover."

"Fair."

As Drea came out, the car pulled up.

"You get in the front."

"No way. We're not breaking traditions. Parents in the front, kids in the back."

"Fair." Her mother kissed her cheek.

"Everybody in?" Her dad rubbed his hands together. "Let's rock and roll."

It made her laugh—another tradition. He'd said the same anytime the family took a road trip.

So off they went with the radio playing her father's favored classic rock.

"So how are the fall rentals?" Sloan began.

"Full up." Her mother shifted to look over her shoulder. "The Bensons are coming in Tuesday for their Thanksgiving week. Two more grandchildren came along this year, so they've booked two cabins. They'll do some skiing, but some of the older kids want to try snowshoeing. We've booked that."

She remembered the Bensons, as they'd been coming to the Rest since she'd been a kid herself. Renting a cabin in the fall and again in the summer. Skiing or hiking in the fall, a boat rental in the summer.

The family business, All the Rest—in its third generation with Drea on board—maintained and rented cabins, cottages and lake houses, boats—motor, sail—kayaks, canoes, and paddleboards.

They booked white-water rafting excursions, winter skiing, snowboarding, snowshoes, arranged guided hikes.

Heron's Rest, deep in the mountains and centered by Mirror Lake, didn't pull them in like Deep Creek and the resorts, but it appealed to those who wanted a quieter, more intimate stay.

And it offered what the tourists wanted in four distinct seasons. All four, Sloan thought, with their own beauty and appeal.

She couldn't go to her own place for a while, Sloan thought, but she could, and would, take short hikes on familiar trails, long walks on the lake path. She'd build up her strength and endurance again.

The route north and west was also familiar. The endless highway that took long, long curves through the mountains, and the mountains that became more serious as the miles passed.

They'd left the hospital in the chilly but dry, but as those miles passed, snow spread over hills and fields. It iced the peaks, ran down the valleys. It clung to the branches of pines and denuded hardwoods so everything looked like an old-fashioned Christmas card.

She loved the look of it, the feel of it, the smell of it when she walked through those deep woods. That appeal had been one of the reasons she'd chosen her career.

She knew the beauty of nature—and its dangers, its capriciousness. And she'd felt, always, a strong need to protect and preserve it.

She dozed off, then surfaced, irritated with herself. Like a child, she thought, or an old lady, unable to stay awake for a couple of hours in a moving car.

No whining, she reminded herself. A nap just made the ride go faster.

And besides, they were nearly home.

The car rolled off the highway now where the road wound and climbed up, snaked and rolled down. Thick woods of green and white, icy rocks, deep seas of snow, the rise of the Alleghenies dominated, as if highways didn't exist.

She glanced over to see Drea scowling at her phone.

"Problem?"

"Hmm? No, not really. Why does it always get me that there's no service on this mile-and-a-half stretch?"

"I bet whatever's on the other end of the phone can wait the three or four minutes until we're through the gap."

"It can wait longer." Still, she frowned at the phone. "Everything's fine. I just hate not being connected. And I know that's a little bit sick. Maybe I like being a little bit sick."

"Maybe you should just hot-glue the phone to your hand."

"I've considered it. Anyway, I need to be connected to work—just like you."

"I hope I remember how to work."

"As if." Drea turned the phone screen down on her thigh. "What kind of shoes is Dad wearing?"

"Boots. Timberland, dark brown. That's not a stretch. It's pretty usual."

"Don't look down and tell me what shoes I'm wearing."

"Black boots, over the ankle, black-and-white-checked laces." Sloan squeezed her eyes shut. "They're Uggs. Nice, look new."

"They are nice and new. Don't even think about borrowing them."

Typical, Sloan thought. "I can get my own Uggs."

"You should. They're terrific. You see, you absorb, you remember. I wish I was half as good at it."

God, she was tired. Unbelievably tired, and fought to stay awake, stay aware.

"It's just paying attention."

"No, it's not," Drea countered.

Either way, Sloan thought, she'd use that particular skill, keep it sharp. Keep her mind sharp.

And surely her body would follow suit.

Connections. She'd taken some yoga classes with an instructor who talked (a little too much) about the mind/body/spirit connection.

She'd use that now and work on all three.

She caught a glimpse of the lake, just a flash as the sun struck water. Then another turn, one more, and there it was, spread as blue as the sky with the mountains, the folds and peaks of them, the brown and white and pine green of the season reflected on the surface.

Her spirits lifted.

She watched a family of swans—mom, dad, and the six nearly adult kids sailing together. They'd migrate soon, and the parents, at least, would return to mate again, to glide the lake with their cygnets.

Another few weeks, she thought, if the weather held, the lake would freeze solid for skating, ice fishing.

Trails cut through the mountains, and skiers, small with distance, swished down.

She saw the trails of smoke from cabin and cottage chimneys tucked into the brown and green, and the lovely lakefront houses.

And in the sun, the glint of glass from her childhood home around the lake.

The tug, a hard one with the strong pull of sentiment, surprised her. She visited at least once a month, stayed the occasional weekend when work allowed.

But this was different, she realized. A different kind of homecoming.

And she found it soothed both mind and spirit.

Until that moment, she hadn't realized how much she'd needed to come home.

She wanted to sit, bundled up by the firepit, and watch the sunset, mirrored in the lake. She wanted to hear the loons, watch the heron's flight, bask in the sight of the majestic bald eagle.

She could catch a glimpse of the bay from her apartment window in Annapolis, but no, she thought. Not the same.

And for now, at least for now, she finally understood she needed the same.

She needed the old two-story house with its working shutters, its generous decks, its big eat-in kitchen, its sit-and-stay-awhile front porch.

She wanted her view of the trees climbing up the mountains outside her bedroom window. She wanted the comfort and the quiet as much as she wanted to feel like Sloan again.

Her father pulled the car into the garage with its apartment above. He shut the car off, turned to smile at her.

"Welcome home."

# CHAPTER THREE

It wasn't her place, but it was home, and the familiarity brought that comfort.

The big, shaggy dog her parents had named Mop lumbered over to greet her. As he wagged head to tail, Sloan scrubbed at his long, fluffy gray fur.

"There's that boy. Been rolling in the snow again."

"Nothing he likes better unless it's jumping in the lake for a swim. I'm going to run up to my place, check on some things. I'll be down a little later."

With that, Drea peeled off in her nice, new boots to climb the steps on the side of the garage to her apartment above.

With the dog leading the way, Sloan went into the house with her parents.

The old stone fireplace with its thick wood mantel and flanking bookshelves dominated the living area of what had been—in her paternal grandfather's day, before his marriage—a one-bedroom cabin.

Ezra Cooper had started the business, bit by bit, then added to the original cabin when he started his family. He'd added a second story, the big country kitchen, and a dining room used almost exclusively for holiday meals and company.

With his two sons, he'd added on the decks, a garage, widened windows. And all the while had invested in other cabins, boats, gear, until All the Rest provided rentals, sales, guides, and more for the tourists who came to Mirror Lake.

Dean's older brother had stepped out of the business, continued his education. A professor of history at West Virginia University, he and his wife had settled in Morgantown.

Though since their parents' retirement, Dean and Elsie ran the business, Archer could and would step in when needed. His oldest son, Jonah, lived a stone's throw away with his young family, and worked as Dean's right hand as well as a white-water rafting pilot—and whatever else All the Rest needed.

With Drea handling marketing, community relations, and sales, and her mother dealing with decor, supplies, and inventory, the business thrived with three generations.

Like her uncle, Sloan had stepped away. But it didn't lessen her pride in what her family had accomplished with All the Rest.

The home her grandfather and his sons had built and rebuilt over the years welcomed her back as if it had been yesterday.

"We put your things away in your room." Elsie skimmed a hand down Sloan's hair when Sloan pulled off her winter cap. "The doctor said the one flight of stairs was fine, but if it feels like too much, we can set you up in the den."

"No, don't. I need to move."

She did so now to the big front window that faced the lake and its reflected snowcapped mountains.

"It never gets old."

"Sure doesn't. How about I fix you a snack?"

"Mom, you're not going to wait on me."

"Just for today." Elsie slid an arm around Sloan's waist, tipped her head toward her daughter's. "Indulge me a little. It's so good to have you home for a while. It's so good to see you looking more like yourself."

"I don't feel like myself yet."

"You will," Dean said. After he shed his coat, hung it in the coat closet (house rule), he walked over, crouched down to set kindling to light in the hearth.

The dog immediately plopped down in front of it.

"Now, big question and no wrong answer." He rose, a fluid motion, an athletic one. "Thanksgiving's Thursday. If you don't feel up to having a houseful of relatives, say so. Everybody understands."

"No, no, it'll be good to see everyone. Honestly. I need some normal, and a houseful at Thanksgiving's normal."

She turned to them, and thought as she always did: Unit. They were as connected as any two people she knew.

And she was a blend of them—as Drea was. She had her mother's coloring, and Drea their father's. She had his eyes, and Drea her mother's.

They'd made her, and not only stood together but stood by her.

"You want to fuss, and I get it. All of this, all of it, had to be scarier for you than it was for me. I was too doped up to be scared. And it's good to be home. Really good. But if I'm going to get back to feeling like me, I need to do things that feel like me."

"A houseful it is." Elsie stepped over, wrapped Sloan in a hug. "Not scared. Terrified. But that's behind us now. So I'm going to fix you something to eat."

"Don't the two of you work for a living?"

"Drea's up in her place right now doing just that. Jonah's got things covered otherwise. Tomorrow we're back to it." Dean patted her shoulder. "We're taking today."

Elsie tempted her with homemade soup, fresh bread, and Sloan did the best she could. The appetite still wasn't there.

But the need to move was.

"I'm going to take a walk—a short one," she promised. "Fresh air. It feels good to be out in it. Feels like me," she added.

"One favor, for today?" Elsie said. "Would you stay in sight of the house?"

"Like you used to say when I was eight?" But Sloan laughed with it. "That's a deal. The soup was amazing, Mom. Like always."

"Mop's going to want to go with you," Drew warned her.

"Mop's always welcome."

And the minute she put on her coat, the dog got up, stretched, and wagged.

Since she wanted the lake, she went out the front. The dog immediately raced ahead, bulling his body through the snow like a canine plow.

The air bit, but felt good, so good, breezing over her face. She scented the lake, the pines, the snow, and all that said home, too. She'd do this every day, she promised herself, as many times a day as she could manage. Down to the lake, or out the back and into the snowy woods when her mother wasn't so worried about her.

And in two weeks, at her follow-up, she'd get the all clear from Dr. Vincenti. And by Christmas, she swore an oath, she'd be back all the way.

She walked down to the dock, where there would be a sailing sloop through the season. This summer, she thought, she'd take a real vacation, come home for it. Spend hours sailing, hiking, kayaking, and appreciating what she had.

Maybe it had taken dying for a few minutes to make her realize she'd let too much of that go. Time for another vow, she decided. She wouldn't fall into that trap again. Work satisfied. God knew she loved her work, but for the last few years, she'd let the balance tip.

As she walked the path around the lake, the dog trotted ahead, trotted back, ahead. And reminded her she walked like an invalid.

"Sorry, Mop, not at full capacity."

In fact, she had to admit she hadn't covered an eighth of a mile, and was flagging.

She felt weak, breathless, and not a little pissed off.

Her ears still worked just fine, so she turned when she heard footsteps. And waited, giving her heart a chance to slow as Drea approached.

"I'm not going to bitch."

"Damn. I was counting on it. Then I'd point out that a week ago, you could barely walk two minutes down a hospital corridor."

"I pointed that out to myself, which is why I'm not bitching. But—"

"Here it comes!"

"Not a bitch, just a fact. I still feel so wrong. Drea, I feel so wrong."

"Here's more fact." Reaching down, blue eyes on Sloan's green, she took her sister's hand. "You look tired, and you're pale, so you've done enough. So go in, do your breathing exercises, take a nap. Then get up and do it all again."

"Bossy pants."

"Worn with quiet pride and innate style. Come on." Drea hooked her arm through Sloan's and gave her little choice.

"Will you do me a favor?"

"Maybe."

The answer made Sloan laugh. "Just talk them down from worrying about me when you can. It's a weight. I don't want to tell them it's a weight. They'll just worry more and try not to show it."

"When they see you following doctor's orders, they'll worry less. And I'll talk them down when I can because you'll follow doctor's orders."

"That's not a favor, that's a deal."

"Take or leave."

"Take." When they reached the front door, Sloan paused. "Start now."

As she opened the door, Sloan plastered a smile on her face. "That felt good! Wore me out a little, which also feels good. I'm going up, do my breathing thing, maybe take a short nap."

"If you need anything," Elsie began.

"I got it all." Deliberately, Sloan hung her coat in the closet, used the basket for her scarf, cap, gloves. "I plan to blow the doctor away at my follow-up."

The stairs felt like a mountain, but she made it. She turned down the hall, used the bathroom to splash cool water on her face.

Her childhood bedroom, just across from it, held a bed with four short, turned posts and a snowy white duvet with a deep blue throw at its foot. The reading chair, another throw across its back, angled cozily in a corner.

Its walls, a misty, soothing blue, held the local art her parents collected. Springs and summers here, of the lake, the mountains, wildflowers streaming through the woods.

Because she'd made the deal, she did the breathing exercises, coughing, as instructed, after the long exhale.

It tired her, too, and made her grateful her mother had put a covered pitcher of water and a glass on the bedside table.

Flowers—mums in rusts and golds—sat on her old dresser and gave a hint of spice to the air.

A short nap, she thought, and lay on top of the duvet, pulled the throw over her. Twenty minutes just to recharge.

She slept for ninety, and didn't wake until the nightmare tossed her out of sleep.

The next day, Sloan laid out a routine. She showered, changed the dressing on her chest wound—which she assured herself was healing well. She studied her body, trying for dispassion.

Day One, she thought. A baseline. Yes, she looked frail. Yes, she'd lost weight and muscle tone. But she could stand and walk, and while things ached, she didn't have active pain.

Like the chest wound, the one on her forehead would leave a scar. But they'd remind her she'd survived.

That made her a survivor.

She dressed, then considered makeup. Then decided some blush, mascara, all the rest wouldn't fool anyone.

When she went downstairs, she found her parents lingering over coffee at the kitchen table. They both looked over at her, and she felt their study down to the bone.

The parental X-ray.

"We thought you might sleep in." Elsie started to get up. "How about some breakfast?"

"Mom, sit. I mean it. I'm going to put some coffee in a go-cup and take a walk—doctor's orders on the walking. Don't the two of you have to get to work?"

"I'm about to head out," Dean told her. "How'd you sleep?"

"Like a rock."

"I thought I'd stay home today," Elsie began. "There's a lot of prep for Thursday, and I can get started."

Sloan detoured from the coffee, sat. She took her mother's hands.

"I need you to go. I need you to do whatever you'd do today. I know you'd take off half on Wednesday to make the pies and all that, but you need to go to work. I need to feel capable of spending a day on my own. I know I'm not a hundred percent. Not even close. But I have to start. I know my limits. Trust me, my body doesn't let me forget them."

Elsie shifted her gaze to her husband. "I can hear you thinking *I told you so*. Knock it off."

He just smiled, shrugged.

"You'll keep your phone with you?"

"Yes, Mom."

"And call or text if you need anything?"

"Yes, Mom."

Elsie's lips twitched at the tone. "And you'll eat something. Then the One Bite More."

Sloan had to laugh at the old childhood refrain. And as she had as a child, rolled her eyes.

"Yes, Mom."

Dean rose, took the empty cups to the sink. "Mop's staying. He'll walk with you—that's the deal."

"I accept. Now go, add to my inheritance."

In the end, she walked out with them, Mop at her side. She waved the humans off, then laid a hand on the dog's head.

"Let's get started."

Though the sun beamed, the air snapped with cold, edged by a rising wind that rippled over the lake and sloughed through the trees. She watched a heron glide and swans sail. Focused on them, she made it to where she'd stopped the day before. Breath labored, she stopped to let her system recalibrate. Mop left her side long enough to leap into the snow and roll.

Ten steps more, she told herself, and took them.

Not pushing, she thought. Improving.

"That's all I've got," she said to the dog. "We'll do it again later, and again. Ten steps more."

Despite the cold, she felt sweat slide down her back as she walked back to the house. Her legs trembled some as she let herself back in, and her head felt light enough she just sat without taking off her coat.

"Just need some fuel."

She added some to the living room fire before tucking away her outdoor gear.

In the kitchen she made herself a bowl of cereal, added half a banana and blueberries.

She managed half of it before even the idea of eating exhausted her. She took a breath, then one bite more.

"Don't rat me out, Mop." She set the bowl on the floor, watched him gobble up the contents.

She made herself get up, fill an All the Rest water bottle.

"Next on a daily agenda: PT."

Obviously pleased with the company, Mop went with her to her parents' exercise/yoga room. Maybe it hurt the pride to pick up two-pound weights instead of twenty, but . . . Day One.

She sat on the bench and did steady curls until her arms burned. Then did two more. After managing a handful of shoulder presses, she tried a few kickbacks.

She rested, drank water, and did it all again.

"And that's all I've got."

She wrote it all down. How long she'd walked, how many curls, and so on.

Keeping a record, she decided, added incentive.

When Mop laid his head on her knee, she stroked his head. "We'll try yoga tomorrow, slow and easy. But I think I'll stretch out on the couch for bit.

After building up the fire, she closed her eyes.

Maybe she'd do one of Drea's famous crosswords—exercise for the mind. Even as she thought it, she dropped off.

She woke up with the dog sitting politely, staring at her.

"You need to go out again?" Groggy, she reached for the phone she'd set on the table. "Oh, for God's sake. I was down for over an hour."

Pushing up, she took mental inventory. She could handle it. "Give me a minute. It's time to walk again anyway."

The wind still kicked, and had pushed the clouds to dim the sun. More snow coming, she thought. She could see people—bright coats against the white—sledding on the east side slope. Smoke streamed out of chimneys. Despite the cold, a pair of kayaks plied the far side of the lake. Someone had built a pretty impressive snowman in front of one of the lakeside houses.

She made it to her first stop, had to rest, breathe, then took the ten steps more to her second stop. She wanted ten more, but stopped at five.

"Know and respect your limits, Sloan."

If she had to stop twice on the walk back, she still made it.

She sat, recovered, and though she didn't want it, heated up a little soup. Ate the one more bite.

When it was done, she looked at the dog.

"Now what? It's barely one in the afternoon. If I lie down, I'll sleep. If I get a book or try a movie, I'll end up asleep. And don't give me that sleep's healing. I've had enough of it.

"Am I really stuck with crossword puzzles?"

She went upstairs, brought down her laptop. She'd make a spreadsheet of her activity, her progress. It would help to see it all laid out. She could even add the times.

Though it burned some, she added sleep into the mix.

There, less equaled progress. At least on her gauge.

She set it up meticulously, and felt organized and accomplished.

And bored beyond the telling of it.

Desperate, she brought up a crossword puzzle on her laptop. Then wandered the house just to stay awake. When wandering, she came across the basket her mother used for her when-in-the-mood knitting or crocheting.

Inspired, Sloan carried it into the living room by the fire, and found a YouTube video teaching the basics of crocheting.

When her brain went fuzzy, she rolled it back, started it again. She had to focus, concentrate, and with hook and yarn created a very precise run of chain stitches.

Because she had to listen, watch, count, it kept her mind engaged. After a painstaking hour she had the beginnings of a Christmas-red scarf.

She rewarded herself with a Pepsi.

"Okay, Mop, I can do this. I'm not sure I actually want to do it, but I can. I'm going to consider it occupational therapy. Now we're going to walk again, then do another round with weights. I'm going to make myself eat some fruit or cheese or something, then we'll get back to this."

Before her parents got home that evening, she'd had to log another nap, but she offset that with more steps, more reps, and what by her measurements equaled about a quarter of a very simple red scarf.

Elsie looked at the yarn basket, the length—about a third now—of completed scarf, then at her daughter.

"When did you learn to crochet?"

"This afternoon."

Elsie picked up the work in progress, studied it front and back. "This is very nice work. How many times did I try to teach you?"

"You always gave up because you said I wouldn't sit still long enough." She heard the sound of the snowblower roar to life, which meant her father cleared paths.

And Mop would be joyfully leaping into the blowing snow.

"I know I kind of have to now. Occupational therapy. You really have to think."

"Good for you? A scarf?"

"Yeah, and when I finish, you have to wear it. The cost of being a mom."

"The reward of being one. How about some hot chocolate, and you can tell me how you did today?"

"How about some wine, and we can tell each other about our day?"

"Even better." Elsie laid a hand on Sloan's cheek. "You look better."

"I do?"

"In those magic eyes of yours, yes."

Sloan felt tears burn at the back of them because she knew her mother wouldn't lie.

"Today was Day One. I made a spreadsheet."

"Of course you did. It's our loss you didn't come into the family business, Ms. Organized."

"I came by that naturally," she said as they walked to the kitchen. "But it's good for me to track my progress. And we'll get to that. You start first because Dad's going to want to know what I did today when he comes in."

"We got another three inches today, so he's hell-bent to clear that before the next two or three fall overnight. Red okay? I still have plenty of sauce frozen from tomato season. We're having pasta tonight."

"Red's great."

"Let's see. We rented about a dozen sleds and toboggans, and sold about half that many. I've got an order in for more. Are you sure you want to hear all this?"

Sloan settled at the counter. "I do."

"We're booked solid for December and January, and damn close to full for February. Drea's Winter Wonders campaign did the job. Long-range forecast says the lake will freeze by mid-January, so we'll have the ice-fishing tournament the first week of February. And we're already half-booked for that."

Elsie took a sip of wine, studied the glass. "Now, this was a fine idea."

"I still got 'em."

"Oh, news in Heron's Rest. You remember the old Parker place?"

Sloan dug into her memory files.

"Great big ramshackle two-story, between here and town, with a wide, saggy front porch. If you walked back that way on a really windy day, you could actually hear the wind whistling through the windows.

"An even more ramshackle detached garage/workshop, all tucked into the woods by a long, narrow driveway always full of potholes."

"Couldn't have said it better myself. Brady Parker let the place go to hell when his father died—what, about ten years ago—and it wasn't in the best of shape back then. Well, he sold it a couple months ago."

"Somebody bought that old place? For the land maybe? It's not exactly prime, and yeah, the house needs serious work, but it'd be a shame to tear it down. It's got all kinds of character."

"Apparently that's not the plan. Some New Yorker bought it, with the plan—I'm told—to rehab it."

Sloan frowned over her wine. "Really?"

"Really. Word is he intends to live here, start his own business. Handyman kind of business, which if he's any good, would be great. Further news, Maggie Wells finally talked Barry into moving to Florida. We depended on Barry to deal with whatever repairs or improvements your dad and Jonah couldn't get to."

"Maggie and Barry, what'll the Rest do without them?"

"We're going to find out. They're leaving December first. I have to hope the New York transplant works out. With the rentals, the shops—and God help us, your dad has his eye on a little cottage that should come on the market around the first of the year—it'll be hard to keep up without someone as good and reliable as Barry."

As she spoke, Elsie took a clip from her pocket. She twisted up her sunny hair, clipped it up and back. Then she took a freezer bag of sauce out, set it in a pot to thaw a little.

"What part of New York?"

"The New York. New York City. Supposedly worked in finance or investments. Wall Street. But I don't know if that's reliable information because I also heard he was in real estate, and someone else said developer, and so on."

Sloan thought of the old Parker place, the size and scope of it, the history, the character. And frowned again.

"He doesn't sound handy."

"He really doesn't, but I'm going to hope, then hope if he is handy, he doesn't expect to get New York prices for labor."

On a sigh, she lifted her wine. "Well, change happens, whether you're ready for it or not."

"I'll say."

Elsie reached across the counter to squeeze Sloan's hand. "I have to ask, and want points for waiting this long. Did you eat today?"

"Most of a bowl of cereal with fruit, and a bowl of your soup. I'm writing all that down, too. And tomorrow, I'm going to do it all again. When I'm not sitting here peeling apples or pulling out pumpkin guts for pies."

"I'll be home by one to get all that started."

"I'll be here."

"I like hearing that."

They both heard Dean come in the mudroom, scolding the dog. "No, you don't, pal. You sit right there until I get the Abominable Snowman off you."

"Now you can get started on your day," Elsie told her.

"Not very exciting. In fact, I bored myself. It's a lot of rinse and repeat."

"We want to hear it. Dean? I'm having a glass of wine with Sloan. Do you want one?"

"Pour away. Give me another minute. Whose idea was it to get a dog who likes to bury himself in snow?"

"Yours," mother and daughter said together.

"Oh yeah."


A good Day One, Sloan congratulated herself as she readied for bed. She'd eaten what counted as three meals, done some strength training, had walked, when you added it all up, just under a full mile. And she'd made close to half a scarf.

Thirteen days to go, she thought, until she got the all clear.

She slept deep and dreamless until dawn slid silently across the eastern sky.

Rising, she welcomed Day Two.

# CHAPTER FOUR

Sipping his first cup of coffee, Nash Littlefield watched the sun burn red across the lake. Or his view of it through pines and skeletal hardwoods.

He enjoyed the brilliant drama of it, the contrast of that drama with the almost preternatural quiet.

From where he stood, he heard only the roar of the fire in the hearth, the whisper of winds that snuck through the failing weather stripping of windows he planned to replace.

Even his well-built condo hadn't masked the sounds of the city he lived with, lived in all of his adult life.

And now he lived with, lived in the quiet.

With the distance and those ancient, inefficient windows shut, he couldn't hear the quacking or honking of waterfowl. If he wanted that, he could gear up and take a short hike.

That short hike wouldn't take him to a restaurant, a bar, a shop but to a lake that earned its name with its reflected mountains and sky.

He could've afforded one of the lakefront houses with their better views and access, their up-to-date fixtures and amenities.

But he had, maybe for the first time in his life, exactly what he wanted.

The challenge of an old place, with good bones, that needed him to bring it to life. And the solitude it afforded. The convenience to town when he wanted that.

He had, imagine it, the possibility of making a living doing something he loved rather than something he'd been expected to do.

He considered he'd started that by tackling the old workshop, buttoning it up, organizing tools—the ones that came with the house, the ones he'd had, and, best of all, the ones he'd bought with his new business in mind.

He'd been good at the expected—investments, managing accounts, making money out of money, gauging the market. He'd even enjoyed it. But he hadn't been happy. Not really happy in the corner office he'd earned, or in his sleek, stylish condo with its very fine view of the city.

He'd had a woman he'd cared for, and who had cared for him. But not enough, just not enough to make it stick for either of them.

Particularly not when he'd decided to change his life.

If he'd stayed, they might have stuck at least for a few years. But he wouldn't have been happy. If they'd started a family, he'd have stuck, no question there.

He knew what it was to be the child of those who didn't stick.

But standing here, in the big, drafty mess of a house, he knew he'd found his place.

And waking here, crossing the creaky floors, shoving wood into the fire to cut the chill, he knew himself happy.

As he'd known it when he'd turned in his resignation, when he'd sold his condo, when he'd gotten his contractor's license.

Now he'd make his home, and earn his living with his hands. Something he'd always wanted.

And he felt more than happy. He felt—and yes, for the first time—free.

No more designer suits and carefully knotted ties, no more weekly trims to keep his unruly waves in check. If he didn't feel like shaving? So what?

So he stood there with his oak-brown hair waving at the collar of a white, insulated shirt, a couple days' worth of stubble on the hard planes of his jaw and cheeks, brown eyes on the drama of a new day's birth, and felt complete satisfaction.

He heard the floor creak, glanced around as his surprise—and welcome—visitor came to the head of the stairs.

His brother, Theo, wore sleepy eyes of golden brown, a mop of sleep-crazed brown hair, and a pair of *Star Wars* boxers.

"It's freezing in here."

"If you're going to walk around next to naked, you're going to be cold."

"Right. Minute."

As Theo turned around, Nash headed back, down a long hall, through a doorway in a wall he fully intended to knock down, and into a kitchen he figured hadn't been updated in half a century.

All that would change.

On the stained Formica counter sat a shining silver machine Nash would have fought to the death to keep.

He made a second coffee for himself and one for his younger brother.

He heard the stairs creak, and the spots on the floor in the hallway. He wasn't sure he wanted to fix all that. He'd miss the old-fashioned sound.

A montage of Marvel Comics characters covered Theo's sweatpants. He'd paired them with his Columbia University sweatshirt. "Got bagels?"

Nash pointed to a drawer.

"Man, it's quiet here. Like spooky quiet. Horror-movie quiet, where it's just you and the guy in the hockey mask. Took me forever to fall asleep, then I slept like a corpse."

He sliced the bagel, then popped it in the shiny silver toaster.

"I couldn't believe you bought this place." In the old fridge he hunted up cream cheese. "Then got a load of the view outside the window this morning. It's you all over."

"Is it?"

"You know it is. That vacay we took here back when? You couldn't get enough. Still, I had to see the house for myself, you know. Plus, Thanksgiving. Can't miss our annual Thanksgiving pizza."

Nash's one regret about the move was Theo. And now Theo toasted bagels in the big drafty kitchen.

"It's gotta be frozen this year. The place in town closes on Thanksgiving."

"It's still pizza." Theo popped another bagel in the toaster, then brought the two halves and the cream cheese to the makeshift table.

Nash had found an old door in the workshop. It now served, with its sawhorse legs, as a table surface.

"We could build a table," Theo said.

"I'll get around to it." Nash picked up his half a bagel. "A lot of other things have priority."

"Like heat. The furnace is probably crap."

"No 'probably' about it."

"The windows are definitely crap."

"They're way beyond crap."

"That wall's gotta go."

"It's going."

Nodding, Theo munched on his bagel. "Insulate, I mean Christ. And the floors. Those babies look original. Firm 'em up, refinish, they'll be a showstopper. Bathrooms are sad, and this kitchen."

"Designing my place now?"

"I know how you think." Rising, Theo went over to get the second bagel. "You'll upgrade, and bring it up to code—and right now, it can't be close to code. You'll bust out that wall, and turn the bedroom next to the one you're using into a kick-ass bathroom, a nice walk-in closet. And a deck, you'll want that to take advantage of the view. Enlarge the kitchen, open it, bring it into the current century."

Theo smiled over his bagel. "Big house, lots of rooms you'll open, combine. It'll cost you more to fix it up right than it did to buy it."

Something Nash had calculated, considered, then accepted.

"You're not wrong on that. I've got drawings in for permits."

Nodding, Theo kept eating. "A lot of work, bro. Plus starting a business, getting that set up. You could use some help."

"Are you volunteering to come down on weekends?"

He'd already planned to earmark one of the bedrooms for Theo's visits. And calculated the travel time.

"No." Theo drank more coffee, then set those golden-brown eyes on his brother's. "I'm asking you to give me a shot."

Because he was still thinking about the distance, the travel, it took Nash a minute. "A shot at what?"

"Partners, in the business you want to make. Teammates in restoring this house. Living here while we do the second part anyway."

"You live in New York. You're a lawyer."

"Yeah, I passed the bar and I've got that shiny new degree."

"And a job at a damn good firm."

"Says the guy who had a job at a damn good firm on Wall Street up until about a month ago."

He waited a moment, giving his brother a chance to process.

"They had a way, you know it, of putting just the right amount of pressure on us to do what they wanted. You in finance, me in the law. So we did it. I didn't see the escape hatch until you opened it and went through."

"Theo—"

"Don't parent me, okay? You've only got a couple years on me." Theo shoved the bagel in the air toward Nash, then pulled it back and bit in. "I don't want to practice law in New York."

"Well" was all that came to him.

"I don't know if I want to live here—maybe that's just temporary. But I'm asking for the shot. I'm good with tools, you know that. I've got some skills and a good eye. You're my family. You're what I've got. I'm what you've got."

Truer words, Nash thought. And sighed. "They're really pissed at me."

"Didn't stop you," Theo pointed out. "It won't stop me. I want to try doing something I want to do. Right now, this is it. Add in, I am a lawyer. Somebody starting his own business could use a good lawyer."

He ate more bagel. "Money isn't an issue for either of us. That's a privilege, and we paid for it, goddamn it, Nash. We paid. Maybe I didn't know how much I wanted out until you got out. But I do now."

He hadn't figured on this, and wondered now if he should have. They'd been close all their lives, linked together as they were shuttled back and forth between parents after the divorce. Watching mother and father remarry, divorce. And in their father's case remarry again.

But all the while those parents had united in the insistence their two sons do what was expected of a Littlefield, socially, professionally.

Small wonder now that he'd broken that chain, Theo wanted to follow.

"Listen, you can stay here as long as you like. Until you figure out what you really want. And yeah, I can use your help with the house, so great. As for the rest, you'd need a contractor's license, and—"

"Taking the test next month." Theo grinned at him. "I'm not deadweight, Nash."

"You've never been. I don't know how much work we can generate, at least in the first year or so. You're right, money isn't a problem, but establishing a business, that's vital. Good work, reasonable prices, reliability."

"No job too small," Theo said. "Need your toilet fixed and your plumber can't make it on a Sunday afternoon? We're there."

"Well, shit. All right then."

"Yes!" Theo shot out a hand. "Partners?"

"Make it legal," Nash said as they shook over the old door.

"Can do. The Fix-It Brothers of Heron's Rest."

Nash started to laugh, then considered. "The Fix-It Brothers. That works."

"And so do we."


For Sloan, Day Two brought progress, and comfort with it. With the faithful Mop, she walked her snowy path by the lake. And effortfully added ten more steps.

She accepted the need to rest by the fire until her breath stopped whistling and her legs felt solid again. Instead of cereal, she scrambled a single egg, added a slice of toast, and managed just over half of both.

A slow, easy sun salutation frustrated her when she couldn't, simply couldn't push her own body into a plank. She lay a few minutes, face down with limbs trembling. Rolling over, she tried a standard sit-up, and failed.

Staring at the ceiling, now she let herself do what she hadn't allowed since she'd walked into the mini-mart.

She let herself wallow, let herself cry.

As if he understood, Mop wandered in, lay down beside her.

When she finished, she found herself surprised. She felt better, maybe a little bit cleared out. She indulged herself, lay stroking the dog, drawing in that unrestricted love.

"Okay, okay. We'll save that for another day. We're not there yet."

She compensated with ten minutes of easy floor stretches.

"Better than yesterday, right?" She hugged the dog, and held there another moment. "Let's go update the spreadsheet."

Doing just that gave her a sense of satisfaction. When her phone signaled a FaceTime request from Joel, she felt a leap of joy.

When she saw his face on-screen, heard his voice, she realized just how much she'd needed that connection with her life.

"Hey, sis. Wanted to wish you Happy Thanksgiving. Tomorrow's Crazy Day for us."

"You'll love every minute."

"Can't deny it."

She heard the sounds of birds, saw the Chesapeake Bay and the gulls swooping. And yearned.

"How're you doing?" he asked her.

"Good. Really. A lot better."

"You don't look half bad."

"Thanks. My days include at least three outside walks, and yesterday I—wait for it—curled two pounds! And started crocheting a scarf."

"You what now?"

"Two pounds curling."

He tilted his head, gave her that look. "Yay. You're crocheting? Like my granny?"

"My novice skills are no doubt an insult to your granny, but yeah." She reached in the basket, held up the crocheted red wool.

"Well, son of a bitch."

"Occupational therapy, that's how I see it. This afternoon, I'll help make pies." She set the scarf back in the basket and laughed at herself. "God, Joel, I need to get back to work."

"You'll get there, sis. I gotta get back to it myself, but I wanted to see your face. Glad I did, because you don't look half bad. Do I get that scarf?"

"My mother's getting this one. If I don't bore myself to death, I'll make you a manly one."

"I'll count on it. You take care of my partner, and have a good Thanksgiving."

"Doing my best. Love to Sari, Mama Dee, and the rest."

"Same to you and yours. I'll check in later."

She missed him, the work, the life she'd led the minute she put the phone down. So she picked up the yarn.

"Occupational therapy," she muttered.

She nodded off over it, but pushed back annoyance when she surfaced. She made progress on the scarf, and had only been under about twenty minutes.

After bundling up, she set out with Mop for another walk.

She spotted the two men standing together maybe a hundred yards or so ahead of her finish line.

About six feet, both of them, she judged, maybe a hundred sixty for the one on the left, one-fifty for the one on the right. Brown hair under ski caps—darker on the left male. She couldn't see their faces well enough with the distance, and both wore sunglasses against the glare off the lake, off the snow.

Black parka for the left, blue for the right. Jeans and boots for both.

Details, it always paid to notice details.

Relatives, probably, she thought, given the similarity in build, coloring, even how they stood. Maybe brothers.

She reached the end of that morning's line, and stopped to catch her breath, give her legs a chance to rest. "Five more, Mop. I can do five more steps."

When she had, she turned back. The house seemed so far away this trip, and her breathing already labored.

"It's okay, one step at a time. Slow and steady. We'll have a mile in, and one more walk to go today. Progress. Jesus, I feel like I've run up a mountain."

She had to stop again, wait until she felt she could manage that slow and steady.

Nash watched her walk, pause, walk.

"Nice-looking blonde," Theo commented. "At least I think so. Hard to be sure from this far away. The way she's walking, maybe she started her day with a few drinks."

"I don't think so. Looks more out of shape and tired, maybe sick or injured, than drunk." A little shaky, Nash thought, and decided to keep an eye on her as long as he could.

"Look at that dog!" On a laugh, Theo pointed as Mop leaped into a snowbank and rolled. "Likes his winter sports. Hey! We should get a dog."

Nash shifted his gaze long enough to look at Theo. "What would we do with a dog?"

"Enjoy. They never let us have one. Then, you know, New York and putting in the hours we both did. Not fair to close a dog in an apartment all day."

She'd stopped and started again, and now appeared to aim for a house up the slope. Good-looking house, great views, sturdy with style.

"And it's fair to have a dog hanging out all day while we're tearing the house up, working—we hope—outside jobs."

"Sure. Job dog." Theo's naturally sunny side shined brighter at the thought. "He hangs with us."

"Uh-huh." Since the woman and the dog made it inside, Nash took a last scan of the lake.

They'd easily walked a mile, he calculated, and that view stayed as alluring as ever. But.

"Let's go back, get the truck, and go check on our permits before town hall shuts down for the holiday."

"Cool. I want a better look at the town anyway."

"That part won't take long."

"I'm going to look at trucks. I'll need my own transportation, and it wouldn't hurt to have two trucks for the business. Hey, we could grab some lunch in town."

"And we'd better hit the grocery store. With you around, we need more food."

By the time her mother arrived, Sloan had pulled herself together. If asked, she could truthfully say she'd had breakfast, and lunch—even if lunch consisted of a few bites of leftover spaghetti.

"Drea's on her way with the pumpkins." Cheeks pink from the cold, Elsie hung up her coat. "I'm going to have both my girls making pies! How was your day, baby?"

"Good. Promise. I'm ready to deal with pumpkin guts, peel apples, and whatever else you've got in store."

"I've got a list." Pulling a clip from her pocket, Elsie looped her tail of blond hair, then secured it up.

She opened a closet, took out aprons. "You're going to need it. Once we get the pies done, I'm going to do the ham. Turkey goes in at dawn tomorrow. We can make the cranberry sauce today, bake some bread, devil a few dozen eggs."

"I don't know how you do it, year after year."

"Loving it helps. If I had to cook for an army more than a couple times a year, I wouldn't love it so much." Obviously primed, and pleased with the work ahead, Elsie got out bowls, knives, baking sheets.

"I'm going to say this before we get started, and I promise I won't say it again. Tomorrow, when you've had enough, need a break, need to lie down awhile, you'll go up and do that. You promise me that, I won't bring it up again."

"All right. I can promise that."

Elsie glanced toward the mudroom. "Here's Drea. Pumpkin in, dog out!"

"Got it," Drea called back. "Out you go, Mop. And I didn't have to tell him twice."

Drea came into the kitchen, pink cheeks, hair braided back, and a trio of pumpkins in her arms. "Let the games begin!"

And like a game, Sloan found it fun as it took her back to childhood. The gooey strings of pumpkin, separating the seeds for roasting. The scent of the pumpkin cooking in the oven, and the feel of a crisp apple in her hand.

As they worked, Elsie consulted her list.

"Your aunt Lauren's bringing a mincemeat pie."

"I've never understood the mincemeat," Sloan commented.

"Plenty do. Amelia's doing a cheesecake. Grandpa's bringing his sweet potato casserole, and Gramma's doing a roasted yam and kale salad."

"Yuck," the sisters said in unison.

"Now, now. Jonah and Gina are doing that snack mix the kids wolf down. Nanny and Pop—forgot to tell you, Sloan, their flight landed safe and on time. Archer and Josie will drive them in tomorrow. Mac and cheese from them. Oh, and your cousin Ray's bringing his boyfriend. Josie says it's serious."

"Serious-serious?" Sloan asked.

"Apparently. Your dad and I met him several months ago. He's really handsome, add funny and sweet. He's a forensic accountant."

"The artist slash art teacher and the forensic accountant. Interesting combo."

"They look cute together. They're bringing . . ." Elsie consulted her list. "Thyme-roasted brussels sprouts with fresh cranberries."

"Yet another interesting combo," Drea decided.

"And your cousin Flynn and Carlie round it out with corn pudding."

"How do you make pudding out of corn?" Sloan wondered.

"We'll find out."

With a pair of pumpkin pies in the oven, and sliced apples covered with sugar, flour, cinnamon resting in a bowl, Elsie rolled out more pie dough.

She did love it, Sloan thought. Every laborious minute of it.

In the spirit, she rose to help her sister clear the current chaos in preparation for the next round.

"Dad's bringing pizza, right?"

"It wouldn't be Thanksgiving Eve without pizza from Ricardo's," her mother answered. "And once we get the ham going, he's on dish duty. Are you hungry?"

"No. It's like you said, it wouldn't be Thanksgiving Eve otherwise." Because she needed a boost, Sloan pulled out a Pepsi. "Anybody else want a drink?"

"Sure. I call for a break after the apple pies are in. Mom needs to sit down for ten minutes before she wears out."

Sloan shot Drea a look. "I'm fine."

"Who's talking about you?"

"I could use ten, and the hell with healthy. Some chips to go with that Pepsi."

Outnumbered, Sloan took the ten.

"Oh, news from the Rest," Drea began. "I ran into Craig from town hall when I was getting the pumpkin. The new owner of the Parker place applied for building permits—right after he settled on the place."

"I hadn't heard that one," Elsie said.

"He'll have them early next week, according to Craig. He and his brother checked on them today. Some serious work's going to happen, according to Craig. Walls coming down, bathrooms and kitchen gutted, new windows throughout, updated wiring, plumbing, and whatever. Craig said the younger one's more talkative and mentioned they're starting up their business. The Fix-It Brothers."

"Brothers." Sloan frowned, thought back. "I wonder if that's who I saw today. Two guys on the lake path, not that far from the Parker place if they wanted a good walk. They struck me as relatives."

Elsie munched on a chip. "Did you talk to them?"

"No, they were well down the path."

And she had enough trouble breathing much less talking by the time she'd walked that far.

"But they had similar builds," Sloan continued, "body language, coloring. A lot of wavy brown hair on both of them. Anyway, it's good someone's willing to do that kind of work on that place. It's needed it.

"What's next on the list, Mom?"


While the pies cooled on a rack, the ham roasted, and Sloan helped peel countless hard-boiled eggs, Janet Anderson left her home near Deep Creek Lake to head to the grocery store.

She couldn't believe she'd run out of butter. For the first time in her life, she'd taken on Thanksgiving dinner, and she'd run out of damn butter. She probably needed more milk, too.

She was cooking for ten people, which terrified her. Her parents, her husband of fourteen months' parents, his brother and girlfriend, her brother and his—annoying and pregnant—wife.

And, of course, the girlfriend decided to go vegetarian, so she had to come up with vegetarian dishes in addition to the turkey—something she'd never cooked before.

She really wanted to do a good job. Her mother-in-law was incredibly nice, warm, welcoming. And a really, really exceptional cook.

She'd taken off the whole day to make certain their pretty little starter home shined. She'd arranged fresh flowers, she had candles, wine, special cloth napkins and rings.

Her mother-in-law volunteered to bring pies. Thank God! But Janet had insisted on doing all the rest.

Because, she admitted, she wanted Drake, his parents, hers, everyone, to be proud of her. And she'd gotten a second chance at being a really good marriage partner, and—hopefully soon—being a mother.

That summer she'd nearly drowned in the lake. Technically, she did drown. But they'd brought her back. Given her this second chance.

She wanted this to be a step toward all of that.

With her mind on the cranberry sauce she'd talked herself into making from actual cranberries—what if it didn't gel?—and all the sides she had to prepare, not to mention the intimidating sixteen-pound turkey, she didn't notice the white panel van turn into the lot behind her.

She parked, gathered her purse. Remembered her keys and dropped them in her outside pocket.

Late afternoon had gone gloomy, and now she worried about snow.

What if, what if they got dumped on and her parents couldn't make the drive? She really wanted them there.

She got out, then nearly walked into the door of the van when it opened in front of her.

A man got out, smiled. He said, "Sorry."

Then jabbed a needle into the side of her neck.

She managed one gasp and started to struggle, but the side door rolled open.

He shoved her inside, climbed in after her.

Dimly she heard the door roll closed again, heard him say:

"Got her, babe. Easy peasy."

She managed to choke out, "Help," before everything went dark.

"Don't you worry, Janet." The woman in the driver's seat glanced in the rearview before she pulled out of the lot. "That's what we're here for. Check her pulse, doll. We don't want her fading out on us before we get her home."

"Slow and steady, babe. She's just under."

But he lifted her onto the cot on the side of the van and strapped her down. Once he had her secured, he climbed back into the passenger seat. He fastened his seat belt, then turned on the radio.

"Easiest one yet." He slid on sunglasses, smiled a happy smile. "Who knew she'd take a drive to the supermarket out of the blue like that?"

The woman drove, carefully, at the speed limit, toward the highway. And gave a silent thanks for the blessing now in the back of the van.

"What's meant's meant, doll," she said. "She's nearly the youngest one we've released. I have a real good feeling about Janet."

He consulted the chart. "Twenty-four, five-five, a hundred and twenty-one pounds. Type O-neg. All good on her last checkup."

He sat back with a sigh, tapped his foot to the beat on the radio.

"Pretty perfect. I gotta say I wasn't sure it was worth it, driving down here after we both worked an early shift. But, babe, you always know best."

"She'll have a story to tell, I know it. Then we'll take what she has and set her free."

# CHAPTER FIVE

When Janet woke with her head floating, her first vague thought was: Hospital.

She heard the beep of a monitor, saw beige walls and the IV needle on her left hand. The narrow bed had guards on either side, and the back was lifted so she half sat, half reclined.

She'd had an emergency appendectomy her junior year at college, then the accident in the lake, so thought hospital.

She'd had an accident? She couldn't remember.

But when she tried to reach for a call button, she found herself strapped down. And panic bubbled up her throat.

She tried to shout, but the single word—"Help!"—came out in a croak. As she turned her head from side to side, she saw a woman rise from a chair. She wore scrubs with kittens playing over them, and that eased some of the panic.

Her smile struck reassuring in a round face topped by curly brown hair.

"Here you go!" The woman picked up a cup with a bendy straw. "Sip some. You're thirsty and light-headed, but everything's fine."

"What happened?"

"What was meant to." She gave Janet's head a light pat. "Everything that happens now was meant."

"Where am I? Drake—"

"Where you're meant to be, Janet. Don't worry about a thing! We're going to take care of you."

"Did I have an accident?"

The woman had blue eyes, so pale, so clear, so calm.

"Nothing's really accidental, is it, Janet? The Almighty has a plan for all creatures, and all His creations are precious. I'm Nurse Clara, and I'm here for you."

"My husband, I want to see my husband. Is Drake here? He must be worried."

"Mm-hmm."

Studying one of the monitors, Clara nodded, then took out her phone, sent a text.

"Why am I strapped down? I need to . . . I was going to the store for butter. Thanksgiving. Oh, I left everything out on the counter! I need to—"

She broke off when a man opened the door. He, too, wore scrubs, plain blue. But she saw his face, remembered his face.

Now panic spurted.

"The parking lot. The van. This isn't the hospital." Terrified now, she strained against the straps. "Who are you? What's happening?"

"Now, now, I understand the urge to struggle, but it won't help. We've secured you for your own protection. This is Nurse Sam," Clara continued as Janet fought against the straps, and the man set up a tripod and camera. "We're here for you, Janet. We're here to help you."

"Let me go. I want to go home! I want Drake." Tears rained as she fought. "You can't keep me here."

"Letting you go is why we're here. Try to stay calm. Now take some deep breaths. We don't want to sedate you again, Janet."

With that reassuring smile in place, with blue eyes calm and clear, Clara picked up a syringe.

"No, no, no, no! Don't! Please."

"It's up to you, Janet. We're given choices in this life, we have the gift of free will."

"What do you want? We—we have some money. Drake would pay. My parents would. We have some."

Insult, sincere and strong, flashed over Clara's face. "Oh, what a terrible thing to say! No one dedicates their lives to others for money. The poor thing, Sam, thinks we're holding her for ransom."

He just shook his head. "Too many people think it's always about money."

But when he looked at Janet, she felt a chill run through her. His eyes, not calm and clear, held some hungry secret. A light-skinned Black man, he didn't smile.

Where the woman edged toward plump, he was lean. He wore his hair in short, neat twists. She tried to judge his height—details to tell the police. Not really tall. Five-eight or nine. Or ten?

Oh, she wasn't any good at that kind of thing.

But she needed to be. Needed to stay calm. She didn't want the needle.

She tried to swallow the panic. "Please tell me what you want."

"Your story, Janet." Clara sat in the chair beside the camera, folded her hands in her lap. "We want you to tell us your story before we let you go."

"I don't understand."

One little window, she noted—high by the ceiling, covered with a blackout shade.

A basement?

"What story?"

"The story that matters, of course."

Clara's voice remained pleasant, her smile encouraging.

"On June twenty-fourth, you died."

"Well, no. I'm—I'm here. I'm alive."

"Brought back by artificial means."

"Not—not—not—" She had to stop, take a long breath. "Not really. I mean. I fell off a paddleboard on the lake. Um, Deep Creek Lake? And hit my head. I went under, and nobody realized for a couple minutes, so—"

"We know all of that, Janet." Sam spoke from behind the camera.

"Now, Sam, she can tell it in her own way. But what he means, Janet, is we're aware, of course, of what led to your death. You drowned. They weren't able to establish exactly how long you were gone before you were brought back to life, pulled back into this world. Two minutes, maybe three. We need to hear what happened in that two or three minutes."

"I don't understand. I was unconscious."

"No, Janet. You were dead. Tell us what you experienced."

"I don't know. I fell, hit my head on the board. I had a mild concussion. They kept me in the hospital overnight, but I was fine."

"Janet." Clara spoke with infinite patience. "The story we need begins and ends with those two or three minutes. It's important for you to tell that story, for that story to be documented. Where did you go? What did you see? What did you hear or feel or learn?"

Long tube lights on the ceiling. The floor looked like concrete. Steps! Steps leading up.

A basement. Yes, a basement room with beige walls.

"Janet, what did you see, or hear, or feel, or learn?" Clara repeated.

"There was nothing. I fell, hit my head, and I went under the water. Then I was choking and heaving up water. My head hurt, and my chest, my throat."

Clara nodded. "You had pain when you were pulled back. Before, before they forced you back into this world, it was peaceful, wasn't it?"

"I don't know. I didn't want to die."

Clara's smile remained pleasant, her voice patient.

"Want doesn't change what is, what was, what must be. Please try to remember, to take yourself back to that two or three minutes. It's what's best for you."

"The board knocked me out, so there isn't anything to remember. I promise I'd tell you if there was. Afterward, I remember afterward how the light hurt my eyes."

"You saw a light?"

"When I coughed up all the water, the sun hurt my eyes. And Drake started crying, and I went to the hospital in an ambulance. Wait, first, I was on the boat. The police boat. I don't remember that very well. I felt really sick.

"That's what I remember. I swear."

"You have nothing to tell us about your death? Where you went?"

"I was in the water, and they pulled me out and saved me."

On a sigh, Clara looked over at Sam. "All right, Janet. I know you did your best."

"You're going to let me go. You said you'd let me go."

"Yes, of course." Clara rose. "A promise is a promise."

She walked over to a sink, scrubbed her hands, then slicked on medical gloves. She went to the table beside the bed, took a tourniquet, and wrapped it on Janet's arm.

"What are you doing? Stop!"

"It's important to be sanitary, Janet." Carefully, Clara used an antiseptic wipe. "We'll use the antecubital fossa. You have good veins! Just relax now. Relax," she repeated as she pulled the skin on Janet's arm taut to anchor the vein.

"No! Let me go. You said—"

"We are. Here now, I'm very good at this. You'll barely feel a thing."

"Don't! Don't! You promised."

"And a promise I keep." She nodded, pleased, as blood appeared in the tubing. She connected it to the plasma bag.

Horrified, terrified, Janet didn't realize Sam worked on her other arm until the procedure was nearly done.

"You're taking my blood! You're taking my blood."

"Yes, of course. It's useful. You want to be useful, don't you, Janet? All God's creatures serve a purpose. Just relax," Clara told her. "This really won't take very long, and you'll be at peace again."

"Why are you doing this to me? Why?"

"Shh!" Gently, Clara stroked Janet's forehead. "Your existence in this world is unnatural. Men forced you back, and we're here to ease your path to where you belong. Only God can perform the miracle of resurrection, Janet."

"Don't, don't! Don't hurt me. Don't kill me."

"We're sending you home, Janet. You'll just go to sleep now, and when you wake, you'll be where you're meant to be. It's our hope that the Perpetual Light shines upon you, and not the everlasting fires of Hell."

Janet screamed, and tears ran down her face. But the screams weakened, and the tears began to dry as the blood drained out of her.

Efficiently, Sam unhooked bags, replaced them with fresh. He labeled and stored them in the refrigerator at the back of the room with the others.

Janet went as pale as the crisp white sheets. When her eyes fixed,

Clara gently closed them. On the monitor, her vitals sank, then flat-lined.

"Rest now," Clara murmured. "Rest in peace."

"We should get close to four liters," Sam told her.

"Very good. We'll dispose of her earthly remains in a few hours. Okay with leftovers tonight?" Clara tossed her gloves in the wastebasket. "Meatloaf sandwiches? I've got a turkey to roast tomorrow."

"Sounds good, babe. Too bad she didn't see anything."

"Oh, I know she did. Those who pulled her back stole that from her, too. Poor thing. Well, she's getting her eternal reward now, whatever it may be."

Clara turned off the machines.

"Go ahead and clean up, doll, while I get us some dinner. I'll have a cold beer waiting for you."

He stopped to give her a warm embrace, a long kiss. "You're the best, babe."

"Better with you."

She went upstairs in their cozy little house to make sandwiches out of meatloaf she'd baked the night before with a little blood of the resurrected.

On Thanksgiving morning, Sloan's Day Three, she woke early. She dressed for her walk, and when she went down for coffee, she smelled it already done. And found her mother, obviously up before the sun, stuffing the enormous turkey.

"You take your walk," Elsie ordered. "I've got this under control."

"I'll be back to help."

"Once this bad boy's in the oven, we're gold for a while. Take the dog, and take your time. We got another inch overnight."

Sloan set out and felt good about it. Felt good she'd slept a solid eight—closer to nine—hours, and without the nagging dreams.

She walked in the crisp air with the brooding sky mirrored in the lake. Just her, she thought, and Mop, the waterfowl. Including the heron she watched glide, then dive.

He came up with a fat fish, then streamed away to enjoy his breakfast.

Stronger, Sloan realized. She honestly felt stronger this morning. When she made it to last evening's stop, then ten steps more, she decided she could try another five.

She wanted five more yet, but reminded herself how easily she flagged on the return trip. Fifteen equaled progress.

"See?" she told Mop. "I'm not obsessive. Not pushing beyond my limits."

She rolled a snowball, gave it a toss—just a light toss up—for Mop to leap and bite. More PT, she considered. The bending, straightening, tossing. So every few feet, she rolled another snowball.

Then stopped, not so much to rest as to exchange long looks with the big buck that stopped at the edge of the trees.

Ten pointer.

"Watch out, buddy. We're moving from archery season to firearms."

She hooked a hand in Mop's collar, just in case. He aimed a series of barks at the deer, and the buck gave them both a superior look before turning and sliding back into the trees.

Satisfied, Mop shoved his muzzle into the snow.

"If I could be at work, I'd be patrolling the woods today. But we'll get back to it."

She only had to stop once, and did that so she wouldn't walk back in breathless.

She went in the mudroom entrance, stripped off her gear.

Elsie sat at the kitchen counter, frowning at the TV.

"Good, now I can turn this off. I don't know why I turn it on the news anyway. Something bad always happened I wish I didn't know."

"What happened?"

"Oh, the usual world bullshit, but close to home? A woman went missing down at Deep Creek."

"How long?"

"They're not exactly sure. Her husband got home just before six last night. She'd taken the day off because she was doing Thanksgiving dinner for their family. She wasn't home."

Elsie poured out two more cups of coffee.

"He didn't think too much of it, but texted her just to see, and the text didn't go through. He tried calling, same thing. Tried some of their friends, nobody'd seen her. Worried enough, he went out looking."

"Any signs of violence in the home? Any problems with the marriage?"

Elsie held up a finger. "No, Corporal Investigator. At least not that they said in the report. He found her car parked at their local grocery store. But nobody'd seen her there either. That's when he called the police."

Sloan had a dozen questions building up, but let her mother finish.

"They started a search, but nothing so far. He did an interview. Poor guy looked terrified. She's ah, let me think. Twenty-four."

"Did they show her photo?"

"Yes, a pretty brunette. Happy eyes."

Sometimes happy took a hard turn, Sloan thought. But why leave the car?

"Keys in the car?"

"They didn't say either way."

"Purse, wallet?"

Elsie gave Sloan's arm a light pat as she walked by.

"They didn't give every detail, baby. I hope they find her. It was down to about twenty-eight last night. Anyway, I shouldn't have turned on the news. Your father's up, grabbing a shower. He's making omelets."

"Sounds good. If we're still clear in here for a while after, I should use the fitness room, do some PT."

"You do what you need to do, then maybe change into something besides sweats."

"I can do that." And find a few minutes to look up more information about the missing woman.

She managed half a cheese omelet and a triangle of toast, which seemed to satisfy her parents. Then she took her phone into the fitness room and looked up what she could find on the missing woman.

As that didn't satisfy her, she made a call.

Captain Travis Hamm not only had been one of her inspirations for joining the NRP, but had been her father's friend since childhood.

She called his personal cell.

"Hey! How's that girl!"

"Doing good, Cap. Happy Thanksgiving."

"Same to you. I'm coming by to see you in a few days, and I expect you to look a hell of a lot better than you did when I dropped by the hospital."

"I can promise that one. Listen, I know I'm on leave, but I heard about the missing woman."

"Janet Anderson."

"Yes. Really, I'm just curious, and wonder if you can give me more details than I can get in the news."

"No harm in that. You're still NRP. It's looking like she stopped working on some casserole—she was making Thanksgiving dinner—and headed to the store. Either she destroyed her phone or someone else did. Her neighbor thinks he might have seen her pull out of her driveway between four and four-thirty. He's not a hundred percent on it. No keys, no purse in the vehicle. No family disputes. They were married just over a year, and by all accounts crazy about each other."

"You're leaning toward abduction."

"It's looking that way, but it's possible she had a meltdown. She took a fall into the lake last summer, had to be pulled out, resuscitated."

"What kind of fall?"

"Paddleboard. Witnesses saw her fall in—no foul play. It took a minute for her husband to realize she wasn't coming back up. She'd hit her head on the board. Officer First Class Wilber was on patrol. They got her into the boat, did CPR, mouth-to-mouth, and got her back."

"Lingering issues? Physical, emotional?"

"Nothing physical. Her husband said she has some bad dreams every so often, some anxiety. And she was nervous about making this family meal. We're not discounting any of that. Search teams are out, with canines. No ransom contact."

"I saw her photo. She's very pretty. Young and pretty."

"Not discounting that either. It takes balls or crazy to abduct a woman in a grocery store parking lot at somewhere around four-thirty in the afternoon."

"Yeah, it does. Thanks for filling me in, Cap. I miss the job."

"I bet it misses you, Corporal. I'll be by to see you in a few days."

"Looking forward to it. Happy Thanksgiving to your family, too."

"And to yours. Tell your old man he owes me that beer."

"Will do."

She picked up three-pound weights, sat on the bench. And as she curled, thought about Janet Anderson.

When she finished, she went upstairs, set her phone alarm, and slept for fifteen minutes. Considering she'd see extended family—and they'd see her—she took time to do her makeup.

Then stared at herself in the mirror. It actually helped. Maybe it didn't cover the healing wound on her forehead, but it helped.

Spirits boosted, she chose a dark green sweater, the dark gray jeans she considered moderately dressy. Weight loss meant she needed a belt, and they still bagged in the ass some, but better.

Since her sister had packed them, she added earrings, two small hoops for her left ear, one for the right.

Then stood back, took stock.

"There you almost are."

Music played on low in the kitchen, and she found her mother and sister sitting at the counter drinking hot chocolate.

"I guess I didn't miss anything."

"Oh, you look nice, baby! Sit down, have some hot chocolate before we get to work. We've still got time," Elsie added before she popped up to pour Sloan chocolate from the red pot with its white snowflakes.

"Whipped cream or marshmallows?"

Because she honestly wanted neither, Sloan grinned. "Why not both?" And saw immediately she's said the right thing, as pleasure lit her mother's face.

"Your dad'll be back before three—and might even beat some of the gang. So much to do over the holiday."

"She's high on holiday," Drea commented.

"I am, and not ashamed."

"I'm getting a little high myself. It smells amazing in here."

"The bird's doing his job. Now, I want the table set before the first arrival."

"Which will be Gramma and Grandpa," Drea put in.

"No question. And we'll put out the nice cheese and charcuterie I have planned. Drea already made a pretty cheese ball."

Sloan angled her head at her sister. "Check you."

"Damn right. Still, it's nothing compared to the baked Brie Mom did. It looks like a little pumpkin."

"I watched a video, and tried it last night. We're going to do some candied nuts, and we already did the cranberry relish yesterday. Add some veg, some fruit, some sliced Gouda, crackers."

"Fancy," Sloan commented.

"I really wanted a little fancy this year." Elsie gripped Sloan's hand, then Drea's. "Just a little special. I've got a lot to be thankful for."

"I've got table duty. I'm good at the fancy."

Now Sloan frowned. "I can be good at the fancy."

"I'm better. You peel and chop."

"You can start with carrots," Elsie told her. "Roasted and glazed for the table, raw for the charcuterie. I need a mountain."

So Sloan peeled a mountain of carrots, trimmed another mountain of green beans, sliced apples and pears to toss in lemon juice. As she started on the next mountain—potatoes—she had to admit, her sister's table managed to hit both the fancy and family with her mother's good china and wineglasses, rusty red napkins in copper rings, and a pair of squat pumpkin-colored candles in glass columns ready to light.

With the lower oven hard at work, the turkey roasting in the top, Drea kept busy cleaning up behind their mother.

She gathered up all the vegetable debris. "I'll run all these out to the composter."

"Thanks, baby."

Sloan waited until her sister went outside. "I'm doing the charcuterie."

"Oh, well—"

"I'll make it fancy."

"It's just I have a lot of other things. Grapes—I want them put out on the vine. Dried fruit, some cute little gourds—just for decoration. And this sweet potato spread I made last night."

"I'll make it fancy," Sloan repeated, determined. "Drea can quarter the potatoes for boiling. What am I using?"

"I got a new board for it."

When Elsie brought it out, Sloan felt her confidence waver.

"It's really big."

"There are a lot of us, but—"

"You don't think I can do it." Sloan pointed a finger at her mother. "I'll show you!"

"All right then." Elsie plastered on a bright smile. "I'll get you everything you need. I'm doing some little slices of baguette along with crackers."

"Jeez, Mom, you went wild."

When Drea came back in, she looked at the board and the variety her mother assembled.

"I'll help with that."

"No!" Eyes narrowed, Sloan held her arms over the board. "Mine!"

"Wow. Fine. Whatever."

Sloan decided to approach it like a puzzle. She liked puzzles. She began to arrange, shifted and arranged again. Started over.

Then slowly began to see a pattern of shapes, colors, textures.

"It's looking very pretty," Elsie said, surprise thinly covered.

"Not done." Rising, Sloan went into the pantry, found the colorful veggie chips her mother bought and her father pretended to like.

She added some in a short, careful curve, then took a whole pear from the fruit bowl and placed it.

"Don't touch it."

She got up, went into the living room and came back with three yellow-orange baby mums from a vase, placed them. Added a few springs of sage leaves, filled spots in with more candied nuts, then another small curve of veggie chips. She carefully sliced some figs she hadn't yet used, placed them.

Finally, she took a handful of the pumpkin seeds they'd roasted the day before, sprinkled them on.

"Now it's done." Folding her arms, she stepped back to survey her masterpiece.

"It's—beautiful. Honestly, Sloan, it looks better than the video."

"I have to admit." Drea walked closer. "I'm seriously impressed."

"I have skills." To memorialize it, Sloan pulled out her phone and took a picture.

Drea took out her phone, then put an arm around her mother. "Bring it in, Sloan. Cooper girls selfie."

She nearly reached up to the wound on her forehead, then pushed the urge back. Flanking her mother, she smiled at the camera.

"All right, Cooper girls, I figure we've got about twenty before my parents arrive a half hour early. Let's get little plates for this magnificent board, light the candles on the magnificent table. Then we're going to be thankful for a glass of wine."

As they opened the bottle, Dean came in with Mop.

"Everything's under control," he announced. "And we've got a nice, clear day. Cold and clear. Hey, it not only smells amazing in here, it looks amazing. Elsie, you outdid yourself on that board thing."

"Sloan made it."

"No, really? Wow."

He started to reach over to sample, and Sloan threw out her hands. "No! It's not to be touched."

"Ever?"

"Until. Here." She handed him the bag of veggie chips. "Eat these."

"That's okay. I can wait." As he'd been trained, he folded the bag, clipped it, and returned it to the pantry.

"We're having a glass of thankful wine," Elsie told him.

"I'm in." And as he looked back at them, his smile spread. "I have everything any man could be thankful for right here."

# CHAPTER SIX

Elsie knew her parents, and had timed their arrival nearly to the minute.

For her part, Sloan prepared herself for questions and comments about her health, probably her weight loss. She reminded herself those questions and comments came from love, and worry laced the love.

Her grandfather hugged her so hard she felt her injured ribs twinge, but warmth, and that love, saturated the embrace.

"Look at you." Miles Riley scanned every inch of Sloan's face before laying his lips, so gently, on her forehead. "There's that girl." He kissed her again. "We knew they couldn't keep you down."

"Let me in there."

Her grandmother's hug, equally fierce, added a whiff of Dior's J'adore. "You look better, and brighter with it. Skinny, but better and brighter."

"You have red hair."

"What do you think?" Blue eyes smug, Ava patted her bold copper wedge. "I decided enough of old lady ash blond and went for it."

"I love it, and the cut's great."

"Got some zip to it. They can take that bullshit about growing old gracefully and stuff it."

"You'll never be old, Gramma."

"Not if I can help it. I have to keep my boyfriend here on his toes."

"And she does," Miles confirmed. "She sure does."

"And always will. Elsie, everything looks wonderful."

"I learned from the best."

"You sure did." With a laugh, Ava fisted her hands on her hips. "Dean, you're not only a handsome devil, but a lucky son of a bitch."

"Don't I know it." He gave his mother-in-law a kiss and a glass of wine.

Within the hour, the house on the lake filled with people, with voices, with the scents of the season. After the initial not-so-subtle studies, words of concern or encouragement, the subject of Sloan's health—to her relief—dropped away.

And she considered the decimation of her carefully created charcuterie a solid compliment. Adults munched, drank, gathered in a crowd or cozied up for more personal chats. Kids, ranging from eleven to four, gave Mop all the love a dog could want.

By the time her father began to carve the turkey—fancily presented with a surround of parsley, cranberries, rosemary, sage—Sloan had fielded all the comments and questions.

Her paternal grandfather carved the ham served on a bed of rosemary and thyme.

Ezra Cooper winked at his daughter-in-law. "I swear, Elsie, I'm putting on the pounds just looking at this spread." Behind his black-framed glasses, his gaze slid to Sloan. "And seeing as we're all of us together, and all of us healthy, wealthy, and wise, I'm gonna be grateful for every one of them."

"Together." Rose Cooper's hand reached for Sloan's, squeezed lightly as the eyes she'd passed to her granddaughter scanned the faces all around. "That's the gift."

When they sat around the big table, when that table groaned with platters and bowls, Dean lifted his glass.

"To family. The best there is."

They feasted.


Roughly a mile away, the Littlefield brothers sat in the chilly, outdated kitchen with a large pepperoni pizza on the makeshift table.

Theo lifted his beer. "Here's to us, the fucking Fix-It Brothers. We're going to kick some handyman ass around here."

"Here's to us," Nash agreed. "To the fucking Fix-It Brothers, to kicking that handyman ass, and Jesus, getting those damn permits so we can start on this wreck of a house."

"I'll drink to all of that." And Theo did before he took his first slice. "It's going to be a great house when we're done with it."

"I'm counting on it."

"Did you ever picture us in a place like this?" As he ate, Theo glanced around the frozen-in-the-seventies kitchen. "In a big, drafty, full-of-potential house near a lake in the mountains?"

"I guess I did, since I bought the place."

"No, I mean back when. I used to think how we'd get out, just out of that mausoleum where you weren't supposed to touch anything. Then after the divorce, out of the mausoleum she kept, and out of the midlife crisis mansion he bought where everything was sharp and shiny."

"The chrome and glass palace."

"Yeah. You needed sunglasses the minute you opened your eyes in the morning. I always figured we'd get out, I just never pictured where we'd get out to."

"I thought about California for about five minutes."

With a nod, Theo gestured with his beer. "Because it's on the opposite side of the country from Connecticut. I thought about Alaska."

Nash nearly choked on his pizza. "Get out."

"I did, for maybe ten minutes. How I'd talk you into heading out there. We'd get a cabin, start a business, live free, right? Then I remembered how it's dark there like half the time. Snow's one thing."

"Let's open it up, then close it again and put it away. I got an earful yesterday. Well, two. One from each."

Theo's brown eyes held all his sympathy with a little guilt tossed in.

"Sorry. I figured that would come once I emailed each of them I wasn't taking the position at the firm, and was starting a business with you here."

"No sorry required or wanted." Nash lifted a slice. "Do I look wounded?"

Theo smiled, shrugged. "You always handled it better than I did."

"Not always." He'd just cared less, Nash thought. And cared less sooner than Theo. "But the point is, it's done now."

Theo gestured with his slice. "And all your fault, naturally."

"Mostly mine."

And he'd let that roll over him. The angry accusations of carelessness, ingratitude, shortsightedness, and his stubborn determination to ruin his brother's life along with his own.

"I'm ungrateful and recalcitrant."

"Can you really be recalcitrant once you hit thirty?"

"Apparently." Nash gestured with his slice in turn. "But you? You're just feckless."

Theo's grin flashed. "According to them, that's my middle name."

"And they're wrong, as usual. You're your own man, Theo. Smart, capable, open-minded and -hearted. Their unique combination of neglect and unshakable demands layered together with constant disappointment hurt you more than it did me."

"You were always there to stanch the wounds. It doesn't hurt anymore, Nash, or not enough to count. Are you going to tell me what you said to them?"

There had been times along the way Nash had held back, held it all in. But, partners now as well as brothers.

"Basically? That we were going to look out for each other, like we always did. He said not to come running to him when we finished screwing up our lives, and I assured him he was the last person either of us would go to, for anything."

"That's a fucking fact," Theo muttered.

"She said she'd washed her hands of us. I suggested she get a towel."

After Theo's mouth fell open, a laugh burst out. "You actually said that: 'Get a towel.'"

"I did, because it's time to say fuck it. It's past time we both said fuck it, so that was my fuck it substitute. Then she hung up."

"He's giving me three weeks to come to my senses. She was a little more generous with a month."

"Marking your calendar?" Nash asked him.

"Nope." Theo took a second slice. "Happy Thanksgiving, Nash."
Nash took a second slice for himself. "Happy Thanksgiving, Theo."

In their little house, tucked in the West Virginia woods and hills, Clara and Sam enjoyed Clara's roasted turkey, mashed potatoes, and corn bread. The creamed corn, green beans, and cranberry sauce came from cans, but the gravy and stuffing Clara made like her grandmother taught her had a nice addition of blood from the resurrected.

This had been an older gentleman from the Farmington area who'd been brought back from a cardiac arrest.

Before they'd drained him, he'd told them he'd heard his mother's voice coming to him from a bright light. How he'd felt young again, his vision sharper, his steps toward that light quicker.

That had pleased Clara very much, and she felt Wayne Carson's contribution to their mission, and now their holiday meal, was something to be thankful for.

"This gravy's terrific, babe."

"I'm so glad you like it." She beamed at him through the two white tapers she'd put out to add some class and romance. "My granny taught me how to make it. I told you how my mother couldn't cook worth spit, but my granny, she knew her way around the kitchen."

"That pumpkin pie's going to go down good, too."

"It was fun making it together." She reached over for his hand, squeezed tight. "You and me? We do everything good together, doll."

He squeezed back, added a wink. "And one thing better than all the rest."

"Oh, you!" Slapping at the air, she giggled. "Nobody ever loved me like you do, Sam. With your heart and your body. I know it was meant for us to meet when we did, but sometimes I can't help but wish we'd met when I was young enough to give you a child."

"Babe, you're everything I could want. You gave me purpose when every day was just a get-through-it. You opened my mind to that purpose."

Her heart just sang. "I'd never be able to do what we're meant to do without you. Before you, I just didn't have the courage. We've got some more possibilities, but I think it's best we wait a couple weeks. Maybe even a month."

"You'll know when it's time. You always do."

"I will," she agreed. "I was given that gift." She ate the last of the potatoes and gravy on her plate. "They're out looking for Janet Anderson. They just don't understand, doll, that she's finally at peace. All those people fretting over her when she's gone to her reward.

"I'm thankful we were able to give her that gift. How about another helping?"

He shook his head. "Like my pap used to say, enough's as much as plenty."

"I'll get the pie and the Reddi-wip."

"I was thinking, why don't we do the other thing we do so well before pie? I sure am thankful for that!"

"Oh, you!" She giggled and slapped the air again. Then she got up. "Gotta catch me!" And ran toward the bedroom.

When he caught her, and they tumbled onto the bed she'd made that morning, complete with neat hospital corners and flowered bedspread, she wrapped around him.

"I sure do love you, Sam."

"I sure do love you, Clara." He nuzzled into her neck. "When I think last Thanksgiving I was on my own. I didn't have you, didn't have love, or purpose, or the enlightenment you brought to me."

"Happy Thanksgiving, doll."

He filled his hands with her big soft breasts. "Happy Thanksgiving, babe."


In the Cooper house, post-dinner/pre-dessert chaos reigned. Some gathered in the kitchen, dealing with dishes, the leftovers, and talked as if they hadn't already talked more than an hour over dinner.

Others flopped down with football on the big screen in the family room downstairs, and shouted their triumph or disappointment.

Drea, their cousin, and his, yes, adorable boyfriend took some of the kids out for sledding and snowman building.

Happy but tired, Sloan gave in to the fatigue and slipped upstairs for a twenty-minute nap.

Though she admitted as she rose, as she freshened up, she could've taken an hour, she told herself the twenty did the trick.

She'd eaten what she could, little bites of everything she liked. She wasn't sure how she'd manage pie, but she'd try.

A lot to be thankful for, she reminded herself. And more if she could manage another walk outside.

Pleased she felt reasonably steady and rested, she went back downstairs in time to hear the shouts of *Touchdown!* and the moans of those rooting for the opposition.

She turned in time to see Jonah's little boy, Austin, let out a war cry as he chased Mop—a ball clamped in his mouth, dark eyes lit with fun—into the home office.

She detoured—not the place to play tug—and got to the door in time to see the little guy slip and fall flat on the floor.

"Oops," she said, then moved in. "You okay, pal?"

He sat up, eyes big and teary, and raised up his arms.

She didn't think, simply reached down and lifted him.

She felt the pop, the sudden stab of pain as the breath went out of her. Her legs gave way.

She didn't drop the boy, but it was close, and crumpled on the floor. She struggled to get her breath back as the four-year-old's tears began to fall.

"What was that?" Drea turned into the doorway, then sprinted. "Sloan."

"Take him. Take him." Her hands shook like her voice. "I didn't think. I didn't think."

"Stay right where you are."

Hauling Austin up, Drea rushed out, and Sloan tried to take stock. Gingerly, she slid a hand under her sweater, found her chest dressing wet.

"Fuck, fuck, fuck."

Drea rushed back, knelt down. "How bad?"

"Goddamn it, my own fault." Her breath wheezed in, wheezed out, but the pain stayed. "Popped some stitches. And I think maybe strained a muscle. Maybe, shit, shit, tore one."

"How bad are you bleeding?" Without hesitation, Drea yanked up her sister's sweater. "Okay, okay, not a gusher. Stay down. I'll get our things, take you to the ER."

Sloan felt her own tears building. "I'm screwing it up."

"You're not. We're going to do what we need to do."

Of course, everyone would have crowded into the room if Dean hadn't shooed them off.

"I'll drive," he said.

"No. Dad, I've got this. And I'll take care of her." Drea put on her coat as Elsie helped Sloan into hers.

"It's not bad," Sloan assured them, though she didn't know for certain, since it hurt to breathe, much less talk. "Stupid of me, that's all. I didn't think about it, just hauled him up. He's about five times five pounds. They'll stitch me up and I'll be back. Save me some pie."

Still, her father insisted on carrying her to the car, and cars had to be moved and shifted so Drea could back out.

"I'm sorry."

"Save it," Drea told her. "You picked up a kid because he was crying. I get it."

"I knew better. I should've sat down on the floor and held him."

"You didn't." Eyes straight ahead, Drea handled the winding roads like a Formula 1 ace. "You're wired to help someone who needs help. Beating yourself up isn't going to accomplish anything. Just like you said all the right things back there about being right back, having pie."

"It could be true."

"We're going to hope it is."

Sloan closed her eyes and focused on breathing. "They listened to you."

"So did you. I didn't give any of you time not to."

"Good trick," Sloan mumbled.

"You need plenty of tricks if you're going to work in a family business and stay a happy family. And I've got plenty."

Drea stayed in charge when they reached the hospital. Quick and brisk, she put Sloan in a chair and marched to the check-in counter herself.

In under ten minutes, Sloan lay in an exam room with a doctor who appeared to have graduated from the same school of quick and brisk as her sister.

During the poking, prodding, needles, X-rays, she made herself go somewhere else in her head. Thinking about the moment, what was happening to her could only lead to thinking about what could happen.

After the tests, the stitching, Sloan braced herself for the results.

"You look better," Drea observed.

Sloan wasn't sure if they'd let her sister into the room or she'd just bullied her way into it. Either way, she was grateful not to wait alone.

"Oh, and the nurse I spoke to said not to be concerned that Dr. Marlowe looks sixteen. She's actually thirty-four and an excellent doctor. I googled her while I was waiting."

"Of course you did."

"She was in the top ten percent of her graduating class at WVU and opted to specialize in emergency medicine."

As Drea spoke, Dr. Marlowe, a tall brunette in a white coat and black running shoes, breezed in.

"Good news. No tears or ruptures."

Sloan's stress level dropped, just bottomed out as quickly as it had spiked. She hadn't realized just how high it had spiked until it plunged again.

"Not as good, you have an intercostal muscle strain—basically you pulled a pectoral muscle. You need to contact your surgeon— tomorrow's soon enough—and we'll send him your test results. I'll consult with him. Meanwhile it's rest, ice—"

"Compression and elevation," Sloan finished. "RICE."

"Yes, exactly. Your surgeon may want to see you, and his instructions override mine. Mine are you can resume light—key word *light*—activity in forty-eight hours. RICE and take your meds for pain and swelling. Ice twenty minutes, three times a day, and keep your chest elevated. I'm going to wrap the affected area in an elastic bandage. When you change it, don't wrap it any tighter than I have. And don't pick up any toddlers."

"That's definitely off my list."

"Sloan Cooper," Marlowe said. "Heron's Rest. You ran cross-country."

"In high school, yeah."

"You ran against my sister in regionals—Willa Marlowe, Cumberland. I remember because you nipped her by about two seconds, and went on to All-State."

"I remember Willa." Another tall brunette, Sloan recalled. "She ran like a cheetah—with an extra battery pack."

"And she said your kick at the end was your superpower."

Sloan managed a wan smile. "Those were the days."

Drea rubbed a hand up and down Sloan's arm. "I'm going to step out and call the houseful of worried family. Before I do, is there anything else Sloan's watchdogs need to know?"

"You'll get a list at checkout. Keep an eye on her for the next forty-eight. And contact Dr. Vincenti tomorrow."

"Done. I'll be back."

"Let's get you wrapped and back home," Marlowe said when Drea walked out. "Your wounds are healing well. I understand this is a setback in your recovery, and it must be frustrating to someone with a superpower kick. But it's temporary."

"Since I imagined I'd torn a muscle and might spend some time in the OR again, I'm not going to complain. Much."

"What's your pain level now?" The tall brunette had clear, direct blue eyes. And they locked on Sloan's. "I'll add it's stupid to lie to a doctor. Don't be stupid."

"Between seven and eight. I have the prescribed pain meds at home. I haven't needed them, but I'll take one."

"Good. Not stupid. You had an excellent surgeon."

"I know. I'm grateful. And I'll contact him tomorrow and confess."

"The problem with being a human is we make mistakes."

The problem with being Sloan, she admitted as she—very carefully—got back in Drea's car—was she just hated making them.

Before she strapped in, Drea handed her an ice pack.

"Where did you get this?"

"I have my ways. Twenty minutes on. It'll take thirty or so to get home. Might as well start now."

Sooner started, sooner finished, Sloan thought, and slid the pack under her sweater.

"I'm going to contact Dr. Vincenti's office in the morning and arrange a video consult. If he wants you to go in, Mom can take you. My schedule's tight tomorrow and so's Dad's, but hers is a little more flexible."

Drea made the turn, started home. "Dad doesn't have a recliner, which didn't strike me as odd until now. My nurse informant said that's a good way to sleep elevated. But we have plenty of pillows, and you'd rather sleep in bed anyway."

"You're organizing me. This is another of your tricks."

"You'll be back to organizing yourself soon enough, so I'm taking it while I can. I like the power." Drea lifted her shoulders, jiggled them. "It may be better than sex."

"You're not having any sex that I've noticed."

"I could say too busy, which is true enough, but mostly? Nobody recently hits the mark. If I'm going to have sex, I want to date first, and unless somebody at least hits somewhere on the target, it's too much trouble."

She glanced over. "How was sex with Matias?"

"Good enough."

"Ooh, ouch."

"I know, right?" Sloan started to laugh, but it hurt. "And I'm not saying that because he dumped me while I was in the hospital. Sex was okay. Just okay. Actually, everything was just okay, and looking back, just too easy and convenient. I guess on both sides."

"Then you're in the hospital, and it wasn't easy and convenient for him." Drea glanced at her sister. "You wouldn't have done that to him."

"No. You know what's weird? I wish, I honestly wish, he'd broken my heart."

"That's not weird." Drea shook her head. "No, not even approaching weird. You wanted more from him, from yourself, and you didn't get it. He only hit the outer rim of your target, and who doesn't want a bull's-eye?"

"I'm retiring my target for a while."

"I like leaving mine out there, just in case. You never know who may hit, or when."

By the time they got back, her father's truck sat in the drive so Drea could take his slot in the garage. Before the garage door closed, their parents stepped in.

"Everyone stayed until Drea called. So much relief," Elsie added. "I've got your bed all ready for you."

"Here, baby."

"No, Dad, no carrying. Walking's fine. It's encouraged. I'm just a little slow. I'm just really sorry this put such a damper on everything."

"No damper after Drea called. Everything's fine now. How about you lean on me a little?"

"Leaning's good. Maybe an extreme way to get out of dish duty, but mission accomplished."

The stairs that had happily become just stairs turned into a mountain again.

So she leaned, took it slow while her mother hurried ahead.

"Plenty of pillows," Elsie said, "to keep you elevated. We've got your book, your laptop, and your crocheting within easy reach. I'll help you change into your pajamas. Dean, why don't you go down and make Sloan some tea?"

"Just the water's fine, Mom."

"I'll be right downstairs."

When Sloan sat on the side of the bed, Dean bent down to kiss the top of her head.

And Drea held out a pill and a glass of water.

"Thanks for organizing me. Sincerely. But don't get used to it."

"I may not be able to give it up. Such a surge of power. I'll be downstairs with Dad."

"Here now, let's get you comfortable."

Before Elsie could help Sloan off with her sweater, Sloan took her hand. "I know I worried you. Worried everyone. I'm not going to do that again."

"Oh, baby, when you're sixty and I'm . . . we won't say that number out loud—I'll still worry about you. Love demands it. You know what your dad's doing right now? He's sending a group text to the family to let them know you're home. Because love demands it."

Gently, she exchanged Sloan's sweater for a soft thermal shirt.

"You've been working so hard to stay inside the lines. I know how hard it is for you not to lift boulders and race the wind, but you've done the work. This is a bump, that's all," Elsie assured Sloan as she helped her undress. "A nasty bump, and you'll get over it and through it."

A tear spilled out; she simply couldn't stop it, or the one that followed.

"I feel weak again, Mom, and . . . breakable."

Elsie drew Sloan's head to her breast, stroked her hair, murmuring as Sloan gave up and let the tears come.

Then she drew Sloan back, met those teary eyes.

"You're only weak physically for now. Your will isn't weak, and trust me because I've run up against it since you were born, it's not easily broken."

"Okay." Sloan took the tissue Elsie offered, dried her face. "Okay."

She helped Sloan into bed, tucking covers as she had when Sloan was a child.

"Are you sure you don't want that tea? Some pie?"

Sloan shook her head. "The pain meds make me sleepy. Drea's a rock, Mom."

"Both my girls are. They take after me. I put your phone right there on the charger. If you need or want anything, text."

"I will. Promise."

"Lights on or off?"

"Off, thanks."

In the dark and the quiet, she settled back, propped up by a mound of pillows.

Just a bump, she told herself. She just had to make sure she didn't trip over it.


Something growled as she walked into the glaring lights of the mini-mart. Light turned to dark, the shelves and spin racks to trees with limbs like brittle bones. The counter became a thicket with thorns that gleamed like sharpened teeth.

She saw tracks in the snow, and drawing her weapon, began to follow them.

Just a slice of moon, barely a slice, to bounce its light off the snow. But she saw well enough, saw the tracks, human tracks.

She needed to stop the one who made them. Needed to do her job. To protect human and wildlife, to protect the forest, the rivers, the lakes.

She couldn't remember why she'd come here, alone, in the dark, but knew the only way to go. Forward.

She heard the quick squeal—a death cry—moments before she watched the great horned owl sweep by, silent as a ghost in the night, with its prey.

Her head throbbed, a dull, draining ache, and when she lifted a hand to her forehead, it came back bloody. Her blood dripped down her face, onto the pristine white of the snow.

But she kept moving forward. To stop was failure, to turn back cowardice.

Even when the tracks circled, turned from human to beast, she moved ahead.

The growl came from behind her, close. Too close.

She spun around. The beast, huge, black, its eyes fiery red, its teeth long and keen, leaped out of the dark.

Its fangs sank into her chest.

She woke gasping, a scream caught in her throat. She had to press her hands against her mouth to hold it in. Shuddering, she rocked herself until the need to scream passed.

Carefully, because her hands shook, she picked up the water on the nightstand, drank to ease the burning in her throat, in her lungs, in her belly.

Because she needed it, she switched on the light and immediately felt calmer. A check of the time showed her three-twenty-five.

As quietly as she could, Sloan got out of bed and into the bathroom across the hall. After she splashed the clammy sweat from her face, she studied herself in the mirror.

The strain showed, and the circles under her eyes spread like bruises against the pallor.

She looked haunted, but she wouldn't be.

Everything hurt, but she settled on an Advil.

Wishing she'd thought to ask for her earbuds, she went back to her room, eased herself back into bed.

She turned her laptop on, considered music, but decided she needed a bigger distraction. She chose a movie to stream instead, then picked up her crocheting.

By five a.m., she'd finished the red scarf.

# CHAPTER SEVEN

Just after nine, her mother brought her breakfast in bed—with a purple mum in a bud vase on the tray.

"Good morning!" Like the flower, the greeting aimed for extra cheer. "We peeked in a couple hours ago, but you were sleeping."

After setting down the tray, Elsie offered Sloan an ice pack. "But you must've been awake at some point because you finished the scarf."

"I slept, woke up, slept. I can come downstairs."

"Why don't you pamper yourself a little?"

Elsie's hand brushed over Sloan's forehead, checking—Sloan knew—for fever.

"You've got a video call with Dr. Vincenti at ten-thirty," she continued. "Drea set it up."

"Still organizing me."

"As long as possible. And, for my contribution there, I'll bring you up some more yarn."

She wanted to get up, do something. Anything. But had to admit she felt as lousy as she'd looked in the mirror.

"I guess I half promised to make a scarf for Joel. A manly one."

"I've got just the thing. I'll go get it for you, and after we see what the doctor says, we'll go from there."

"If he orders me to stay in bed another day, I will. But otherwise."

"We'll go from there. I'll go get the yarn."

Her mother had scrambled eggs with chunks of ham—a childhood favorite. She did her best with it as she stared out the window at a pretty snow shower.

And yearned to walk in it.

Elsie came back with the yarn. "Definitely manly. A nice ombré that goes from black to light gray." She glanced at the tray. "One more bite?"

"I took one already." Sloan crossed her heart.

"All right then. I'm going to set this aside, then show you how to do a double crochet stitch."

"Now you're scaring me."

"You can handle it." She added a smug smile. "And now you have to sit still long enough to learn."

After a few poor attempts, Sloan got the rhythm. And found herself ridiculously pleased.

"Soothing, isn't it? And satisfying."

"I stand—well, sit—corrected."

"I'm going to take your tray down and give you privacy for your call with your doctor. And because I trust you to tell me everything he says."

"That's sneaky."

"And it works. Drea's sent you a link for the call. Let me know when you're done, and—"

"We'll go from there."

Sloan set the yarn aside, shifted her laptop. Bracing herself, she made the call.

He came quickly on-screen. "Sloan."

"Dr. Vincenti, thanks for talking to me. I want to say I'm sorry I screwed up. Honestly, I didn't mean to. I just—didn't think. He was crying, and held up his arms, and I just reacted. I promise you I've been following the discharge instructions. I have a spreadsheet. I can send it to you."

Even in her rush to explain herself, Sloan caught his mild amusement. "A spreadsheet of?"

"Daily activities, food intake, sleep, all of it. I've been making progress, but I've been careful. Until."

"I'd like to see the spreadsheet. Meanwhile, Dr. Marlowe's report and attachments are very thorough. You estimate the boy's weight at twenty-five pounds."

"His parents weighed him, and he came in at twenty-three."

"You're lucky there's no tear, no internal bleeding or damage. What's your pain level this morning?"

"About four. I took an Advil earlier. It's not severe enough for the heavy stuff. I'd take that if I needed it."

Once again, she crossed her heart, and made Vincenti smile.

"I'm on RICE. Dr. Marlowe indicated I could resume light activity forty-eight hours after the injury."

She'd expected a lecture and when she didn't get one, couldn't decide if she felt relieved on mildly disappointed.

But she answered the battery of questions, lifted her top, eased off her compression bandage so he could see the wound.

"It's unlikely I'd order anything Dr. Marlowe hasn't. If your symptoms increase, I want you down here. Otherwise, we'll keep our current appointment for the follow-up. Understand, Sloan, a pectoral muscle strain will take a few weeks to resolve. No lifting, not even light weights, for the next couple days. I'm going to send you an exercise plan tailored to your injury."

"All right."

"You're motivated," he added. "Dr. Marlowe and I fully agree on that. And this is a setback, but only an additional two or three weeks."

"Do you mean two or three weeks before I'm cleared to go back to work? Even desk duty?"

"This is going to add a couple of weeks, yes. We'll reevaluate when I see you. Any increase in symptoms, contact me. Send me the spreadsheet, and follow the plan I send you."

She ended the call, closed her eyes.

Like starting over, she thought. Day One all over again, and today wouldn't even count for that.

Since he hadn't ordered her to stay in bed, she got up. Went across the hall to brush her teeth. Since the movement of brushing her hair caused pain to flare, she left it alone.

She went down and found her mother in the home office with Mop snoring on the rug behind her.

"Sloan, I'd have helped you downstairs."

"Walking's okay. Not a lot of it. And everything else is off the table for a couple days. I'm trying not to be a baby about it, but—"

"You're my baby." Rising, Elsie crossed over to hold her. "He doesn't need to see you today?"

"No. That's a bright spot."

"I know it's hard for you to stay planted, but it won't be for long. You can keep busy sitting down for a couple days."

"Can we go outside, just for a few minutes?"

"All right. You don't have to get dressed. We'll just bundle up, put some boots on, and take Mop out."

She got her few minutes while the snow fell cool and light, and the lake went to silver.

And in the cool and light, felt calmer.

"It's so beautiful. Every season, it's just so beautiful. Look at all the people sledding."

"Long weekend, no school. We've got a lot of kids. Snowpeople contest tomorrow in the town park."

"That'll be fun. I remember one year Drea and I—and Hallie, Hallie Reeder—did Captain America."

"Drea had such a crush on Captain America."

"Probably still does. It was fun. All the Rest always brings the fun."

"We do our best. Hallie's engaged."

"Really? She sent me a card in the hospital, but didn't mention it."

"He's the head chef at the Seabreeze. I think the wedding's this spring. Maybe you'll get in touch while you're home."

"I will." Relaxed again, Sloan let out a sigh as Mop settled on a mound of snow like a man might in an easy chair. "This is better than eight hours' sleep for me. Just a few minutes outside. And with this view."

"I've always loved it here."

"So have I. I know I moved away," she added when Elsie said nothing. "That didn't mean I didn't love it here. Don't love it."

"You needed to spread your wings. And you did."

"Won't be able to spread them for a while now."

"The business wasn't for you. Your dad and I understand that."

"Drea's worth two of me there. Possibly three of me."

"It's what she wants. We want what our girls want. And now I want you inside by the fire."

"Yeah. I've got a scarf to make."


On the first Monday of December, the Littlefield brothers drove into Heron's Rest. A small town with only a couple thousand year-round residents, it bustled. The winter season brought the skiers, the snowboarders, the hunters, and plenty who just wanted a cozy getaway.

The Rest offered the mountains, the lake, the slopes and trails, the campsites and cabins, and the lake houses and docks. A scatter of restaurants and bars, plenty of shops—retail and rental—a small library lined its Main Street.

The town had a reputation for friendly and picturesque. After all, it depended on tourists to eat, drink, shop, play, and stay.

Nash knew the town enjoyed glowing write-ups in magazines and blogs touting places to visit, hidden gems, vacation destinations.

He'd made the dramatic change in his own career and location because the practical part of his brain calculated he could make a decent living there doing what he'd finally admitted he wanted.

Then the house, the dilapidated wonder of it, had hit him hard. It was, to his eye, a sad and neglected treasure, and he could make it shine again.

Would make it shine again.

The challenge of it appealed to every part of him and stood as the perfect start of the new phase of his life.

Theo was the big bonus, the whipped cream and the cherry on top. There was no one he'd rather work with, partner with, build something strong and good with than Theo.

And today, on this first Monday in December, they'd begin.

"Where do you want to start?" Nash asked him.

"I figure to hit the All the Rest place. They own most of the vacation houses, the boat and equipment rentals."

"And like I said, I checked before I settled on the house. They've got a contractor."

"Yeah, but a lot of cabins and houses to deal with. Plus, you have to figure they know everybody. I'll spread on the charm, then work my way, hit the shops, the rest."

He patted the box on his lap. "The flyers look good. So do the business cards. We're marketing, bro."

"I'll pick up the permits and catch up with you."

"Don't forget your flyers. You've got some charm in there."

"I'll see if I can dig it out."

At the first of three traffic lights, Nash made a turn, then turned again at the next corner and drove into the town parking lot.

"Do you know where you're going?" Nash grabbed his briefcase—flyers and business cards inside—before they walked back toward the corner of Main and Mallard.

"Yeah, I scouted it out. I'm that way." Theo pointed left. Then right. "You're that way. It's pretty," he added as they waited for the walk light. "Got the postcard vibe going. We've got to start coming in at least two times a week. Grabbing a burger, a beer. That's marketing, too."

"We'll get to it. Later," Nash said, and started his walk—or climb—up the slope of the sidewalk.

Theo tucked the box under his arm and strolled across the street.

He really did like the look and feel of the town. Maybe it should've struck him as weird that he felt so free just walking here. He'd enjoyed New York, he really had, but he'd always felt pressure. Constant pressure, he thought now, through college, through law school. Get the grades, push harder, intern at the right firm.

And he'd liked the law fine, but he'd never loved it. Not the way he'd loved the first summer he'd hooked up with Nash for Habitat for Humanity.

Building something, doing good work, learning how to make something last. And meeting people from all over who wanted to do the same. All that had left a deep impression.

He marked that summer, after he'd turned twenty-one, had defied parental expectations and done exactly what he wanted, a precursor to this.

He'd pull his weight, he'd learn more. And he wouldn't let Nash down.

Optimistic, and pulling on the charm as easily as he pulled on a hoodie, he walked into All the Rest's town offices.

It surprised him. It had a homey rather than a business feel with its focal point of a brick fireplace, logs simmering, the couple of cozy chairs angled toward it.

The mantel held artfully arranged greenery and pinecones, red and silver balls, red and silver candles.

Clever framed photographs on the spruce-green walls showed the hills, the lake, the trails, and people enjoying them in all four seasons.

A long table held an arrangement of flowers, a laptop, and several neatly placed brochures, maps, and, hey, flyers.

A Christmas tree stood in the corner by the street-facing windows. Its lights gleamed icy white, decorations sparkled on the boughs. A real tree, he realized, with a star on top, that scented the office air with pine.

They needed to get a tree, he decided on the spot. A real one, and stuff to go on it.

Then she walked in, and his brain glazed over.

She had long hair, kind of golden brown, that spilled down past her shoulders. And a face that made his mouth go dry. Blue eyes, like a summer sky, lips, Christmas red, that curved into a smile.

She wore a blue dress and short, high-heeled boots.

And when she spoke, he actually felt a little dizzy.

"Good morning. How can I help you today?"

"Ah . . ."

He couldn't remember. Honestly couldn't remember for a minute where he was, why he was there.

She filled everything.

"Are you lost?"

"Am I . . . No, no. Sorry. I, ah, lost my train. Of thought. I'm Theo . . . Ah . . ." Jesus! "Littlefield."

Her widening smile had the tiniest little dimple flickering at the top right corner of her gorgeous mouth.

He feared he might drool.

"Are you sure about that?"

"Pretty sure." He had to get a grip. He held out a hand, and when he gripped hers, lost his again. Her hand, so warm and smooth, felt perfect in his.

"Nice to meet you. I'm Drea."

"Drea. Beautiful."

"Thanks. What can I do for you?"

"Right. Right. I want to say it's really nice in here. Welcoming. And reminded me we need to get a tree. And the lights and the rest."

"If you want to shop in town, Happy Trails has a nice selection of ornaments and decor, and a few artificial trees. Otherwise—"

"In town's good. In town's best. But that's a real tree, right? It smells great."

So did she. Boy, so did she.

"It is. Your best bet there is Wilford's Tree Farm. I can show you on the map."

"That'd be great. So All the Rest means it. Full-service."

"We do our best." Taking a map and a pen, she drew a route. "Where are you coming from, Mr. Littlefield?"

"Theo, just Theo. New York, but I live here. We live here now."

"Oh?" She glanced up with those beautiful blue eyes.

"My brother bought a house a couple months ago. Ah, it's off North Lake Drive."

"The old Parker place? That's you?"

"Well, Nash, but I talked him into letting me move in. We're— forgot what I came in for. Distracted."

He opened the box, took out one of the flyers he and Nash had designed.

Angling her head, Drea studied it.

"The Fix-It Brothers. That's clever. Licensed contractors."

"Nash is already. I will be in a few weeks."

"Mm-hmm. Home repair, remodeling, new builds. No job too small. Friendly, reliable service, seven days a week."

"That's the plan. We're just getting started."

"New businesses are always welcome. Why don't you give me about a dozen flyers? Any business cards?"

"Yeah, thanks. Really." He fumbled out the flyers, a small stack of cards. "We appreciate it. Ah, Nash would've come in, too, but he's picking up our building permits. The house needs a lot of work."

The phone rang. Drea held up a finger, picked it up. "Good morning, All the Rest. This is Drea. Could I ask you to hold just one minute?"

"So, I'll get out of your way. Thanks again. And . . . just one thing? I have to say you're really beautiful. Really seriously beautiful. That would've been stuck in here if I didn't get it out."

"We wouldn't want that. Thank you."

"Yeah, sure. So . . . thanks again."

As he walked out, he heard her say:

"Thanks for holding. How can I help you?"

His heart just sang.

While Theo worked a candle and rock shop—purchasing some of each for community relations—then the bookstore—a buy of a history of Heron's Rest by a local author—Nash dealt with the business at town hall.

He met the mayor, a sharp-eyed woman of about fifty who barely topped five feet. She and her husband also owned the hardware store on the far end of town.

Since Nash figured they'd do plenty of business there—keep it local—he had no trouble cooperating when she pumped him for information.

He left flyers and business cards.

Since it was right next door, he did the same in the town library, where the head librarian, a gangly guy of around thirty with a massive black beard, pinned a flyer to the bulletin board, took another handful.

Then asked Nash what he would charge to replace a bathroom vanity and sink, and paint.

They discussed; Moose, as he introduced himself, called his wife. Before he left, Nash had an appointment to meet Mrs. Moose at eight the next morning before she left to teach third graders at Heron's Rest Elementary.

More than satisfied, he stepped out, texted Theo.

Where r u?
**Happy Trails.**
I'll work my way up.

He handed out flyers, had conversations. And booked another job at the Snip and Style when Suze—with pink-streaked hair and freckles—asked him to come look at a leaky faucet.

"My no-good, lazy ex-boyfriend promised to fix it," she told Nash, "but I booted him out before he did. Like he ever would anyway."

After two more stops, he met Theo on the street. And stared.

"What the hell, Theo?"

"You give some to get some." Theo shifted his mass of shopping bags. "Plus, we need Christmas stuff. And, this isn't even the big news, we've got a job."

"Doing what?"

"Replacing three bedroom doors. Ms. Haver knows what she wants—I got pictures. Her husband was going to do it, but he broke his foot playing with the dog, and they're having their kids for Christmas. I checked, and the lumber center between here and Deep Creek has them in stock—I got them on hold, contractor's rate. I gave her our hourly rate, an estimate of time, considering we have to pick up the doors, and said we could do it tomorrow."

Theo grinned. "She pinched my cheek."

"Let's get this crap you bought to the truck. I'm nearly out of flyers anyway. And we've got to be back in town tomorrow to look at two other jobs."

"Two?" Stopping, Theo beamed like the sun. "Are you serious?"

"Eight a.m., possible bathroom vanity and sink replacement, and new paint. Another's just a leaky faucet, but—"

"No job too small. We did good, man."

"We got lucky on top of it, as the local guy who'd probably handle most of this retired and moved south. Just. We've got an opening."

"Charging through! We could pick up those doors now. Get them installed tomorrow. She wants these glass doorknobs—they're in stock. Then if the faucet just needs a washer, or tightening, a simple fix, we could say it's on the house. Good marketing."

"Good marketing. And the faucet owner just kicked out her boyfriend. She's cute. Looked like your type."

"Nope." Theo shook his head as they reached the truck and loaded the bags in the back. "Not for me."

"You haven't even seen her. She has freckles. You always went for freckles."

"Not anymore." He got in the shotgun seat, laid a hand on his heart. "Big news? Nash, I met the girl of my dreams."

"That was quick."

"Years in the making. Maybe centuries. I really have to marry her."

"Does my future sister-in-law have a name?"

"Drea."

"Drea what?"

"I don't know." He sighed it out. "Doesn't matter. She threw me off my game, just by existing. But I'll do better next time. She's the most beautiful woman in the world."

"Okay. Well, now that you're getting married and, I assume, starting a family—"

"Absolutely."

"Then you should be happy to know we've got our permits. We're starting demo."

Theo rubbed his hands together. "Nothing like demo. Oh, wait, one more thing. The tree farm's on the way to and from the supplier. We can stop either way and get the tree."

"We have dozens of trees."

"Christmas tree, Nash. We need a Christmas tree."

"We're about to tear the house up. Where the hell are we going to put a tree? When are we going to have time to screw with a Christmas tree?"

"Here's my motto," Theo told him. "You gotta make time to screw with Christmas."

"If we made pillows, that belongs on one."

"We'll find a place. I already got lights and a stand, and a shitload of decorations. Nothing like what they used to have decorators bring in and put up. Our tree, our way. Our Christmas."

It had never been Nash's favorite holiday. Always formal, stilted, perfection as fake as the soaring tree.

But he heard the yearning in his brother's voice.

And why not? he thought. They could make it their own.

"Then here's the plan. Doors, tree, unload back at the house. Then we're tearing down a wall."

Theo rubbed his hands together again. "I like this plan."

They picked up the doors—good and solid—the doorknobs, the hardware. Nash took a turn through their lighting section, cruised the bathroom vanities, faucets.

In his judgment, somebody replaced a vanity, a sink, painted a bathroom, they'd decide to change the lights.

He let Theo talk up the manager, pass off flyers, business cards. His little brother had a knack for it.

Because he didn't have a preference, he gave the choice of the tree to Theo as well. From what looked like acres of them, and plenty of people already in the holiday mood on the first week of December.

He tried to ignore the Christmas music playing on the outdoor speakers.

They strapped the tree—a nice six-foot blue spruce—to the top of the truck and headed for home.

"Damn good morning for the Littlefield brothers," Theo declared.

"And a better afternoon when that wall comes down. I ordered the windows, and we're going to need some help there when they come in. Maybe you could ask your bride-to-be if she knows anyone."

"I'll do that. Good opening. Now, about that dog."

"Don't push your luck, Theo."

"Yeah, the dog should wait a few weeks anyway."

When Nash made the turn back to the house, he saw the woman and the dog, slow walking on the lake path.

"There's Lake Walker again."

"Yeah, I see. That's gotta be routine, right?"

"I guess." And Nash had to admit it struck his curiosity.

Who was she, what did she do besides walk with the dog? And why did she walk like someone recovering from a long illness?

And because she did, he felt more admiration than sympathy, because she just kept taking one more step.

Sloan saw the truck, the tree strapped to the roof. The Coopers would put up the family tree tonight, and she wished she could push herself into the spirit.

She'd finally made it to the mark she'd hit on her very first walk out of the hospital. But she was out of breath, and her chest hurt.

Not enough for the big guns, but enough she'd take a couple of Advil when she got back.

"A few steps more tomorrow, Mop. But that's it for this trip."

At least she'd convinced her family she didn't need watching and tending twenty-four/seven.

She'd lost progress, but she'd make it up.

Back in the house, she dumped her coat. She'd hang it up later, but she needed to sit, steady up.

When she felt able, she rose to get the Advil, drink water. She needed to eat something. She heated up a bowl of the turkey noodle soup her mother had made from Thanksgiving leftovers.

When her phone rang, she saw her captain on the readout.

She'd dreaded this. She'd put a call in to him—she had to tell him about her setback.

Nudging the soup aside, she answered.

"Captain, thanks for getting back to me."

"Sorry for the delay. How are you, Corporal?"

"Well, sir, I had a little incident a few days ago, and pulled a pectoral muscle."

"Well, damn, Sloan. I'm sorry to hear that."

"Yes, sir. It's not serious, and I can treat it at home, no problem. It will take a couple of weeks, possibly three, to fully resolve."

"I see. And that's a damn shame, Sloan. A damn shame. You're missed here."

"Thanks. I could possibly do some remote work. Paperwork, searches, background checks."

"We're covered there, of course, if something comes up . . ." He let that trail off. "I think it's best if you remain on leave until after the first of the year. Your duties have physical requirements, and you can't resume those duties until you have full medical and psychiatric clearance."

"I understand."

"I know it's hard, I recognize that this is hard on you. But we have to think of your health and safety, and the health and safety of your fellow officers."

"I understand."

"I appreciate you telling me. We'll make arrangements here to cover your duties. Take care of yourself, Sloan. You're a valued member of the Natural Resources Police."

"Thank you. I will."

And that was that, she thought as she set the phone down.

She'd known it, and in her captain's position, she would have said and done the same.

"No whining," she ordered herself. "Absolutely none."

Reaching up, she rubbed the scar on her forehead.

"I'm not going to bitch, not going to give in to that. Just because I can't walk without huffing, can't lift over a couple pounds. Can't even brush my own damn hair without it hurting."

She looked down at the dog, who sat faithfully at her feet.

"I can't brush my damn hair. I hate seeing this reminder of that night on my stupid face. So, why don't I just fix that? I can fix that."

She pulled open a drawer, took out scissors.

"This is probably a terrible idea. I'm doing it anyway."

# CHAPTER EIGHT

Like farmers, resort towns rise and fall on the weather. When Elsie came in with Drea, her thoughts centered there.

"Hitting the fifties this weekend means boat rentals. How about we run a weekend special?"

"Already in the works." Drea shed her coat. "We're doing a flyer, and housekeeping's putting one in all the units."

"Should've known you'd have it covered. How about we . . ."

Then her thoughts drained away as Sloan came slowly down the stairs with the kitchen scissors in one hand, a long hank of blond hair in the other.

"I just wanted it gone."

As she heard both tears and defiance in her daughter's voice, Elsie moved into support mode. "You wanted a change."

"You sure got one," Drea added, and got a quick elbow jab from her mother.

"I just couldn't deal with it—the motion right now. Washing, drying, brushing. So I thought, *I'll get rid of it.* Oh my God."

In something close to horror, she stared at the tail of hair in her hand.

"I whacked it off. I just whacked it off."

"We can fix it. Here now." Elsie moved up, took the scissors out of Sloan's hand. "I can fix it, and if I can't, we'll call Aileen, and she'll come and fix it."

"I look like I put a bowl on my head. I didn't!"

"You went heavy on the bangs," Drea observed, and ignoring

Sloan's snarl, considered. "I like that part. It's a good look. The rest's a disaster, but the bangs work. Once they're evened up a little."

"Drea, third drawer, my side of the bathroom vanity. Get the kit I use when I cut your father's hair, and a towel. Did you forget I cut your father's hair, and have actual tools for it?"

Miserably, Sloan stared at the sheared-off hank of hair. "Yes."

"So I can fix it, and if I can't fix it good enough, we'll call Aileen. She's been doing my hair for, lord, fifteen years. Come on, come sit in the kitchen. Cut it dry, with kitchen scissors, didn't you?"

"Yes."

She felt like an idiot. She *had* been an idiot. The tears she couldn't stop added to it.

"I was so angry and upset. I had to tell my captain what happened. I thought maybe I could do some remote work. Just background checks and that sort of thing. Something. But he said . . . basically, it was 'See you next year.'"

"And that hurt." Elsie pulled out a stool so she could walk around it, eased Sloan down. "I'm sure he thought he was doing the right thing for you, but it hurt."

She went for tissues, handed them over, then filled a spray bottle with water.

"He said I was valued, and all that. But it doesn't feel like it. I've been away for weeks now, and everything's just fine without me."

"Did you want your department to fall apart?"

"No." She blew her nose, sighed. "Maybe a little."

After a one-armed hug, Elsie kissed Sloan's cheek. "I don't blame you a bit."

"You don't?"

"Who doesn't want to feel like they're needed, even essential? And you are, baby, but why would you feel that way right now?"

"I feel useless, Mom. So what do I do? I screw up my hair. That'll teach them."

"You changed your hair." After prying away the tail of hair Sloan gripped like a lifeline, Elsie set it on the counter. "And why not? I'm going to ask Aileen about donating it. It's thick, healthy. There are places you can donate it to, and they make wigs for cancer patients. So a good cause."

Sloan sighed again. "Too soon."

Elsie just patted her shoulder as Drea came in.

If part of her hit terrified at tackling the uneven chop of a mess, Elsie didn't show it. After draping the towel over Sloan's shoulders, she sprayed the hair with water.

"Drea, why don't you get us all a glass of wine."

"I can get behind that. More a box than a bowl," she added.

"Drea." Elsie's single word issued a warning.

"No, let me finish. Now that I see it, I really think short hair's the way to go. You've lost weight, Sloan."

As she spoke, she got out a bottle, glasses.

"Until you gain it back, the long hair sort of drew your face down, accentuated that weight loss. The shorter hair, and it's a crap cut, but even with the crap cut, it's lifting your face up. It's bringing out your cheekbones, and adding to those weirdly wonderful eyes. Plus, pulling those bangs from the crown? I'm calling that accidental genius."

"I didn't want to see it every time I looked in the mirror." Sloan lifted a hand under the bangs, rubbed at the wound.

"Now you don't," Drea said easily, and drew the cork. She studied Sloan as she poured. "I'm doing your makeup."

"No."

"Shut up. I'm getting my bag and doing your makeup."

She handed Sloan a glass as Elsie ran her fingers through Sloan's damp hair.

"Dad's probably another hour, right? He and Jonah went by to see the Littlefields, talk to them about taking on some general maintenance.

"I met one of them today." Drea sipped her wine as Elsie took out her haircutting scissors. "The younger one, Theo. He came into the offices with flyers. Cute, seriously cute. A little strange."

"What kind of strange? Like serial killer strange?"

Smiling at Sloan, Drea leaned against the counter. "You would go there. No, not at all. He just seemed flustered. The flyers were well done, and the business cards."

"Flustered's normal enough," Elsie put in as she worked. "In a new place, starting a new business, needing to connect with strangers."

"He did, on the way out, tell me I was beautiful."

Sloan's eyes narrowed. "He hit on you?"

"No, not like that. Anyway, UPS Pete dropped off a package, and said he'd dropped one off to Moose at the library, and Moose said he'd met the older brother, and they were going to take a look at the bathroom Maisie wants fixed up."

"They were making the rounds." Elsie kept snipping. "I ran into Kate Burkett this afternoon, and she'd met the younger one. She said he seemed very sweet."

"Did he hit on her, too?" Sloan wondered.

"She didn't mention it. And telling your sister she's beautiful is just stating a fact."

Drea sipped her wine, fluttered her lashes. "I see where you're going, Mom. It's going to work. I'm getting my bag, and Mom's hair dryer."

"Bring a mirror!" Sloan called out.

"No! Not until it's all done."

"Your hair's beautiful, Sloan. Every color of blond, right up to a bit of soft doe brown. It'll be easier for you to take care of short, and when you're all better, if you want it long, it'll grow."

"It looks like I've got until next year to look like an idiot anyway."

"Next year's only a few weeks away, and I didn't birth or raise any idiots."

"You know how impulsive I am, Mom?"

"You mean not at all?"

"Exactly. I think through, calculate, weigh, self-debate pros and cons. But my hair? Whack! I think getting shot's made me stupid."

"Stop."

Elsie said it with enough feeling to lift Sloan's shoulders into a hunch.

"Getting shot made you feel vulnerable, which you dislike. It made you feel weak, and that you hate. You're not weak, baby. I've watched you deal with what happened, day after day. Get up every morning, face it, and work toward putting it behind you."

She came around the stool, took Sloan's face in her hand. "But it's never going to be behind you. It's part of you now. You'll get through it, and you'll get the life you want back. But it's always going to be part of you. I'm proud of you."

"You have to be."

"No, I don't. I have to love you, but pride's a choice."

She stepped back, picked up her wineglass, sampled. Nodded.

"I see where I'm going, too. I'd actually go shorter."

"Shorter?" When Sloan lifted a hand toward her hair, Elsie slapped it away.

"No looking, no touching. I would go shorter, but I won't—no more than necessary. Drea's right about it lifting your face and the rest."

"Drea's always right," Drea said as she walked in with a brush, comb, hair dryer, and some styling gel. Along with her makeup bag.

"I can't believe you carry that entire bag of makeup in your purse every day."

"Be prepared. What if I was somehow trapped in one of the cabins during a blizzard, then was dug out and rescued by Mr. Gorgeous? Wouldn't I want to look my best? I raided your makeup, and you have this excellent eye shadow palette, so I'm combining yours and mine."

She began to set out palettes, brushes, tubes, compacts. "This is fun. Oh, I didn't mention it before, considering, but you really need to invest in a good face serum. I'll send you a link to what I use. You're pretty good at this, Mom."

"I've been trimming your dad's hair for years. Not the same, of course, but I know the method. Did I ever tell you about the first time he asked me to trim his hair?"

"No." Sloan lifted her wine again for a slow sip.

"We didn't have anything but regular scissors, and this other tiny pair, but we sat down, and I snipped and combed and snipped. We were both very pleased and excited with the results, and . . . celebrated. So much so that nine months later, Sloan came along."

That had a laugh bursting out so Sloan had to press a hand against her chest. "Oh, don't do that! I'm not ready for that yet. OW!"

By the time Elsie wielded the hair dryer, and Drea finished up with her own mascara—deemed superior to Sloan's—Sloan felt easy again. And resigned. However her hair looked, she'd live with it.

It couldn't be worse than what she'd done herself.

"What do you think, Drea?"

"Well, I love it. And the makeup?"

"Excellent. Sloan, sit where you are. Drea, sweep up the hair, will you? I'll go shake this towel out. Then we'll do the big reveal."

Sloan waited until Elsie stepped outside. "Drea."

"I'd tell you if we needed an SOS to Aileen. We don't. I can't tell you if you'll like it or not, and at some point, you'll want a pro. But I really like the look. It's hard to give this up."

Drea lifted the tail of hair from the counter.

"I get it, but I not only really like the look, I'm coming down hard on this needs to be your look."

Elsie came back. "Ready for the mirror?"

"Yes. And before I look, thanks. I was a mess, and you fixed it. So thanks."

"You're welcome. Now let's take a look in the powder room mirror."

"Don't scream," Drea warned. "You could pull another muscle."

They went together, crowded into the powder room.

"God. I look like Tinker Bell."

"Sexy Tink," was Drea's opinion as Sloan lifted a hand, brushed at the thick bangs.

It didn't seem possible, but her eyes looked bigger, longer. It did lift her face, she had to admit. The short, sort of shaggy cut diminished some of the drawn look she'd gotten used to seeing in the mirror.

Maybe it seemed weird to have her hair cut above her ears on the sides, but it wasn't bad.

"I think I like it. I hate to admit your mascara's better."

"I'll send you a link."

"I won't have to spend time working it into a bun for work. It's kind of a shock, but I think I like it."

"We can still call Aileen."

"No. I need to get used to it. I haven't had short hair since middle school, so I need to get used to it. It's a big change. I think . . . I think it feels good to make a big change."

She breathed out, nodded.

"Thanks, both of you. You turned a low point into a high point."

"Good. Drea, stay for dinner. Your dad's making the beer pork chops and noodles. Let's go top off our wine."

While Sloan sat and her mother snipped, her father and cousin got a tour of the old Parker house.

Jonah, former high school quarterback and Dean's right hand, had sandy hair under a Ravens ball cap. He had a good start on the beard he grew every winter, then shaved off in the spring.

"Got your work cut out for you," he said in his cheerful way. "Gonna have yourselves some fun."

"We had some today." As the four men trooped back down to the main level, Theo nodded at the demoed wall.

"You're going to have a lot more natural light in the kitchen with this wall gone," Dean pointed out. "I don't always go for the open concept in these old houses—takes away some of the character. But you needed it here."

"We're vaulting the ceiling, adding skylights in the kitchen."

Dean looked up, then over at Theo. "I can see that. Nice. It's going to keep you busy."

"We'll take it as it comes," Nash said. "No rush. The business, and whatever clients we get, come first. Along with a dumpster, which should've come first. Be nice if the snow holds off until it gets here."

"Work around here doesn't stop when the snow falls. Work's why we stopped by," Dean told him. "Jonah and I are licensed, and we take care of some of the general work. But we lost our contractor."

"I heard."

"We've got eighteen vacation units, five rentals, five retail spaces in town, and eight apartments, plus our own offices. Too much for just me and Jonah. With our contractor and CJ, we kept up. There's always going to be a list, but with the four of us, and an occasional laborer, we kept up."

"You need another contractor."

"We do. Me, Jonah, CJ? Not enough."

"CJ? He'd be willing to work with us?"

"She," Jonah corrected. "Catherine Jane. Licensed plumber, and a hell of a good carpenter. Like Dean says, the three of us? Not enough to keep things running by All the Rest's standards. We keep 'em high."

"We do. And we're always happy to give a new business a boost."

"But," Nash finished, "you need to know more about what we can do, have done, and are willing to do. How about we have a beer and discuss it?"

Dean came home with Jonah in tow.

"Brought this moocher home for dinner. Gina's got a girls' night, and the kids are with her mom," he began, then his jaw dropped when he saw Sloan at the counter.

"You—your hair. You cut your hair."

"I whacked it. Mom fixed it."

"It looks— You look—"

"Hey, Tink." Jonah dropped down at the counter beside her to scrub at Mop. And earned a sour look.

"You look beautiful." Dean walked over, wrapped around her.

"Dad?"

"My girl again."

"Without her hair?"

He shook his head before he eased back. Then kissed her forehead, her cheeks, her lips. "Look at that face. There you are. Nobody holds Sloan Cooper down. Jonah, we're having another beer."

"I hear that. I like it, if that counts."

"It doesn't." Sloan drilled a finger in his side. "But thanks."

Since Dean would make dinner, Elsie got the two beers. "What's the word on the Fix-Its?"

"I liked them, too," Jonah said. "It's going to be a cool house when it's finished. Pretty much have to touch every inch of it to get there, but they've already busted out a wall that needed it."

"Both of them spent some summers working with Habitat, and that's a solid few steps up the ladder for me." Dean took a swing of his beer as he opened the fridge for the chops. "Got a nice vibe between them, and reasonable rates. We looked at the plans for the house. And yeah, they've got some work cut out, but it's a damn good plan."

"Nash had a friend, an architect in New York, work on them with him. Solid," Jonah declared. "We're going to have them start on the tile work and paint in Water's Edge next week, see how they do."

"They may have work for Moose and Maisie," Drea told her father.

"They let us know. Putting in some interior doors for the Havers tomorrow. I'll be checking with them, with Moose and Maisie, and we'll see how it goes."

"The younger one hit on Drea."

"He did not." Drea rolled her eyes at her sister. "He told me I was beautiful."

"That's a fact," her father said. "I'd think less of him if he didn't notice."

"They've got a Christmas tree in the corner of the living room," Jonah added. "Got to decorate it yet, but I give them credit for it."

"We'll be doing ours after dinner." Dean slapped a hand on Jonah's shoulder. "You're drafted."

"And I need to take my scheduled walk."

"Want company?" Drea asked Sloan.

"I've got Mop for that. Drink your wine. Trust me, I won't go far."

"It's getting dark," Elsie said.

"Flashlight in my pocket, and I really can't go far."

Jonah sipped his beer when Sloan went into the mudroom for her coat, and Mop wagged his way to follow. He waited until the door closed behind her.

"She needs to walk, be outside. What happened on Thanksgiving wasn't her fault. She's careful."

"You're right." Elsie let out a breath. "You're absolutely right. I'm going to make some quick biscuits to go with the pork and noodles."

"And keep your hands busy."

Elsie glanced at her husband. "And keep my hands busy."


Sloan made it to her afternoon mark, rested thirty seconds, then took ten more steps.

Stopping there, she watched dusk settle over the lake and turn its water deep and dark.

This was here for her, she thought, if she looked out the window, if she stepped outside. As were the mountains, the woods, the trails.

She'd grown used to living in the city, in an apartment. Now—maybe it was the strange Big Change—but she realized she'd grown used to this again.

She just needed to get back to work, back to routine, back to her plans.

She stood another moment, as her mind wandered toward the brothers in the old Parker house. Obviously, they had plans, but what were they, exactly? None of her business, she told herself, except . . . They might be doing work for her family, and didn't that make it her business?

She could run a background check, but admitted since she was on leave and they weren't doing anything to warrant it, she'd walk into a gray area.

Her father was a good judge, and she needed to leave it at that.

She just missed being a cop.

What about Janet Anderson? she wondered. No harm, really, in looking into that. Maybe asking Travis what he knew, if anything.

Maybe just looking at media reports, making some notes, thinking it over would help her feel less useless.

What could it hurt? she decided as she started back.


In their little house, Clara fried up some chicken. As a nurse, she knew oven-baking some skinless breasts or thighs made a better choice. But she used her grandmother's recipe—rest in peace—and Sam just loved it.

So did she.

They'd both put in a long day, her at the hospital, Sam at the nursing home. They deserved it.

She'd fry up some potatoes, too. Why not go for the gold?

She'd start them both off with a cup of tomato soup—with just a drizzle or so of what Sam sometimes called the magic juice.

Though she'd been on her feet all day, she felt only contentment as she cooked for her man.

To think she'd given up on having a man after her husband died, more than twelve years before. God had called him home, and she'd learned to be content with that, too.

He'd been a good man, Rufus had. A good man, a hard worker. Though she didn't hesitate to admit he hadn't lit her up in bed the way Sam did.

God had called him home because it was meant. He'd been meant to fall off that ladder on that windy Sunday afternoon.

Meant to fracture his skull, break his back, bust up his leg.

They'd lost him on the table twice, and brought him back.

A strong man, he'd lingered for days and days, nights and nights on the machine that did the breathing for him, kept his heart beating.

And she'd had to make the choice, and she chose to send him home to God because she understood he was meant to go. And she'd come to understand the machines were wrong, against what was meant.

Machines pitted man's will against the Almighty's.

Sinful.

She'd come to understand *she* was meant to make that choice for others. To send them back, send them home.

Their blood wasn't magic—that was just Sam making jokes. But it was holy. It was blessed.

And taking it into themselves, a kind of communion. A way to bring them both strength to do what they were called to do. A way to add those lives, sent home, into their own.

She fried the chicken to a turn, if she said so herself. Then called Sam to wash up.

"I tell you, babe, this day about wore me to the bone."

"You work so hard."

"So do you."

"Well, we're going to have a fine meal, and I'm going to tell you about the one who came into my mind today. How I think it's time to start tracking him. He's a year out, but he's the one who came to my mind."

"You know best. I swear, Clara, that chicken looks like heaven."

"A little soup first. For strength and purpose."

She poured from pot to cups.

They sat, tapped the cups together, and drank.

After the meal, she put her feet up because Sam did the dishes and pots. (Her doll!)

They sat together at the computer and started the real research on Arthur Rigsby, age fifty-six, a dentist in Cumberland, Maryland, who'd been brought back after a car accident and collapsed lungs.

"This one might be a little tricky considering he lives and works in the city. Probably rich, too, since he's a dentist. Got a wife. She's got an art gallery—don't that beat it?"

"Artsy-fartsy," he said. "I bet she can't cook near as good as you, babe."

"This is the one, Sam. We just have to take the time we need to make a good plan. It might take a few weeks, but he's the one."

"If you say he's the one, then he is." He turned his head to kiss her. "Tricky won't stop us from doing what needs doing."

"There's nothing we can't do together, Sam. That poor man." The thought almost brought tears to her eyes. "They dragged him back into this world."

"We'll help him into the next. Let's see what else we can find out about him. And next day off, we take a nice drive down to Cumberland and scout things out."

He gave her that eyebrow wiggle she loved. "And maybe do a little Christmas shopping."

"And buy a tree!" Delighted, Clara clapped her hands. "Just a small one, doll. We can put it right there by the front window. I've got ornaments stored away, but I haven't felt like decorating in such a long time. Now, this year, with you? I want the works!"

"Then we'll have it. Whatever my girl wants."

# CHAPTER NINE

By noon the next day, the Littlefield brothers contracted the bathroom job—which would include new lighting, new faucets, double sinks, a tub/shower combo, and a pair of floating shelves. They installed the three interior doors while talking football with the man of the house—a rabid Ravens fan—who hobbled around with his cane and stabilizing boot.

After examining the work, Bill Haver shook his head. "Well, damn it all."

"Is there a problem?" Nash asked him.

"She was right. They look good. And now she's going to come home, take a look. She's gonna say: *Bill, these new doors make the rest look bad. We gotta do the rest now.* I know that woman," he said with another head shake. "Been married forty-eight years, so I know that woman. She's gonna want the closet doors switched out, and all the rest. And she's gonna want them before Christmas."

He shook his head again. "I know that woman."

"I bet she'd be happy if she came home and you told her we'd have them in next week." Theo added a flash of grin.

"Yeah, she would." Now Bill smirked. "I'm going to beat her to the punch and tell her I came up with it, and got you going on it. So, best do a count and measure then."

He opened and closed one of the new doors, nodded. "You boys do good work. I'll write you a check."

From there they moved on to fix a leaky faucet for Pink Hair and Freckles. No charge.

"I'm starving," Theo announced when they walked back outside.

"Yeah, I could eat. Why don't we grab a burger, and I'll order the doors and hardware for Bill and Rita? With any luck Mrs. Moose will've settled on what she's after, and we can pick it all up at once."

"We did a good morning's work. And this afternoon? More demo."

"That downstairs john's a gut job."

"And what's more fun than a gut job?" Theo asked, then answered. "Not much. Oh, wow, there she is! She's coming out of High Country Kitchen."

Nash didn't have to ask who, not with the dazzled look in his brother's eyes.

She was a beauty with a sparkly black cap over a long fall of golden-brown hair, a black coat open to a just-below-the-knee red dress paired with tall black boots.

She had a purse the size of a baby elephant on one shoulder, and a large take-out bag in her other hand.

When she spotted Theo, she smiled, and Nash imagined his brother's heart rate spiked through the roof.

"Well, hi," she said.

"Hi. Thanks again for the help yesterday. We got the tree. Oh, this is my brother. Nash, this is Drea."

"Nice to meet you." She held out a gloved hand.

"You, too. You work for All the Rest. We'll be doing some work for them."

"So my father told me."

"Your father?"

She smiled back at Theo again. "Dean Cooper. My father. He said you'd already started demo on the old Parker place. I guess that makes it the new Littlefield place."

Nash knew his job as wingman was to make nice and disappear.

"It'll take a while before much of anything looks new. I've got to place that order," he said to Theo. "See you inside. Good to meet you, Drea. Give our best to your father."

"I will. I won't hold you up," she said to Theo as Nash walked down to the restaurant. "And I have to get this food to the hungry horde at the office."

"Right, but . . . Could I buy you a cup of coffee sometime?"

"Coffee?"

"Or dinner. Maybe a trip to Barbados."

Her eyebrows lifted. "I've never been there. Sounds tempting, but . . ."

"Are you with someone? I should've asked that first."

"If I were, I wouldn't say you could buy me dinner tonight. I'll meet you at By the Lake. Seven o'clock."

Everything in him sang, joyfully.

"Great. Where is it?"

She passed him the take-out bag, then took a map and a marker out of her purse, and outlined the route.

"Great," he said again, and pocketed the map. "I could carry these up for you."

"That's all right." She took the bag back. "I've got it. See you tonight."

He watched her walk away, then floated into the restaurant on puffy white clouds.

Nash already had a table, and worked on his phone.

"I've got a date with the most beautiful woman in the world."

"Quick work. I ordered already—burgers, fries, Cokes. You usually go for the cuties. Like Pink Hair and Freckles. The bouncy ones."

"Bouncy?"

"Yeah, the kind that see a friend, squeal." Nash mimed bouncing a ball on the table. "Bounce, bounce, bounce. This one strikes as smooth."

"I don't know what it is. It's like getting hit by lightning. I like it. I'm taking her to dinner tonight."

"Just some brotherly advice? Hold off on the proposal, at least until dessert."

On top of the world, Theo flashed a grin at the server when she brought their Cokes. "Thanks. We did a good morning's work, got a gut job coming, and I've got a date with Dreamy Drea.

"I'm having a real good day."

When their mother mentioned the date, Sloan began to fret. She'd talked herself out of digging into the Littlefields, and now regretted it.

She spent an hour after dinner doing just that. Not through official channels, but you could find out a lot through other means.

What she found out had her fretting more, then waiting downstairs while her parents watched TV in their bedroom until she saw the headlights.

At eleven-twenty-three.

She stepped outside into the rush of night air, and called her sister.

"Sloan? What're you doing? Is something wrong?"

"You tell me. Come in here."

She'd done some fancy fishtail braid with her hair, Sloan noted. And wore heels—high ones—with a short, snug black dress.

"What are you thinking?" Sloan demanded.

"What are you thinking?" When she stepped inside, Drea loosened the scarf around her neck. "You didn't actually wait up for me?"

Because the amusement in her sister's voice burned, Sloan ignored it. "You went out with someone you don't even know."

"Sloan, here's a little clue. The point of dating is to get to know someone."

"Did you know he's a lawyer? What's a New York lawyer doing in Heron's Rest hammering nails?"

"Starting a business with his brother." The amusement vanished like smoke. "You did *not* run a background check on Theo."

"Not an official one. I can google some stranger who's after my sister."

"You know, I only had one glass of wine with dinner since I was driving. I'm about to have another."

She clipped her way back to the kitchen to pour one. "I had a really good time," she added as Sloan came after her, more slowly. "A nice dinner with an interesting, attractive man. So what?"

"Did you know they're loaded? I mean seriously loaded?"

"He didn't mention it, but I gleaned, since he was wearing Hugo Boss, knew his wines, got his law degree from Columbia, and grew up in a swanky area of Connecticut.

"Want some?" Drea held up the wine bottle.

"No. Listen—"

"No, you listen first. You're working yourself up over me going to dinner with someone you can't pin down. I'm torn between being really pissed off and amused. I'm going to take the middle ground there. I like him. I liked talking with him. I liked finding out he's a crazy fan of the Marvel Universe. You know how I feel about Captain America."

"You were going to marry him."

"Since, regretfully, that's not going to happen, I enjoyed spending a few hours with a very attractive man. And?" She jabbed out a finger. "That's attractive on more than the physical, where he gets tops marks. I understand his tight bond with his brother, admire his work ethic and their mutual ambitions for their business."

"His brother's some Wall Street honcho."

"Not anymore."

"They're like fourth-generation rich. No, wealthy. *Wealthy*'s a step up from *rich*. It doesn't make any sense."

"This is what they want. He didn't spend the whole time talking about himself, which is a major point in his favor. But I got enough. Family pressure's my opinion. He didn't talk about his parents much, but when he did it was 'he,' 'she,' 'they.' Not 'my mom,' 'my dad.'"

"They're divorced."

"I gleaned that, too. I didn't push there because it's clearly a sore spot. He loves it here."

"He's barely unpacked."

"They vacationed here when they were younger. Once at least, from what I got. It's why Nash bought the house, wanted to start the business here. And Theo, in his words, horned his way in. Nash is his family, and he wanted his family. He wanted a chance to build his own, or help build their own. I admire that."

"You've already got a thing going." Sloan pointed at her. "I know you. One date, and you've got a thing going."

"He's the first man I've had dinner with in . . . I can't remember, who started a thing going. So deal with it. We're going kayaking Sunday afternoon.

"Now I'm going to bed. We've got a lot of weekenders coming in."

She walked toward the mudroom door, paused. "I could tell you to mind your own business, then you'd say that I'm your sister, so your business. And round and round. Instead, I'll remind you you're not the only Cooper who can take care of herself."

She paused another moment. "And I'll add he's an excellent kisser."

Sloan just sighed as she heard the outside door open, close. "Of course he is."


She had her follow-up with Dr. Vincenti, and clung to the bright spot. She was cleared to drive again. Short distances for now, but at least she'd be mobile.

Of course, her car remained in Annapolis, and since work stayed off the table, no access to her official vehicle.

But she could borrow her mother's car, her father's truck.

The rest seemed like a long road of tiny steps.

She promised herself she'd take one the next day. Borrow the car, drive into town. She'd walk, do some Christmas shopping that wasn't desperate online purchases.

She'd see people, talk to people.

"I know you're a little disappointed," Elsie said as they drove home.

"Not really. Honestly, not really. And not at all surprised."

"He gave you good marks—on everything but the weight."

"I'm working on it."

"I know you are. I'm going to hitch a ride to work with Drea tomorrow and leave you the car."

She didn't even have to ask. "Thanks. I'd really like to drive into town, do some shopping."

"I'm a homebody, to the bone, but if I'd been stuck all this time the way you have, I'd go stir-crazy. You hardly ever complain."

"Oh, you don't hear inside my head. It's an endless bitch fest."

"And you can bitch out loud to me whenever you want. I wish you would."

Sloan laughed. "You want me to bitch?"

"Yes, I do. Start now."

"Okay, here's a list. I miss being able to roll out of bed, take a run or hit the gym before work. And I miss work. I miss the purpose. I miss feeling strong. I knew that was important to me, but not how important until I lost it. I miss being able to go out at night when I feel like it, meet up with friend, or a date. I miss sex. I miss looking in the mirror and thinking: *Well, you look pretty hot today, Cooper. Go get 'em.*"

She glanced over. "Too much?"

"Not even close."

"Okay. I miss feeling useful. The job gives me that. Every day, I felt useful."

"That would be the worst part. Not to feel useful. But you are and have been." Reaching over, Elsie rubbed a hand on Sloan's arm. "I can wish it wasn't under these circumstances, but you've been so useful to your dad and me."

"Helping with the dishes? Peeling vegetables?"

"No. We've had this time with you. We've been able to watch you come back over these weeks. You've let us see how hard you try. I never wanted you to join the NRP."

"But . . ." Shock struck and spread. "You never said. Ever. You always supported me there."

"Supporting my daughter in what she wants doesn't mean it's what I wanted for her. My girl wearing a gun on her hip every day? No, not at all what I wanted, and I can't count the number of times I had to stop myself from trying to push you in another direction. But if I had, I knew I could push you away. I'd never risk that."

"It's been hard on you." Shifting, she studied her mother's profile. "I didn't know, I never thought."

"Sometimes—and I wouldn't have wanted you to know. But having these weeks, watching you try, seeing how hard you'll work to get back? It's changed my mind. It's not just what you wanted to do, but what you were meant to do. So now, I want it for you, too."

She shot Sloan a smile. "So you've been very useful. And by Christmas? You'll be that much closer."

"I should bitch out loud more often."

"Are you up to it if I get off in town, catch that ride later? You can drive yourself home."

"I will be. Mom." She had to stop and take a breath as emotion swamped her. "God, you always know just the right thing."

"Not always. But this way, we can both feel useful."

Twenty minutes later, Sloan sat behind the wheel. Maybe it was silly, she admitted, but the act of driving a car, even for a few miles, made her feel better.

One more step, she thought as she turned up the radio and navigated the roads. Everything looked bright and sparkling, the sheer, cold blue of the sky, the deep green pines with the carpet of snow at their feet. The white-smothered peaks shining in the mirror of the lake.

When she caught sight of a hawk, she pulled over just to watch it circle against that pristine sky.

She'd mark today as a turning point, she told herself as she drove on. She'd consider it the end of the beginning.

When she got home, she pulled into the garage. Instead of going through its mudroom entrance, she went back outside. After a four-hour round trip, she could—and should—walk.

This time she didn't push for steps, but studied the hills, the way they rose up, the way they swam in the lake. She watched the birds, listened to their calls. She spotted deer tracks in the snow.

And realized when she stopped, she'd passed her last mark.

Backtracking, she counted.

Fourteen steps more.

After pumping a fist, she walked home.

Tired, she thought, taking stock. But not exhausted, not really shaky.

Inside, she lit a fire, then started to sit down, update her spread-sheet. Then remembered her low marks on weight gain, so went to the kitchen instead.

She made herself a grilled cheese sandwich, then took it to the living room and ate while she updated. Then gave herself a mental pat on the back when she managed to eat it all.

She washed the pan, then accepted she needed to sit awhile. Maybe even take a nap.

She sat, picked up her crocheting because she'd discovered it not only gave her something to do but lulled her.

She'd managed a few stitches on her newest project when someone knocked on the door.

Assuming delivery, she nearly ignored it, then made herself get up and answer.

"Cap!"

She found herself enveloped in a hug by a man who smelled like the forest.

"Let me have a look at you."

"Come in first. Let me get your coat."

"I've got it, I've got it. I know the rules."

The visit brightened her day a little more.

At six-five, her father's oldest friend, Travis Hamm, hung his parka in the closet, tucked his uniform hat in with it.

Then stood, giving her a long study out of eyes the color of faded denim.

"You cut off your hair."

"Impulse. I'm getting used to it."

"Well, you're looking a hell of a lot better than the last time I saw you."

"I sure hope so. Sit down. I'll get you coffee."

"No, you sit, too. I've already had a gallon of it today. Where's Mop?"

"He's job dog today. Mom had to drive me down to Hagerstown for my two-week follow-up, and Dad decided to take him along."

"How'd that go, the follow-up?"

"Not bad."

He sat, stretched out endless legs, crossed his big feet at their booted ankles. "Your dad told me what happened on Thanksgiving. I was sorry to hear it."

"It's healing up. I'm healing up. Hey, if I don't screw anything up, I can start using five-pound weights next week. I'm nearly up to a mile and a half round trip on walks outside.

"And I've crocheted two scarves. Now I'm making this."

She held up a long strip of soft white wool.

"What is it?"

"It's going to be a baby blanket."

His eyebrow shot up. "Got something to tell me?"

She laughed, and that still hurt a little. "Not for me. You know Joel—he and Sari are having a baby next spring."

"Good for them. Good for you, too."

"I've been bored brainless, Cap. Fighting off the bitchy with it. This helps with both. Tell me what's happening, what you've got going. I was thinking of calling and asking you about the Janet Anderson investigation."

"I wish I had good news on that. Or any, really. We assisted in the search, but it's not our case. I've gotten updates. No trace of her. Nothing. The family's put up a reward. Twenty-five thousand for bringing her home. They've done interviews, made statements pleading for whoever took her—and there's no doubt that's what happened at this point—to let her go."

"I've followed what I can. The husband looks sick, devastated."

"They were married just over a year, together for three. Saved up, bought a nice little house. Everybody who knew them—family, friends, neighbors, coworkers—says they were crazy about each other. No pissed-off exes on either side, no trouble, no nothing.

"She drove to the grocery store. The investigator figured she went for butter because she had a recipe out and didn't have enough in stock. And nobody saw a damn thing."

"Somebody's holding her, sold her, or she's already dead."

His eyes on Sloan's, Travis nodded. "That's the hard truth. I wish I could say different."

"What about other abductions in the area? Her age group?"

He smiled at her. "Can't stop, can you?"

"I guess not. And it happened when I was down. It keeps pulling at me."

"Nothing that hits the notes, no. As it happens, I came to see you, and also to talk to you about work."

"Oh? Something I can help with while I'm on the DL?"

"No, but something maybe when you're off it. I understand why you went where you went, and I know you've done good work there. If you'd consider a change, I could use you."

"Oh. Cap."

He held up a hand. "I don't want to pressure you, and I won't. I will ask you to think about it. You know Sergeant Masters."

"Sure."

"He put in his papers. He's got thirty in, and he's buying an RV. He and he wife want to hit the road, travel the country."

"Really?"

"Their kids are grown. One out in Montana, another up in Michigan. They plan to take off, head south for a long vacation starting the first of February. I need another good officer. I need another sergeant."

"I'm a corporal."

"I can offer you your next chevron. You've earned it. It's a big change. I just want you to think about it. You decide you're not interested, no harm, no foul. I don't need to know either way until after the first of the year."

"The first of the year," she murmured. Everything was next year. "You really caught me off guard with this."

"I expect I did. I haven't said anything to your dad about it. This is just you and me. Mull it over."

"I will. Of course I will."

"I'm not offering this because you're family to me, I want that clear between us. I've kept tabs on you since you joined the department— because you're family. You're good police. Smart, capable, and damn well dedicated. I wouldn't make this offer to anyone who didn't meet those standards."

He pushed to his feet. "Now, I've got to get back. If you have any questions about this, you just give me a call."

"I'm so thrown off, I can't think of any."

"I bet you will," he said, and when she rose, hugged her again. "It's good to see you looking more like Sloan, even with the new hair."

He gave her a light pat, then got his coat, fit on his hat. "No pressure. I mean that."

"Okay, and I will mull it over. It's a lot to take in."

Since she couldn't think of anything else, Sloan sat down and let it all roll over her.

Normally, she'd take a long walk to think it through, but that was too big a physical push. Instead, she went with another of her go-to methods. She opened her laptop and began lists pros and cons.

Number one pro, the promotion. Who knew how long it might

take her to make sergeant in her current unit after two months' medical leave?

Number one con, leaving her current unit—and most especially Joel.

The lists grew on both sides until she realized she'd started to argue with herself.

Putting that aside, she texted Travis.

> I do have some questions. If it's all right with you, I'll write them out in an email so you can answer when you've got the time.

His answer came back in under two minutes. (Another on the pro side.)

> That'll work.

Then she had to debate whether to address him in the email as Travis or Captain. (One for the con side.)

Stick with Cap, she told herself.

> Cap, first I want to thank you for offering me a position in your unit. It's a possibility I hadn't considered, so I have a lot to think about.
> I see the filing deadline for applications is December 18, with the written exam for Sergeant scheduled for January 4. I understand upon passing the written, I'll have an oral board interview in late January.

Which explained why he'd brought it to her now, she thought. There would be a vacancy in February, and she could fill it.

> I've already familiarized myself with the material for the Sergeant's Promotional Exam in anticipation of a possible promotion within my current unit.

If I decide to file an application to fill your vacancy, I'll study the
material again. I understand your recommendation carries weight,
and if we move forward, I won't let you down.
Before I make that decision, I have a short list of questions.

She listed them, and ended the email with another note of appreciation for his confidence in her.

When she sent it, she noted the time. And realized she'd been
awake and active for hours.

Not a single nap!

Doing a mental check, she found she didn't feel the physical drag
that meant she needed one.

Her parents would be home in a while, so she'd do something wild.
She'd make dinner.

In the kitchen, she checked for ingredients, supplies. She'd never
known her parents not to be prepared, and wasn't disappointed.

Taking out a large bag of frozen red sauce, she got to work.

It felt good to do something productive. Something not just for
herself, for her recovery. For company, she switched on the TV.

When she had to sit down, she didn't bitch at herself. She just sat,
sipped some water, watched a pretty, perky woman with amazing red
hair transform a very sad main suite into a calm and stylish oasis.

"Nice job, Red," Sloan said, then got up to set the table before
texting her sister.

Come in when you bring Mom home.

Okay. Why?

For me to know, you to find out.

Fine. Leaving in about twenty.

"Perfect." Sloan signaled her acceptance with a thumbs-up emoji,
then got back to it.

A half hour later when they came, she had a bottle of good Chianti breathing, wineglasses out, and the meal ready.

Elsie took one look at the kitchen, another longer one at Sloan. "You made dinner."

"Well, you'd already made the sauce and the bread. I just defrosted them. It's Italian night at the Coopers'. Lasagna, also known as Sloan's Kickasserole, insalata mista, and garlic bread."

"Smells good, looks good." Drea accepted a glass of wine. "You're feeling feisty tonight."

"Why not? I got a doing-good from the doctor, drove a car again, walked fourteen—count them—additional steps, didn't fall asleep on the couch. Oh, and Travis stopped by. It was good to see him. When do we expect Dad?"

"He should be on his way." Elsie walked over to take a good look at the lasagna. "This looks just right, Sloan. Thanks."

"You've all been taking care of me, and doing a reasonably good job of pretending not to be taking care of me. Tonight, table's turned."

"And a pretty job of setting that table. Why don't we all sit down and enjoy this wine?"

"See?" Sloan tapped a finger in the air at Elsie. "Taking care of me, pretending not to. But sitting down works."

# CHAPTER TEN

She didn't tell them about Travis's offer. She valued their input, but this had to be her decision. And she already knew they'd be thrilled if she opted to stay in the area.

Because she loved them, that weighed heavily on the pro side.

But she'd lived on the other side of the state for years, and they'd never lost their bond, the connection. Her family ties stayed tight.

She had family on the other side of the state, too, in Joel, Sari, his mom, and the rest. Would that bond hold, that connection remain? Would those found family ties stay tight?

With that on her mind, she texted Joel.

Can you FT?

The answer came barely a minute later when her iPad signaled.

"Hey, sis! Whoa, what? The hair."

"Yeah, I went a little crazy."

"What about her hair?" Sari moved on-screen. "Girl! I love it. You cut your way to some sexy sass there."

"You think?"

"I know what I know." Sari, her amazing cloud of hair dancing around her pretty face, put her cheek close to Joel's. "You're looking good! You're looking so good!"

When her big brown eyes teared up, Sari rolled them and smiled. "Hormones, honey. I got a million of them. And hey, check this."

She stepped back, turned sideways, and pointed at her belly. If Sloan looked hard enough, she could make out a tiny pooch.

Sloan widened her own eyes. "Holy shit, Sari, you're enormous!"

"I think maybe I felt her move. It's a little early, but I think maybe. I'm so glad to get a look at you and your sexy, sassy do! We miss the hell out of you."

"I miss the hell out of you. Maybe you could come up for a couple days. I could see about getting that house you guys liked last time."

"I can't speak for my man— Hell yes, I can. We'd love it."

"We would. Let me see about schedules and all. But it's likely you'll be back before we can work out the time. Just another few weeks, right?"

"It's looking like I'll be cleared within the month. I had my follow-up, and Vincenti was happy enough. I have to follow up with the doctor up here for the pec muscle thing to cover the bases. But something's come up, and I wanted to talk to you about it."

"You're okay, right?" Joel asked. "You look a lot better, sis. You sound better, too."

"I am better. Captain Hamm came by today. You know him."

"Sure."

"I don't. Do we like him?" Sari demanded.

"We do," Sloan assured her. "He's the Western Region commander. And a friend of the family. He and my father go way back. He's losing a sergeant to retirement, and wants me to take that position. Wants me to apply for it, test, and join his unit."

"I'm sitting down now." So announcing, Sari pulled up a chair beside Joel's.

"He's too good a commander to offer this to me because of the personal connection. If I wasn't sure of that, I couldn't even consider it. This just happened today. I haven't said anything to my family yet. I know where they'd come down, and know they'd tell me it's my decision, and support either way. But since I know, I don't want to tell them about it."

"Made a list, didn't you?" Sari kept up the conversation when Joel said nothing. "Reasons to, reasons not to."

"Pros and cons, yeah. I'd say they're running pretty much neck and neck. I still need to think about it. I have some time before the application deadline. But I wanted to hear what you thought."

Joel put a hand over Sari's. "I got a question."

"Okay."

"Are you stupid?"

"No! Come on, I—"

Now he held up his other hand to cut her off. "Then you're going to take what you want, what you've earned, because you're not stupid."

"It's not just a matter of a promotion, Joel. It means moving across the state, leaving people I've worked with—especially you—for years."

"I know that, sis. I didn't say it was easy. I said you're not stupid. None of this should've happened to you. You shouldn't've walked into that goddamn mini-mart and into a bullet. But it did happen."

He took a breath.

"It did. Now, whatever the reason, something good's come out of that bad. That terrible bad. I'm not saying turning it down's wrong, because it has to be right for you. I'm saying when something you want and worked for lands in your lap, it's stupid not to pick it up."

"I gotta love this man." Sari pressed her lips to Joel's cheek. "He doesn't give me a choice."

"You'd take it?"

"It's not about what I'd do, sis. It's you."

"You're right. It's me. I'm going to think about it some more. I've got time to be sure, either way, before the deadline. Thanks for hearing me out."

"Always will."

"That goes for both of us. We love you, Sloan."

"I love you guys. I love all three of you. We'll talk again soon."

She set the tablet on charge. After she got ready for bed, she stood at her window looking out at the shadows and silhouettes her view offered.

It amazed her she wasn't yet tired enough for sleep. She settled down, picked up her crocheting, and got to work on the baby blanket.

As they finished up their first job for All the Rest, Nash and Theo met CJ Kirpeckne.

Since it was Theo's turn with tunes, the Bluetooth speaker played a lot of alternative music Nash didn't necessarily get. Apparently, neither did CJ Kirpeckne.

When she walked in, she put her hands on her hips. "What's wrong with genuine rock and roll?"

"That's what I said." Nash came down from the ladder he stood on to finish painting the ceiling.

"Country's fine as long as it's not whiny. Does Dolly whine? No, she does not! Not even on 'Jolene.'"

"Dolly Parton's a goddess."

"You got that."

Nash pushed back the Mets cap he wore, gave the woman a quick study.

Maybe five-three, possibly a buck-ten. The purple hair under her purple Ravens ski cap said teenager to him. But her face said she'd seen forty.

"Can we help you?"

"Turning that bullshit down'd be a start."

"I got it." Theo, a blue do-rag covered in Baby Yodas tied around his head, set his roller in the pan and turned down the volume.

"Better. CJ Kirpeckne." She stuck out a hand as hard as an oak plank. "I'm just here to check your progress. Who's who?"

"Nash." Then he pointed. "Theo."

"Okay then."

She wandered the open kitchen, dining, living area, hazel eyes narrowed. "Well, you haven't made a mess of it. You should be about wrapped up by my clock."

"This is the last coat. Tile's done."

She walked into the bathroom, studied the work. Gave a nod, a grunt. Walked back.

"Didn't make a mess of that either. The boss said you might could use some help over at your place."

"No 'might' about it. We've got a couple dozen windows coming in next week. The old ones leak. A lot of demo yet, but we're living there, so one section at a time on that."

"We're rehabbing top to bottom," Theo put in. "Or right now, middle to top."

"I'll give you an hour or two when I've got it. Same rate I get from the Coopers, and I'm worth it. I got a nephew at loose ends when you need a laborer. He's not lazy, and he'll cart and carry, and do what he's told. You don't want to set Robo off on his own. He's mostly willing, but he's only half-able."

"Robo?"

"His sister couldn't say *Robert* back when, and *Robo* stuck. Gimme your phone. I'll put his number in. You call him or don't, up to you."

"Okay, thanks." Nash handed it over. "Why don't you put yours in there, too?"

"All right. A couple hours here and there, and that's if the boss doesn't need me. Otherwise, I'm your job boss on ATR jobs unless Dean's on that."

"No problem at all." Nash took back his phone.

She gave them both another measuring look. "How come you left New York City? Women trouble, trouble with the law?"

"No."

"Actually, I guess you could say I had some trouble with the law." Theo lifted his shoulders. "I got to be a lawyer and decided I didn't want to be one. At least not there."

"A lawyer? How old are you?"

"Ah, twenty-eight."

"And you're a lawyer."

"Today, I'm mostly a painter. Next week I'll be a licensed contractor."

"You know the thing about people? They never make any damn sense. Make sure everything gets put back as it was," she told them as she headed for the door. "Elsie'll come in, hang the art and such, fluff it all up.

"They've got a family booked in here over the weekend."

"We'll get it done," Nash told her.

"I really like your hair," Theo added.

"Ravens rule," she declared, and walked out.

"Well, that was interesting." Nash adjusted his cap. "Let's finish up."

Theo picked up his roller.

"Nash, I'm loving this."

"Seashell Blush paint?"

"No, but it's a nice color for this room. I'm loving it here. I mean, holy Jesus, look at the view."

"Your view should be a wall of Seashell Blush."

"I'm doing work I actually like, hanging with my big bro, and okay man, dating Dreamy Drea." He did a quick shuffle. "Third date Friday night."

"Should I find another place to stay, or are you just going to put a sock on the bedroom door?"

"It's not just about sex. I want the sex, but I'm not going to push. She's worth waiting for."

Nash looked down. "Boy, you are truly gone."

"I am truly gone. I'm loving that, too."

While the Littlefields finished that last coat, Sam drove with Clara to cruise Cumberland.

She'd always liked the look of it, the hilly streets, all the redbrick buildings. And a lot of churches. If she'd had a yen to live in a town— and she didn't—she'd have put Cumberland on the list.

She liked old buildings. People should respect and honor what came before. She liked the views, and she planned to enjoy the shops.

She wanted to find something fine for Sam for Christmas.

But first, they had work to do.

Dr. Rigsby closed his offices on Wednesday—so it said on his web page. Taking him from work, coming or going to it, could prove too risky, especially since his offices housed themselves in one of those nice old buildings shared by other offices and practices.

"It'll be interesting to see if he does anything on his day off. Maybe he just lazes around the house."

"Or watches porn all day while the wife's away."

"Oh, you!" Snickering, she slapped Sam's arm.

He navigated the curvy streets, kept right on the speed limit as they left the downtown area with the shops she wanted to browse. They moved into a pretty little neighborhood where Clara checked house numbers for the address they'd found in their research.

"That one there, doll. That nice redbrick on the slope. Three stories! Can you imagine? Double porches, and all slicked up for Christmas. A really nice yard, too. I just bet they have gardeners taking care of it."

She noted they had Christmas lights up, and approved, and caught a glimpse of a tree in the big front window.

"Don't see a car, but they've got a garage. Neighbor on the left's a little close. But we could figure it out."

"We always do," Clara said as he drove by. "We'll circle around, park on up. There was that house with a For Sale sign."

He had to smile. His babe thought of everything.

"If anybody says anything, why, we're just taking a look. Out in the area looking for our forever home."

"That's just right." She sighed a little. "You know, I was thinking how I liked Cumberland, but didn't want to live in a town. But this part here doesn't so much feel like a town. And the houses aren't so stacked up together. They're not that cookie-cutter deal you get either. I couldn't stand that."

"I love our little house."

"Oh, so do I. I like we got a little bit of land to keep us nice and tucked away. But it's fun to think what if."

When they parked, she hauled up her purse. "I'm going to get out, take some pictures of the house for sale. The sign and all. Most don't pay much mind to a woman, and it'll look like I'm interested in the house for sale."

As she started to open the door, he put a hand on her arm. "Hold on. Babe, you got the touch. You said we needed to come look-see this morning, and look-see that. The garage door's opening."

"It's got to be him! Unless his wife's really late leaving for work."

The gleaming gray Mercedes sedan drove right by them.

"It's him, all right. You got the touch." Sam pulled into the driveway of the house for sale, reversed, then followed. "Let's see where he goes."

The Mercedes cruised leisurely through town, out of it, and onto Interstate 68, east.

Sam kept his distance, kept his eye peeled as the Mercedes racked up nearly twenty miles.

"He's getting off! Put his turn signal on."

"I see it, I see it." As Sam exited behind the Mercedes, Clara noted down the exit.

Rigsby drove another mile, past a strip mall, fast-food places, then pulled into the lot of a motel.

He got out, carrying a small overnight bag.

"He's checking in, Sam. Twenty miles from home, day off, and he's checking into a motel?"

"Got something on the side! Bad boy!"

Rigsby came out, got back in the car, then drove around to the back of the motel.

"Give it a minute. We'll know which room. He'll park in front of his room. We'll drive around, park a few slots down, and see when whoever he's cheating with shows up."

He'd parked in front of 122, so they pulled in at 126.

Within ten minutes, a blue Toyota slipped in beside the Mercedes.

The woman who got out didn't carry an overnight, but a large purse. A blonde, she wore a short coat over a short dress, sunglasses, and high heels.

"She's got to be twenty, maybe twenty-five years younger than that cheating man."

Sam grinned. "The old dog. I'm going to get us those Sprites out of the cooler, and that bag of barbecue chips. This may take a while."

It took an hour and twenty minutes before the blonde came out. She shook back her hair, then slipped on her sunglasses before she slid into the Toyota and drove away.

"We could take him now, babe. He's alone, and I bet he's real relaxed."

"Not yet, no, not today, doll. We're not ready for him. It's not time for him. And we've been sitting here too long so somebody might remember the van."

"When you're right, you're right."

"We'll follow him again, just to see. Then we'll make ourselves a plan."

He came out, looking sleepy and satisfied.

The follow home proved easy, as that's just where he went.

"Drive on by, and back into town, doll. I'm going to take you to lunch, then we'll do that shopping. I've got a plan coming on."

"I know you do. One thing? The way you've been cooking for me, I'm taking you to lunch."

"Oh, Sam. You're the sweetest man in the world."

"It's easy to be sweet to you, babe."


Sloan took another day, then another. She borrowed her mother's car and drove into town. Christmas shopping headed her list, but she wanted to take stock during the trip. Of herself during the walking, standing, choosing, carrying. Of the town with its hilly streets, chatty shopkeepers.

She wanted to evaluate, weigh, compare objectively. If she went forward with Travis's offer, this would, once again, become her home base.

She found objectivity challenging, as Heron's Rest pumped out the charm in all its holiday finery.

Garland wrapped the posts of the old-timey streetlights, wreaths hung on doors, and trees stood in windows with their smaller cousins nestled in pots along Main Street.

When dusk came, lights would twinkle around windows, along roofs, down porch posts and doorways.

If you looked for small-town Christmas, you'd find it right here.

By the time she drove home, she'd talked to at least a dozen people she knew (and felt undecided on pro or con), racked up a few thousand steps walking inside and out, and considered her Christmas shopping complete.

In the kitchen, she heated up a bowl of soup, eating while she sat at the counter updating her spreadsheet, her pro and con list.

She studied both of them, reread Travis's answers to her questions before she sent him her decision.

The right one, she determined, for her. For this time, for these circumstances.

At dinner, she listened to her parents' easy replay of their day. Her mother had restocked books and puzzles in two vacation units, placed and decorated a tree in another, as requested by an incoming guest, inventoried linens, culled out those she felt needed replacements.

Her father and Jonah had completed the refresh of one of the apartments in town.

According to her father, the Fix-It Brothers' work proved more than satisfactory, so they'd contract that team to overhaul the kitchen in another.

"I need the final measurements," Elsie told Dean. "I'll go to the suppliers, choose the new counter surface, new cabinet doors, hardware, lighting, and the rest tomorrow. I've got a look in mind."

"You always do. I'll get you the measurements." He gave her a look. "And the budget."

"You always do. You're quiet tonight, Sloan. Is everything okay? Did you get your walks in? The temperature dropped again, and it's windy with it. But that's never stopped you."

"Yeah, it is, and yes, I did. With more steps added. I'm quiet mostly because I was listening. You know, when I was a teenager, and the two of you would talk about work, I always thought: Boring. It's not. It's genius."

Dean laughed. "Never boring to me and your mom, but I don't know if I'd lift it to genius."

"No, it is. The way you both focus on your strengths, but still blend the work. The fact that you can and are professional partners and still have a loving, solid marriage—and a life outside the work. That's the genius."

"Take the 'genius,' Dean." Elsie toasted with her water glass. "She's not wrong."

"Add that one of your daughters joined that business, with her own strengths, opinions, perspectives, and she gets professional respect from you, but is still your daughter first and last."

"There are times—plenty of them," Dean said, "when I wonder how we managed without her. Drea's got her own genius. But so do you, baby. And you're first and last our girl."

"I know it. I've always known it."

And maybe, she thought, taken it, at least a little bit, for granted.

"But I think coming home this way brought that, well, home. When I told you I was going to join the NRP, you didn't try to talk me out of it. You didn't pressure me when I decided to move to Annapolis. You asked questions, good ones that made me think. But you never tried to change my mind."

"That's never been the easiest thing to do, has it, Elsie? Add the fact you think things through. It's a rare thing for you to take a jump without calculating the distance, time, wind velocity. So when you decide, you've decided."

"You've decided something." Elsie folded her hands together under the table. "Something important."

"Yes, I have. When Travis came to see me a few days ago, he told me his sergeant was retiring in February. He offered me that position. I'd have to file an application, take the written exam, the oral, pass. I'd have to leave my unit, relocate."

Now Elsie reached for Dean's hand under the table.

"I didn't say anything about it because I needed to think it through—calculate," she added with a glance at her father. "It's a very big jump, so a lot of calculating."

She took a breath. "I filed the application this afternoon."

"Sloan—"

"Wait." Dean waved off his wife. "Are you making this change for us? Because we don't want that, Sloan."

"Do you factor into those calculations? Of course you do. But I'm doing this for me. I'm being given a chance for a leadership position, and I want it. I believe I'd get the same, at some point, otherwise, but this could be mine now.

"And why now?" she added. "When I ask myself, it seems like fate. And I've never really believed in that. Why does this opportunity drop down after I've needed to spend weeks back home? Weeks when I've started to realize how much I miss it here. I had to leave and make something, be something, on my own before I could come back."

As simple, she'd realized, and as complex as that.

"Now I've come back. I want to stay, for me. I want that chevron, for me. I want to serve under someone like Travis, for me. I want to be close to my family again, for me. And I want to be here, for you."

"Am I allowed to tell you how happy this makes me? Makes us?" Elsie added.

"You can be happy after I pass the exams."

"You know you will."

"I damn well will. The written's right after the first of the year. I'm on it. But there's one more thing. I'm going to need my own place."

"Well, Sloan—"

"Mom."

"No, no, you're all grown up, of course you want your own place. I was going to say there's no rush. And I am going to ask you to wait until you're fully recovered, and until you're sure of what you want."

"I know what I want, and what I don't. I don't want to live in town. I considered that because I've gotten used to it. But that's not what I want now. I don't want an apartment, I want a house. It doesn't have to be big and shiny—I'm not ready for anything like that. But a little house where I have some room, some outdoor space, too."

"Rent or buy?" Dean asked, and made her smile.

"Either, but I'd rather buy something. I've been careful financially. I think I could afford a little house. A fixer-upper, since I'm fairly handy, and more, I happen to know people even more handy who could help me out there. But no rush, Mom. I know I need at least a few more weeks. At least."

"I might know a place."

Sloan glanced at her father. "Does this surprise me? I think, no."

"It's a nice little bungalow—needs some work. Well, a lot of work, but—"

"Good bones?" Sloan commented.

"Good bones. Two bedrooms, what they're going to list as a den or home office, two baths. Updates needed. Eat-in kitchen, and that needs updating, too. Wood-burning fireplace—though I'd want that checked out before I lit a fire in it. It's about eleven hundred square feet and on a little under a quarter acre."

"Room enough in, and that outdoor space."

"Wooded lot," he continued, "no dock, but with lake access. No porch, no deck, and the back patio needs a complete overhaul. It's not on the market yet, but the owner came to see me, so I took a look. I've been thinking about making an offer."

"What kind of offer?"

"Investment property for resort rental and a first-home buy—two different things." Considering, he rubbed his knuckles on his trim beard. "Let me do my own calculations. Anyway, you might want to take a look at it. It's closer to town—the other side of the Parker place, and tucked back some. The driveway's rough, so that needs to be dealt with."

"Okay, I'll take a look, and if I don't hate it, this is one area I'm going to put myself in your hands." She gestured, both palms out. "You're the expert."

"You take a look," Elsie agreed, "and if you don't hate it, if it's what you decide you want, we'll help with the down payment."

"I don't need—"

"It's not about what you need," her mother interrupted. "It's what we're going to do. When and if your sister decides to buy a house, we'll do the same. It's something we've always planned for."

"Say 'thank you,'" her father advised.

It took her a minute, then Sloan reached out a hand to both of her parents. "Thank you."

On the Wednesday before Christmas, Arthur Rigsby checked into a different motel. He switched them up, which Clara thought made him smart.

A cheater, a sinner, but a smart one.

As they had on the two previous Wednesdays, they watched the blonde arrive shortly after. Then, since they'd have about an hour and a half, they drove to a nearby Burger King for takeout and munched on Whoppers and fries while they waited.

They timed it to pull back in the motel lot beside the Mercedes at that ninety-minute mark.

Ten minutes later, Clara shook her head. "Taking more time here than I like. We may have to wait a week. But . . ."

"You said it's today, so it's today. Look, she's coming out. See how she's fiddling with her earrings. I bet he gave her those in there. Christmas present."

"I bet you're right. Now she's pulling down the vanity mirror, admiring them. Well, just shame on him. Last present he'll give her."

It took him nearly another ten to exit. Clara opened the van door, blocking him from the driver's door.

"Oh my goodness, excuse me!"

"That's all right."

She eased that door closed, stepped back and put a hand on the side door.

"Safe travels," she said. "And Merry Christmas."

Rigsby took one step forward before Sam slipped up behind him and plunged the needle in.

Rigsby's eyes went wide, and he made a "*Gah*" sort of sound. He struggled, but between the two of them they pulled him into the van.

"You drive, babe. He's still fighting it."

As she got behind the wheel, Rigsby rolled, kicked while Sam tried zip-tying his hands. So Sam pushed him back, punched his face twice until he went limp.

"Sorry, Clara, I had to."

But he'd enjoyed it.

# PART TWO

# THE
# CALLING

*Men never do evil so completely and cheerfully*
*as when they do it from religious conviction.*
—Blaise Pascal

# CHAPTER ELEVEN

Sloan studied over and through the holidays. She took time to enjoy Christmas, helped bake cookies, wrapped presents—plus kept up with her physical therapy.

And walked along the path, with the snow-smothered hills reflected in the lake.

The walking and the PT increased when she earned an all clear on the muscle pull.

She looked at the bungalow that immediately brought a secluded, and neglected, cottage to her mind.

Tucked back from the road just enough, the location suited her. Close enough to her family, but not too close. Close enough to town, but again, not too. The same with neighbors. A small lot, with plenty of trees, and if she wanted the lake, she could walk to it in a couple of minutes.

Or, in another few weeks, run.

The house itself struck her as the right size for a single woman with a demanding job who'd handle her own cleaning and yard work. Right size, right place, so she overlooked the lack of a porch, the sad brown siding, the leaky windows.

If the exterior struck her as sad, the interior hit next to desperate and teetering on ugly.

But though she hadn't gone into the family business, she'd absorbed plenty. She saw the potential. Maybe she winced at the popcorn ceilings, but the original white oak floors made up for it. Or would after refinishing.

She'd just look down instead of up.

Over time, she thought, step-by-step she could transform it into a pretty, cozy cottage.

Resurface the brick fireplace someone had painted fire-engine red, gut the bathrooms, eventually, and the small, frozen-in-the-eighties kitchen. A little here and there—some sweat equity and a lot of paint—but she could deal with all of it.

In time.

She sat down with her father, and together they calculated what she could afford for monthly payments, mortgage, utilities, taxes.

Because she knew his level of expertise in real estate, she left the negotiations in his hands.

She made the offer, and as her father predicted, they countered. And, as he'd assured her, they met in the middle.

A little terrified, a lot excited, she signed the contract two days after Christmas. In thirty days, she'd own a house.

And in a week, she told herself, she'd take—and damn well pass— the written exam and start gearing up for her oral interview.

On New Year's Eve, she stood firm on her parents attending their annual party at a friend's. She didn't feel up to that kind of socializing yet. She was perfectly happy seeing in the New Year with Mop, her studies. And maybe finishing the baby blanket.

At midnight, she toasted the New Year with a glass of wine. It would be, she promised herself, a year of change, accomplishment, and one of fully taking her life back.

"This is Day One," she said, and drank her wine.

Nash wandered his house with a beer. Good progress, he thought. And the biggest came from new, efficient windows throughout—no small feat. Gutting the half bath and redoing even that small room top to bottom made a difference.

Robo turned out to be exactly what his aunt had outlined.

Not a real self-starter, not especially skilled, but tireless, willing, and (to his aunt's surprise) reliable.

Like their own motto, no job was too small for Robo.

Progress in the business included a small job here, a small job there. And another, not so small, courtesy of the Coopers.

He kept the TV on in the living room to mark the end and the beginning. The screen would have to move when they tackled that room, but for now, it, the fire in the hearth, and the Christmas tree kept the holidays going.

When he looked ahead to the New Year, he saw more. A good life doing good work was what he wanted. And clearly, so did Theo. A home he enjoyed even in its current sorry state.

And the possibilities for more yet. He didn't know what the more might be, but everything stood wide open.

As the ball began its descent, the crowd in New York counted down. His life had been there once, and now it was here, watching.

He didn't regret any of it.

At midnight, he lifted his beer and toasted change.

"We're ready for it."

As he sipped the beer, the puppy he thought safely sleeping—finally—gave a yip. Then, looking up at Nash with adoring eyes, peed a river on the floor.

"Jesus Christ, what was I thinking?"


In Drea's apartment, after slipping out of another party early, she snuggled with Theo on her sofa. They watched the same ball drop together.

When they kissed, it was long, slow, sweet, and exactly the way she wanted to end one year and start the next.

"Happy New Year."

"Happy New Year, Theo."

On-screen, thousands cheered, but when he kissed her again, he heard nothing but the quiet hum in her throat.

He made himself shift away—because how much could a man take—and top off the champagne she'd opened when they'd come back from a party.

He left his own single glass half-full, then clinked it to hers.

"I did the Times Square thing once. Once was enough. It's insane."

"Clearly." She reached for the bottle poured more into his glass.

"I really need to keep it to one. It's not far to drive, but—"

"Smart and responsible." Drea lifted her own glass, watching him over it. "And I wonder, are you always this slow?"

"Slow?"

"We've been dating for about a month now, and I wonder why you've never asked to stay." After another sip, she smiled all the way into her eyes. "Then again, it might be you just don't want to sleep with me."

"I . . ." Words failed him, so while she watched him, lips curved just the perfect amount, he dug some out. "I do. I—I think about you all the time. The first time I saw you, it was like getting hit by lightning. It was so fast, hell, instant for me. I wanted to give you time. I want to give you time and space."

"Theo, when I want time and space, I'll ask for it, or I'll take it. I think, in these first minutes of a brand-new year, I'm telling you time's up."

She set her glass down. Rising, she held out a hand. "Why don't you come with me?"

"That's a really good idea."


In their cozy house, Clara and Sam also had champagne. The label couldn't compare to what Drea opened, but the bubbles added sparkle.

They had sex before midnight—to end the old year. And after, to ring in the new. In between, they watched the recordings and munched on chips and salsa. With a little blood of the resurrected adding some sparkle there.

She found Arthur Rigsby the best yet.

Not because he'd begged, promised to tell no one, offered them money. Mostly they all did that at some point.

But because he'd spoken of looking down at his own body, how it felt like he'd been bathed in warm light while he had.

He'd spoken of his life running through his head like a movie on a screen, and how he'd felt disappointed he hadn't done more, taken more chances, enjoyed some forbidden fruit.

Clara paused his recording. "He's so detailed, doll. I know he's blubbering, but it's what he's saying. How he felt sad because he'd married while he was in the dental college, and worked so hard, raised two kids. He got to be a grandfather and what the hell there? How he felt he'd never really lived, and now he was dead before sixty."

Though he trusted her above all, Sam shook his head. "Blubbering, begging, and whining's what I hear when we review that one."

"But he *felt*, doll. We've gone half and half with the four we set free before this one. Two said how they didn't see or hear anything. One said he saw a light, heard his mother's voice, and the other said she heard her daughter calling and crying while she did the CPR on her. Rigsby, well, he breaks the tie, doesn't he?"

"I guess he does."

"And more, Rigsby felt. Emotion, Sam. Before they pulled him back, he felt sad and angry and disappointed."

She turned to him with her eyes avid. "I knew it. In my heart and mind, I knew it. Because death's not the end. It's a new beginning. And when you're on that next journey, you not only see and hear, you feel."

Her heart just overflowed with the joy and wonder of it.

"Feeling, that's the miracle, doll! Because it's another kind of life. It's why we let them go, Sam, why we send them home. We're leading them into that new life."

"I hadn't thought of it like that, I guess." He looked at her, his eyes filled with admiration. "You're so deep, babe."

"We'll start working on a new one. I think it might be we got more detail because more time had passed since he died, as was meant. More time for him to miss that door we're opening. For his soul to remember more clearly."

"Vacation first," he reminded her.

"Vacation first." Pleasure had her pressing her hands to her cheeks, wagging her shoulders. "I still can't believe you did that for me, doll. Four days and three nights in Aruba! You work so hard, and now you've spent all that money on me. I've never had such a wonderful Christmas present."

He wanted to give her everything. This trip, their very first together, marked a start.

"We're going to have a fine time—and out of this winter for a few days. We'll sit on the beach and drink cocktails with little umbrellas in them."

"And when our time comes, we'll never regret we didn't live this life."

"Let's live it some more now."

Giggling, she went into his arms. As they rolled together, Arthur Rigsby's terrified face, tears caught on his cheeks, stayed frozen on-screen.

During the month of January, Sloan strapped on snowshoes and handled a mild round trip. She moved up to ten-pound weights, and put back five pounds she'd lost.

When she studied her body, she concluded most of that five pounds was—finally—muscle.

She took and she passed her written exam, and began to prep for her oral interview.

Because she had no way around it, she had three sessions with the department shrink. Reluctance turned to relief before the end of the first session.

It helped, she realized, to talk to someone who wasn't family, wasn't connected emotionally. She could admit her frustrations with what felt like a slow recovery without feeling bitchy.

And when she talked about the occasional nightmares and flash-backs, she didn't feel weak and foolish.

She decided maybe the truth could set you free when after the third session, she was cleared for duty.

When Joel and Sari came for the weekend, she enjoyed every min-ute they spent together. Then she drove back to Annapolis with them with Sari stroking the baby blanket nearly all the way.

It felt right, it felt good to pack up more of her things, to arrange for movers to bring her furniture.

She walked out of her apartment for the last time with good mem-ories and no regrets.

The drive back to Heron's Rest in her own car felt like freedom.

The freedom of knowing she'd made the right choice.

She spent the first night in the house that now belonged to her wakeful, but not worried. In time she'd grow familiar with the creaks and sighs of the place, as well as with the views outside her windows. And with the sense of being alone and on her own again.

Twice she got up, just to walk through it all again, to see her furniture where she'd put it, to consider and reconsider changes she'd make over time.

When snow began to fall, she opened her front door just to watch it from her own threshold.

She reported for duty the third week of January, and that fed her mind, her spirit. Light duty at first, standard patrols, reminding those on public land of the rules and enforcing them when necessary.

It felt good to be back in uniform, doing the work.

She took an early call to a vacation cabin adjoining the public land buffer strip in Deep Creek Lake.

A woman peeked through a fractional crack in the door. "Who are you? What do you want?"

"I'm Corporal Cooper, ma'am, with the Natural Resources Police." Sloan held up her identification. "You reported a possible assault."

"In the woods! In the dark." She flung open the door. Bundled in a thick robe over flannel pajamas, her feet in fuzzy pink slippers, the woman gestured wildly. "She—I'm sure it was a woman—screeched, and he—I'm sure it was a man, maybe more than one—howled. Terrible sounds. Oh, and he had a dog, too. Vicious barking."

"Mrs. Colbert?"

"Yes, yes, yes." She gave Sloan the come-ahead, closed and locked the door behind her, then pointed toward the back of the cabin. "I'm sure it was back there, somewhere up in this wilderness."

"Ma'am—"

"This is my brother's cabin." Dragging her hands through brown hair that stood up in tufts, she cast a withering glance toward the open stairs leading to a loft. "And where is he? Why, he's in Florida, fishing or

God knows. And my husband insisted we camp here—because that's what it is—for a *week*. Do I look like a pioneer?

"No, ma'am, but—

"'It'll be quiet,' he says. 'Peaceful,' he says. So I'm dragged up here from Richmond and civilization, and he wants to go snowboarding. Sixty-two years old, and he wants to go snowboarding? Now he's got a bruise the size of a ham shank on his butt. Serves him right! And now there's women getting raped and murdered, likely eaten by that vicious dog, and I say I could be next, but he's 'It's just some animal, Patty, go back to sleep!'"

"Actually, Mrs. Colbert, your husband's correct."

"Correct?" Patty Colbert stopped with her hands pulling at those tufts of brown hair. "About what?"

"The sounds you describe—screeching, howling, barking. Foxes. It's mating season."

"Foxes? Are you out of your mind?"

Sloan simply pulled out her phone, hit an app, and played the shrieks and screams. "Is this what you heard?"

"Yes. Yes. That's it!"

"Those are red fox calls, Mrs. Colbert. They're common in this area, and they breed during the winter. What you heard are mating calls."

"Well, for God—" She huffed out a breath, scrubbed her hands over her face. "She didn't sound like she enjoyed it."

On a laugh, Sloan put her phone away. "It can sound human, and scary."

"Tell me about it!"

"She'll have the kits in early spring, and he'll help tend them. They often mate for life. They're inquisitive. You might spot one."

"You mean near this—this shack?" The woman looked toward a window as if expecting an attack. "Are they dangerous, aggressive?"

"Inquisitive," Sloan repeated. "Clever and timid around humans. A fox is much more likely to run away from you than approach."

"I feel like an idiot."

"You shouldn't. You heard what you thought was a woman being attacked. You reported it, and that's the right thing to do. I hope you enjoy the rest of your stay."

Sloan grinned all the way back to the truck.

Yes, it was good to be back.

If the days in November and December had dragged, January rolled toward February with barely a breath.

The lake froze and opened itself to the ice fishermen, the skaters, pickup hockey games.

And Travis asked her to take on a rookie.

"She's smart, she's enthusiastic, and she's green. You've trained a few before so you could ripen her up a little."

"Sure. No problem."

"Just keep it simple and routine for the first few days. You can patrol Mirror Lake—a lot of activity on it right now, so license and safety checks. Take her on some of the easier trails."

He sat at his desk, scanning reports, schedules. "Let's say three months, then write up an evaluation."

"Yes, sir."

He sat back, studied her now. "Are you ready for your board interview?"

"I feel ready, and I'd better be. It's coming right up."

Still at ease, he gestured. "Why don't you tell me why you want to be a sergeant?"

Since she appreciated the support, and the opportunity to practice, Sloan dived right in.

"There are a number of reasons I want to be a sergeant. Becoming a Natural Resources Police officer was a goal I worked toward since college. Having served as a member of the DNR for more than six years, I have tremendous pride in the work we do. I grew up in Heron's Rest, on Mirror Lake in the Alleghenies, and consider that a gift.

"My background instilled in me a sense of duty to protect and value our public lands and waterways. As a sergeant, I would use that leadership position to motivate the teams I work with as well as the communities we serve to preserve and respect the resources that belong to all of us."

"Good. You worked in, and smooth with it, your motivation,

background, and experience. Also good you looked relaxed, made eye contact, and sounded sincere."

"I am sincere."

"I know it, but you don't have to convince me. They'll see it and feel it because you mean it. Go ahead, get Officer Sanchez and get started."

Elana Sanchez appeared thrilled to patrol with Sloan. As far as Sloan could see, Elana appeared thrilled by everything.

She remembered the feeling from her first weeks and months in uniform. The pride, the sense of accomplishment, and the boundless enthusiasm.

"I know I'm brand, shiny new, Corporal Cooper, but I really want to do good work."

"We all start off brand, shiny, and new. And it's Sloan."

"Thanks. Can I tell you my family thought I was crazy when I signed up to train for the Department of Natural Resources?"

"You just did."

"Oh, right."

And Sloan laughed as she drove. "It's fine. How do they feel about it now?"

"Proud, but kind of baffled, too. I mean, I grew up down in Montgomery County. Nice quiet neighborhood, sort of sheltered. Youngest of four and the only girl."

"Ah."

Elana laughed. "So yeah, maybe a little spoiled."

"A girlie girl?"

"Oh, absolutely! My idea of natural resources was the pool in the backyard. I figured to be a supermodel, even though I'm only five-four, or a super something as long as it was glittery."

Since the rookie obviously wanted to talk, and to help train, it paid to get to know the person inside the uniform, Sloan kept it going.

"So why are you wearing a uniform instead of stilettos and spangles?"

"I do love heels, the higher the better, right?"

"If I'm wearing them, they're high or what's the point?"

"Exactly! They make me feel tall and powerful. But anyway, I went to college and took this natural resources course. I thought it was a filler, but it changed everything.

"I'm so glad I got assigned up here. It's so beautiful. You grew up here?"

"I did. I spent my first years in the department away from family, too. This was the right time to come back."

Elana hesitated, adjusted her Stetson on her hair—glossy and black and worked into a tight bun at the nape as Sloan had once worn hers.

Then she turned liquid brown eyes to Sloan. "I know you got hurt. I hope it's okay to say."

"Sure it is. I got hurt. I got well."

Sloan made the turn to Heron's Rest. "It wasn't in the line," she added. "Just wrong place, wrong time. There's the lake."

Elana leaned forward, and her Cupid's bow mouth curved in a smile. "It's so pretty! It's a lot smaller than Deep Creek Lake but really pretty. And busy!"

"Once it freezes, they're all over it. Natives and tourists. If you come here in the winter, you probably come for winter sports."

She thought of Mrs. Colbert.

"With exceptions. We'll just do a check on fishing licenses and alcohol consumption."

"Alcohol? This early in the morning?"

"Some think it's a way to stay warm. A breakfast beer, a thermos of Bloody Marys, a flask of whiskey. Or it's just *Hey, I'm on vacation*. We're friendly. We educate rather than push. Safety first, Elana. Like that guy over there, near the shore. Ice fishing near the shore's a bad idea."

"Ice is thinner near the shore."

"Exactly right. Why?"

"Um, the shallower water and the underwater vegetation melt the ice faster."

"Yeah, and that's what you'll tell him."

"I will?"

"With courtesy." She parked the truck. "Let's strap on the cleats."

She'd always enjoyed walking on the lake, and skating over it on a cold afternoon with the mountains dressed in white rising up.

The skaters zoomed around it now, though this was no Zamboni'd rink. Ripples and bumps sent more than one into a spill.

She counted sixteen ice fishermen—and women—taking advantage of the early morning. More than one had already pulled up a catch or two.

Their cleats gripped, and the wind blew light and steady as they crossed over to the man all but buried in a black hooded parka. He had a red plastic sled he might have borrowed from a kid. It held an auger he'd already used to drill a hole in the ice, and the chisel he'd used to widen it.

He sat on a portable seat that looked brand-new. So did the flag on the tip-up in the hole, and his fishing rod.

"Identify yourself," Sloan instructed, "and me. Call him sir, always polite. Once we see his fishing license, you can refer to him as Mr. whatever it is. Make conversation," Sloan added. "Then educate him on the spot he's chosen."

"Okay. Here goes."

Elana put on her pretty smile as they approached. "Good morning! I'm Officer Sanchez, and this is Corporal Cooper with the Natural Resources Police."

He looked up, squinted with most of his face hidden by the hood, and a thick scarf that came up past his chin. "The what? They got cops for that?"

"Yes, sir! It's sure a beautiful day out here."

"If you like frozen tundras. I've been sitting here freezing my ass off for damn near an hour. I got nothing."

"I'm sorry to hear that. Would you mind showing us your fishing license?"

"Jesus." With his gloved hand he dug into a pocket. "Right here. All the good it's doing me. Do you know how much I spent on all this stuff? I don't even want to think about it."

"Thanks, Mr. Garrett. You might have better luck in another location. This near the shoreline, the ice is thinner. You might increase your luck, and definitely your safety, if you moved farther away from the shore."

He looked at her like a man who'd been asked to climb Everest in his underwear. "You want me to go through all this again?"

"For your safety, Mr. Garrett."

"I've fished on this lake," Sloan began.

He switched his miserable gaze from Elana to Sloan. "This kind of fishing?"

"A few times, yes, with my grandfather. He has a favorite spot, and he catches whoppers. Every time."

Now Garrett eyed Sloan with more interest.

"I only need one. One damn fish. Then my wife, who's sitting up there"—he gestured to one of the lakeside houses—"sitting up there in front of the fire reading a damn book, and getting up every now and again to go to the window and laugh down at me, can't say *I told you so*."

"Take your gear about ten feet that way, another four or five to the right. That's one of Pop's favorite spots. That's a good electric auger you've got, so it shouldn't take long to drill your hole. What bait are you using?"

He pulled up his line, and Sloan nodded.

"Rapala Jigging Rap, excellent. Try that area, and with that lure, I'm betting you catch a couple of those whoppers. You'll be the one laughing and saying *I told you so*."

"Well, hell, I'm in this far." He got up, started to pack up. "Problem is those crazy skaters, especially the ones pretending to play hockey, are probably scaring the fish away. Yelling, zipping around, falling all over themselves."

Sloan glanced around in time to see three of them collide, hard. Two of them fell on their asses, laughing, and the third tried to break his fall.

Sloan didn't hear the wrist snap, but she nearly felt it.

"See?"

"Yeah. Good luck, Mr. Garrett. Call for medical assistance, Elana. Probably a broken wrist."

By the time Sloan crossed the ice, the injured man, maybe twenty-five, sat where he was, cradling his arm while the others gathered around him.

"Natural Resources Police. Let's take a look."

"I think I broke it."

"I think you're right. Paramedics are on the way. Are you hurt anywhere else?"

"This is enough, thanks." He hissed out a breath. "Hurts like hell."

"I broke mine in gymnastics when I was eleven," Elana told him. "I know how it feels."

"Let's get you off the ice. Get a blanket out of the truck, would you, Officer Sanchez?"

"We've got you, Matt." Two of his friends helped him stand, and slowly skated with him off the ice.

"This sure screws guys' week."

"Where are you from?"

"Me, Hagerstown." Though pale, the injured man spoke and walked steadily. "We've been planning this trip for months. First day out, we run into Mr. Chainsaw Massacre, and today, I break my wrist."

"They'll fix you up, Matt," one of his friends assured him. "And you can still hoist a beer with your good hand."

"There's that."

"Tell me about Mr. Chain Saw Massacre."

Matt looked at Sloan as Elana dropped a blanket over his shoulders. "Some weird mountain-man type. Big belly, big beard. We were snowshoeing—or trying to—on—what was it?—Deer Track Trail, and we heard the chain saw going."

"Saw a couple fresh-cut trees," one of the others added. "We didn't think you were supposed to cut down trees up there."

"You're not. What happened?"

"Well, we spotted him and he spotted us. He turns around with that chain saw, and he picks up an axe with his other hand. He yells for us to get the hell off his land."

"We thought it was public land."

"It is."

"There were four of us, one of him, but." Matt let out a breath of relief when they heard the siren. "He had a chain saw and an axe, and he looked crazy enough to use them."

"We walked back down the trail," his friend finished. "We just figured we'd made a wrong turn or whatever and ended up on private property."

"Deer Track Trail. About how far along?"

"Less than a mile." Matt smiled wanly. "First time with snowshoes."

Sloan waited until the paramedics took over.

"Hey!" Matt shouted as she and Elana walked back to the truck. "Thanks!"

"You're welcome."

When they got to the truck, Sloan turned. "Ready for the next adventure?"

"Chain Saw Massacre Mountain Man?"

"That's the one. Call it in, give the situation and our location. Deer Track Trail. Can you snowshoe?"

"I'll bet I'm better than those guys, but I need more practice."

"You're about to get it."

# CHAPTER TWELVE

Because Elana did need more practice, Sloan slowed her usual pace. But she already knew part of her evaluation would likely label Officer Sanchez as game, and someone who knew how to take direction, follow orders.

About a half mile up the trail, Sloan heard it. Not the roaring buzz of a chainsaw but the steady thump of an axe against wood.

"Hear that? That's not a woodpecker."

"I can't believe he's cutting down trees. Why? Oh, Sloan, look!"

"Yeah, I see it."

A stump, the cuts no more than a day or two old. And prints—human ones—drag marks where he'd hauled the tree up the trail.

"Poaching trees. For firewood, maybe, to sell or use. Maybe both. The trail levels out a few yards ahead."

"I won't mind that. I think I'm in good shape, but I have to admit, my quads are burning."

"I'll be taking the lead with this one."

"It's all yours. And," Elana added with a big smile of relief, "whew!"

He'd taken down two more trees, and when they topped the rise, she saw another down. And the man—big belly, big brown beard—using the axe to split the logs he'd made on the fresh stump.

Sloan judged him at mid-forties, five-ten, and carrying about two hundred pounds. He wore a flannel coat, yellow work gloves, and a ratty black cap.

He shifted when he spotted them, then gripped the axe handle with both hands.

Sloan put hers on the butt of her weapon.

"Get off my land!"

"Sir, this is public land."

"I'm the goddamn public. My taxes pay for these trees, and I'm taking my share. Fuck off."

Sloan kept her hand on her weapon, and her eyes on his. And blocked out the dread crawling up her spine as she had one quick flash of the mini-mart.

This was now, she reminded herself. Right here, right now.

"Sir, we're with the Natural Resources Police. You're not permitted to cut down trees on public land. Please put down the axe."

He shook it. "Why don't you come over here and take it? Try it, and you'll lose an arm. No bitch is going to tell me my rights."

"You're threatening police officers with a deadly weapon. Please put down the axe and step away from it."

"If I give it a toss, I'll split your head in two where you stand. Get the hell off my land. I've got a right to defend it, and I damn well will."

"No, sir, you don't, but we do."

Since he looked perfectly capable and just crazy enough to throw the axe, she drew her weapon.

"I really don't want to fire my weapon, but if you make any threatening movements, I absolutely will. Now put the axe down and step away from it."

"You gonna shoot me?" Through the thick beard, he bared his teeth. "You gonna shoot me over trees? A million goddamn trees around here, and you'd fucking shoot me over them?"

"No, sir. I'm going to arrest you for that. But I will shoot you if you continue to threaten us with that weapon."

He did throw the axe, but down into the stump. Then he lifted fisted hands. "Come on and try it."

Sloan holstered her weapon, pulled out her baton. As she approached, he charged forward. She ducked his wild swing, sidestepped.

Then whipped the baton hard against the back of his knees.

He went down like, well, a tree.

"Stay down!" She yanked his arms behind him, snapped on cuffs.

"Officer, report in. We're bringing a prisoner down Deer Track Trail. We need a team up here to record the scene, to confiscate the prisoner's axe, chainsaw, snowmobile, and sled and to clear the downed trees.

"Sir, what's your name?"

"Fuck you!"

"Fine, Mr. Fuck You, you're under arrest for defacing public land, for threatening police officers with bodily harm, for assaulting a police officer and resisting arrest. On your feet."

She started to haul him up, waited to feel that snap and pain in her chest. It didn't come, but neither did he.

She drew in another breath, relieved, so relieved, it came steady and clear.

"Give me a hand, Officer Sanchez. Mr. Fuck You's still resisting."

They managed to haul him to his feet. Sloan patted him down, removed a knife from his belt—over the legal limit—but found no other weapons. No wallet, no ID.

"Go ahead and read him his rights," Sloan said as they walked him down the trail.

Elana maintained a professional demeanor, remained silent a great deal of the time. At the foot of the trail, Sloan gave the arriving team directions, a brief report.

After they'd transported the prisoner, Sloan asked Elana if she felt confident to write the incident report.

"Yes. It's etched in my brain. My first assisted arrest. Wow, what a morning! What's the rest of the day going to be like?"

"Probably a lot quieter."


Sloan dreamed that night in her creaky new house.

She walked into the mini-mart and into the raw winter air of the forest. The man at the counter turned. He had a big belly, a big beard, and an axe in his gloved hand.

"Get off my land!"

When he threw the axe, the blade struck her dead center of the chest.

The shock of pain, so real, so intense, woke her. Struggling for air, she sat up, both hands clutched at her chest.

The dream faded before the pain did, and the pain faded before the shaking.

Switching on the bedside lamp, she got up to walk across the hall to the bathroom. The pipes banged when she ran water in the sink, but she found the reality of the sound a comfort.

Her house, her pipes. Just a bad dream, and she hadn't had one in a couple of weeks.

She'd handled the incident. She hadn't frozen, she hadn't panicked. She'd done her job.

She was fine. She looked at herself in the mirror. No longer pale, no longer so drawn. A few more pounds to go to get back to her fighting weight, but she'd made progress.

Most important, she'd done good work that day.

So she'd get up in the morning, put on the uniform, and do the same.

Until her board interview, Sloan put off all but the most urgent repairs. Prettying up her house could wait. The ancient water heater and the chimney cleaning couldn't.

Once the interview was behind her, she made some time and a plan. The two bathrooms equaled gut jobs, but she opted to focus on one as her first genuine home improvement project.

The one across from the bedroom she'd chosen had a shower the size of a broom closet, a nasty vanity someone had tried, unsuccessfully, to paint a pea-soup green, a sink the size of a teacup, and rusting faucets. The room also held a tub that was barely big enough to accommodate a ten-year-old, that someone had somehow cracked, and linoleum flooring covered in bright yellow daisies that had begun to peel.

Rather than obsessing on the board's decision, she researched tile, showerheads, finishes, paint on her off time until she had a solid vision.

She saw her family, and twice ran into her father while she and Elana were on patrol.

"Your father's so handsome. And so fit."

"He is. Also just great."

"My dad's great. He made a New Year's resolution to get fit. Bought a tracker watch, joined a gym. My mom says it's going very slowly."

"One day at a time."

When they'd finished their shift, she took Elana back to headquarters. Travis called Sloan into his office.

He rose, held out a hand. "Congratulations, Sergeant Cooper."

She gripped his hand, and when he came around the desk to hug her, hugged back.

"Oh God. I've been trying to convince myself if I didn't get it, it wouldn't matter."

Laughing, he hugged her again. "How'd that work?"

"Not even a little. Thanks, Cap. Thank you."

"You did the work. And starting tomorrow, you'll do more of it. Full duty, including supervisory duties. I'd like you to report a half hour earlier so we can go over all those duties. I lean hard on my sergeant."

"I'll be here."

"Now go home. Celebrate. Dean and Elsie are going to be over the moon. My family's going to jump over it right behind them when I give them the news."

"I'm already celebrating. In here?" She pointed to her heart. "Champagne's popping."

She let out a happy sigh.

"You're a big reason I'm wearing this uniform, doing this job. I grew up listening to your stories, what you did, how you did it, what you saw, how you felt."

"Stories? I got a million of 'em."

"And I loved every one."

As she drove home she remembered her parents planned to go out to dinner. And Drea had a date. She didn't want to tell them the news over the phone. No, she wanted to see their faces.

So she'd go over later. Her parents should be home by nine, since it was just dinner. She'd wait, tell them face-to-face.

Meanwhile, she had to do something to celebrate.

She could buy that champagne, but who wanted to drink champagne alone? She could turn on the music and dance in her own house.

Then it struck her.

Or she could start getting herself a new, up-to-date bathroom. One where she didn't smack her elbows whenever she washed her hair.

A bathroom with good lighting, with a floor that didn't hurt her eyes and sensibilities, with a toilet that didn't threaten to buck her off.

She'd already decided not to ask her father and Jonah on this one. This wouldn't be a couple-hour project, or a weekend job. They had enough going without her poking every time she wanted something done.

This would be her personal celebration. One she wanted and could afford. She could afford it because her parents had helped with the down payment, because her father had negotiated a deal below what she'd expected to pay.

And because she'd just gotten a promotion.

She drove past her own bumpy drive—a project for the spring— and up to the old Parker house.

She'd already pulled up and parked when she remembered Theo— the brother she'd actually met—was out somewhere with her sister.

If the other one wasn't home, she'd just contact the Fix-It Brothers later.

She got out, approving the fact they'd cleared snow—falling again—from the walkway, the drive. She noted the vast improvement of new windows, and the smoke curling out of both chimneys.

When she knocked, she heard the yip-yip-yip and remembered Theo saying his brother had gotten him a puppy for Christmas.

That single fact made her disposed to like him, at least a little.

When he opened the door, her first thought was he didn't look much like Theo. A little taller, more muscular. His hair and eyes hit a few shades darker, his face more sharply angled.

He had a few days' worth of stubble going where she'd only seen Theo clean-shaven.

"Mr. Littlefield?"

"Yeah. Is there a problem, Officer?"

"It's Sergeant, actually."

"Okay, same question. Oh, man, have a little pride."

He spoke to the dog, who'd shoved its way between his legs to jump on Sloan.

"He's fine. Just fine." She gave the dog—a rambunctious yellow Lab—a good rub. Then she pointed, said, "Sit!"

When the dog's butt hit the ground, Nash stared. "What did you do and how did you do it? How did you get him to sit?"

"I told him to."

In response, Nash shoved at all that thick, wavy brown hair.

"You think I haven't tried that? He never listens. Hell, it's snowing again. Come in out of it. We're in the middle of a major rehab, so it's a wreck."

The dog raced in ahead, ran in crazed circles, then grabbed a paint rag between his teeth and raced with that.

"Can you make him stop doing that? I'll give you a thousand dollars."

"What's his name?"

"Tic. We call him Tic. Short for Lunatic. Reasons obvious."

"Tic!" She pointed. "Sit."

He sat, tail thumping, eyes filled with adoration.

"No charge. This time."

"It's like magic. Witchcraft. Sorry." Baffled, Nash shoved a hand through his hair a second time. "Are you with the State Police?"

"No. I'm Natural Resources Police."

"No kidding? I never heard of them before we moved here. Now the woman my brother's dating has a sister . . . You're the sister."

"I am. Sloan Cooper." She offered a hand.

He took it, gripped hard. "Are they okay? Did something happen?"

"No. No. This has nothing to do with them. I stopped by to see about hiring you. I bought a house."

"Oh. Well. Okay then."

The dog, rag still clamped, bellied over to Sloan and laid it like a tribute at her feet.

"You're a good dog, aren't you?" She crouched, rubbed. "Yes, you are." She made an uh-uh sound when he jumped at her. "You're going to be too big for that really soon. So no jumping, or no pets."

Tic wagged and rubbed against her knees.

"Are you like Dr. Dolittle?"

"No." She looked up. "I'm an alpha, and he knows it. Be an alpha. I don't think this is yours, Tic." She picked up the paint rag, handed the now slobbery thing to Nash. "What do you have that is?"

"He's got balls, bones, squeaky things. He had a stuffed rabbit but he tore it to shreds. A massacre."

"Go ahead and get him something that belongs to him."

"Ah . . . There." He walked over, around a pile of lumber, and picked up a bright orange bone.

Sloan took it, offered it. "This is yours."

Tic clamped around it and sat at her feet, staring up at her with heart eyes.

"Would you consider living here for maybe six months?"

Looking up again, Sloan decided she did like him and his flustered, frustrated ineptitude with a puppy.

"We never had a dog," he continued. "We don't know what we're doing. I read this, and it doesn't work. Theo reads that, it doesn't work."

"Be an alpha. Correct, reward, repeat. Anyway, I just bought a house."

"Right. You want to hire us to fix something."

"My bathroom. It's a gut job. My father, you obviously know, could take it on, but I don't want to ask him and/or Jonah to carve out that kind of time. It's not a big space, about ninety square feet, but it's easily a week's work. Maybe ten days, especially if you need to juggle jobs."

"Okay. Let's go take a look."

"Now?"

"Why not? It's practically next door, right? Theo said Drea's sister bought it."

"All right."

"I need to block the dog into what will, one day, be my home office."

"Bring him. Like you said, it's practically next door. Put some dog treats in your pocket."

Obviously baffled, he frowned at her. "I should put dog treats in my pocket?"

"Always."

He did what she said before they walked out into the snowfall together.

The dog immediately raced around, leaped in the air, rolled in the snow.

"Mop does that. My family's dog. Some of them just love the snow. Tic!" Sloan snapped her fingers. "Come."

When he did, Nash just picked him up. "You could take him for six months. Name your price."

"You'll do fine."

"Be an alpha," Nash muttered as he carried the dog to his truck. "I thought I was an alpha. Between you and the blond wood nymph, suddenly I'm a wimp."

He followed Sloan the short distance while Tic leaped from front to back, back to front. Navigating the bumps and potholes of her drive, he hoped she'd budgeted enough for a grader and gravel.

And he immediately saw half a dozen things he'd do to the exterior of the house. New siding, paint the trim, new windows, a new front door, a porch. Add window boxes to play up the cottagey feel.

But maybe she liked a shit-brown house.

All the charm came from the location. The surrounding white-flocked trees, the falling snow, the shadows spreading as dusk approached, and the sense of being tucked away, just a little secret.

It seemed like a good choice for a woman who looked like she might sprout wings.

After leaping from the truck, Tic dived into the snow. Rolled, ran, paused, sniffed.

"Tic, come."

With a snap of her fingers, magic happened, and the dog pranced over to her.

Maybe she actually was a wood nymph.

"Exterior work." She chin-pointed at the house. "Spring or summer."

"Exterior work?"

"The siding's crap," she said as they walked to the house. "It needs a porch, new windows, and I grew up with a mudroom so I want one. But all that can wait."

She unlocked the front door, which required a quick hip bump as it stuck. "I'll be replacing this eventually."

When he walked in, the contrast struck him. Dull walls, cheap trim, brick fireplace painted screaming red—and poorly—with a poky mantel, open to a roomy enough but very sad kitchen.

And everything in the space was neat, organized, well-placed, and had style.

The size of the sofa, in a strong blue, suited the size of the room. She had a wingback chair in minute blue-and-gray checks facing the fire with a gray throw draped over it, a small armchair in a surprising red that worked. None of the tables matched, but looked old and polished. Like family pass-downs, he thought, that added warmth and character.

Tic immediately raced around, wagging, sniffing.

Then nosed into her basket of yarn. "Uh-uh! Come."

He wagged his way to her.

"Give him a treat for being a good boy."

Nash dug one out of his pocket. Tic leaped for it.

"No. Tell him to sit. Mean it."

Since it worked for her, Nash added the point. "Sit!"

Tic tried one more leap, then sat.

"This is not a small miracle."

He looked around as the dog all but swallowed the little biscuit whole.

"It's a good space."

"It's ugly, but I can live with it."

She hung up her coat in a narrow closet, unrolled a scarf, and put it in a tub on the shelf. The undeniably sexy Stetson went beside it.

And the hair, full in the front, short and shaggy in the back, only added to that fairy-gliding-through-the-trees image.

She held out a hand for his coat.

"You have a gun."

She gave him a nod and a slight smile. "Yes, I do. I'm a police officer."

"I guess I figured . . . you arrest people?"

"When necessary. We educate, and we enforce."

He couldn't quite figure out why seeing her in uniform gave him a buzz.

"Interesting." Now he had to look up the Natural Resources Police. "First house?" he asked her.

"Yeah. Home, college dorm, apartment, this. You?"

"Pretty much the same."

"You don't start small."

"The house spoke to me."

"Really. What did it say?"

"*Help.*"

She had a quick laugh, and one that sparkled in those amazing eyes.

"It's been saying that for years. You're the first one who listened. You'll hear the same plea from my bathroom. It's this way."

The living area split off into two—they didn't rate as wings—sections. She went to the left into what barely qualified as a hallway, then right.

He walked in as she stood in the doorway. The dog raced in to sniff, tried and failed to climb into the tub.

"Yeah, I hear it. It needs it. What crazed mind picked this flooring?"

"Can't say, but I curse them daily. It goes. It all goes."

"Good choice. Even somebody your size must barely fit in this shower."

"You are correct. I want bigger. I don't need the tub, so a nice-sized shower goes there, and what's now the shower could be open shelves. I thought about a closet, but the room's small, and open shelves would give some breathing room."

Since he couldn't argue with her choices, he nodded. "You know what you want."

"I do."

Tic wandered out.

"He's housebroken—through too much trial and error to speak of—like ninety-five percent of the time. But—"

Sloan just shrugged. "If this is the five percent, you'll clean it up. Listen, I've drawn up a plan if you want to take a look."

He glanced back at her. Yeah, the uniform was a killer. He just couldn't figure out why.

"Sure."

She led the way into the kitchen, where the dog bounded back. With a ball of yarn in his mouth.

Sloan pried it free. "This is not yours." Opening a cupboard, she took out a rawhide stick. "For when the family dog visits," she explained, then pointed.

Tic sat.

"This is yours."

He collapsed on the floor with it in ecstasy.

"It'll keep him busy." She gestured to the square oak table and its pair of chairs. "Have a seat. I'll get my file."

He saw she'd set up a small room off the kitchen as an office. Decent desk, ugly walls to go with an ugly light on a popcorn ceiling.

She opened a drawer in the desk, took out a file folder.

"I've decided on the fixtures, the tile, the flooring, and all that. That's in here, too."

When she took out a sheet of graph paper and he saw her drawing, he shook his head. "You're a Cooper, all right."

"I am. Sorry, I should've asked before. Do you want coffee, a Coke?"

"Coffee if it's handy," he said as he studied the drawing. "Black's fine."

She'd measured everything, very precisely. She had the square footage of the room, the shower space, the size of the vanity, even the mirror, the side lights.

And she had printouts of everything. The tile, where she'd calculated how much required for the shower, the floor, new trim, a compact, floating vanity, fixtures, towel rods, all of it.

"Thorough."

"My middle name. I'm sticking with the one-room-at-a-time plan. My dad and I already pulled up the bedroom carpet. Hardwood under it."

"Why do people do that?"

"A question for the ages. New paint and trim in there, a little closet work, get rid of the popcorn—that's everywhere. So that's a quick and easy. This?"

She set down his coffee, then with her own sat at the table as she looked around the kitchen.

"The cabinets are in good shape, just blah. So paint them, new hardware, all good. New countertops—probably quartz to replace the ancient Formica. In that question for the ages, there's hardwood under this weird linoleum. The stove's okay, the fridge is crap, the lighting's horrible, as is the school bus–yellow paint."

"Goes with the daisies on the bathroom floor."

She smiled at the basic mind meld.

"I think that was the plan. Anyway, that can wait until we add on the mudroom. Come through that—a good drop zone—into the kitchen."

"Laundry room?"

"Currently down in the serial killer basement. I might move it up when we work out the mudroom."

"You could put the laundry where you have your office, use the second bedroom as a combo guest room and office."

"Under consideration, but right now I have my home gym set up in the second bedroom. I thought about setting that up in the serial killer basement, but just no."

"That's where mine is. Well, it doesn't reach serial killer status, but it needs a lot of work. It's okay for now."

She smelled like the woods, he thought. The woods she looked as if she wandered in moonlight.

"I've got one suggestion on your bathroom plan."

"All right."

"If you put in a small cabinet, the shelves over it, you'd add storage without displaying the stuff. Can I?" He took a sheet of graph paper, and though he free-handed it, the design was precise.

"Gives you three, maybe four shelves depending on how much space you want between, and a cabinet below, which gives you another flat surface for whatever."

He glanced up again as she frowned over the design. "I'm surprised Dean didn't suggest it."

"Now that I see it, I'm sure he would have. I haven't shown him, or mentioned moving on this. If I did, he'd want to do it for me, and he just doesn't have time during the workweek. That means his weekends—

when he doesn't have to go fix something in one of the units—is eaten up with more work."

"He's already offered to lend a hand around my place."

"It's what he does. I like this. This would work. I can start sourcing cabinets."

"We can build it, match it up with the vanity you've picked out."

She sat back, considered. "How about you work me up an estimate on the work, including the cabinet, give me a start and end date."

"I can do that. I can tell you now . . ." He pulled out his phone, checked the work calendar. "We can start Thursday morning. I'm going to say two weeks because we don't know what we might find when we start tearing things out."

"I figured that. Second bath on the other side of the house. Not as bad as this one. Close, but not as bad. I'll be fine."

"Okay then. If you put your contact in my phone, I'll get you an estimate by tomorrow."

"I see why Dad likes you." She took his phone, put in her number, her email.

"It's mutual." He pointed to the chevrons on her sleeve. "Doesn't a sergeant have three of those?"

"Yes. I just got the promotion today."

"Today? Well, hell. Congratulations, Sarge."

"Thanks." In that moment, she realized he was the first one she'd told.

"My parents are out to dinner tonight, so I'm going over a little later to tell them. So, if you happen to see them before I do, do me a favor and don't mention it. Or the bathroom."

"No problem."

She tapped his drawing. "Did your dad—or mom," she added, "build things?"

"No, they never built a thing." He rose. "I'll go get started on this. Thanks for the coffee, and the dog pointers."

"I appreciate you moving on this so quickly. I'll get your coat."

Tic scrambled up, bounded after her.

"He already likes you better than me."

She gave that quick laugh again. "A dog like this? It's love at first sight whoever he meets."

"I'm surprised you don't have a dog. You're really good with them."

"I'm gone all day. Luckily, I have Mop—the family dog."

Then it clicked. Theo talked about Mop. The Cooper family dog.

"I saw you."

"Sorry?" She turned from the closet with his coat.

"Walking with the big shaggy dog. A few times along the lake." Slowly, he remembered, as if recovering from a long illness. Not at all like the woman he'd spent most of an hour with.

He replaced that with "Your hair was longer."

"It was, then I cut it."

"I like it, if that matters. It suits your face." Those magical eyes.

Thinking it wise to switch gears, he nodded toward the fireplace as he put on his coat. "Tell me you're not going to leave that fire-truck red. You're going to repaint, resurface, something."

"It's on the list."

"That's a relief. Let's go, Tic. I'll be in touch."

He walked out through the thickening snow, boosted the dog into his truck.

He'd work up the estimate—he already had some of it figured anyway. And he'd look up the Natural Resources Police to find out why she carried a gun. And what he thought was a baton.

And though he felt strongly about privacy, his curiosity hit stronger. He'd see what he could find out about Sloan Cooper.

# CHAPTER THIRTEEN

The short visit to the tropics had Clara yearning. She loved her little house, but maybe—someday—she and Sam could take regular vacations to places like Aruba.

They both worked hard, and they stayed frugal so they had some savings.

Then occasionally, as with the dentist, they hit a small gold mine of cash. He'd had three hundred and sixty-seven dollars cash in his wallet.

Obviously, those they let go couldn't use it. It certainly didn't qualify as stealing, not in Clara's mind.

They'd taken his fancy watch, and the fancy cuff links in a fancy box in his bag. She couldn't help but wish Sam could wear the fancy watch, but like with the other things from the others they'd let go, they kept it stored away in a box.

She felt it wasn't worth the risk to wear any of it, sell any of it.

But cash was cash.

She was, and always had been, law-abiding. She wore her seat belt and drove at the speed limit. She filed her taxes and considered herself a good citizen.

What they did for the resurrected rose above man's laws.

They kept the cash money they harvested in a freezer bag. Sam called it Cold Cash, which made her giggle every time. Last count, they'd had eight hundred and fifty-eight Cold Cash dollars.

Not enough for a real vacation, but if they kept saving, and—God willing—they hit a few more gold mines through their mission, they might be able to take a whole week in Aruba next winter.

Or pick some other sunny, romantic place.

They hadn't had much time for the mission, what with the vacation, and her pulling double shifts, Sam drawing the night shift for nearly three weeks.

But the idea of those palm trees, that blue water, of making love with Sam in a hotel bed incentivized her.

When they finally had a full day off, she let Sam sleep in.

By the time he came out, she'd finished the last of her research, had the bacon fried crispy, and had eggs—he liked them over easy—in the skillet.

"I heard you stirring, so I got breakfast going. You get enough rest, doll?"

"Feel like a new man." He crossed over to nuzzle her neck. His hands snuck up to her breast. "And you feel like my woman."

"Oh, you! Now, you sit and have your coffee while I finish this up."

"You sure treat me right, Clara. Get you coffee?"

"I've already had two cups, but . . . maybe just a half. I got up thinking about our vacation. Best vacation I ever had, ever thought I'd have."

"Wish we could've stayed longer. It sure was fine."

"And that's what I'm thinking. We got that resurrection money saved up in the freezer."

"Our Cold Cash."

She giggled, as always. "We could earmark it for a vacation fund. Add to it. Next year, we can take each other back to Aruba, or where we want, for a week."

"I sure do like your thinking, babe. And don't this look good! Just the way I like my eggs."

As Clara sat across from him, Sam cut into them.

"That thinking got me going. We've been so busy, and worn out when we're not. It's time to get back to it. And I've got the one."

"The woman you were thinking about before?"

"No, we're putting her off. I'd put this one by because he tried to take his own life. You know how I feel about that."

Sam gave her a sad, sober nod. "I do, babe. Biggest sin there is."

"It is, it surely is. But when I started thinking, started looking things over, I realized I was judging. It's not for me to judge, and how he died doesn't matter. It's cheating death that does. It's pulling him back from his journey taking him home that matters."

As he ate, Sam nodded again. "You're wise, babe. Tell me about him."

"He's thirty-one, works as a hotel bellman." And hotel bellmen pocketed plenty of cash money. "Works in a hotel over in Uniontown. His wife left him. She works at a law firm, and got her fancy lawyer to fix it so he only got to see their little boy—just two years old at the time—every other weekend. In his despair, he hanged himself. Hanged himself over a woman who didn't want him."

Pausing, Sam laid a hand over his heart. "I wouldn't have to take my own life if you left me, Clara. I'd just die of a broken heart."

"As if I ever would or could! His daddy found him. He was staying back with his parents because the wife got their place in the divorce."

"Fancy lawyers." Sam shook his head in disgust as he ate.

"His daddy got him down, and turns out he was a paramedic. He brought him back, and they got him to the ER. He had to go for a psych eval, get some treatment. That was back last April. That's ten months."

"And we're trying to find ones with some time between, like the dentist."

"He still works at the hotel. He's got his own place again. And I feel good about it, as he appears to have made his peace. I don't like the thought of us letting him go when he's covered in darkness."

Reaching out, Sam squeezed her hand. "You have such a good heart. We never did a suicide before."

"I think it might add to things. Hearing what he saw and heard, maybe felt, since he died in the deepest of sins. Are you up to a drive to Uniontown?"

He smiled at her. "You know I am."

"Then that's what we'll do. I checked the weather. Snow's maybe coming, but not until tonight. We should have clear sailing."

"We'll finish breakfast and set sail."


Nash learned his newest client worked for one of the oldest law enforcement agencies in the country. And reading that made him feel woefully uninformed.

And yeah, she could arrest people.

She—they—had the authority to enforce all laws in the state—anywhere in the state. The only agency that had that scope.

Maybe the focus was public lands, waterways, fish—which struck him funny—wildlife. Add search and rescue. But if she ran across someone robbing a bank, she could slap on the cuffs.

And he found that fascinating.

He supposed he'd found her fascinating. The way she'd handled the dog, how she'd had her plan in place—every detail—before she'd hired him and Theo.

She looked fragile, and that was probably the eyes, but she didn't come off that way.

Thorough, he thought again. Add in decisive, straightforward.

He started to look for some personal information, and stopped himself.

"Can't do it. Feels wrong."

Instead he laid out the samples he'd gotten for the kitchen.

"Time to pull the trigger, Littlefield."

He spent nearly an hour debating with himself, told himself he'd finalized. When Theo came in, and Tic went wild, he got up.

"Dinner's served! I went with spaghetti and meatballs."

"Works for me. Thanks for picking it up."

Theo put the takeout on the counter before crouching down to send Tic into delirium.

"I heard back from Drea's sister."

"Already?" Theo straightened to pull off his coat. "We only sent her the estimate this morning."

"She's no time waster. And we're hired."

"Excellent! How about we go with wine? Spaghetti, meatballs, wine."

"Fine."

Theo looked at the samples on their temporary table. "Again?"

"At last. I just finished writing up the order. No going back."

"You're going with the two-tone cabinets. Slate-gray uppers and lowers, dark blue on the island and coffee station."

"I better not regret it."

"You won't. It's classy, and this hardware? Yeah, the matte black's good. We want a manly kitchen."

"We have to start actually cooking. Not just making sandwiches. We'll finish the Haver job by noon, latest. Then we'll start demo."

"Good deal." Theo added fresh water to Tic's bowl, put his nightly food in the other. When Tic scrambled to the bowls, Theo took a glass of wine from Nash. "The Fix-It Brothers are rocking it."

"Into month three, and it doesn't suck." Nash shoved the samples to one end of the door table, put plates on the other.

In the morning, they worked, with Robo and Tic the job dog, on what the client called her second-best guest room. Now that she had all new interior doors—her husband hit that on the nose—she felt that second-best guest room needed some sprucing.

Which included a window seat—storage beneath—more shelves in the closet, and fresh paint—walls, ceiling, trim.

They only had a couple of hours' work left, but they'd hit the finale on her day off. And she eyed them like a hawk.

Tic settled in to watch, chew on his toy, or occasionally attack bootlaces.

"I want you to take a look at the laundry room after this. I spend a lot of time in there, and the light's not good, the folding counter's too small. Maybe paint there, too. It should be more cheerful."

"Happy to do that."

As he spoke, Nash caught the pleading look from his brother. Rita Haver all but sat on his back as he installed shoe shelves in the closet.

"Why don't I take a look now? We're nearly done here. Theo and Robo can finish up."

"Can't wait to put this room back together. I got new bedding. Robo, you be careful not to drip that paint."

Robo just smiled at her as he did the touch-up. It turned out his superpowers included cutting in and touching up. "I sure won't."

"How's Bill?" Nash asked as he walked downstairs with her.

"All healed up and ready to dance. I can tell you he's not giving me any guff about having you all do the work around here. More time for ice fishing. He's not at work, he's on the lake. You try that?"

"No, ma'am, and not likely to. I like my ice in a glass."

She hooted at that, then pointed him into the laundry room off her kitchen.

"You're right about the light."

"And plenty of times I'm in here after work."

Rita pointed out what she wanted. Nash took notes, measurements.

"You give me a fair price, now." With a smile, Rita wagged a finger at him. "Well, you have so far, so I expect you will. You boys do good work. Wouldn't have you back otherwise. And Dean Cooper sure wouldn't. I heard you're doing some work for his daughter. Sloan."

"Redoing a bathroom in her new house."

"It's good hearing she got a place. She's been gone down to Annapolis these past years. Most figured she'd go back working there after she healed up."

Nash started to check himself, then, deciding being told information wasn't the same as digging it up on the internet, asked the natural question.

"Healed up? Was she sick?"

"Oh my goodness, near to death! The girl got shot. Shot twice at that."

"Shot?"

He was from New York. He knew people got shot. Cops got shot. But the shock of it had him turning, staring.

"In the head—but that was mostly a miss, I'm told. But the one that didn't miss hit that poor girl right in the chest."

Rita smacked her own.

"I don't know what's wrong with people, I swear I don't. She walked into one of the gas station markets, and some hooligan was robbing the place. He just shot that girl, shot her and ran. They got him, though."

"Shot." Nash could only repeat it.

"In the hospital for a time, then back here, as she wasn't in any shape to be on her own. When I saw her the other day, I said a prayer of thanks that she looks like herself again. A little thinner I guess, and she went and cut off her hair. But she looks like herself. She was always a strong girl."

She'd have to be, Nash thought.

It stuck in his head as they finished the job. Noting the time, he pulled out some cash.

"Robo, why don't you go pick up some subs? I'll take a cold cut, the spicy."

"I'm all in on that," Theo said.

Robo took the cash. He had sandy blond hair pulled back in a tail and the face of a choirboy with guileless blue eyes and a crooked incisor.

"Okay if I get the roast beef?"

"Whatever you want, Robo," Nash told him. "Theo and I will finish getting the kitchen ready for demo, and we'll break for lunch when you get there."

"Sure thing, boss. That room turned out real nice, didn't it?"

"It did. You did good work."

Beaming at the compliment, Robo boosted up into his truck.

Nash got behind the wheel of his own as Theo climbed in the passenger side after Tic jumped in the back.

"Do you think, whenever we spring for lunch, he'll stop asking permission to get what he wants?"

"I'm hoping that wears off."

"He's a good guy. And a hell of a painter." Since the dog pushed his head over the back seat, Theo reached up to rub it. "Demo day, Tic! What's more fun than that?"

"Did Drea tell you Sloan was shot several months ago?"

"What?" Theo's jaw dropped. "Shot? What?"

"Obviously not."

"Like with a gun, shot? On purpose?"

"Rita just dropped that, yeah, with a gun, on purpose. Twice. A few weeks before Thanksgiving. She walked into some mini-mart. Sounds like this asshole was robbing it at gunpoint, and shot her."

"Bad? It's always bad, but I mean bad-bad?"

"Sounds like it, yeah. Hospital, then here, with her parents. We saw her, remember, walking with the dog."

"Yeah, yeah." At Tic's whine for attention, Theo stroked absently. "I forgot about that. I remember now. We saw her walking with Mop, and like she was ninety. Drea's never said anything about this. Holy shit. She's okay now? She looks okay, and she's working and all, got her own place."

"She seems okay."

"That's a hell of a thing, Nash."

"It's a hell of a thing," Nash agreed, and made the turn toward home.

The next morning, Nash drank his coffee, standing in what had been the kitchen. And would be again, he thought. New and vastly improved.

They'd added that space on sometime in the last fifty years or so. Now he'd taken it down to the studs, and the ceiling down to the beams.

Then they boxed up the newspapers and magazines they'd found behind the drywall.

He now knew John Sirica had been *Time*'s Man of the Year in 1973 and Woodward and Bernstein wrote their first Watergate article in June of '72.

Seeing the space now, Nash decided to leave the beams exposed. They'd clean them up, sand them, seal them. When the weather allowed, they'd add the skylights.

They could start there while the electrician he'd contracted worked on updating the wiring, and CJ dealt with the plumbing.

Inspection, he thought, insulation, drywall.

Tic loped over to him carrying a sock.

"What is this obsession?" But remembering the routine, Nash grabbed a dog toy. "This isn't yours." With some tugging on both sides, he retrieved the sock. "This is yours." And gave Tic the toy.

As he did, Theo came in the front door.

"He's been out, had breakfast."

"Thanks. Sorry. Hey, pal, hey, Tic." He crouched to rub the dog all over. "I wasn't going to stay over last night, but—let me get some coffee."

They'd set up a kind of kitchenette in the living room. The refrigerator, the microwave, coffeemaker, toaster, the door table.

"I asked Drea about Sloan. She and the guy she was working with stopped to gas up. They'd been up this way, a little south of Deep Creek. These three guys had been robbing hikers, stealing from campsites, even roughing some people up. They tracked them down. I didn't really get they did stuff like that."

Because the dog wanted more, Theo sat on the floor, drinking coffee with one hand, rubbing Tic with the other.

"Anyway, they got them. Drea said Sloan didn't tell her, but the guy she was with, Joe—no, no, Joel. Anyway, these guys were armed and everything. He told Drea, Sloan took one of them down herself. Can you beat that?"

"I can't." Looked fragile, he thought again. But wasn't.

"So they're on their way back, and stop to gas up. She goes in to get some drinks, and Jesus, Nash. The first shot grazed her head, and the second hit her right in the chest. He ran, shot at the Joel guy, but missed, so Joel ran in, called for an ambulance.

"She started crying. Drea. Said how Joel probably saved Sloan's life. Pressure on the wound, all that. And in surgery—man—her heart stopped and they had to like shock her back. Drea said Sloan didn't tell them about it, but the doctor did. They put her in a coma for a couple days because it was pretty dicey."

He blew out a breath as Nash said nothing, only walked over to get another cup of coffee.

"And get this. After they let her come home—well, here—and she was being really careful to do everything the doctor and all told her, on Thanksgiving one of the little kids fell down, started crying, and she just automatically picked him up. Pulled a pec muscle, and pretty much had to start all over."

He gave Tic one more rub and stood. "She's doing good now, but man, it's a lot."

"How much spine do you think it takes to get through that, then put a uniform back on?"

"Pretty sure more than I've got."

Nash glanced over at his brother. "You've got plenty of spine. But she's got more than most."

Drea caught Sloan as she was leaving for work.

"Early for you," Sloan said as she let Drea in. "I've got maybe five minutes."

"I told Theo about what happened to you," she blurted out. "I didn't tell him, he found out, then I told him. I'm sorry. I'm sorry."

"Oh." Sloan opened the closet for her coat. "Okay."

"I didn't say anything about it before, but once he asked me, it all came pouring out. I needed to tell you I told him. I needed to tell you I'm sorry."

"It's all right. I mean it," she added when she saw Drea on the point of tears. "It happened. It's not some big secret, and he was bound to find out, working in the Rest. I appreciate you didn't say anything before, but you could have."

In response, Drea threw her arms around Sloan. "It all came back, and out. When it happened, I was so scared. I tried so hard not to show it, but I was so scared."

"You did a good job. All of you did. You helped me get through it, all of you helped. And I am through it."

"I didn't want you to think—"

"I don't. He asked; you answered. It's fine."

"He's in love with me."

"What? I'm so shocked, I may fall over."

As Sloan pulled back, threw up both hands, made her shocked face, Drea laughed. "Okay, not a real surprise, but it may be that I really think I'm in love with him."

"A somewhat surprise. I like him, if you need to hear that. What's not to like? He strikes me as smart, he's hardworking, personable, he takes cute all the way to adorable, and he looks at you like you're the only woman in the world."

"It seems so fast. Doesn't it seem fast? I don't know."

When Drea paced in circles, Sloan let it run.

"It seems fast, but it doesn't feel fast. We've only been together a short time even though it feels . . . I didn't tell you, but I had to move on him. New Year's Eve. He didn't want to push there."

"This needs to be a longer conversation."

"Let's just say, he'd already hit all the notes, and that night, a symphony."

"Definitely a longer conversation." Sloan wrapped on her scarf. "I have to go to work." Curious, she studied Drea's face as she put on her coat. "Did Theo tell you they're remodeling my bathroom?"

"What? No."

"He gets another point. I asked his brother not to say anything, so he obviously told Theo the same. And that tells me he can keep his mouth shut when asked. Don't say anything to Mom or Dad, okay? Let the Fix-Its get started first. Then I'll tell them."

"I won't. Dad's going to sulk a little."

"I know, so I'm waiting until it's started to tell him. Then he can come by, make sure they're doing it right."

"That's a given. He won't be able to stop himself."

They walked out together as Sloan put on her hat.

"Have a good day, Sergeant Cooper."

She intended to, and didn't intend to worry about the newcomers—as the Littlefields would be for about five years—learning about her incident.

She'd worry a bit about her sister falling for Theo. So she'd run a background check, and justify it as he and his brother would be in her house when she wasn't.

She'd run that after work, and because Janet Anderson still pushed into her mind, she'd do a search for like crimes in the area. Maybe in the state. She'd include West Virginia, Pennsylvania.

Probably wouldn't hit anything, but as she saw it, you couldn't hit if you didn't aim and fire.

But now, like the mountains, the day spread out before her.

In her duty as sergeant, she assigned her teams, then reported to Travis.

"Cap? I got a report of a poacher off the Sky Hill Trail. I'm taking that with Elana."

He looked up from his own paperwork. "The hiker report of a bear trap?"

"Loring's on it." She ran through the other assignments. "I know you want the evaluation on Elana after a full three months, but I wanted to tell you I'm finding her a quick study, eager, and smart."

"That's good to hear. Before you go, let me give you an update on your arrest of the tree killer. Paul Jacob Moseby has refused legal representation. All lawyers are liars and cheats. His mandatory psych eval found him competent to stand trial. You'll be called on to testify."

"Understood."

"It's not his first run-in. He's been fined for poaching several times, skipped out on bail after assaulting the owner of a hunting cabin where he'd decided to squat. He'll be squatting behind bars for some time."

"He earned it."

"That he did."

She stepped out. "We're up, Elana."

They put on their outdoor gear, walked to the truck. Elana hopped in. "Another day of adventure!"

"Bound to be. Poachers carry weapons, so stay alert. They're usually not aggressive, and more likely to run or make excuses. But you still handle with care."

"Officer First Class Loring and I fined one my first week here. He was pissed off—not like Chainsaw Tree Killer—but pissed off. Didn't put up a fight or anything, just argumentative."

"That's pretty standard."

"He went on a bitch rant about how man was made to hunt. Loring was really polite, suggested he get a hunting license, which he didn't have anyway, and follow the posted hunting seasons."

"That's how it's done."

As they trooped up Sky Hill Trail, Elana marveled. "Everything just sparkles. It's warmer today. Warmer and sunny. The snow's melting some."

"February thaw. It won't last long, but we'll take it while it does. There's the deer stand." She pointed up the trail and to the east. "Fifty feet more, two o'clock. He's tried to camouflage it so anyone using the trail won't see it."

"You sure did. Now I do."

Sloan's eyes went narrow and hard. "He's baited the ground around the stand. Not enough for him to hunt off-season, but baiting on top of it."

That infuriated her, but she reeled it in.

She watched the man in full camo gear, carrying a Winchester with a scope in one hand, start hustling down the ladder of the stand.

"Sir, you don't want to run."

When he did, Sloan shook her head and picked up her own pace.

Her quarry, glancing behind, slipped on slushy snow and face-planted.

He said, "Son of a bitch."

"Sir, I'm taking your rifle."

Sloan picked up the rifle he'd been foolish enough to run with. She checked the safety, shook her head when she found it off. She engaged it, then handed the rifle to Elana.

"Are you injured?"

"Maybe."

She thought: Bullshit, but she spoke pleasantly.

"We'll call for medical assistance and help you down the trail."

"Nah, I'm not hurt." Rolling over, he pushed himself to sitting.

"Sergeant Cooper, this is the individual Officer First Class Loring cited and fined a few weeks ago."

"Is that so?"

"Yes, sir. Mr. Ernst, I don't believe you learned your lesson."

"Son of a bitch," he repeated. "Listen, I was just sitting up there. No law against just sitting in a stand."

"With a Winchester XPR," Sloan added.

"For protection."

"Are you aware there's a cabin about a hundred yards due west, and it's illegal to discharge a firearm in a national forest within a hundred and fifty yards of a resident, a cabin, occupied area, or campsite?"

"I didn't see any damn cabin. How am I supposed to know that shit?"

"Basic safety principles, Mr. Ernst, which I'm sure Officer First Class Loring relayed to you."

"Yes, he did," Elana confirmed.

"You also have bait spread on the ground. I see grain, acorns, a protein block."

After a glance, Ernst shrugged. "I don't know where that came from."

"Now, Mr. Ernst, that's a new protein block, and I'm betting you just bought it. I'm betting we can track that block back to you without much trouble at all."

He sneered, but came up with a whine. "So what? Baiting's legal in plenty of states."

"Maryland's not one of them if it's on state-controlled property. The last time you got off with a fine. Now you're going to be charged. For erecting a deer stand, baiting deer, hunting during the closed season, and I'm betting you don't have that hunting license."

"Licenses are just a way to gouge hunters."

"Actually, the funds from hunting licenses go to conservation, to wildlife management."

He said, "Son of a bitch."

# CHAPTER FOURTEEN

Sloan considered it another very good day. She'd regained her rhythm physically, professionally, and—for the most part—emotionally.

The occasional nightmare hardly counted.

When she needed a mental health break, she worked out, or she crocheted—something she could now do passably well while watching TV.

In anticipation of her gutted bathroom, she took everything out of the vanity, the shower, pulled towels off the rods and transferred them to the second bath.

In the kitchen she made herself some stir-fry with chicken as protein. Then sitting at her little table with her dinner and her laptop, initiated a background check on Theo (not Theodore, but Theo) Littlefield.

No criminal, so good there. No civil suits, no accusations of domestic abuse, no criminal charges period. A couple of speeding tickets. He'd passed the bar six months before, and as of December sixteenth, became a licensed contractor.

"Nothing to see here," Sloan concluded. She took a moment to evaluate herself, and found she wasn't just relieved but happy.

Drea deserved a good man who loved the air she breathed.

Since she'd started it, she ran the same on Nash.

No criminal, unless she counted the underage drinking violation. Which, from the dates, the location, she took to be a senior high school kegger.

She couldn't hold it against him, as she'd have the same on her record if she'd gotten caught.

She'd either been luckier or more strategic.

She found more than a couple of speeding tickets in his late teens, early twenties. But apparently he'd regulated himself in that area.

She came up with one civil case, from three years prior. Then found herself shocked to see his own parents had brought it against him.

They'd sued their son to try to cut him off from the chunk of money he'd receive from his trust fund at thirty.

They'd lost, and in fact had been ordered to pay Nash's legal fees. She just couldn't get over the fact parents would go so far against their own son.

And for money. The reason somehow made it even worse.

"Not my business. It's really not my business. So enough. Nothing to see here either."

She could hand over her spare key to the Fix-Its without a qualm.

She put it aside, did her dishes.

After building up the fire, she brought her laptop to the living room. Feet up on the coffee table, she started her search for like crimes.

She found nothing that fit the specific and narrow parameters on Janet Anderson, so widened it.

She paused for a text from Joel.

> Just checking in, Sarge! Have to tell you Sari really, truly felt our girl move!! She said it felt like a bunch of butterflies flying around and flipping over. Had her checkup, too, and I heard the heartbeat. They said we're all a-okay, and our girl's about the size of a banana. Saw her in there, too. And didn't need them to show me. Sending Auntie Sloan a pic.

Studying the ultrasound warmed Sloan's heart. And this time she could make out Joel's girl—because Mama Dee hit that target—easily.

> This is so exciting! And she just gets prettier. So glad you're all a-okay. Butterflies. You could name her Lotis for the lotis blue—one of the rarest. I can't wait to meet her. All's good

here. Getting my bathroom ripped out and redone. That's my excitement. Love to all of you. Keep me updated on the baby.

Joel sent her a baby emoji as a sign-off.

Still feeling that warmth, she nearly put the search away. She could watch a movie instead, or get back to reading the book she'd started the night before.

Or try her luck on crocheting a hat.

She decided to give it another hour, then shift to the book before bed. Early to bed, she reminded herself.

She wanted to be up, showered, and dressed before the bathroom crew arrived.

One hour drifted into two. She found a missing woman, reported by her adult daughter, from Hazelton, just over the West Virginia border. In September of last year, Sloan noted, no abandoned car this time. Celia Russell had taken her dog—Misty, a miniature poodle—out for a walk.

Neither had been seen since.

The daughter reported that Russell, divorced, had no signs of depression, no known enemies, no gambling or drinking problems.

Investigated as abduction, but that ran cold.

"More than twenty-five years older than Janet, and there's the dog." She moved on.

So many, she thought. So many missing. Some found, some not. Some found when it was too late.

A dentist from Cumberland intrigued her. That abandoned car. But male, middle-aged. And having an affair with a woman about half his age.

She made notes on him, and on Celia Russell simply to satisfy the investigator inside her.

Realizing she'd missed that early night deadline, she made herself shut off her laptop and get ready for bed.

As Sloan climbed into bed and turned off the light, Clara and Sam sat parked on the far end of the hotel's parking lot in Uniontown, and directly beside Zach Tarrington's Saab.

"We're really lucky he's working the late shift, babe."

"Not lucky," Clara corrected, and kept a hawk eye on the doors. "It's meant."

"You're right." He patted her hand. "It's meant."

"He should be coming any minute now. You should get out, doll, go around the back of the van. We don't want him seeing a big, handsome man like you."

"Black man." Sam gave a resigned shrug. "I know how it is."

Now she patted his hand.

"Just like we planned."

Sam got out, used the van as cover.

The security lights worried him some, but Clara said this place, this time, this resurrected was meant. That was that.

Plus, it was goddamn cold. He could think the *goddamn*, but he had to be careful with certain swears around Clara.

And sometimes he thought she could read his mind. She was spooky, his Clara. He loved that about her.

He heard her open the door of the van, and got ready.

Clara slipped out, pretended to have some trouble opening the side doors.

"Pete's sake!" she said loud enough for the man approaching to hear her. "Stupid thing's sticking again. Wouldn't you just know it!"

"Need some help, ma'am?"

She turned, gave Zach a frustrated smile.

"I sure could use some if you don't mind. Door's stuck again. It takes some muscle to get it open."

He smiled back, a pleasant-looking man with a good haircut and horn-rimmed glasses.

"Let's see if I've got enough."

He gripped the handle with both hands, gave it a hard sideways pull. It opened so smooth, so fast, he nearly tumbled.

He started to laugh, and Sam shoved the needle in.

Zach managed a half shout. His arms waved wildly. Sam locked his arms around him, tossed him inside.

"I got him." As he climbed in, he glanced toward the hotel.

"Jesus, somebody's coming."

Clara slid the door closed, and wearing that frustrated smile again, walked over to a tall Black man who crossed the lot.

"Excuse me, I must've made a wrong turn. My daughter's going to wonder where I am. Can you tell me how to get back on 40, headed west?"

"I sure can."

He gave her directions where she had no intention of going.

"Thank you. My old bucket doesn't have the GPS, and I got turned around."

"No problem at all. Drive safe."

"Oh, I always do."

She walked back to the van, put on her seat belt. Started the engine. She gave a wave to the man who'd given her directions as he unlocked a car several spaces down the row.

As she drove, safely, out of the parking lot, she flipped a glance in the rearview mirror.

"You shouldn't take the name of our Lord and Savior in vain, Sam."

"I know, Clara, I'm sorry. It just jumped up. And aren't you cool, walking right up to that guy that way."

"I couldn't see any other way to do it. Had to distract him."

"Smart. But now he's seen you, babe. He's seen you and the van."

"We won't worry about that right yet. Let's get this one home. He's good and out, isn't he?"

"He is now."

Sam climbed in the front, put his seat belt on.

"He didn't see you, doll. Didn't see you put this one in, or get in after. He came out after that, when I was closing the door. But this one was putting up a ruckus, and I couldn't be sure the other wouldn't hear. I needed to keep him away some until you had him all secure."

"Fast thinking, babe. Those security lights . . . Still, it was pretty dark, and you're wearing a hat, got your scarf bundled up. I bet he didn't see much of your face."

"Probably not, but you're right, doll, he surely saw the van."

"We'll paint it. We can paint it."

"Now who's thinking fast! We'll paint it. Oh, let's pick a pretty color. Dark blue, I think. Navy blue. That's not flashy, but it'll be a nice change."

"Dark blue it is." It pleased him he'd thought of something that pleased her. "I'm going to take care of this for us, babe. I'll look up how it's done and take care of it."

She sent him a quick grin. "Now that it's all done with, Sam? That was kind of exciting. It got me wound up some."

He grinned back. "We get home, get this one secure, I'll take care of that, too."

Promptly at seven-fifteen in the morning, Sloan answered the knock on the door.

"Right on time." She stepped back. "Hi, Theo, nice to see you."

"You, too. Thanks for the job."

"You'll see that it needs a lot of work."

Theo flexed his biceps. "We're up for it."

She had to smile at him. "Nothing like demo day, right?"

"You got that. I guess you've done your share."

"And enjoyed every minute. If I had any spare weeks, I'd tackle that ugly bathroom myself. But."

She offered Nash a key. He still had some stubble, she noted. But more like a night's worth.

"In case you have to go out and come back, and to lock up when you leave. I probably won't be home until you've knocked off for the day."

"Do you want us to leave it somewhere when we do?"

Her quick background check made this part easy, and had her mind easy, too.

"No, just keep it until the job's finished. I'm on call twenty-four/seven, so it's better you have a way to get in, in case I'm not here to let you in. Some of the replacements are due to be delivered today."

"We'll take care of everything."

"Thanks. Where's Tic?"

"Oh, he's home," Theo said. "In his crate."

On a frustrated breath, Sloan rolled her eyes—mostly at Nash. "Well, go back and get him. Don't leave him crated all day."

"Really?" Theo's face brightened. "Are you sure?"

"Really, and I'm sure. Go free the dog. Make sure you bring him some toys and treats."

"I'll be right back."

As Theo ran out, Nash sighed. "You're asking for trouble."

"Train your dog, Littlefield."

"He's Theo's dog."

"He's the Fix-It Brothers' dog. There's coffee, and soft drinks. Help yourself."

"We brought our own, but thanks."

"If you run out, help yourself. I stocked for a crew. Now I'm going over to confess to my father I knocked him out of a job. He'll only have five minutes to sulk before I leave for work."

"Good luck with that."

"I may need it."

She got out her scarf, her coat, stuck gloves in her pocket.

Then put on her Stetson.

And turned to see Nash smiling at her.

"What?"

"You look damn good in that hat, Sergeant Cooper."

"I do, don't I?" She gave the brim a finger swipe. "Tear it up, Littlefield. I never want to see that yellow daisy flooring again."

He watched her walk out. Maybe it was the hat, he thought, but she had a definite swagger.

He thought of the way she'd walked the first time he'd seen her. Like every step required pain and effort.

"Sure wouldn't know it now."

He started to shut the door, but Robo pulled up so he waited.

"Ready for demo, Robo?"

"Ready, boss."

He stepped in, looked around. "It's some better in than out. Maybe. She's got nice furniture. That fireplace is dead ugly, though, and the kitchen's not much prettier."

He tipped up one shoulder as Nash grinned at him.

"I've been paying more attention to that kind of thing since I started working for you and Theo."

"And you're not wrong about the fireplace or the kitchen. Wait until you get a load of the bathroom we're gutting."


It would be a busy morning for Clara and Sam. Because they'd wanted sex and sleep, they used deep IV sedation on Zach to keep him under.

Bright and early, Clara mixed up some Bisquick pancakes and pork sausage so they'd both start the day off right.

She dressed in scrubs, not only for the procedure, but because she needed to be at work by one for her shift.

She'd chosen her rainbow smock, a favorite, as rainbows were one of God's miracles.

She understood the gays had taken the rainbow for their symbol, and she didn't approve of homosexuality. But she didn't judge, as only the Almighty could judge.

And she liked the smock.

She went in to Zach, checked his vitals, then turned off the drip. She checked his pee bag—not enough to change out as yet, she decided. Then went back for another cup of coffee to give him time to wake naturally while Sam did some of his online schoolwork.

It made her proud he was studying to be an RN. She knew he made a fine caregiver at the old folks' home, but he could do more and was working hard to better himself.

"Sorry, doll, he's waking up now."

"I'll be along in two shakes."

"You take your time."

She took hers, getting up from her coffee and the monitor to walk to the locked door, then down to the basement.

Clara turned the key and stepped in where Zach lay propped on the hospital bed, eyes glazed and fearful, heart rate on the monitor spiking.

She spoke kindly, calmly. "Good morning, Zach! You got some good sleep. How're you feeling?"

Behind his glasses, his eyes rolled wildly, left, right, left again. "Who are you? What's happening? Where am I?"

"Questions, questions! And not even a 'good morning'?" She tsked as she smiled. "I want you to try to slow down your breathing a little, and remember everything's going to be just fine."

"But—I was leaving work. You were there. Your door was stuck. I helped you."

"And thank you for that. You showed good manners and consideration. We're going to help each other now. I'm here to help you."

His breathing stayed labored as he stared at her. "Why am I strapped down? I don't like being strapped down!"

"We don't want you to hurt yourself, Zach. You hurt yourself before, didn't you? You took your own life."

"I was—I was in crisis. I got treatment. I go to therapy."

"Those are choices you should've made before you killed yourself. But that's done." She gave his shoulder a comforting rub. "Still, we need to hear your story. That's all we're asking."

"You need to let me go. Please. People will be looking for me."

"Well now, that might be, but you wouldn't report in for work for hours yet. You tell us your story, and we'll let you go long before that. We'll send you home, and those waiting for you will give you your homecoming."

Clara noted he strained against the straps, as they all did. In her nurse's heart, she wished to give him minimal sedation to ease his fears. But even minimal could interfere with the process.

"What story?" he demanded. "I don't understand. Who is that!"

His agitation grew as Sam came in with the camera.

"Zach, Zach, slow your breath down. Try to relax for me. We're here to help you."

"Help me with what? I'm fine. I'm fine. Why are you doing this?" Anger burst out first, then despair followed. "I'm nobody. I'm nobody."

"Now, don't you say such a thing. You're one of God's creations. All we want is for you to tell us your story. If you can't do that right now, we'll sedate you, give you a chance to relax, and try this again tomorrow."

"No, no! Don't do that. I need to pick up my little boy from preschool tomorrow. I have a little boy. His name is Ben. I'm taking him to a monster truck rally on Saturday. I have to go home."

"Of course you have to go home. Didn't I just say we're going to send you home? You just need to tell us your story first."

And as with the others, a spark of hope lit in his eye. Clara always took that as a good sign. They might not believe they were ready to leave this world and go to their true home, but they'd tell their story.

"All right. All right. I'll do whatever you want, but I don't understand. What story?"

"Ten months ago, Zach, you closed yourself in your room at your parents' house. Parents who took you in, gave you shelter when you were sad and upset."

"Yes, yes. I thought I'd lost everything. I thought my life was over anyway, and I just wanted to end it. I was wrong. I was wrong."

"You bought a rope, a good, thick rope, and you tied it into a noose, and you secured it up on the pole of the ceiling light. You got up on a chair and put that rope around your neck."

"I thought I didn't want to live. I thought death was the answer." Tears rolled down his cheeks. "I was wrong!"

Calmly, Clara continued.

"Your father heard the chair you kicked over. He didn't think anything of it at first, and then he worried some. He knocked on your door. When you didn't answer, he beat on the door, then he slammed his body against it until he broke it down."

"He cut me down." Zach couldn't wipe the tears away, so they kept rolling down his cheeks. "He yelled for my mom to call nine-one-one, and he got up on the chair, used his pocketknife to cut me down. I'll spend the rest of my life trying to make that up to him and my mom."

He choked on a sob. "I hurt them. I hurt them so much."

She paused a moment, then stepped closer. "You understand what you did was deeply hurtful to those who birthed and raised you? And more, a terrible sin?"

"Yes, yes! Please, let me go!"

"And have you repented that sin, Zach? I'll know, I promise you, I'll know if you lie. Have you made atonement for that most grievous sin?"

"Every day! I swear it!"

Her face, her eyes lit with genuine fervor. "I'm so happy to hear that, Zach. I believe we can atone, even from the most grievous sins."

"I got treatment, I'm in therapy. I wake up every single day grateful I've got another chance to live a good life. To be a good dad, to be a good son. Please, that's the truth. That's my story. I want to go home now."

"Soon. But that's only part of your story. After you died on that rope, your father cut you down, and he pulled that rope away from your neck. He did CPR, and he pushed his breath into you."

"He's a paramedic, and he knew what to do. My mom got the portable defibrillator. They had to shock me twice."

"And using that machine, they pulled you back into this world."

"Yes. They saved my life."

"You took your life," Clara corrected, but gently. "What we need to know is what happened between the time you took your life and your parents pulled you back into this world."

"I—I wasn't breathing."

"Yes, we know. Tell us what you saw in those few precious minutes."

"I was clinically dead."

Patience, Clara reminded herself. They always needed her patience.

"It's very important, Zach. What did you see, hear, even feel during those minutes? Where did you go?"

He wet his lips, swallowed. "I was on the floor, and when the ambulance came . . . You want to know if I had an afterlife experience?"

"You gave up this life, and only came back into it through human intervention. Tell us what you saw, heard, felt before that human intervention. Then we can let you go."

He looked away from her, looked toward the camera and the man behind it.

Both his body and his voice shook. "You're recording this."

"Of course. It's very important, and we need to hear your story in your own words. In your own voice. Then you can go home again."

They always clung to the idea that home meant here, on this worldly plain. That was the trick this artificial life played on them.

"I'm not really sure. I was so out of it for a while after. I thought I heard voices, but I couldn't tell what they were saying."

"Did you listen, Zach? Did you listen close?"

"I don't exactly remember. I . . . had a dream."

"A dream?" She glanced back at Sam. This was new. "Tell us about the dream."

"I was a little boy and playing with the dog. With Hetty. My grandpa's dog. He had lots of acres, and always planted a big garden. He had chickens, and there was a creek. He taught me to fish. I was at Grandpa's, playing with the dog. Everything was bright with summer, and everything was good. I didn't have anything to worry about."

"Has your grandpa passed this life, Zach?"

"He died two years ago."

"Did you hear him call to you?"

"I don't know. I was playing with the dog. The dog they had when I was a kid. I think I heard the chickens, and the creek bubbling."

"You were happy there. Peaceful there."

"I loved going there. I take Ben over to see Grandma when I can." Zach kept his gaze locked on hers. Fear lived in it as she smiled. "She still keeps chickens, and Ben likes to see them."

"You dreamed of a place where you were happy, peaceful, carefree. Where you knew you were safe and loved."

Tears filled her eyes at the beauty of it. They thickened in her voice, spilled into her heart. That heart sang hallelujahs.

"You dreamed that wonder, that peace, during those precious minutes before you were dragged back into this life."

"I think. I don't know. Maybe later, in the hospital. I don't know."

Enraptured, Clara shoved his doubts aside, because she *knew*. Even with his great sin, he'd been welcomed into the next life and shown love.

"That's a beautiful story, Zach. I've never heard one so beautiful, so inspiring. It's a story I'll hold in my own heart forever. Thank you for sharing it with us."

"I need to go home now. Please. I need to go home."

"Of course you do."

She walked over to the sink to scrub her hands, put on her gloves.

He screamed when she hooked up the tubes. Begged and wept and cursed. She felt sorrow. Sorrow that he didn't understand they were setting him free. Sending him back to that happy, peaceful dream.

But his story kept her heart, her very soul lifted and joyful.

After the blood ran out of him, when the color and the false life left his body, she gently removed his glasses.

They would go in the box, and she would think of them as a remembrance of a man who'd atoned, and whose homecoming was, even now, filled with the light of a summer day.

"Don't you cry now, babe."

"They're good tears, doll. Tears of gratitude for the beauty he gave us. For knowing he's at peace again. A little boy, playing with a dog on an endless summer day."

Overcome, she leaned against Sam. "No one ever gave us a story like that before. I can get discouraged when they can't or won't tell us anything at all. Now, after this. I'm lifted, Sam. The gift he gave us, the gift we've given him? It lifts me."

She laid a hand on her heart before they labeled the bags of blood, stored them. Before they cleaned and sterilized the medical equipment.

Looking at the fragile flesh and bone in the hospital bed, Clara pictured Zach's freed soul welcomed into his reward. And considered the job well done.

"Now, I've got to get some laundry going or we'll be working in our altogether. I'll make us a nice lunch before I go to work."

"I'm on nights again. Couple more weeks of it. I sure do miss sleeping beside my woman."

"And she misses you."

"But I guess it gives me enough time to take care of his earthly remains."

"That'd be best, since you've got the day for it. If you're still busy with it, I'll leave you a sandwich from last night's chicken."

"Appreciate that, but don't you forget to come in and kiss me goodbye."

"Here's one for now." She caught his face in her hands and kissed him. "And I'm saving a better one for goodbye."

When she went out, Sam hauled Zach's body up and over his shoulder. He went through the next door into the small workshop.

Clara's dead husband had liked building things. Clara had kept all his tools, and kept them neat as could be.

The room was a little tight for the work Sam did there, but he made do.

He dumped the body on the worktable, on the plastic sheeting already prepared. He turned on the Bluetooth speaker Clara had given him for Christmas.

Bless her heart, she knew how he loved his music.

He put on his playlist, then the rubber apron. He shoved his feet into the old galoshes, secured them. He put on the plastic cap—though he'd shower and shampoo good when he finished the work. He added goggles and the long rubber gloves.

He picked up the bone saw.

He didn't mind this duty, or the mess. His father had been a butcher, and what was on the worktable was just meat. What counted had gone to his grandfather's, after all.

He turned on the saw, and sang along with Rihanna as he got to work.

# CHAPTER FIFTEEN

Dean Cooper dropped in three times while they worked on his daughter's bathroom. Nash figured he couldn't help himself.

Dean also made clear he wanted whatever Sloan wanted, which, with Nash's history, came as a novel parental stance.

He swung in twice at the Littlefields' next door while the subs worked on the electric and plumbing. He even walked around with the inspector—another friend, no surprise to Nash at this point.

It took some juggling and a lot of long days, but they managed to keep the balls in the air.

Dean dropped by again as Nash and Theo finished up the bathroom job.

"It looks damn good. I wondered about the tile, but Sloan knows what she wants."

"Clearly," Nash agreed.

Pride showed as Dean looked around the bathroom.

"She got the design gene from her mother. Some of that's rubbed off on me over the years, but she got it from Elsie. Good, quick work here, Fix-Its."

"We were lucky we didn't run into anything behind the walls."

Nash installed a towel rod while Theo handled switch plates.

"She's going to be happy with this. Where's Robo?"

"I sent him to start a paint job. He can more than handle it solo, and it's pretty tight in here."

Tic bounced over to attack Nash's bootlaces.

"Speaking of which. Theo, I can finish here. It's just a little punch out and cleanup. Take this idiot dog home. Walk him over and you can start taping drywall."

"Got the drywall up? I'll give you and the pup a lift, Theo. Going your way."

"Good deal. Come on, Tic, let's go for a ride."

The word *ride* always sent Tic into yips of joy. He rushed out toward the door before Theo edged out after him.

"You and Theo sure came along at the right moment," Dean commented. "First time I've had breathing room since my contractor started making serious retirement noises."

"We aim to please."

"You're hitting the mark." He glanced around the bathroom again. "She's going to be happy with this," he said again. "See you around."

No doubt of that, Nash thought.

He considered himself lucky that he sincerely liked Dean and Elsie Cooper—and it appeared to be mutual. On a personal level, because his brother was well and truly stuck on their younger daughter. Professionally, they did excellent work, and valued others who did the same. They'd given the business he and Theo began a good solid jump in Heron's Rest.

He finished installing the rod, then the smaller one for hand towels by the sink. The robe hook. He took a good look around, making sure he'd missed nothing, that the paint didn't need touching up anywhere.

He carted out the trash first, and noticed Theo had neglected to grab the dog's chew toy. Picking it up, he stuck it in his pocket, then returned to pack up his tools.

He carried them out, then went back to wipe up.

He set her house key on the kitchen counter and had reached for his coat when the front door opened.

"You're here early."

"You're here late."

He glanced at the time. "Looks like we're both right." He picked up her key. "All done," he said, and put it down again.

"Done? As in finished? I figured another day on it. I've gotta see!"

Still wearing coat and hat, she strode toward the bathroom. She'd seen the progress, he thought, but finished? A whole different ball game.

"Well, God. Yes!"

He strolled over to stand in the doorway while she touched everything.

"Good pick on the shower tiles," he commented. "I wasn't sure about that blue until it started going up. It's got movement, variation in tone. Doing the subways horizonal, floor to ceiling, adds depth. Wasn't sure about the wall color either, but that barest hint of blue in it works, and so does continuing it on the ceiling.

"Light wood on the vanity," he continued, "that bit of blue veining on the white countertop, the other cabinet and shelves, those natural wood touches. Good choice on the penny tile, carrying it from the shower floor and out."

"It's beautiful. It's really beautiful." She ran her fingers over the top of the cabinet he'd built, imagined putting flowers on it, or candles. Or both!

"You were right about the cabinet. It's perfect, and such good craftmanship."

"Thanks."

"It's such good light now. I won't look like a ghoul in the mirror."

"That would take some doing."

"I can't believe how perfect . . . damn it!"

"Problem?"

"Yes, there's a problem." She waved him aside, marched out, then pointed at her fireplace. "How the hell am I supposed to have that perfect bathroom, and look at that?"

He only said, "Ah."

"I'm supposed to wait at least two months—I planned it out. Three's better, but I could do two, then hit this room. Then a few months later maybe—maybe—think about the kitchen. Or if the weather allows, start on the exterior, leave the kitchen for now. The bedroom can wait. I mostly only sleep there, and I sleep with my eyes closed."

"Hey, me, too. That's amazing."

"Shut up. But I spend time out here in the evenings, and I'll want a fire in that brick ugliness right into April. And if I cave and do something with that ugliness, I can't leave the walls like this, or the trim, and that horrible popcorn ceiling must go."

Nash glanced up. "Should be illegal anyway."

"Yes!" She high-fived him. "And I can't keep that hideous ceiling light up there. You know this!"

Diplomacy mattered in business, Nash thought. He decided on "Well, hmm."

"And I can't just paint over the ugly of that brick because all that brick is too heavy for the size of the room. Heavier yet with that stupid skinny mantel."

She turned, stared at him.

Diplomacy and honesty mattered.

"I sense you might want me to disagree with that, but I can't."

"If you did, I'd know you lie."

Studying, surveying, she pushed the brim of her hat up about an inch.

And he felt something stir inside him he recognized as pure and simple lust.

"Then if I do something with it," she went on, "I'd need to bring out the hearth another couple inches because it's too narrow, and replace the mantel because it's too small and flimsy-looking, and the hearth frame is old, dated, stupid-looking."

"I don't lie, as a rule anyway." Amused by her, Nash spread his hands and hoped the lust died down. "When you're right, you're right."

"But I'm not tearing that brick out."

"No need to. It's sturdy, and they mortared well."

"I'm going to go with stucco. A simple look, a chunkier mantel. I have to at least ask my dad on that. I can't give him two hits in a row. But the rest."

Now she pointed at Nash.

"Popcorn ceiling goes away. New trim, paint. New light."

He glanced up at the close-to-ceiling trio of flute-edged amber glass. "Yeah, that's an unfortunate ceiling light."

"Recessed lighting. Four cans would do in this size space. Five," she corrected. "One right as you come in the front door."

"Cleaner look. On dimmer switch?"

"Yes. And shit, another down each hallway, on separate switches. Damn it, damn it. I'm getting a glass of wine. Do you want one?"

The offer surprised him, and he realized it shouldn't have.

The Coopers had friendly in their DNA.

If he had to live with the lust, at least he could have a drink.

"I can handle one, considering my short commute. Do you want me to measure while I'm here?"

"I've already got the measurements." She brought out the wine, what he recognized as a very nice Cab.

"Why don't I pour that, and you can take off your coat? Hat's optional."

"Right."

She walked to the closet, and to his mild disappointment, took off the hat, too.

"Well, damn it, this closet door has to go, too, doesn't it?"

At this point, he couldn't stop the grin.

"I didn't want to mention it."

"Single-panel Shaker style, same natural wood as the bathroom. And I am not replacing the rest now. Just the closet. Okay, fine, the closet and the bathroom door, but that's it."

She walked back, picked up her wine, drank deep. "If I'm doing this, the floors need to be sanded. The ones in the bedrooms are fine. They were protected under the ugly carpet. These, sanded, stained to match, sealed."

She drank again. "This is going to cost me. I can't even really blame you because I'm the one who decided to redo the bathroom ahead of schedule."

Damn it, over and above the lust, he just liked her.

"We did have the nerve to do exceptional work. I can take part of the blame."

This time when she sipped her wine, she smiled over it. "I guess I can't hold it against you. I was perfectly happy just to have my own place. Thrilled, actually. And I love this spot. Now I have that perfect little bathroom, and the rest of the house is jealous."

"I hear that."

"Do you?"

"We redid the main-level powder room in our place. I figured we'd just get our hands in, get a simple—fairly simple—room done. Now we've torn out the kitchen, and there's nothing simple about it."

"Because the kitchen said: *What about me?*"

"What it said to me is: *What the fuck? You're just going to leave me like this?*"

She laughed, quick and throaty. "It was pretty bad according to Drea. Worse than mine. Do you cook?"

"I didn't until I moved here. Now it's a very dubious event. Do you?"

"I'm not bad. Ranking in my family goes Mom, Dad, Drea, me, but my mother sets a high bar."

She looked around again. "I'll send you the measurements after I talk to Dad. And I'm not talking to him until tomorrow. I may still come to my senses."

"You won't."

Now those eyes of hers gave him a measuring stare. "Won't I?"

"No, because you already see it."

She sighed once and sighed long. "I do already see it. And I know I'm going to spend too much time tonight looking through my paint fan, looking up fireplace fronts."

"I'll let you get started on that. I've got to get going. Somebody has to nuke dinner, and Theo's worse than I am. Thanks for the wine."

"You earned it. Let Theo and Robo know it's exactly what I wanted."

"I will. Talk to you later."

When he went out, she topped off her wine.

She supposed liking Theo's brother was a positive thing. She liked his looks, sure—who wouldn't?—but she liked his style just as much.

And she'd think about the little extra buzz she'd felt later.

Right now, she'd cart her things back to her pretty bathroom, hang her towels—which should probably be replaced with new now. She'd set candles on her new little cabinet, and enjoy a nice long shower surrounded by lovely blue tiles.

Then she'd get in her pj's and make herself . . . something for dinner. And she'd look through her paint fan.

Sipping, she scowled at the brick wall of her fireplace. "This is all on you."

February ushered in a respiratory virus that knocked people down like bowling pins. Because she managed to dodge it, Sloan spent the next two weeks juggling schedules and covering for those who were laid flat.

Since she'd seen Drea's misery, and heard Travis's lingering cough when he returned to work, she pulled out all her gratitude. But even grateful, double shifts and covering weekends took their toll.

She knew her dad jumped right on the fireplace project, as she noted his progress whenever she managed to get home for some sleep, but she didn't see him.

Or Nash—Drea had passed her clogged head, tender throat, and low-grade fever on to Theo. But she noted the despised popcorn ceiling was no more, and neither was the clunky, too-big, too-dark trim and baseboard.

But the fever—literally—began to break. The day she drove home under ten hours since she'd driven away, she vowed to make herself an actual meal.

Maybe catch up on the like-crimes research she'd had to set aside. Hell, she might even read a chapter of her book or watch a little TV before getting a regular night's sleep instead of dropping into oblivion.

To add to the miracle, she had the whole weekend off. At last.

The brief February thaw had swung back hard to serious winter. Snow might have held off, but the frigid air winging down from Canada kept the lake frozen.

She had some regret she couldn't light a fire, but the wait would be worth it.

When she pulled in, she saw both her father's truck and Nash's. So no silence and solitude, she thought as she squeezed in beside Nash, but she'd happily trade that for more progress on her living room.

She had to climb over the seat, get out the passenger side and into about a foot of snow.

Also worth it, as she wouldn't need to come back out to move her truck to let the others out.

She knocked off her boots at the door, then just pulled them off before she went in.

And found her father, and her mother, standing in the living room with Nash. Elsie let out a peal of laughter, then turned.

"Sloan! We weren't sure when you'd get home. I came over with your dad. I left you some chicken soup. I made a tanker full. Nash is taking some home, and we're dropping off some for Drea. She's doing much better—Theo, too—but chicken soup never hurts."

"Yours especially. I— Oh!"

She'd started to take off her coat when the room itself rather than the people in it registered.

Instead of dreary, her walls now gleamed in the palest of pale green that reflected the last, lingering light of the day. Instead of an eyesore, her fireplace now stood as focal point, with its smooth stucco in a deeper, moodier green and chunky white oak mantel.

Dean grinned. "I think she likes it."

"It's wonderful. I don't have enough wows. My dad's a genius."

"Well, yeah." He laughed when she threw her arms around him.

"You've already got a fire set and ready to light."

"That's for you," he told her. "You've been working such long hours, we didn't want to start one before you got home. Go ahead, light her up."

"I will. Thank you." She kissed his cheek. "Thank you." Then the other.

"You're welcome." He kissed hers. "You're welcome." Then the other.

"And the walls look great, Littlefield," she added as she walked over, then crouched to light the fire. "You got the lights in the popcorn-free ceiling. The crappy trim's gone."

"Robo's a painting machine."

"That may be," Elsie said to Nash, "but he didn't know it. He's do-ing good work for you, and looks happy doing it." She turned a half circle one way, then the other. "It's starting to look like you, baby."

"Not finished? Work still required?"

"Pretty," Elsie corrected. "With easy style and the occasional flash."

She gestured to the red chair. "I want to know when you're ready to tackle the kitchen. I've got ideas."

"I'll take them, but that's going to wait awhile."

"Do you have to work tomorrow?"

"I don't." She pumped both fists in the air. "The weekend is mine at last."

"Terrific. Dinner Sunday then. You and Theo, too, Nash."

"Oh, well—"

Elsie pointed at him. "Man does not live by microwave alone."

"Are you sure about that?"

"I am. Sunday dinner, six o'clock. Dean, we should get going. I want to get this soup to Drea." As she spoke she stepped over to hug Sloan, slid the back of her hand under Sloan's bangs to check for fever.

"I'm fine, Mom."

"Just making sure. Oh, and I brought over some mirrors I had in storage," she added as Dean got her coat, helped her on with it. "In the box on your counter. That wall there? Mirrors, if you like them. Enjoy your fireplace."

"Believe me, I will."

"See you and Theo Sunday, Nash."

When they left, Nash began to pack up his tools as Sloan hung up her coat.

"You don't know Elsie Cooper all that well yet," she said casually. "I'm going to help you out. There's no point in trying to think of an excuse for Sunday."

"I don't want to horn in on family."

"She wouldn't have asked if she considered it horning in. She likes to cook for people. Hence, you and Theo, and I, are having home-made chicken soup tonight. It won't be fancy," she added. "She'll fuss a little because you're company, but you'll know what fork to use and can leave your tux at home."

"But I look so good in it."

Head tilted, she gave him a sweeping glance. Workingman's jeans and flannel shirt, tool belt, Mets cap, boots. He looked good in it. And in a tux? Yeah, she could see it.

"Bet you do. How's Theo?"

"He's crawled out of the hole. He was still sitting on the edge of it this morning, so I told him I'd kick his ass if he came near me for another twenty-four."

"Smart. Drea's taken a few solid steps from the edge, but she caught it first. Being in love means sharing germs."

"That's one way to look at it. Is she?"

"What?"

"Stupid question." He made a wiping away gesture. "One I shouldn't ask." She was too easy to talk to, he realized, and that made him forget the boundary lines. "Pretend I didn't."

"Oh, Drea. Why shouldn't you ask? You're his brother, I'm her sister. She's crazy about him. I don't have to ask the question in reverse because I have eyes. But you could let him know, if you so choose, if he screws this up, hurts her in any way—"

"You'll kick his ass. I can't make that statement in reverse for obvious reasons. I'll just buy him the beer he can cry into."

"It'll be wine and ice cream on this end. But I don't think they will. Screw it up."

"Why not?"

"Because they've got something."

She said it so simply it sounded like truth.

"And they're both nice people," she continued. "Not stupid, not spineless, just nice people who know entirely too much minutia on the Marvel Universe."

"Her, too?" Amused, he reached for his coat. "We used to hide the comic books under the mattress."

"Why would you have to hide them?"

He caught himself for the second time, had to wonder how that had slipped out. "No time to read about Iron Man when you're supposed to read *Moby-Dick*."

"I always liked the first sentence. 'Call me Ishmael.' Then, for me, it goes downhill from there."

"It's all an allegory."

"Yeah, so was *Buffy the Vampire Slayer*. I'll take that over the white whale any day."

He laughed. "I missed that one. The *Buffy* thing."

"Stream the first season sometime. Little blond girl doesn't run from darkness. She walks into darkness to fight evil, finds her power and purpose, all while navigating the many, many terrors of high school."

"I'll keep it in mind."

"And thanks for dealing with the popcorn in the kitchen, too."

He hadn't seen her so much as glance at the kitchen.

"While we were at it. Your father is a genius, by the way. That's one great-looking fireplace."

"It really is. See you Sunday."

He winced at that, but had the sense to wait until he'd walked outside. He liked the Coopers, and liked them a great deal.

He wasn't antisocial. He wasn't on Theo's level of social, which hit way over his limit. He was, Nash decided, social neutral. He liked people well enough, even though people constantly made a mess of things for other people.

And when they got done, the people they'd made a mess of things for made a mess of things for them.

It just went round and round.

He had a circle of friends in New York, and stayed in touch. Even though most of them thought he'd lost his mind when he'd made this life change.

He even intended to have some friends come down for a weekend once he had the house done.

He stood by his truck a moment and studied how close Sloan had parked to the other side. Maybe an inch to spare. The woman was lean, but not that lean.

She'd climbed over to get out the passenger door.

He found her an interesting mix—of what, he hadn't decided, but an interesting mix.

He couldn't figure out why a woman looked sexy wearing a tie, but she pulled that one off.

He eased into reverse, then navigated a three-point turn to head down her bump-filled drive.

Sunday dinner. Might as well admit why that had his shoulders tensing. Whenever they'd happened during his childhood, they'd marked a day of stress, stiffness, interrogations, disapproval, and misery.

Sitting in the formal dining room like characters in a badly written play. The starch in the collar of his white dress shirt—required attire—rubbing at his neck. Sit up straight, don't slouch. Two hours—set your watch by it—and five courses served by the silent staff, who, on occasion, might send a look of sympathy to him and Theo.

If you didn't like what they served, you ate it anyway, without complaint or comment.

Otherwise, you still had to eat every bite, but you had to swallow the lecture with it.

He'd have preferred a solid smack to those endless, soul-sucking lectures.

No one physically slapped, but those Sunday dinners still left a mark.

"Deal with it, Littlefield," he muttered as he pulled up to his own home. "You're all grown up now."


Sam spent whatever free time he could steal working on the van. The February virus caused both his work and Clara's to run shorthanded, and for Clara, added patients.

But he'd managed an hour here, two hours there, carefully followed the instructions and videos he'd found online.

He had to be glad they'd decided to keep their cars and save the van for the mission. They'd considered selling at least one car—he still had payments on his—but they'd decided the mission was too important to risk adding unnecessary miles, risking a breakdown, even an accident.

He'd had his ear pressed to the news, too, but hadn't heard anything about the police looking for a white van.

Still, he knew—he watched TV!—the cops held stuff back. So happy they could keep the van home and he could get it all painted fresh and new.

It was damn cold work, even though he'd jury-rigged a kind of tent over it, had a space heater going.

When he had it finished, tested to make sure the paint was good and dry, he went inside for Clara.

He found her just pushing up from the couch.

"I'm sorry, Sam, I meant to get a meal going, but I fell asleep, just dropped right off sitting here folding laundry."

"No wonder, you've been working night and day. You're looking flushed."

"I think I've got a fever. Throat's scratchy. It's no surprise I'd catch this damn thing."

"You're calling in sick to work for tomorrow. Monday, too."

"I hate doing that." She held a hand up to her neck, as even speaking felt like broken glass scraping the inside of her throat. "But I can't go in if I'm running a fever."

"You're going to get yourself into bed, babe. I'll make you some soup, some toast, some tea."

He laid a hand on her forehead. "You're warm, all right. I'm going to tuck you in, but first, I've got something might perk you up."

He wrapped a throw around her shoulders, walked her to the door.

He opened the door, said: "Ta-da!"

"Sam!" His name came out in a croak, but didn't lack enthusiasm. "It looks beautiful. Why, you'd think it just came off the lot and was that color all along!"

"The navy blue you wanted."

"I just love how it looks. Why, it's painted just like a professional would."

She didn't mention the blue hazed some under the windshield wipers, or on the edge of the right headlight.

He'd worked so hard!

"When you're feeling all better, we'll take it out for a drive. Now, let's get you in bed. Don't you worry about the laundry. I'll get it folded."

"Oh, Sam, that's not your job."

"It's my job until my woman's well again. I'll take care of you until you are."

Emotion choked her; fatigue drained her. "You always take care of me."

"Extra-special care."

He helped her off with her shoes, helped her change into a night-gown. Then plumped up the pillows so she could sit up in bed.

"I'll get the thermometer and some cold meds. Then make you that soup."

"I do feel poorly."

"Don't you worry. I'll be right here. We'll take your temperature, and you call in. You need a couple days, babe, and you've been pick-ing up the slack for others who needed it. You got sick because you were there to help others."

"That's what we do. We were called to help. I could sure use that tea, doll, with some honey. My throat's just raw." A cough snuck up on her and hurt like fire.

"I'll put the kettle on, and get your phone. How about I set up the laptop in here for you, so you can watch a movie or something?"

"You think of everything."

"I think of you, Clara." Gently, he smoothed a blanket over her. "Night and day, day and night. You just rest now, and let me take care of everything."

She lay back, closed her eyes. She was the luckiest woman in this world.

She sent out a prayer of thanks.

# CHAPTER SIXTEEN

Sloan spent her finally free Saturday doing what she hadn't had time to do over the past two weeks. Starting with a workout in her makeshift gym.

While she curled and pressed, she imagined the possibility of turning her serial killer basement into the perfect fitness area, maybe including a three-piece bath—with shower—and an organized storage area.

After she gathered her laundry, carted it down the steep, narrow stairs, crossed the pockmarked concrete slab to the washer that had surely left the showroom in the previous century, she admitted that possibility would mean a serious budget and time crunch.

Not an impossible crunch, but serious.

And she could probably cross off that bathroom.

Upstairs, while the fire crackled, she gave the house a good Saturday cleaning, and that felt gratifying.

She headed downstairs again to shift the first load into the equally ancient dryer, and put in the second.

And thought, maybe, depending, she could do the bathroom if she held off and saved for a year or eighteen months.

So that project went on her mental list. At the bottom.

Next on the current list: groceries.

She left her clean, quiet house for town and with the plan of coming back, putting away the groceries, folding laundry. And then, chores complete, sitting down by the fire and continuing her search.

She couldn't say why Janet Anderson stuck in her mind. Maybe,

maybe because her disappearance coincided with when she herself had felt helpless and pulled away from her own life.

A pretty young woman running to the store for groceries as Sloan did now. Then gone, just gone.

After pulling into the crowded lot, she reminded herself why she tended to food shop after work rather than on the weekend. Add the forecast called for snow. But since she hadn't managed a stop in the last harried couple of weeks, she needed some essentials.

Coffee, Cokes, frozen pizza topped that particular list.

So she braved the madness, which proved not as bad as she'd feared. She followed the list on her phone, and considered it a sign of her returned health that she added some Flamin' Hot Cheetos to her cart. They called to her, and she remained four pounds shy of her prehospital weight.

She wanted those pounds back.

By the time she got in the checkout line, she calculated she had about two weeks' worth. In Annapolis, she'd tended to shop more often because it was easy to swing in for a few things, or if work crowded her schedule, have groceries delivered.

Here, grocery shopping became more of an event, and one—with careful planning—she could limit to two, maybe three times a month.

"Sloan Cooper! You cut your hair. I almost didn't recognize you."

She turned to the woman who'd slid into line behind her.

They'd called her Diane the Disher in high school, as Diane Howe, now Blakley, always had the latest news.

She had her curly brown hair in a jaunty tail scooped back from her pretty face. Deep brown eyes sparkled as she leaned in for a hug.

And Sloan felt the baby bump, and a quick, decisive kick.

"Diane! You're going to be a mom!"

"Five weeks to go. He's going to be a hell of a field goal kicker, like his dad."

Jim Blakley, Sloan remembered. One of the stars of the Heron's Rest High School football team.

"You look wonderful," Sloan told her. Easy to say, as it was absolutely true.

"Oh, I'm starting to waddle like a platypus, but it's worth it. But you."

Diane gripped her hand, and Sloan felt the genuine warmth. "I can't tell you how good it is to see you, how good it is to see you looking just absolutely terrific. I hope you feel the same."

"I do. I appreciate the card you and Jim sent when I was laid up."

As she spoke, Sloan started unloading her cart.

"Hannah—you remember Hannah Otts—she said she saw you out on the lake not long ago. And in your uniform. I'm so happy you moved back to the Rest and you're working again."

"So am I."

"And you bought a house! I'm glad somebody who knows what to do bought that place. I don't know what the Johnsons were thinking. They hardly ever came up here to use it, then trying to make it a vacation rental without sprucing it up. You'll spruce it right."

"That's the plan."

"You always had one. We were all so shocked about what happened. I won't dwell on it because I know you won't want to."

Sloan paused, felt that warmth again. "You were always a good friend, Diane."

"I try to be. And with the baby coming, I'm trying to—I know it sounds New Agey or something—but I'm trying to bring in the light."

"It sounds like somebody's going to be a great mom."

Diane's dark, expressive eyes teared up a little. But she managed a laugh. "That's the plan. It's hard when there's just so much, well, dark out there. It can be such a mean world," she said as she set down the separator and started putting her items on the belt.

"What happened to you, and I don't know if you heard about Sarah Glenn's cousin Zach. You might've met Zach a million years back. His family used to come to the lake for a week every summer. They always rented Serenity—that's one of your family's rentals."

"I remember Sarah. I'm not sure about her cousin."

"He's had a rough time. His wife left him, got custody of their little boy. Broke Zach's heart, and his spirit. He actually tried to kill himself last year."

"I'm sorry to hear that."

"He was doing so much better, Sarah told me. Then a couple weeks ago, he just walked away."

As Sloan set the Cheetos on the belt, she paused. "Walked away?"

"It looks like he did just that. Got off work—he's a bellman at a hotel in Uniontown—and left. Didn't even take his car."

The back of Sloan's neck prickled.

"He left his car? Where?"

"Right there in the hotel lot. Clocked out of work, then just walked away, I guess. Not a word to his family since."

Sloan heard the cashier give her the total, and fumbled for her wallet as she focused on Diane.

"They reported him missing?"

"Oh, sure. His family's beside themselves, worried they'll get word he tried again, you know?"

"Zach Glenn?"

"No, no, it's Tarrington. Sarah's mom's sister's son. Sarah and I—oh, and Hallie Reeder—get together, for sure once a month, on book club night. You should join our group, Sloan. We have a lot of fun."

"It sounds like it, but right now, work and the house keep me really busy. It was wonderful seeing you, Diane."

"Welcome home, Sloan. And I love your hair!"

Sloan sent her a smile, a wave, then got out fast.

Left the car—no, not logical. Possible, yes, possible. If he'd been in crisis, logic didn't always play. But. But.

Left his car, like Janet Anderson, like the dentist in Cumberland.

Three locations, three different types of people.

A woman in her twenties, a middle-aged man, and—she'd check on Zach Tarrington. If he'd come with his family to vacation, during her high school years, she pegged him as not much over thirty.

Verify, she told herself. Don't speculate.

She wanted to verify immediately, but made herself put the groceries away first. The laundry sitting downstairs could wait.

Then she sat at her kitchen table with her laptop, and verified.

Zach Tarrington of Uniontown, Pennsylvania. Age thirty-one. Divorced, father of one. Employed as a bellman for nine years.

Last seen leaving work at approximately midnight on February 6.

She read the details of the report, then, Saturday be damned, contacted the Uniontown police.

She identified herself, gave her badge number, her phone number, and requested a callback from the lead investigator at his earliest convenience.

Knowing she might have to wait until Monday, or later, for that callback, she dug where she could.

She pulled up his photo, studied it. Average-looking guy, she determined. Average height and weight.

An average-looking guy who'd tried to hang himself, she discovered. And was lucky his father was a paramedic with a portable defibrillator on hand.

Lucky, too, she thought as she read details, and read between the lines, to have supportive parents and extended family.

By all appearances, he'd pulled himself out of the hole. He'd gone back to work nine weeks after his suicide attempt.

She made notes.

> Treatment?
> Ongoing therapy?
> Relationships?
> Work absences?

Diane hadn't mentioned abduction, so obviously Sarah hadn't mentioned it to her, or she would have.

That didn't mean the authorities weren't looking in that direction.

She pushed up, got herself a Coke, and let the info roll around.

Why abduct an average guy from a hotel parking lot? The ex-wife— new relationship, jealousy, revenge?

An attempted robbery gone wrong?

Wrong place, wrong time—as it felt for Janet Anderson?

Sitting again, she gave a push on social media accounts and managed to find some wedding pictures, some new parents and baby shots.

From there she jumped to the ex-wife's social media. Jenny Malloy—she'd taken back her maiden name—had accounts primarily, it appeared, to hype an organic skin care line—she was one of the top salespeople thereof. But she personalized it with chatty videos.

Busy single mother—how the line's tincture added to water every morning helped keep skin glowing even under stress.

A photo, looked recent, of her building a snowman with the little boy. With commentary about the importance of sunscreen even in the winter and the miracle of the overnight mask restoring the moisture winter stole.

She clicked through the lists of friends and finally landed on one with an open account with a huge chunk of social posts.

Including one with Jenny Malloy and two men all posing in cocktail-type wardrobe.

> At last! Double date time with my honey, my bestie,
> and her new beau!

Who actually used the term *beau*? Well, Sloan thought, apparently Jenny Malloy's bestie Dani did.

The post was dated February second.

So the ex had a boyfriend, and that could have tripped Zach back into depression.

Had to factor it, Sloan admitted. But she'd be damned if that explained the car. Or the fact she now had three missing persons cases, all with abandoned cars left in parking lots.

Then the time frame, she considered. The end of November, the end of December, and the first week of February.

She pushed up to finish the laundry, and to let it cook in her head.

She beefed up the fire, then, remembering those four pounds, heated up another bowl of chicken soup.

As she ate, she wrote down more questions.

Part of her wanted to contact Joel, brainstorm it with him as they'd used to. But these weren't DNR cases.

They were, she admitted, just a pebble in her shoe. The only way she'd remove it would be to find some answers.

She couldn't drive to Uniontown, interview his ex, his family, his coworkers. That crossed a line.

In any case, those leading the investigation would have done so.

But nothing said she couldn't work them on her own.

She moved everything into the tiny office space.

She printed out photos, newspaper articles, search results.

Slowly, meticulously, she built a case board on a wall someone for some reason had painted Barbie pink.

Since she had no intention of keeping it that way, she used a marker to add times and locations of last-seens, the make, model, year of the cars left behind.

She added spouses, residences, the distance between residence and last-seen.

With her mind focused on possible connections, she answered her phone absently, and in police mode.

"Sergeant Cooper."

"Detective Frank O'Hara, Uniontown PD. What can I do for you, Sergeant?"

"Detective O'Hara, thanks for getting back to me. And on a Saturday."

"No problem. I've got some curiosity why the NRP in Maryland have an interest in a missing persons case in Uniontown, Pennsylvania."

"I'll make it clear this is more a personal interest. A woman went missing from Deep Creek Lake in November. She's believed to have been abducted from the parking lot of her grocery store, where her car was located."

"Yeah, I heard about it. A connection's stretching it."

"A man went missing from Cumberland in December. His car was located in a motel parking lot. In both cases, there's been no trace, no ransom demands, no credit card activity. Both had cell phones, deactivated."

"Did they know each other, Deep Creek and Cumberland?"

"There's no indication they did. From what I know, Arthur Rigsby left behind a successful dental practice, a new model Mercedes sedan, a house worth about eight hundred thousand, a hefty portfolio, a wife—one he was cheating on—a couple of adult kids, grandkids.

"Janet Anderson from Deep Creek had been married just over a year, and from all reports happily."

O'Hara's response was flat. Cop flat. "People don't always know what they think they know."

"Agreed."

But she pushed. If nothing else, she'd lay it out to another cop.

"Anderson was making Thanksgiving dinner for her family and her husband's. Investigators concluded she'd run to the market for a couple of ingredients. She'd spoken to her mother earlier that day to check on a recipe. Her mother states she was nervous but excited.

"There's no evidence she walked away on her own."

"And the cheating dentist?"

"Left a hell of a lot behind, as I said. If it had come to divorce, he'd have lost some, sure. This way, he loses everything."

"You gotta look at the wife."

"Yes. I can only look so far."

"Why are you looking?"

She hesitated, then decided if she wanted a favor, she'd need to be honest.

"Anderson's close to home. I'm in Heron's Rest."

"Been there once. It's nice."

"It is. I was formerly attached to the Criminal Investigative Bureau of the DNR. I've transferred back home. Between that, at the time of Anderson's disappearance, I was on medical leave."

"Hold a minute." The flat, the rote, went out of his tone. "You're the one who got shot outside of Hagerstown a few months back?"

"Yeah. Not my best day."

"How're you doing?"

"Five-by-five now, thanks. I missed the job, Detective, so when I was able, I dug a little into the Anderson case on my own. Have you ever had one that just sticks with you?"

"Sure I have. Look, Sergeant, Zach Tarrington got hit with a hard divorce and it sent him down. He attempted suicide last year."

"I know. He has some family connections here in Heron's Rest."

"Hmm. So it pinches there, too. His ex has a new boyfriend."

"Jesse Roper."

"Family connection tell you?"

"Social media search. I understand the wife's new relationship might have triggered him. But if he hasn't contacted anyone, if there's been no sightings, no credit card transactions. No body. Over two weeks now."

"There hasn't been. You want a look at the file."

"I'd really appreciate a look at the file. Leaving the cars might not be much of a connection, but it isn't zero. And all from parking lots where someone could also park a vehicle."

"I'll give you that. You give me it's more than an hour's drive from Uniontown to Cumberland, has to be a solid hour from Cumberland to Deep Creek."

"I'll give you that. I'd say, if I decided to go into the abduction business, I'd want to put some distance between where I grabbed people. Different jurisdictions."

"Tell you what I'm going to do. I'm going to make a couple of calls, then if I'm satisfied, I'll send you what we've got. It never hurts to have a fresh eye. And the fact is, this one bugs the crap out of me."

"Thanks. I'll save you some time and give you my captains' names and contacts from Annapolis and from up here."

Once she had, O'Hara said, "All right. I'll be in touch."

Something, Sloan thought as she looked back at her very unofficial case board. She had something, if only because she'd shopped on a Saturday.

She made herself step away, and with her phone in her pocket took a walk to clear her mind and keep it clear until she had that something to focus it on.

She walked down her drive, across the road, and down to the lake path.

Lots of Saturday activity, she thought, and those who enjoyed it would probably get another week or two before the ice began to thin. Then, before much longer, there'd be boats, kids fishing off docks, joggers on the paths, more hiking on the trails.

Winter would give way to spring with its bursts of wildflowers. Kits and fawns and cubs would arrive.

But for now, she thought as the first flakes fell, winter kept its grip tight. Tight enough she decided to head back to her fire.

As she did, her phone rang. And reading the display, felt another step of her own coming back.

"Detective O'Hara."

"You passed the audition, Sergeant. I'm sending you the file. And, FYI, we'll be reaching out to the investigators on the Anderson and Rigsby cases."

"That's good news, Detective. It's appreciated."

She quickened her pace back home.


Since he couldn't think of a way to comfortably duck out of dinner at the Coopers', Nash pulled out a bottle of the same wine Sloan had poured for him. He opted to take Sloan at her not-fancy word and pulled out black jeans and a dark green crewneck sweater.

But he shaved first, a process he disliked. He'd tried a beard once, but had liked that even less.

As he shaved he considered the bathroom. Not as bad as the one they'd gutted at Sergeant Cooper's, he thought, but nothing to brag about.

Along the way someone had tried to punch it up with wallpaper, so he had various illustrations of seashells everywhere. The weird yellow shower/tub combo had probably been the rage in the seventies, along with the matching toilet and the sink about the size of a goldfish bowl.

He reminded himself, since there were three on the bedroom level—the second done in baby blue, the third in vomit green—at least he didn't have to share with Theo.

Eventually, they'd rip everything out of this one, make it a good hall bath. Take out a couple walls and turn two of the five bedrooms into en suites.

As he walked back to his bedroom, he heard music thumping from Theo's room, and Theo singing along with Billie Eilish.

Eilish, in Nash's estimation, had no worries about competition there.

As he dressed, he visualized taking down the wall to the next bedroom. He couldn't say why he needed the walk-in closet, as his life no longer required dozens of suits and all that went with them. But he wanted one anyway.

With a coffee station.

More, he wanted the big-ass bath, the wet room, the heated tile floors, the small but snazzy electric fireplace.

A gas one for the bedroom, and the French doors he'd already installed would, eventually, lead out to a deck. A deck where he could drink that coffee and watch the sun shimmer through the trees, catch glints of it on the lake.

Sometime in May, June latest, he promised himself, he'd stand on that deck.

He'd estimated a year, and maybe longer, to complete his plans for the house. Half that if the business stagnated or just crept along.

So far the business was steady enough, so the year seemed right.

No rush on it.

He walked to the French doors that led, for now, to nowhere. After dumping about ten inches, the snow had stopped. Now everything spread still and white. From this height he could see a section of the lake and where someone had built a snowman.

And that, just that, struck him as one more reason he'd made this drastic move and at the perfect time.

He wanted to look out at the still, the quiet, and see a snowman on a frozen lake.

He walked down to Theo's room, gave the door a couple of fist-pounds over the music. Eilish had given way to Imagine Dragons.

"We should get going."

"Right there!" Theo shouted, and Nash went down to get the wine and his coat.

And got a lift when he walked back to scan the kitchen cabinets. Cabinets he and Theo and Robo had set themselves—with some unexpected assistance from Dean Cooper.

Lofting the ceiling and leaving those exposed beams, the bigger, better window, absolutely the right call. Since he rarely cooked, he'd nearly ditched the pot filler, but it looked good. It all looked good.

And tomorrow, they'd install the countertops, maybe even get a start on the backsplash before they'd shift to a client. Another week maybe for the new lights, the new appliances, to finish up the coffee bar, the pantry.

But standing there now he knew whatever talent he had for finance, that work had never given him this visceral sense of pride and accomplishment.

He'd designed this, he and Theo had made it real. This belonged to them as nothing else ever had.

He glanced around as Theo came in—Tic wagging at his heels—gave him a long study.

"I'm clear. Hundred percent over it. I swear to God."

"You better be. Let's go. You're actually taking the dog?"

"They said to bring him. He and Mop are friends."

"That dog would think Jack the Ripper was a friend."

As if he agreed, Tic pranced outside.

"Feels good to go out, with people, I mean. You didn't worry too much when I ran the snowblower this morning while you plowed the drive."

"You weren't sitting beside me in the truck with the windows closed."

"You hardly ever get sick."

"Because I avoid people who are."

Theo gave him an elbow nudge. "You brought me food on trays. Dosed me with the Quils."

"I held my breath. And pushing the NyQuil stopped you from hacking half the night and keeping me up."

Theo just kept smiling. "You brought me Skittles and changed my sheets when I got them sweaty."

"I was doing laundry anyway. What's the deal here? You've been to dinner at the Coopers', so what's the deal?"

"Easy, friendly, and Elsie can cook. It's nothing like, you know. Nothing like that."

Nash figured he'd see for himself as he pulled up at the Coopers', nosing in behind Drea's car because he figured she wasn't going anywhere.

Drea answered the door. Tic rushed in to wrestle with Mop, and Theo immediately wrapped around Drea. She wrapped back.

It occurred to Nash they'd done the same the day before when they'd been well enough for her to stop by during kitchen cabinet installation.

And he admitted, found himself glad, the sergeant had it right. They had something.

"The return from the cold wars," Sloan said as she walked out from the kitchen. While she gave Tic—and Mop—quick rubs, she, too, gave Theo a careful study. "Okay, you pass. Let's have your coats."

Nash decided his jeans and sweater suited, as she wore the same— dark blue jeans, Christmas-red sweater. Some dangles on her ears, but women would do that.

Dangles, he thought, for family dinner. Little studs or tiny hoops with the uniform.

"Come on back."

She led the way to the kitchen that smelled really good. Damn nice kitchen, too, but he'd expected no less.

With her hair free to fall a few inches above the shoulders of a navy V-neck, Elsie closed the door on the top wall oven, turned. Before Nash could offer the wine, Theo walked around the island, kissed her, then exchanged a man hug with Dean.

Family, Nash thought again. Theo soaked it up like a sponge.

"Thanks for the soup, Elsie. It helped me over the finish line."

"You're so welcome. It's good to see you up and around. Wine or beer?"

Nash held out the wine he'd brought. "Thanks for having us."

"Glad to, and oh! This will go so well with the baked tofu! Dean, would you open this lovely wine?"

She handed off the bottle, turned back to smile at Nash. "Tofu really makes a Sunday dinner special, don't you think?"

"Ah, sure."

"Well, that's too bad, because we're having pork roast."

She laughed, then surprised him with a quick hug, a kiss on the cheek. "Such good manners! Sit down, have some wine. The roast is resting, the potatoes are just finishing up. I need to sauté up the green beans."

It was easy, and friendly, and nothing like his Sunday dinner memories. They sat around the table where the food was delicious, served family style, and the conversation flowed.

Not just shop talk. Add sports, movies, flavor it with bits of local gossip and family stories.

They clearly loved and understood each other, Nash thought, but more, they liked each other. And they'd folded Theo right in, had given him what he'd never had.

Family.

"Did you get the rest of the cabinets in?" Dean asked Nash.

"This morning, yeah. Appreciate your help with them yesterday."

"I saw the truck, couldn't resist."

"Theo said you went with color."

"It's a big space. It can handle it. The countertops are coming in the morning so we'll find out if it all works."

"Oh, it's going to work," Theo said.

"One way or another we'll be over at your place by early afternoon," Nash told Sloan. "We might still be on it when you get home, but we'll clear out."

"No problem. I'm going to be late tomorrow."

Elsie sent Sloan a worried look. "You're not working another double?"

"No, no. I need to go to Uniontown after work, talk to somebody. It's just something I'm working on."

"Cop thing." Drea offered Theo more potatoes. He took them. "Do the cop thing, Sloan. Entertain us."

"Yeah, it's good," Theo agreed. "You did me already. Do Nash. Make him a suspect."

"What am I suspected of?"

"Armed robbery. That's a good one. Come on, Sloan. You did me, and we're kind of a set."

"Fine. Suspect is Caucasian male, early thirties, six-one, about one-sixty-five, brown and brown."

"That's hair and eyes," Theo said helpfully.

"I got it."

"Suspect is currently clean-shaven—that's a change," she added. "No visible tattoos or piercings. Suspect has a small, crescent-shaped scar below left thumb. Last seen wearing black jeans, dark green cashmere sweater, black Frye lace-up boots. Suspect fled the scene in a black 2025 Ford F-150 King Ranch with rear tow hitch, Maryland plates Echo-Charlie-Tango-four-six-zero."

She took a sip of wine, magic eyes smiling at Nash over it. "Suspect is armed and dangerous."

Theo let out a cackle. "Cool, right?"

"I'm going with spooky."

"She could always do it," Drea put in. "Even when we were kids. Somehow, it never gets old."

Sloan just shrugged. "It's a handy skill considering my line of work."

Nash picked up his own wine and studied her over it. "I bet."

# CHAPTER SEVENTEEN

Before she drove to Uniontown, Sloan got the okay from O'Hara, and laid out her reasoning with Travis.

"I want to talk to Tarrington's coworker. He's the third I found that fits a pattern. Unexplained disappearance, vehicle left in a parking lot, no trace of the missing. Then you have the three locations, no more than an hour to two hours apart."

"With no known connections or similarities in the MPs," Travis added.

"That we've found as yet. The coworker, Adam Rusk, is the only one who saw anything. And the timing, Cap? That's one of the elements that stuck with O'Hara, too. Rusk states he left work no more than five or six minutes after Tarrington, and he talked to a woman in the parking lot who wanted directions. She got in a white or light-colored van parked beside Tarrington's car."

"Rusk thinks it was parked there," Travis reminded her, as he'd read the file, too.

"So I'll talk to him."

"I'm not going to tell you no, Sloan. It's your own time, and I know you're invested in the Anderson case. Our jurisdiction ends at the state border."

"Understood. I'm just asking questions. Cap, if Tarrington had another crisis, why did he talk to coworkers about taking his kid to a monster truck rally? When they checked his apartment, the tickets were on the fridge. He'd gone out and bought juice boxes, had the weekend marked on the wall calendar with a big heart. But he comes out of work, and instead of getting in his car, walks off and poofs?"

She paused a moment. "When Detective O'Hara cleared me, he let me know he didn't feel the walk-away either.

"And the dentist? Rigsby has his weekly roll with his midlife crisis, gives her important earrings for Christmas, and she gives him—she states—a pair of silver cuff links. But he leaves his Mercedes in the motel lot and, again, poofs?"

"You make a case."

"All evidence indicates abduction with Anderson. It's the same pattern."

"I can't disagree." Travis slowly swiveled back and forth in his big chair. "I'm saying that the investigators on Tarrington have very likely wrung all they can get out of the coworker or any other potential witness. But it never hurts to run it all through again."

"That's what I'm going to do."

He nodded. "If there's a drop left to wring out, I figure you'll catch the drip."

She didn't mind the drive, not through the icy and winter-white hills, along the curving roads. She'd enjoyed her weekend off—such as it was, as she'd spent her Saturday night reading the file on Tarrington, working on her case board, making notes, rolling around theories.

She remembered when she'd squeezed in a date and some comfortable sex on the weekends. Even on weeknights here and there.

While she missed the comfortable sex after a three-month hiatus, she had to accept that activity appeared to be off the table.

One of the officers in her unit showed interest. Attractive, good police, quick wits. But she had three reasons why that added up to one big no. Dating someone in the same squad? Bad idea. She outranked him—bigger, badder idea.

And last, not inconsequential, she just didn't share the interest.

The only real buzz she'd felt in months came from the guy next door.

She had solid reasons why that equaled no.

He lived next door, or essentially next door; he subcontracted for the family business. And his brother and her sister were sleeping together. Not just sleeping together, starry-eyed for each other.

But she comforted herself that at least she'd felt a buzz for someone. Her injuries and long recovery hadn't killed that very human urge.

Since her radar worked just fine, she felt that buzz was mutual.

He'd so obviously felt out of his element, and wary with it at dinner. Initially. She'd watched him relax, sort of step-by-step during the actual meal.

It hadn't been the food, she concluded.

From what she'd read of his background, she imagined Sunday dinners hadn't been a laugh fest during his upbringing.

Theo had adjusted quickly, but then he had Drea. And he seemed the more optimistic type than his brother.

Anyway, too many reasons against getting involved with the interesting and attractive guy next door. Including the fact she had other priorities.

No harm admitting to herself, she thought it a damn shame.

She pulled into the lot and looked over where the file had showed the abandoned car. Staff parked there, farther from the hotel entrance, giving guests the closer slots if they didn't use the valet.

Security lights, she noted, but again, the distance compromised that.

She parked, then went into the hotel and straight to the bell station. She spotted Rusk—she had his photo—standing in his uniform beside a trolley loaded with luggage.

"Mr. Rusk. I'm Sergeant Cooper."

He gave her one nervous look, then glanced toward the reception desk.

"Oh yeah, right. Ah, listen, I've got to load some luggage. The guests are at checkout. I've got a break coming in about ten minutes."

"I can wait, no problem."

"Honest, I don't know what else I can tell you I didn't already tell the detectives."

"I appreciate you giving me a few minutes. I'll wait over there until you're free."

His expression went from nervous to bright and friendly as the checkouts walked their way. "All set? That's good timing. They're just pulling your car up."

She took a chair while he wheeled the trolley out, watched him competently load the luggage, pocket the tip—discreetly.

As the guests drove off, he came back in, went to another man at the bell station.

That one, a couple decades older, shot Sloan a look, frowned, nodded. She rose as Rusk crossed to her.

"I can take some time now. Ah, there's a break room in the back if that's okay."

"Sounds good. Have you worked here long?" she asked, though since she'd run him she already knew.

"A couple of years. I'm taking some courses, accounting, so I mostly cover evenings."

"You and Zach worked the same shift."

He led her through to a small break room. "Yeah, mostly. Ah, you want something?"

"No, I'm fine."

"I'm going to get a ginger ale."

When he had, he sat with her at a small table, then turned the can in slow circles.

"You know, Zach and I weren't real tight. I mean I liked him fine. Like him fine," he corrected. "But we didn't, you know, go out for a beer or hang out and like that. He has a kid and all that, and I'm taking courses. He's older, you know, and got seniority. Not like he shoved that in your face. He's nice. You know how he had some shit—stuff—a while back."

"The divorce, the attempted suicide."

"He was a little sketchy when he first came back, but that eased up. Man, he lived for that kid. Days before he went wherever, he talked about taking the kid to see monster trucks."

"He had tickets for that Saturday."

"Yeah. I don't get that deal myself, but the kid was crazy for them, so Zach got crazy for them. He knew a bunch of those weird names and all that. He went and bought the ear protection for the boy, because they're really loud."

"He left right before you that night."

"Yeah, I was still getting changed. He said, 'See you Monday.' And I told him to have a good weekend like you do. And he said how he couldn't miss. He was really happy, kind of whistling a tune."

"Whistling?" That hadn't been in the file.

"Yeah, I forgot that before. I don't know the tune, right? Just something that sounded happy. We'd had a bunch of check-ins. I had a solid three hundred in tips. He probably had more. So happy."

"You finished changing, then went out."

"Yeah, just a few minutes after him. Just five minutes maybe."

"You saw his car was still in the lot."

He turned the can a few more times.

"I really didn't. I was looking toward my own. I wanted to get home, unwind some, get a good night's sleep so I could study most of the next day."

"Walk me through it from there."

"Okay." He finally opened the ginger ale, took a drink. "As I headed toward my car, this woman walked over. I told the other cops I just couldn't describe her much. She was all bundled up. It was really cold that night. She had like a hat, scarf, parka—I think. Anyway, she asked for directions, said she'd taken a wrong turn. So I gave her directions, and she said thanks and something about her daughter or sister or somebody wondering why she was late."

"This was after midnight."

"Yeah. Not long after, I guess. I went to my car, and she walked back toward this van. Maybe white or beige, maybe light gray. I don't know if I'd have noticed, but as I was getting in my car, she pulled out and gave me a wave."

"You didn't see anyone else in the van?"

"No, ma'am, I didn't. I only know it pulled out from beside Zach's car—I think it did—because I heard when he didn't pick up his kid, his dad went to his place, then he came here, saw the car. He called the police. Then they came and talked to a bunch of us. Some think maybe he walked off so he could go somewhere else and do himself for real."

"You don't."

For the first time, he met her eyes and held them.

"No, ma'am, I don't. I've thought and thought about it, and I just don't. He was happy when he clocked out. He's always happy when it's his weekend with his kid, but he was especially happy because he was giving the kid this big treat, you know? How could he be so happy, then turn around and walk off like that in five minutes?"

Then he shrugged, drank again. "I don't know. I'm going to be an accountant, not a psychiatrist."

She talked to him a few more minutes, but the only new element? A happy whistle.

Since she'd driven up, she talked to his supervisor, then a couple more coworkers.

Opinions varied, but one stuck hard.

His son was the center of his world.

By the time she got home, dark had fallen. Light shined in her windows, and the Ford truck sat outside.

Not good timing, she thought, not when she felt frustrated on so many levels. She wanted a drink, her pj's, and quiet time.

Tic rushed her at the door, wriggled as she petted.

Then she walked in to a fire in the hearth, her walls shining under new lighting, the Shaker door on her closet.

And Nash on a ladder, installing what looked like the rest of her trim.

He looked particularly good—due no doubt to her level of sexual frustration—in a faded denim shirt, work pants, and boots and holding a nail gun.

He glanced down. "Thought you'd be later."

"I'm not." With a kind of purr, she ran her hand down the new closet door.

She took a few steps, studied the matching one on her bathroom, then turned a circle.

"This is exactly right. So are the lights, and the trim. And—you hung the mirrors."

"Your mom came by. She wouldn't take no."

"Well, she's exactly right, as usual. It's cozy, but not cramped and dark and sad. You're working alone?"

"Theo and Robo had a date."

She'd walked into the kitchen for a dog biscuit, and glanced back. "They're dating each other now?"

"Ha. Theo's still heart-eyes over your sister."

She pointed; Tic sat. And the biscuit was his.

"I should go back and just say, with some surprise: Robo has a date?"

"Yeah." The nail gun did the whoosh-bang. "I've never seen anybody so worked up about going bowling."

"Maybe he fears gutter ball humiliation."

"Could be it." He glanced down at her. "Look, I can clear out, but if you give me another twenty, I can finish, clean up, then clear out. Robo can come in tomorrow while you're at work and seal this trim."

"That works for me. All of this works for me." She made that purring sound again when she opened the closet, saw the new shelves. "Yes, it does."

"I've given the matter some thought, and evaluation. My conclusion? That's the most organized coat closet in my experience with coat closets."

"I like to know where things are, which means they need to be where they're supposed to be."

She took off her gun, put it in its holder on the top shelf.

"I'm having a drink. Do you want a drink?"

"Not when I'm working."

*Whoosh-bang.*

He measured for the next piece, then came down from the ladder to cut it.

She waited until the saw went quiet.

"How'd the counter install go?"

"Like my nanny used to say, like butter."

"You had a nanny." She saw him stiffen, just a tad. Then shrug.

"Sure, doesn't everybody? I started on the backsplash. Just wanted to see how it would look. I wanted a pop there because we went with white, minimal graining, on the counters."

He measured for the next, turned. Stopped.

She stood in front of her ugly kitchen, holding a wineglass. She'd loosened her tie.

"What?"

"You loosened your tie. It's a look. It's a good look."

Since he went back, measured again, she smiled.

She could read signals, and she'd caught a few from him. But this one was the clearest.

The buzz absolutely wasn't just on her end.

"Why don't you have a date?" she asked him.

"Because I'm trimming this window. Why don't you?"

"Because I drove to Uniontown after work to talk to a guy."

"That sounds like a date."

"No."

"What then?"

She started to brush that off, then changed her mind.

"Have you eaten?"

"Not yet. I'll mic something when I finish here."

"I'm not going to cook, even if it wasn't nearly eight. But I have a frozen pepperoni pizza I'm willing to share."

He glanced back at her. "Like a date?"

"Again no. Call it an exchange. Pizza, wine or soft drink. I don't have any beer. I lost my taste for it after tossing it and everything else in my system after a college kegger."

"Been there. What's the exchange?"

"You're not a cop, but you seem like a reasonably smart and logical person."

"Thousands agree."

"The guy I used to partner with, professionally, is having his first kid pretty soon. I don't want to pull him into bouncing this around with me. You're already here."

"It's a cop thing?" He paused in his work. "Isn't Uniontown outside your borders?"

"Yes. I have strong reason to believe what happened there is connected to two cases in Maryland."

"Sure, why not? I can listen. I get pizza out of it. And you've got good taste in wine."

"I dated a sommelier for about ten minutes once. I'll get the oven going."

When she had, and he put the nail gun in its case, picked up the Skilsaw, she walked over to take one of the sawhorses.

"I'll get those."

"I've got it."

Without bothering with coats, they carted tools and supplies out to his truck with Tic following happily both ways.

On the second trip, she looked over at him. "I should be up front and tell you I can't sleep with you."

His eyes, heavy-lidded and what she thought of as dark chocolate, met hers. "Well, that's direct."

"Direct's best."

She went back in, and since she wouldn't go out again, pulled off her boots.

"Even direct," he said as he came in behind her, with the dog on his heels, "begs the question why."

"I've got a lot going on, and not much time for . . . recreation," she decided. "But more, our siblings are sleeping together, and very likely dreaming of a wedding, a honeymoon, a couple of kids. You and me having sex while they're having sex and dreams? Just weird."

"Maybe. But they'd have it where they have it, we'd have it elsewhere."

"True. With or without the element of siblings, I draw a hard line at group sex."

"We have a point of agreement."

She got out a bag of dog food, filled a bowl from a cabinet, added another bowl of water.

As she took out the pizza to unbox, Tic made himself at home.

"You also live essentially next door, so potential for sticky. Stickier, you subcontract for my family. It's smarter to keep it at pizza."

When the oven dinged, she slid the pizza in. "Want that wine now?"

"Yeah, I do. What makes you think I want to sleep with you anyway?"

"I'm a trained observer."

He glanced down at the tiny scar under his thumb. "I've got to give you that one."

"Have a seat. I'm going to start bouncing."

At ease, he leaned on her counter. "I could make a crude sexual innuendo about bouncing."

"But again, in my observation, you're not. Crude. Maybe when it's just the guys, sure. I work with men, add cops. I know crude. So."

She joined him at the tiny square table.

"On the day before Thanksgiving, a woman goes missing from Deep Creek Lake. Middle twenties, white, middle-class. Married just over a year—together since college. By all accounts happily. They'd saved up, bought their first home, were talking about starting a family. They were hosting their families for Thanksgiving, for the first time."

Picking up her wine, Sloan frowned into it. "She's excited, nervous, took the Wednesday off from work to prep. Checked with her mom on a recipe, made a pretty, seasonal centerpiece for the table. Then, evidence indicates, she realized she needed something from the store. She drove to her local grocery. And that's it."

"What's it?"

"Gone. Her car was found in the lot. Her phone was disabled or destroyed. She had nothing but her purse with her."

Now Sloan drank.

"No ransom demands, no crazed exes, no addictions, no affairs, no witnesses or signs of struggle on the scene. And no trace of her since."

"Don't you guys always look at the husband, or wife depending, first? I read," he added. "Watch the occasional cop movie."

"Yes, and he's clear. The investigators believe, with solid reasons, she was abducted. And at this point, she's either forcibly imprisoned, was sold, or, most likely, dead."

"Did you know her?"

"No. Though the department assisted in the search, I wasn't involved at that time. Medical leave." Her eyes lifted to his, held evenly. "You'd have heard about that."

"Yeah, I heard about it."

When he left it at that, she found herself surprised, and grateful. Rising, she got out plates.

"For reasons, her case stuck with me. Since I had a lot of time on my hands until recently, I followed the investigation, then I started a search. Missing persons, like crimes, narrowed it to Western Maryland, West Virginia, Pennsylvania."

"Kept your hand in."

"You could say that."

She got napkins, a jar of red pepper flakes, the pizza cutter.

"I had a file going. In it, I had a male, middle fifties, a dentist with a solid practice in Cumberland."

She gave him those details as she checked on the pizza, stepped back to top off his wine and hers.

"The connections. A car left in a parking lot, gone with no trace, and leaving a life behind. At the same time, you've got a pretty young woman in a happy marriage, and a middle-aged man having a weekly round with a woman about half his age in various motels. So it's in the file, but it doesn't stick out."

"Until?"

When she took out the pizza, Tic got up, sniffed the air.

"This isn't yours," Sloan said, but got out a bully stick. "This is for good dogs. Are you a good dog?"

She pointed, he sat.

"Yes, you're a very good boy."

Thrilled, Tic plopped down to gnaw.

"Until," Nash prompted again. "You've got my attention."

"Uniontown."

She laid it out as she sliced the pizza, slid two pieces on each plate, the spare two on another. She set one plate in front of Nash, one for herself, and the third in the middle of the table.

She shook red pepper over her two slices; Nash did the same.

She wound through Zach Tarrington while they ate the first slice.

"So now I've got three, different locations, different lifestyles, different types, even different times of day, but all with a car left behind in a parking lot, all missing without a trace."

"Except for a woman and a white van in the last one."

"Yes."

"Why would a woman, apparently alone, park so far from the hotel if she needed directions?"

Sloan lifted both hands, snapped them in the air as she said again, "Yes! You're lost, it's midnight, most logical is a gas station, and she'd have passed more than one in either direction. Even if you decide to ask at the hotel, you pull up to the entrance."

"Could've pulled in, parked to look at a map, or make a phone call."

"Yeah, yeah, yeah." She blew out a breath, picked up her second slice. "But she just happens to park beside Tarrington's car?"

"Probably," he reminded her. "But say she did. How does she get this guy into the van, within a few minutes, without a struggle, some noise? How did she know when he'd come out to his car in the first place? Same with the other two, right? The first, she's out of eggs or whatever, runs to the store. Not planned. The second, you said he rotated motels. The last, okay, a regular sort of schedule, but they'd have to know his car."

He drank some wine.

"You said there's no—what was it?—intersect between the three. Like they went to the second guy to get their teeth cleaned, or used the hotel where the third one worked. No friends or relatives in common or in the other areas—you were pretty thorough. Didn't use the same gym, shops, that sort of thing. So how does this woman know them? Has to know them to pick them, right?"

Sitting back, Sloan studied him. "You're good at this."

"Thanks." He toasted her. "It's my first time."

"She could be cruising. They're in the wrong place at the wrong time, she's in the right place, right time for her purposes."

"What's her purpose?"

"I don't know that yet." So saying, she nudged the extra plate toward him.

"You're done?"

"Two's my limit."

"I can do three," he said, and took a third slice. "Okay, say she's cruising, how'd she hit on the first one?"

"She might've been there already, waiting for someone else to come out, then there's Janet Anderson, and opportunity."

He studied her as he ate. "But you don't really think so."

"No, I don't really think so. Shit. I think all three were targets, but I don't know why. Except a lot more people than most think are just crazy."

"I hear that. Do you really want to hear what I think?"

"I'm sharing my dinner and giving up my breakfast pizza, aren't I?"

He smiled at her. She had to admit he had a good one when he used it. "You stock the same brand we do. I think you're right."

"About what?"

"All of it. I'd have to think the woman in the van has help. Like even if she forced the bellman into the van at gunpoint, wouldn't there have been some noise? And why would he stay in the van when she walked over to talk to the second bellman?"

"You paid attention," Sloan murmured.

"That was the deal."

"There are two of them," she agreed. "Could be more than two, but at least two."

"So a team, of uncertain number. They pick somebody. Maybe they were in the news for some reason, maybe they cut the van off down the road somewhere, posted something the bad guys didn't like in some comment section, outbid them on eBay or whatever. It doesn't take much to set the crazy off."

She took the plates to load in the not always reliable dishwasher. "Not if the crazy's already there."

"They've been about a month apart so far as you know."

"That's right." Yes, she thought, he paid attention.

"There has to be a common denominator. You said the dentist had money."

"I'd put him just above rich into the wealthy category."

"People like him, who work out a plan to cheat with a young blonde?

They don't walk away from wealth. If he planned to walk, he'd have found a way to secure some of the money first. The woman? I can see there might've been some shit happening inside the marriage nobody knew about. But if she'd decided to run, she'd have kept driving. Plus, you said she had a tight relationship with her parents, her sibling."

"She did. And a close circle of friends."

"The last guy? Maybe he has a breakdown, decides to go off."

"Between his locker and the parking lot?"

"He might've walked off whistling because he knew he was going. People leave their kids behind, Sarge, all the damn time. But he left the car. No reason to leave the car. If he'd decided to go, or decided to kill himself again, why not take the car and drive off a bridge somewhere?"

Nash shrugged. "What do I know? I'm a contractor. But from where I'm sitting, you've got a common denominator in the car—that's aftermath. You just need to find the common denominator in the before."

"Because I'm right, and all three were targets of the same person or persons."

"Because you're right."

"Because I'm right," she repeated.

He wasn't Joel, wasn't Cap, but she felt vindicated. The time, the effort, the trip to Uniontown, the ones she planned to take to Deep Creek, to Cumberland.

Vindicated.

"Thank you!" Grabbing his face in her hands, she leaned down, kissed him.

And quickly—maybe not quite quickly enough—pulled back.

"That was reflex," she told him.

"Okay." He got to his feet. "So's this."

He yanked her back. She had time to think: Trouble's coming, before he drew her up to her toes and covered her mouth with his.

# CHAPTER EIGHTEEN

He woke urges she'd tried to quell, then sent them racing through every cell in her body. Giving in to the moment, she moved in rather than away and let herself soak in the pleasure of just feeling again.

His hands moved up her sides, strong, sure, then down again.

Tic, wanting his share of attention, tried to wiggle between them.

Easing back, eyes still on Sloan's, Nash snapped, "Sit!"

Because her lips felt tender, warm and tender, Sloan lifted a finger to rub over them. "You have considerable skill."

"Thanks. I've been working on it for a while."

"Good job. Ah, the reasons against this still apply."

"Do they, though?"

"We should talk about them. I like to think things through, weigh the pros and cons, rather than act on impulse, so we should talk about them. Later."

Hands gripping his shoulders, she boosted up to wrap her legs around his waist and fuse her mouth to his.

"I know this is stupid," she managed as he skirted around the dog and started for her bedroom.

"Odd. It feels really smart to me."

"Stupid," she said as she pressed her lips to his cheek, his neck. "It's just that I haven't done this since . . . for a few months. I'm probably overeager."

"There's no such thing. If it matters"—since the dark was deep, he slapped on the switch for the dinky overhead light in her bed-room—"I haven't either."

"Well, why—" She broke off when he dumped on the bed, and his body pressed hers into the mattress. "We'll talk later."

"Sure."

His mouth took hers again, and his hands began to move.

Her system soaked in sensation like rain after a drought. For too long everything in her had focused on healing, on feeling whole again. This, this elemental need met was another kind of healing.

She was alive, a woman with appetites and desires who was desired in turn.

She reveled in it, and wanted more.

His weren't the soft hands that had last touched her this way, but hard, strong, and sure. They demanded exactly what she wanted to give.

She shoved away the denim shirt, tugged up the dark tee under it. To take exactly what she wanted to take. To feel with her own hands that solid wall of chest that pressed against her, to dig them into the muscled shoulders, his back, the ripple of biceps.

And purred as she had over her new closet door.

He'd wanted her like this more than he'd admitted. Still, he'd have slowed his pace, gentled his touch, but she clearly wanted neither. So when she rolled, he went with her.

Those eyes, wicked fairy eyes now, stayed on his as she unhooked her utility belt.

"Not smart, not smart," she said, but let it drop on the floor.

But when she started to tug off her tie, he pushed up to do it him-self.

"The uniform kills me. Makes no sense, but it kills me. Let's see what happens when I get you out of it."

He made quick work of the tie, then the shirt. Then his gaze fo-cused on the scar inches from her heart.

In the dim light, it struck him as surprisingly round, still pink around the edges. A vicious souvenir of violence.

When she started to lift a hand to cover it, he closed his hand over hers, looked back into her eyes. Because he saw distress, he followed instinct and laid a hand over the wound and her heart as he brought his lips back to hers.

This time tenderly.

She trembled, started to pull away.

"I'm not fragile."

"No, you're sure as hell not." Keeping her close, he flipped open the hook of her bra. "And so far, even out of uniform, you just kill me."

He laid her back again, kissed her again. This time not so gently.

He took her back where she wanted to be, where there was no thought, only feeling, where she could let go of everything but that single, focused, desperate need.

Those rough, seeking hands didn't make her feel fragile, but demanded she give and she take in equal measure.

As her heart pumped wild under his hands, she yanked at his belt. She wanted all of him, everything, and now. Could barely breathe for the urgent beat of her own blood as he dragged her pants down her legs. As his hands followed them down her thighs.

"I want—I want—"

He said, "Shh." Covered her mouth with his, slid his hand up between her legs.

She erupted, cried out in release as the first glorious orgasm tore through her, ripping off scars she hadn't realized closed off emotions, need, longings.

Pulsing pleasure spread through her, bringing back to life what she'd feared had died while the rest of her survived.

She quaked under him, hips arching, nails digging in. Her eyes met his again, the green of them madly beautiful. Then she wrapped her legs around him once more.

"Now. Right now."

He drove into her, wasn't sure he could have stopped himself if someone had held a knife to his throat. The hunger for her, for this, clawed inside him, an animal he couldn't cage.

Fast, rough, he took and he took while the air burned in his lungs, while she met his every desperate thrust.

She came again. He watched those eyes go opaque, felt her body shudder, then go lax. But still he didn't, couldn't, stop.

With a half sob she began to move again, to meet him again.

She fisted a hand in his hair, dragged him down into a kiss that burned into the savage.

"God! God, yes. Again."

This time when she peaked and she fell, he had no choice but to follow her.

She lay splayed out on the bed. Used up. Melted. Burned out.

Even the barest whisper of tension in her body had been snuffed out. Any hint of stress in her mind, blown away into utter contentment.

Keeping her eyes closed, she basked in it.

"I know that was stupid, and I don't care. Jesus, Littlefield, you're really good at it."

He lay sprawled, staring blindly up at the popcorn ceiling, the dinky light. "I can honestly say: Back at you, Cooper. That's a hell of a body you got on you. What do you curl?"

"I'm up to fifteen. I had to start back at two. The dog's whining."

"Yeah, I hear him. Needs to go out. I'll be back."

He sat up, yanked on his pants. "You want anything?"

"Maybe water. A half gallon should do it."

"I'll take the other half."

When he went out, she let herself float. Not toward sleep, she thought, but into bliss. Then remembered her utility belt, and rose to pick it up, set it on the dresser.

He walked back in, the dog loping with him, as she stood naked by the bed.

"There's a picture." He handed her one of the two glasses of water.

"Thanks." She sat, then decided the hell with that. She piled up pillows, lay back against them.

He sat, work pants low on his hips and still unbuttoned.

"I saw you before."

"Hmm."

"Back late November, early December, walking with Mop."

"Oh. Right." She remembered seeing him and Theo, thinking them tourists. "And thought poor, pathetic woman. Felt sorry for her."

"No, actually." He raked his fingers back through his hair, which did nothing to tame it. "I thought you looked tired, shaky, and like every step brought you pain. But you just kept walking. I admired you for that."

Her gaze shifted to his.

"I didn't know who you were then, or what had happened to you. I admire you more now that I do. Coming back from that takes guts."

"What choice was there? Come back, and it felt like an inch at a time, or give up?"

"That's a choice."

She let out a sigh, finished the water, then set the glass aside. "I nearly made the other one. At least I think I did."

"Think?" Though he enjoyed looking at that excellent body, he tossed the throw at the foot of the bed over her, then propped himself up beside her.

"I don't know why I'm telling you. Why not? Maybe it was a dream, but . . . No, it wasn't. I died on the table in the OR, just a few minutes, but . . ."

"I know. Theo told me."

"How did he—"

"Drea."

"Drea." She shut her eyes. "I didn't think they knew that. I never told them about it."

"If we're playing that game, she told Theo the doctor told her and your parents. And the guy who was with you when you got shot."

"Of course he did. Of course. I just shut that out, and they've never pushed. Well, I'll deal with that later. When it happened, when my heart stopped, I saw myself. I looked down at myself."

"Seriously?" Rather than the doubt, even amusement she'd expected, he looked interested. "Like a near-death thing?"

"Not near. I was. And I felt so calm, so quiet, weightless, and well, free. *Look how hard they're working, and I'm fine up here.* Or wherever I was. I didn't feel panicked, but—have to use the word—peaceful."

She could bring it back, see it all again.

"I'm just sort of floating, and I saw Joel. He'd have been out in the corridor. He was talking to his wife, telling her I was in surgery. And he told her I wouldn't give up. I'd fight. I was tough, I was strong. I wasn't finished yet and I wouldn't give up. My blood was on his uniform. He was crying.

"I thought, well, I guess I can't just go. And I didn't. I don't remember anything else, not clearly, until I woke up a few days later."

She shrugged. "I'd say most people don't believe in that sort of thing."

"Sounds real enough to me."

She tilted her head toward his. "Does it?"

"Why not? Maybe it's just a consciousness thing. Heart stops, but that part's still working. So you see, feel, hear, or get impressions. Somebody who matters to you is telling you not to give up, and you don't. Add a medical team zapping you back."

"I can still see it. It's like . . . Wait!" She shot straight up. "Wait! Zapping me back. Wait."

She rolled off the bed, grabbed his shirt because it was handy. Swinging it on, she rushed to the door.

"What? That's my shirt."

He rolled off himself, hitched up his pants, and went after her.

Hoping for more playtime, Tic followed.

He caught up with her as she pushed open the door to the room she used as an office. She hit the lights, then beelined for her laptop.

As she booted it up with one hand, grabbed a file beside it with another, he stared at the wall.

Pictures—of people, cars, parking lots, and more—crowded together with printouts of articles, handwritten notes. More notes she'd obviously written with a marker right on the wall itself.

"Interesting decor. A bold choice."

"Zapped him back. Tarrington's father, paramedic, portable defibrillator. Brought him back."

"So you said."

"Janet Anderson, paddleboarding last summer, fell off, board hit her head, and she went under. It's in the file. You look at the husband. Cleared him, he's clear. Didn't pay much attention before. But . . . Yes!"

"What?"

"Required CPR, mouth-to-mouth. Got her on the patrol boat. Officer First Class Wilber—I know him—resuscitated her. He brought her back. I forgot. I didn't connect it."

Since the room didn't boast another chair, Nash stood, shoved his hands in his pockets. "Okay."

She sat, and her fingers started flying over the keyboard.

"Maybe Rigsby—the dentist—maybe he had an accident, a heart attack, something, and required . . . Cumberland's not that big a town, but there's a local paper. He's had a practice there for more than twenty-five years. Big house, fancy car, prominent citizen."

Curious now, Nash walked around behind her.

"See, here he is, last October—Halloween bash."

She brought up another, highlighting his practice's pediatric dental work, another in the spring when he and his wife attended a local fundraiser.

"Here! Single car accident a year ago last December. Icy road, Mercedes versus tree. Tree wins. Critical condition. Need more."

"You can't just go into somebody's medical records. HIPAA."

"Yeah, yeah, the investigators can get more, but . . . His wife uses social media. And he has a professional page. I didn't go back this far."

So he watched as she sat, swamped in his work shirt, going back through Karen Rigsby's social posts.

Food pictures, kid pictures whizzed by. Photos of Karen and her husband beaming, Karen with a group of women, happy birthday posts.

She stopped at a post in March topped by a header.

**ART COMES HOME TODAY!**

It's been a long haul with a lot of tears, a lot of worry, and a lot of work. Art and I, and our whole family, want to thank

all of you for your prayers, your support during this diffi-
cult time. We will never forget the friends and neighbors
who did so much to help. I don't know what I'd have done
without you.

Our deep and sincere gratitude goes out to the wonderful doctors and nursing staff at UPMC. Your skill, dedica-
tion, and kindness meant everything to all of us. At every
step and stage, you went above and beyond.

So, so many thanks to the first responders. Without your
quick action, your skill, I would have lost my husband, our
children their father, our grandchildren their pop. You
brought him back to us, and now he's coming home.

"Brought him back."

"I get it, but that could just mean they got him out of the wreck."

"Going back, back to February. She'd have posted on it."

She skimmed over progress reports—she'd read them later—and
scrolled back to the first post on the accident.

"Here. Just happened, she's calling for prayers. Worked late, accident. She's scared, not as coherent as her other posts."

"Small wonder."

"Concussion, internal injuries, in surgery. Collapsed lung, and bang.
'Art's big, generous heart stopped on the way to the hospital. They had
to shock it to start it beating again. Please, please, send all your prayers
that it keeps beating, that he heals and comes home to us.'"

"Son of a bitch," Nash muttered. "Looks like you found that common denominator."

"Three for three?" He saw those fairy eyes go fierce. "That's not
coincidence. That's deliberate. That's the reason."

"What kind of a reason is that? We're going to grab people up
who've been dead for a minute?"

"Probably not that simple, but that's the crux. Three different hospitals, different locations. How do they know? How do they pick? Where
are they holding them? Or more likely, where are the bodies? A lot of
questions.

"But this is the reason." She nodded, tapped the screen. "This is the motive."

"So what do you do now?"

"Talk to my captain tomorrow. Pass what I've got on to the investigators in each case. Start looking for more with this connection, as Janet Anderson might not have been their first. Find the answers to the lot of questions."

"They were grabbed up about a month apart, right?"

"Yes, and yes, they'll have another picked out."

"You fit. It could be you."

Tic wedged in, so she rubbed his head.

"I was in Hagerstown—the hospital. Out of their range. And it's really risky to go after a police officer. But since I've been there, I can tell you they stole that second chance, wiped out all the pain and effort of healing and moving on. Killed the joy and relief of the families at having their loved one alive.

"And that pisses me off."

She switched off the computer.

"I've got regular duty tomorrow, but I'll make time for this. Hell, maybe this is another reason I came back. I'll make time for this."

"If you want me to take off, I'm going to need my shirt."

She glanced up over her shoulder, then shifted her chair so she could stand up in the limited space.

"You know how I said we'd talk later about the thing we shouldn't be doing?"

"Now you want to talk?"

"No, I think we should go back and do the thing we shouldn't be doing again. Then we'll have more to talk about later."

"That works for me. I still want my shirt back."

She smiled. "Come and get it."

He left early, but had a chance to try out her new shower—with her in it.

She surprised him. Not just the sex, and he could admit now he'd imagined that before the reality of it.

The reality far outpaced his imagination.

Having her ask him to listen to her theories on police work, that had surprised him. The way her mind worked surprised him, though it shouldn't have, he thought. He'd seen how she approached the improvements to her house.

Step by logical step.

He'd enjoyed being with her—and not just in bed, or the shower. He'd enjoyed sitting, listening, talking over pizza in her ugly kitchen. And standing in that poor excuse for a home office watching her dig for answers.

That wall, he remembered as he let himself and the dog in the house. That showed a lot more than casual, professional interest.

It showed an investment of time, of effort, and over three people she'd never met.

He went back to the kitchen, fed the dog, got coffee, looked out the big window at the snow, the trees, the path he'd cleared to the workshop.

He'd surprised himself, he admitted, telling her he'd seen her walking, that he'd admired her. Usually, he tended to be more cautious in sharing his personal thoughts.

But there'd been something about her, sitting there, that excellent body marred by that scar so close to her heart.

Not marred, he corrected immediately. More a badge, he decided, for someone who'd faced the worst and fought back.

Now, he realized, he was thinking about her too much. They'd had sex—really good sex. He found her interesting, appealing, all fine. No need to dwell on it.

He looked down at the dog. "And I guess, since we never did reach that later for talking about why not, we'll keep the whole thing between us. No blabbing out of you."

Tic wagged, then rushed over to pick up the old pair of socks Theo had knotted together.

"Not now." But Nash gave the other end of the socks a couple of tugs. "I have to go change my famous shirt. Got work to do, and the appliances are coming. Thank Christ."

He'd started downstairs again when Theo came in, and Tic raced to greet him.

"Finished the trim at Sloan's," Nash began. "I've got Robo going over to poly it. I'm going to work on the backsplash. Since we've got the appliances coming, and aren't scheduled to start the Kildare job until tomorrow, you can start on the crown molding in the dining room."

"Yeah, sure."

Giving Tic an absent pat, Theo walked by him in what Nash considered a daze.

"You okay?"

"Huh? Good. Great. You?"

"Fine." Unsure, Nash followed his brother back to the kitchen. "No coffee at Drea's?"

"What? Oh, coffee. Yeah, I'll get some."

"Did she suck out your brains through your ears last night?"

"We had a really good time," Theo said, and dreamily. "We decided to stay in, so we made dinner."

"And did a lot of drugs?"

Theo stopped staring into space long enough to laugh. "Come on, man! We put on music, and talked. So, I need you to come with me."

"Where?"

"To buy the ring. The engagement ring."

"The—" They didn't have the counter stools yet or Nash would've sat on one. Immediately. "You asked her to marry you?"

"Not yet. I need the ring first. I'm going to do this right."

At that moment, Theo looked so young to him. Impossibly young and open, and the next thing to shiny.

"Maybe doing it right should involve a few more months of being with someone."

"I know it's quick." The dreaminess cleared with an easy smile. "But she's it. Nash, she's it for me. I knew it the first time I saw her, and I feel it more now. I didn't know I could feel this way about somebody, anybody. Like I can see us together in a year, in ten years. Building a life together, having a family."

Theo gave a quick little shrug. "When you come from what we did, you wonder if you can ever have that. I know I can with Drea.

"You like her."

"Sure I like her. She's likable. Her whole family's likable."

"I love her," Theo said simply. "She loves me. So I need you to come with me when I buy the ring. I don't want to screw up there."

"What do I know about buying a ring? I've never bought one."

Because Tic made his needs known, Theo let him out.

"You won't let me go overboard. She wouldn't want something overboard. It's not her. She'd want classic. And if she says yes, you'd be my best man, so you could start now."

"Jesus Christ. You're absolutely serious."

"Absolutely serious. Positively sure. I haven't ever been this sure about anything. Coming here, talking you into taking me into the business, that comes close."

Theo finally made the coffee.

"And I was right about that. So, you'll come with me, won't you?"

"Yeah, I'll come with you." Nash dragged both hands through his hair. "It might—hell, it will take me a while to process this."

"If she says yes, I'm hoping we can get married in the fall, whatever kind of wedding she wants."

"One giant step at a time, Theo."

"Yeah, but. Drea deserves whatever kind of wedding she desires, and time to plan it. I don't want to push for sooner because I really want to get started."

He turned back with his coffee. "I'm not going to invite them, Nash." His eyes went hard, determined. "I know if they find out, they'll hit at you about it more than me."

"Don't think about that now."

"I have thought about it. We both know how they'd react, how they'd take shots at Drea, and I won't have it. And I'll make it clear it's my decision."

"Have you talked to Drea about them?"

"Yeah. She knows it all. She knows why it's just you and me. She said how some people don't know how to be parents, or family. And we were lucky to have each other, you and me, because we knew how to be family."

A little dreamy again, Theo let Tic back in.

"See why I love her?"

"Yeah, I do. I may end up half in love with her myself. Where the hell do you buy an engagement ring around here?"

Theo grinned. "I'll find out."

"Later. Now get to work. Since it looks like you'll be moving out by or before the fall, I need to wring all the work out of you I can."

Then it hit him. "Do you want her to move in here?"

"No. I mean there's room, sure, but it's going to be a construction zone for a while."

He bent down, obliged Tic with some tug.

"We'll find a place. I'd really like us to find a place we can start building that life together. So you're stuck with me until."

"Then stop playing with the dog and go get a hammer."

# CHAPTER NINETEEN

Sam caught the bug at the tail end of its run through the tristate area.

He didn't get as sick as most—and Clara credited that to his strong constitution, boosted by some extra doses of blood mixed in the soups and stews she made for him.

At his insistence, she'd gone back to work. Though they'd hit a nice jackpot with Zach Tarrington's cash tips, they couldn't afford to have both of them off work for too long.

She came home on his third day down to find him not only up and around, but with supper waiting.

"Sam! You shouldn't've done all this. You only kicked that fever out yesterday."

And to make sure it had stayed out, she put the back of her hand on his forehead.

"Feeling pretty good, and I figured we both deserved a steak dinner, so I went out and bought us some T-bones."

He gave her a wink out of eyes she found, with relief, clear.

"I can't fry up chicken like my Clara, but I know how to fry up a steak. You let me know when you were heading home, so I got them and taters staying warm in the oven. Got some peas and carrots going because I know how you are about putting something green on the plate."

Delighted, she gripped her linked hands under her chin. "This is such a treat!"

"You sit right down at the table, babe. I'll get us some cold beers."

"I could sure use one. I put in a day and a half on shift, I swear. Three-car pileup, and we got the injured." She sat, sighed as her feet thanked her. "A couple treated and released, another concussed, and we got two in surgery. I'm glad to put this day behind me."

"You do that now."

He brought the beer, then took out the plates to add the carrots and peas from the saucepan.

"This looks so good. Biscuits, too!"

"Not your homemade ones. I popped them out of the Doughboy roll." Grinning, he mimed slapping the package on the edge of the table.

"They look just right. I'm so glad you're well again."

"Me, too, babe. We sure had us a down-and-out February and right into March between us. But that's over now, and we're good to go."

"Spring can't come soon enough." She ate a bite of steak. "This sure hits the spot. You're my hero, doll."

"You're my queen, babe. With all the blowing and hacking we've done, we haven't had much time for our most important work."

"That's the God's truth." She cut open her baked potato. As the steam rose, she loaded on the margarine. "I did do some looking and calculating while you were down. But I can't deny I was distracted with you so sick. Just couldn't clear my head of the worry."

"No worries now, babe."

"There were two I kept going back to, but I need to look again, see if I get my feeling."

"Tell me about them."

"I got a man, sixty-two if I recollect. In for gall bladder surgery. Should've been routine, but he coded on them in recovery. Now we know, doll, there's a reason for that."

With the sober nod of the faithful, Sam cut another piece of meat. "His time. Just that simple."

"That's right, but they brought him back. He's up Farmington way, has his own little hardware business."

"We took the last from Uniontown."

"I know it's close, but that's why we wait awhile, and we got the van painted up. I haven't heard anything about them looking for a white van either."

"If he gets your feeling, babe, we're heading for Farmington."

They clinked beer bottles.

"The other's a woman. About forty-six, I think. This one electrocutes herself. Not on purpose. She's changing out a ceiling light for a fancier one. And didn't she forget to turn off the power? I swear, it strikes me as meant to be."

With a shake of her head, Clara scooped up some peas and carrots.

"Gets that bad shock and falls off the stepladder, knocked herself out. Her daughter was there, pregnant daughter at the time, and called nine-one-one, did CPR. She was gone for about four minutes before the EMTs got there and used the paddles. She's outside Kingwood."

"When she die, babe?"

"Last March—near a year now. And the man, he died in May."

"After dinner, we'll take a look at both. Maybe me being with you and back a hundred percent'll help bring on your feeling."

She sent him a slow smile. "I get all kinds of feelings when you're with me."

He wiggled his eyebrows. "We'll work on those after. I sure have missed making love to you, babe."

"We'll make up for lost time. For the mission, and for us. Sam, I swear, this steak's done to a turn."

"I rubbed a little something extra on it, let it sit awhile, before I fried it up. I knew we both could use it."

"It'll help get us back to full strength." She ate another bite. "Plus, adds flavor."


As Sloan debated coffee or Coke for her drive to work, someone hammered on her door. She wrenched it open to find Drea with a jacket thrown over pajamas.

"Who's hurt? Are you hurt? Mom and Dad—"

"I'm fine, they're fine. Everything's fine. Everything's amazing."

"You're in pj's," Sloan said as she shut the door.

"I couldn't wait. What's different?" Drea demanded. "Come on, come on, you see everything! What's different?"

"Having you beat on my door in your pajamas to start. What's—"
Then she grabbed Drea's left hand, stared at the ring. "Oh my God."

"Isn't it beautiful? Isn't it perfect? I'm getting married!" She threw
her arms around Sloan and bounced.

"Wait. Wow. Wait. Didn't you meet him like five minutes ago?"

"Three months!" When she drew back, Drea's eyes sparkled like
the diamond. "And I know that's fast, but I'm so in love with him.
He's in love with me. We're looking at next fall for the wedding.

"Be happy for me!"

"I am." A quick internal evaluation found that truth. "God, of
course I am. You just knocked me back. Way back."

Drea turned two circles.

"I had to work a little late yesterday, so he said he'd take care of
dinner. I figured he'd pick up a pizza or whatever, but when I got
home, he'd *made* dinner."

"He cooked?"

"Shrimp scampi, and it was good, too. I thought he was flustered
and nervous because of that. I mean, he cooked, and he had the table
set with candles and flowers. He had a bottle of champagne and music on. It was so sweet. So romantic."

Sloan knew Drea prized both the sweet and the romantic.

Now tears added more sparkle to Drea's eyes. "Then he—oh,
Sloan—he got down on one knee."

"He did not."

"He did, he did! Then I knew, of course I knew, but I couldn't even
speak. He said he loved me, that I'd shown him what it was to love.
He wanted to build a life with me, make a home, a family together.
And he promised to work every day to be the man I deserved, to be
the partner I could count on."

*Nailed it, Theo*, Sloan thought.

"Who could say no to that?"

"Not me." On another circle, Drea held her left hand high to admire the ring from another angle. "I knew you'd be leaving for work,
so I ran over here as soon as he left this morning. Now I have to run
back and tell Mom and Dad. You'll be my maid of honor, won't you,
like we promised each other when we were kids?"

"If you didn't keep that promise, I'd find a way to make your life hell. My little sister's getting married. I need to process."

"You've got until September or October."

"I don't have to ask if you're sure. It's all over you." She took Drea's hand again to take a better look at the ring. "And he gets you. It's a pretty big rock, but it's classy, not flashy. Classic and elegant and very, very you. He's a really great guy, Drea. He almost deserves you."

Drea wrapped around her, and on a long sigh swayed. "I'm so happy. I have to go tell Mom and Dad." She gave Sloan a long, hard squeeze.

When Drea rushed out, Sloan walked slowly back to the kitchen. She grabbed a Coke—quicker—then put on her outdoor gear.

She needed to think about this. Yes, it was Drea's life, and her sister was more than capable of making her own decisions.

But she needed to process.

She thought about it on and off during her workday, and made her mental list of pros and cons.

Since Travis was family, she shared with him at the end of the day. But started her roundup end to beginning.

"We had a couple of guys racing their snow machines. Damn near ran over a group of snowshoers. I let Sanchez take the lead with them, and before they got pissy—and they were about to—she charmed them."

She went through the rest, back to their first call involving a birder who'd gone off the trail and gotten lost.

"We got him back on track, and suggested he get an actual compass rather than depending on a phone app. And Drea's engaged."

"Sounds like— What? To the new guy? The carpenter guy?"

"That's right."

"That's quick work."

"I know, right? But after—" She tapped her index fingers to either side of her head. "I have to say, and I hate using the phrase, but they're made for each other."

"Did you run him?"

"Yeah. He's a good guy, Cap. I can wish they'd known each other longer, but it's their life. And they're looking at a fall wedding, so that's time. I really like him, and when I push the that's quick aside, I really like him for Drea."

"Yeah, I can see that." He angled his head. "You're a good judge of people, and their character, and Drea's a smart, more-than-capable woman. What's your dad think?"

"I haven't talked to him, since I just found out this morning. But he likes both Littlefield brothers, a lot."

"Yeah. So he's said."

"Next time you get a chance, you can come by, see what they've done at my place. Just a couple of rooms, but it's good work."

"Good work's always valued. You did some of your own. I've heard from the leads on the Anderson and the Rigsby cases. They're not completely convinced of the connection, your motive theory—you got O'Hara on board with Tarrington—but it's a new angle, and one they'll pursue. They'll share their files with each other, and with us."

At the last, Sloan let out her held breath. "It's not a coincidence, Cap."

"I agree with you, but then I know you, they don't. My impression is Detective O'Hara gave this a firm push on your behalf."

"Then I'm grateful for it. Cap, they're already at four weeks since Tarrington. The pattern's been four or six weeks between."

"Understood. And understood by the leads as well. And you understand the difficulties."

She'd gone over it all herself countless times.

"Different jurisdictions, only one—potential—witness. And medical intervention's used routinely and often to shock someone back. I should know. I'm one of them."

He leaned forward, his face stony. "You've convincingly laid out a theory where you fit the description of a target. If I believe your theory, and I do, that person or persons unknown are abducting people who've received that medical intervention, and who live in the radius you outlined, you fit."

"I was treated outside that radius," she pointed out.

"You're my sergeant, Sloan. You're also my family. On both levels, I want you to stay alert and aware."

"That I can promise."

"You'll get the files by tomorrow. Go home. I need to call Dean and tell him he's on the next step to being a grandpa."

"You would."

Grinning, Travis leaned back in his chair. "Oh, I can't wait. Payback for him buying me a cardigan with patches on the elbows when Marlie got pregnant. I've got my eye on slippers when it's his turn."

Amused, she headed out. She felt pumped at the idea she'd be able to work all three cases—on her own time, in her own office, but she'd have more details.

Whether the devil was in them or not, answers often were.

And she had plenty of questions.

She'd go home, change out of her uniform. She'd toss something together for dinner and eat in her office, where she'd try to find some answers with the details she had.

But first, she decided, she had to make one stop.

She drove past her house and turned into Nash's drive.

Just his truck out front, which she'd expected, since she'd talked to her mother earlier and Elsie had bubbled over about planning a wedding.

She imagined Drea and Theo enjoyed one of her mom's home-cooked meals while celebrating and planning.

When she knocked and didn't hear Tic's happy bark of greeting, she imagined he enjoyed his dinner with Mop.

Nash opened the door; she felt a quick sting of regret.

He looked like a man who'd put in a hard day of work, and that appealed to her. Some might say he needed a trim and a shave, but she wouldn't, because the just-a-little-scruffy look appealed, too.

"I wanted to talk to you if you're not too busy."

"If you're here to discuss wedding plans because I'm best man and you're best woman, I'm closing this door and I'm locking it."

"That's not what I want to talk about." Or only indirectly, she thought as she stepped in.

"Fine. I'm about to make a grilled cheese sandwich. I guess you want one now."

"No, really—"

"Come on back. I want a beer."

"This really won't take long. And you don't sound thrilled about my sister and your brother."

"I'm fine with that," he said as he walked back to the kitchen. "It's the whole wedding thing. I've had friends do the wedding thing. It's enough to make your eyes bleed."

"At some point we'll have to get in on that, but it's not what . . ."

She got her first glimpse of the kitchen.

"You—" She pushed back her hat. "What? This is . . . You don't even cook."

"Technically, grilling bread and cheese is cooking. It requires heat and a pan."

"But this is . . ." She ran a hand over the smooth surface of the counter on the enormous island. "This isn't why I came either, but I'm taking a minute.

"You have a six-burner stove, double ovens, and the biggest refrigerator I've ever seen."

"It's a big space."

"The wine rack." A vertical series of diamond shapes stained to match the exposed beams on the lofted ceiling. "You made that?"

"Yeah."

"It's good. It's all really good. Enough rustic with that, the exposed beams, the original wood floor, the open shelves to keep it from pushing into slick and sleek. It suits the house."

"I think so."

When she turned back to him, he held out a glass of wine.

"Oh, I really . . . thanks. Okay, I'd rate this kitchen as a cook's dream, so you'd better start collecting cookbooks. Did you know Theo cooked Drea dinner?"

"Yeah." He got out bread, cheese, butter. "CJ gave him the recipe because he couldn't stop obsessing. He tried it out on me first. Pretty good. Are you cold?"

"No. Oh, coat."

"Just toss it on a stool. You can pretend you've hung it up."

"Did you know he was going to propose?"

"Yeah." He got out a skillet, set it on a burner. "I went with him to pick out the ring. He wanted backup."

Nash glanced at her. "If you're pissed I didn't mention that to you, get over it."

"I'm not. If you'd told me, it means you don't have a vault." Resigned, knowing he had one added more appeal, she drank some wine. "It's a beautiful ring."

"He didn't really need me. He took one look at it, and that was that. Sort of like when he took one look at your sister."

"It's really fast."

"That's what I said. But."

"Yeah, but. I really like Theo."

"Good. I really like Drea. And if we didn't, it's still up to them."

"Right. Better that we like them, though. And they're good together."

"Agreed. But I'm warning you, if this is leading up to best people duties, I'm kicking you out."

"That can wait until after the wild joy settles down some. Besides, all you really have to do is throw him some guy party, show up, and give a toast."

"You're getting dangerously close to the boot, Sergeant Cooper."

"It applies to why I'm here. My sister's going to marry your brother. That makes us in-laws."

"Does it?"

"Sort of, anyway. So it's awkward for you and me to continue to sleep together."

"How do you figure?"

"My family's big on gatherings. Not just holidays, but Sunday dinners once or twice a month, summer cookouts, and all of it. It feels awkward for us to have a sexual relationship when our siblings are married—and knowing Drea, probably starting a family within the year. Which adds a mutual niece or nephew to the mix."

"You can overthink. Probably makes you good at your job, but boy, can you overthink." He flipped the sandwiches, gave them a little press with the spatula. "You do realize the two of them getting married doesn't make sex between us incestuous."

"Don't be ridiculous." She tossed back some wine. "I said 'awkward.'"

He got plates out from one of the glass-fronted cabinets, then flipped a sandwich onto each one. After walking with them to the island, he set them down. Then pulled her off the stool, kissed her.

"Doesn't feel awkward to me."

"Because you want sex."

"There is unquestionably that. Add, I find you a very interesting woman, one I enjoy spending time with even without the sex. But I still want that," he continued as he walked over to what she saw was an enormous and mostly empty walk-in pantry with lowers that matched the island and coffee station.

He brought back a bag of chips.

"I love my brother, and since I'm already solidly in serious like, I'm probably going to end up loving your sister. You love your sister, and you'll end up loving my brother. And none of that has anything to do with two consenting adults having sex.

"Now eat your sandwich."

She stared down at her plate. "It's weird, you have to admit it's a weird situation."

"I'll give you slightly strange. Slightly strange doesn't bother me or I'd never have bought this house."

She looked around the kitchen. "It's going to be a terrific house."

"It's on its way."

Since it was there, and looked good, she picked up the sandwich. "I'm not starting on my kitchen. This makes me want to even though mine's less than a quarter of this size. But I'm not because I have to start thinking about the exterior as soon as the weather breaks enough for that. The size says I should probably go for white cabinets."

"Not in that house."

"No, not in that house. But—not thinking about it." She bit into the sandwich. "What are you going to do with all this storage, and a pantry as big as—no, bigger than—the room I use as an office?"

Like her, he looked around. "I don't have a clue."

She shifted to him. "You'll figure it out. Figuring things out's something we have in common."

"What are you figuring out?"

"Oh, I've got multiple things going. On a personal level, what color house do I want, how wide do I want for the front porch I need. How to handle the inevitable questions when people find out we're sleeping together. Which they will."

"How about—just try this on: *None of your business.*"

"I don't say that to my family." She waited a beat. "Would you?"

"To Theo? Unlikely, as he wouldn't judge."

"I'll figure it out." She shrugged and ate another bite. "On a professional level, I'm trying to figure out what drives someone to abduct people who've been resuscitated."

"How's that going?"

"It'll go better when I get the files on the Anderson and Rigsby cases. My captain said we should have them by tomorrow. When I'm cleared to talk to the wife and girlfriend—Rigsby—and Anderson's husband, family, I might scratch up a little more."

She reached for some chips. "The lead investigators on the three cases are cross-checking with each other, and that may break something open. For now, I'll go home and work with what I've got."

Picking up her wine, she smiled at him. "And I don't have to make my dinner."

"Let me know if you need somebody to bounce things off of."

She considered him. "If you give me an hour to go back over some things, make some more notes, I could use that. Since I've decided to go with 'slightly strange,' you could bring a change of clothes."

Coolly, he went for more chips. "Sounds like you assume I'll sleep with you."

"I do. I do assume that."

"Then finish your sandwich and get lost. I'll be there in an hour or so. I want to run some baseboard first."

She nodded. "I'm going to tell you something about the guy I was with for a while before I got shot."

He shifted enough to meet her eyes. "See, that's something I find awkward, and unnecessary."

"Maybe it's both, but I just want to say I never bounced work around with him, I never even considered doing that. Not only because I had Joel, but because he wasn't interested. He never asked and wouldn't have listened. And he couldn't have run baseboard if you held a nail gun to his head."

"So those are points for me."

"They are."

"I'll make sure to add them to the scoreboard." He ate some chips as he studied Sloan's face. "In return I'll tell you one thing about the woman I was with for a while before I moved here. She'd hate this place."

He glanced toward the wide window and the sprinkle of moonlight through the dark.

"That's not a dig, it's just fact. New York's her place. And this really isn't."

"So, my point?"

"I guess it is."

"I'll add it to my spreadsheet." She rose, kissed his cheek. "Thanks for the sandwich."

Later that night, the blue van parked at the far end of the lot, and kept watch.

One by one the shops in the strip mall closed. Owners or managers came out, locked up. Drove off.

They watched Lori Preston do the same.

"A little later than yesterday," Sam noted down the time as he had the night before. "That tattoo parlor's the only other place still open, and that doesn't close for another hour."

"I swear I don't understand why people want to mark up the body the good Lord gave them."

"If I was to get a tattoo, it would be right over my heart. It would say CLARA, because that's the name that lives inside my heart."

"Oh, you!" She swatted and giggled.

"We could try for her, babe."

"Not tonight. No, not tonight, doll. We keep an eye tonight."

But because that feeling grew in her, she nodded. "Soon, though. I got an idea on it. Let's follow her on home. I think this is the place to do it, but let's follow her on home again, just to see what's what."

Impatience scraped, but love smoothed it out again. "You know best, babe."

She gave his hand a pat. "I believe I do. Just wasting this stolen life she got. Working late every night, going home in the dark to an empty house. And how many people did we see going in that place of hers this last hour?"

"About three, and only one left with a shopping bag."

"Wasting this stolen life."

The *wrongness* of it struck Clara to the core and brought her pain. To ease that hurt, she thought of Zach Tarrington's repentance, and his homecoming.

"We'll send her to a better place." She patted Sam's hand again as he started the engine. "But not tonight."

# CHAPTER TWENTY

March didn't come in like a lion but more as a bear that lumbered its snowy way over the mountains. It took its time, blew its winds.

The swans returned to thrash their way through the thinning ice and signaled the slow approach of spring.

Sloan took an hour's personal time at the end of her week to make the drive to Cumberland.

She found the Rigsby house with the last snowfall cleared off the drive, the walkway, shaken from the azaleas that would put on a show once spring took over.

The Cooper in her noted the house had been well built, well maintained with a welcoming, covered front porch and double entrance doors. The LEO hoped for some new detail or angle from Karen Rigsby.

She rang the bell.

She recognized the woman who answered from photos. Karen Rigsby, tall, stately, and square-jawed, had a short, stylish swing of chestnut-brown hair. The color set off the ice-blue of her eyes, as did the long-sleeved, cowl-necked dress of nearly the same blue.

"Ms. Rigsby, I'm Sergeant Cooper with the Natural Resources Police. We spoke on the phone."

"Yes, I expected you. You're prompt."

"I don't want to take up any more of your time than necessary. I appreciate you taking that time to speak with me today."

"Come in. I have coffee if you'd like."

"I don't want to put you to any trouble."

"I'd like some myself. How do you take it?"

"Just a little milk, thanks. Your home's beautiful."

"Thank you."

Karen stood in the foyer a moment, looking around as if judging it herself.

"I thought, and seriously, about putting it on the market, then I thought, the hell with that. I love this place. I helped make this house.

"Sorry. Let me take your coat."

"Thanks."

When Karen took it and Sloan's hat to a closet, Sloan noted no men's outerwear inside.

"Please, sit. I'll only be a minute."

Cleared out his coats, Sloan thought as she scanned the living area. But still had photos of them together, of the family together, a kind of journey through the years in a well-arranged gallery wall.

"You own an art gallery in town," Sloan said.

"Yes. Those who can't, sell. Or try to. On the phone you said you're looking into Art's disappearance, as it may connect with another missing person."

"We want to explore every angle, Ms. Rigsby."

"I spoke with Detective Trent, and with a Detective O'Hara. Detective Trent agreed it might help. To my ear, Detective O'Hara respects your input."

She brought the coffee in on a tray, with a pitcher of cream.

"They believe Art's dead," she said flatly. "You do, too."

"I can't determine—"

"You don't have to spare my feelings." She set the tray down, added cream to both cups. "I know he's dead."

She sat, crossed her legs, sipped her coffee.

"At first I . . ." She paused, pressed her lips together as if blocking the words. "That hardly matters at this point. I understand now Art may have left me, but I can promise you, he'd never have left the children, the grandchildren, without a word. He wouldn't have left his practice, our portfolio, and he'd have fought me for this house in the divorce."

"You were divorcing?"

"No, but if he wasn't dead, with my knowledge of his infidelity and deceit, we would be. And I'd take everything I could get."

Ice-blue was her eye color, Sloan thought, but the hard frost in them was fury.

"Imagine being clueless, simply living your life, believing you had a solid marriage, a husband who loved and respected you. Then imagine the fear, the panic when he doesn't come home, when you call the police. And the shock, the humiliation, the open wound when you learn he'd been with a woman half his age in a motel room. Cheating every week for months."

Fury, yes, Sloan thought, and the grief that shadowed it.

"Lying to you, living with you, sleeping with you, and all the time . . ."

Once again, she pressed her lips together.

"We were married for thirty-four years, together for thirty-six. I helped him through dental school, helped him start his practice. In turn, he helped me when I wanted to open the gallery. Art supported me in that dream. We raised children together, welcomed grandchildren into our lives. And we loved them."

She sipped her coffee, sighed once.

"We loved them," she repeated. "We fought and laughed and worried and celebrated together, all that time."

She took a long breath. "And in the end, he made a fool of me. He made a mockery of me and my life, and made himself into a pitiful cliché."

Karen paused, leveled her gaze at Sloan.

"I don't wish him dead. I want him, I desperately want him to walk through that door. So I can kick him out again."

Sloan felt the cold fury, the drag of grief. And with it, heard the last notes of dying love.

"I know you've been asked before, but it's possible when some time has passed to remember something that didn't seem important or relevant. Did he ever make a comment, however offhand, that he felt someone followed him?"

"No, not to me. Maybe to the blonde, but not to me. He was happy, looking forward to Christmas, having the family all here, seeing the grandchildren open presents. We'd had our holiday party here the week before, and he still talked about what a good time it was."

"You stated you'd never met the woman he was seeing."

Sloan could all but see Karen Rigsby wrap dignity around her like a cloak.

"No, and I never intend to. She chose to have an affair with a married man, but Art made the choice to be that man.

"I've tried to pinpoint Wednesdays. He liked to cook on Wednesdays. I'd come home from work, and he'd have made dinner. We'd have a drink, talk about the day. We'd discuss what was going on in the world, what was going on in the family, and so on."

She looked down into her coffee. "We'd have dinner, and we'd chat the way friends do. Because we were. I thought we were very good friends. But." She sipped more coffee. "I was clueless."

Nothing, Sloan thought when she left. Just nothing fresh from that source. Except, she admitted, her own sympathy and respect for the widow.

For she was surely a widow.

If he hadn't been taken, would Rigsby have come to his senses, cut off the affair, kept his marriage intact?

No way to know, but maybe she'd get something from the blonde.

Maci Lovette lived in a downtown apartment. By day she worked as a hostess for an upscale restaurant. Five nights a week she served cocktails in the lobby bar of a local hotel.

Where Karen Rigsby was tall and stately, Maci ran petite and curvy. Blond hair tumbled past her shoulders in careless waves.

She wore a short, snug red dress with stilettos to match.

If Sloan had cast the other woman, the much younger trophy wife, Maci Lovette would nail the part.

"I expected someone a lot older." Her voice bubbled a bit as if a laugh waited to happen. "Come on in. You said you'd make it quick. Have to. I've got a date."

Obviously neither grieving, angry, nor humiliated, Sloan thought as she entered the colorful chaos of the apartment.

"'Scuse the mess. Who has time to clean?" She dumped what

looked like a pile of laundry out of a chair onto the floor. "So have a seat. I never heard of the National Resources Police."

"Natural Resources."

"Oh." Her lips, red like the dress and heels, curved. "Like oil or something?"

"Public lands, waterways, wildlife. I appreciate you making time to speak with me, Ms. Lovette."

"Oh, no problem. As long as it's quick. Jerry's picking me up in about a half hour. I talked to the regular cops a bunch of times about Artie. Do you really think he got snatched up? Like kidnapped?"

"We have reason to believe that, yes."

"Well, I guess maybe. He's pretty loaded. Everybody's got teeth, right?"

"He'd often come into the restaurant where you work for lunch. That's how you met?"

"Sure. He's a real sweetie. Always remembered names, had something nice to say. I just couldn't help but flirt with him. First he got kind of blushy, and some nervous. So cute! After a while he started flirting back some, so I slipped him my number. Took his time calling, but he finally did, and we flirted on the phone. Then we met for drinks, not around here because, well, you know."

"He's married."

"Correct," Maci said with a smile. "He just wanted to have a little flirt, a little fun. Cut loose a little. I mean, God, he's been married longer than I've been alive. Can you imagine only being with one person for decades?"

"Actually, yes, I can."

"Yeah?" Maci seemed surprised, then shrugged it away. "Not me. You got one life, right? So live it. Anyway, we had drinks, got snuggly in his car after. Then Wednesdays. We had fun. Different motel, like intrigue, and that was fun. He's good in bed, too. Really considerate. Generous, too. He liked buying me things."

She tapped her sparkling earrings. "He gave me these for Christmas. Men like buying me things."

*I bet*, Sloan thought.

"He gave you those the last time you saw him?"

"Now that you mention it, that's right. And we talked about our getaway."

"Your getaway?"

"Artie always goes to this dentist convention the first week of February. But this year instead, he was taking me to the Caymans. See, he got another credit card, and he set up a new account for the bills and all that so they'd come to his office, not to his house. And with the earrings, he gave me a couple thousand for clothes. For the tropics."

Her lips moved into a pout. "I was really looking forward to that."

"I imagine so," Sloan murmured. "You met him at different motels."

"Yeah. Like I told the regular cops, we'd pick the motel for the next Wednesday, then Artie would get there and check in. He'd text me when he had it all set, with the room number. I'd already be on the way because he never wanted anyplace too close to home. I'd go to the room, we'd have some fun."

"You'd always leave first?"

"That's right."

"Did you notice a white van in the parking lot on any of the Wednesdays?"

"Sure didn't."

"Did Dr. Rigsby ever mention seeing one, or tell you he thought he was being followed or watched?"

"Well, he worried about the wife sometimes. Not that she'd follow him or anything, but that she'd just sense something. Whenever he worried about it, I'd just distract him. It's not hard."

She shook back her hair, laughed. "Men are easy to distract."

"Did any of your other dates know about him?"

She pursed her lips, tilted her head.

"No. I don't see how. When you date solidly married men like Artie, they can't worry too much about what you're doing with someone else, can they? And when it's done, it's done. I usually let them call it off because it's easier. Then, no harm, no foul, and move on to the next.

"I mean a girl's gotta do what a girl's gotta."

After the interview, Sloan had to sit in the truck for a few minutes to level off.

But whatever she thought of Maci Lovette—and the woman was cannier than she let on—she couldn't see any duplicity. She doubted if the woman would have seen a white van if one had pulled up in front of her.

Too self-absorbed.

So she'd go home with nothing. But nothing was something. She agreed fully with the lead investigators. Neither woman had any part in the abduction.

She'd write it out, mull it over. Maybe pick up her crocheting, turn something on TV she didn't have to pay attention to, and give it more thought.

Then in between, she'd put something together for dinner.

A hell of a way to spend Friday night, she supposed, but it suited her.

As she approached Heron's Rest, she decided to grab some takeout and save herself the chore of making something herself.

Pleased with the idea, she detoured and pulled into the small lot behind Ricardo's. Then, amused, parked beside Nash's truck just as he got out of it.

Inside, Tic jumped from back to front and back again.

"Take-out or dine-in?" she asked.

"I'm on dog duty. Take-out. You?"

"The same. Want to join forces?"

"Maybe. What do you want?"

"I was thinking about the chicken parm, then I'd have leftovers for tomorrow. But I'm flexible."

"I've noticed," he said, and made her laugh. "You take the dog, I'll get the food. I just need to stop at home on the way and get some dog food."

"I restocked the last time I went to the grocery."

He gave her a long look. "Did you?"

"And look how smart that turned out. I'll take the dog."

The minute Nash opened the truck door, Tic leaped out, then sat at Sloan's feet, thumping his tail.

"He doesn't jump on you."

She bent down to give him a scrub. "He knows better."

"Tell that to everybody else." He slammed the truck door; she opened hers.

"In, Tic. Let's go for a ride."

Nice, she thought, to have a dog around on a Friday night. Nice, too, to have his human. Better yet, she could replay the interviews to someone who listened, had thoughts and opinions.

And though she didn't mind socking in alone for the weekend—excepting the Sunday dinner her parents had already claimed—she'd enjoy the company.

"I can tell you," she said to Tic, who sat staring at her with adoring eyes. "You're no blabbermouth. I like spending time with him. Even if you remove the sex factor, which let's not, I like spending time with him. And you, too."

She'd get herself a dog just like him, but she couldn't take a dog to work the way the Littlefields did.

When she got home, she let Tic out, let him roam and sniff, mark some territory.

Winter hadn't finished yet, but she could feel spring creeping up behind it.

"And I'm ready for it." She looked at her house. "I'm ready for new windows, a new front door, nice new siding. I'm leaning toward horizontal lap either a cream—not white—or a nice blue. Have to decide. And a porch the full width of the house, center the steps."

When the dog came to lean against her, she rubbed his head. "Yeah, that's what we'll do. Next month. Let's go inside."

She gave Tic the chew toy she'd picked up with the dog food, then lit a fire. With the dog occupied, she stowed her weapon and changed into warm leggings and a sweater.

She freshened her makeup because, well, it needed it.

And was just pouring wine when the dog raced to the door yipping.

"I left it unlocked," she called out as Nash knocked.

When he came in, he lifted the take-out bags high as Tic jumped up, planted his paws.

"Knock it off!"

Shaking her head, Sloan walked over. "Down," she ordered, and pointed. Tic got down, sat down, and got another rub.

"Good dog. One direct word's better than three when training a young dog."

"I often use the single word *fuck*, but he still doesn't listen."

"One consistent word. If *fuck*'s your code for *down*, use it consistently. There's a bowl in the kitchen. You can feed him, and I'll deal with the human food."

He passed her the takeout, noted with some annoyance Tic didn't jump up to try to steal it. Then saw the two stainless steel bowls. "You got him a bowl?"

"Mop visits, too, so yeah, I got a bowl. Two actually. Food. Water."

Following house rules, he hung up his coat before he crossed over.

"After you've filled his bowl, I'm keeping the bag in the broom closet. You got jalapeño poppers!"

"And now I suppose you expect me to share."

"I do. You also got a meatball sub. You can't eat all the poppers and this sub."

"I beg to differ. But I'll trade three of them for sex."

"Done. I'm having wine, but I stocked some beer."

He straightened from the dog bowl. "You bought beer."

"I'm a thoughtful host. And my father drinks it, too."

"I'll take the beer." He opened her fridge, pulled one out while she set down the food. "Let me ask this straight. Are you looking for something here?"

"I'm looking for my share of these poppers," she began, then it hit her. Insult slapped temper into high gear.

"Because I bought beer? Jesus, you think I'm trying to, what, *ensnare* you with beer and dog food?"

"'Ensnare'? There's a word." His cool tone hit the polar opposite of hers. "I didn't say or mean you were trying anything. I asked if you're looking for something."

Her spine snapped straight; her shoulders tensed to rocks. "Why is it men think women are always trying to trap them into something? I met one today who's really good at that. It's not my style."

"Again, I didn't say or mean that, so ease back some."

"Oh, really?"

Maybe he realized his mistake, maybe not, but he held up a hand.

"Let's try this instead before I get a knee in the balls or a fist in the face, because you look like you could do both. I'm not seeing anyone else, you're not seeing anyone else. I'm good with that."

"That doesn't mean I—"

"Down," he said, and pointed. Her mouth fell open.

"I don't take commands from you. I'm not a dog."

"No. But you've got a temper like most every other human, and in this current situation, it's misplaced. Let me flip this around and say I'm not interested in anyone else. Not for sharing takeout, not for sharing a bed. That doesn't mean I'm trying to—what was the word again?—ensnare you."

"If you decide someone else interests you, you just have to let me know."

"That works both ways."

"Great. We understand each other."

"But I wouldn't like it." He set the beer down, then took her by her tensed shoulders. "I'd back off from someone who didn't want me, but I wouldn't like it if that was you. I'm trying to get a read, that's all."

He felt her shoulders relax—just a little, but enough.

"I wouldn't like it if I had to back off."

"Okay." He kissed her forehead where the scar rode under her bangs.

"You phrased the initial question in a stupid, insulting, *male* way."

He kept his eyes on hers a moment, then nodded. "It stings some, but I'm going to have to give you that one."

Damn it, she liked he could admit a mistake, without laying on qualifications. So she did the same with acceptance.

"All right then."

"Since we've cleared that up, how about we eat and you tell me about this woman who's good at trapping men?"

She rolled the rest of the stiffness out of her shoulders and sat. "I should start with the wife."

He listened as they ate, as the dog went back to his chew toy. When she'd finished telling him about Karen Rigsby, he said something that hit home.

"She still loves him. He broke her heart, and if he were alive, she'd divorce him—and make sure it hurt. But she still loves him."

"Yes, she does. Part of her is a widow, grieving for the man she loved more than half her life, and the other is a woman angry and humiliated by her husband's betrayal."

"It must be hell to have that fighting it out inside you."

"I thought the same. When I talked to her, I thought exactly that. She's in hell, and will be for a long time. Even after we find the answers, she'll be in hell."

"You're sure she didn't have any part of it. I don't have to ask if, because I can hear it."

"If I wasn't before, I am after talking to her. And the leads have cleared her. They looked hard because she'll end up with everything—which is a lot of everything. But she'd end up with it faster with a body."

"So if she'd known, wanted to get rid of him, how would she have done it?"

"The smart way, kill him in the motel room right after the blonde leaves, plant evidence that implicates her. Not that she'd get away with it, but she'd try to punish them both."

"Why didn't the blonde do it?" He took a swig of his beer. "It's a classic, right? He decides to end things, and she doesn't want things to end."

"She didn't care enough. Let me tell you about Maci Lovette."

When she'd finished, Nash ate a fry, washed it down with another swig of beer. "That's the blonde on the wall of your office. She's got the sexy going, sure, but she doesn't look like a player."

"Is that so?"

"It's only one picture, but yeah, that's so. And that's part of how she gets away using middle-aged men stupid enough to think she wants them for anything but what they can and do buy her."

What did it mean, she wondered, that his thoughts ran right along the same line as hers on the subject?

"She can play guileless, and she's not."

"That works for her, too. Can't call it extortion or even sex for pay.

I imagine she didn't have to wheedle much for the gifts. And I'm betting she rarely pays her own rent."

Impressed, Sloan sat back.

"You'd win the bet. She has a system. She works one sucker at a time, but starts the flirt, as she calls it, with the next either when the first guy starts talking about leaving his wife or breaking things off. She prefers the latter as that usually involves a nice parting gift.

"She's got a very nice nest egg." Sloan lifted her wineglass toward Nash. "She could probably use your financial management skills there."

"No, thanks. She's scary. But not scary enough, I take it, to have made the dentist disappear."

"No. She's cunning, calculating, but that doesn't make her bright. Nice apartment, good location, but it's chaos. She's disorganized and careless as well as dishonest. Sex work's honest, a business transaction."

His eyebrows lifted. "That's one way to look at it."

"You want a blow job, here's my rate. You want the full round, this is what it costs. Want me to dress up like a high school cheerleader, that's extra. Business."

He considered her for one long moment. "You don't happen to have one of those uniforms? The little skirt and sweater? Maybe just the pom-poms?"

"Sorry. I ran track and cross-country. The thing is, it doesn't bother her a bit to damage a marriage—and she doesn't take full blame there because she's not forcing anyone. But she's good at spotting a man who's vulnerable to the flirtation, to the *Ooh, Daddy, I'm so attracted to you.*"

She batted her lashes and made him laugh.

"Then she exploits that for whatever she can get out of him. And she wants them older and married because she isn't interested in the long term."

"You didn't like her."

"Not even a little. Not because she had an affair with a married man. That happens, people get caught up. But she had no feelings for him. He's missing, likely dead, and she's pouting because she's not going to the Caymans.

"He was a means to an end," Sloan sat flatly. "Expensive jewelry and a trip to the Caymans, and now she can get all that from some schmuck named Jerry."

Blowing out a breath, she rose to wrap the rest of her chicken parm.

"And all that's irrelevant. None of that helps find Rigsby or what's left of him."

"You're taking this hard."

"No. Maybe." On a sigh, she looked back at him. "Yeah, maybe. You deal with hard things. A search and rescue where the rescue's too late. Hunting accidents, drownings, or assholes like the ones we took down right before I went on medical leave. But this? Someone's stolen three lives—that we know of—upended the world of three families. And not for gain."

Since he'd nudged his plate away, Sloan wrapped the portion of the sub he hadn't finished.

"Not for gain," she repeated. "But because—and I know it—because those three people were given another chance to live."

"Like you."

"I hate you're not wrong. The Janet Anderson case pulled at me before I knew about that, but at this point? It's part of it for me, it resonates for me."

"It has to. Sit down a minute."

When she turned, he grabbed her hand, pulled her onto his lap.

"Here. Theo almost drowned when he was seven."

"How?"

"Backyard pool. He liked to pretend he was Aquaman, and he went under. My job was to count off how long he stayed under. Like, one Mississippi, two Mississippi. I can't remember what I'd gotten to—that's gone blank—when I realized he was in trouble. I pulled him up. He was just limp, I remember that. I remember he wasn't moving. Sophia—our nanny—had jumped in. I don't know if I could've gotten him to the side and out if she wasn't there."

Saying nothing, nothing yet, she laid a hand on his cheek and just listened.

"For a minute that seemed like hours, I thought he was dead. I thought I'd just floated and splashed around while my brother died. Then he was coughing up water, and he was fine.

"Nothing before, nothing after has ever scared me like that."

"You saved him."

"Actually, it's more Sophia saved us both. We still send her flowers every Mother's Day. Anyway, the point. Nobody has the right to decide someone else doesn't have the right to live. And you're entitled to take it hard."

Touched, she brushed his hair back. "You gave me the other side of the coin. Thanks to you and Sophia, my sister's going to marry the man she loves, start a life with him. And between them, they'll make new lives. A happy ending, and I needed one today. Thanks."

Angling her head, she laid her lips on his.

When she started to ease back, he put his hand on the back of her head, took the kiss deeper, spun it out longer.

"It's Friday night." Now he ran that hand down her back. "Have another glass of wine."

"I think I will. I suppose you want another beer."

"It's Friday night. We can take them in the bedroom so you can hold up your end of the deal on the jalapeño poppers."

"I only ate two, but a deal's a deal. We need to take Tic out first."

"At home we can just open the door. He stays close, comes back."

"So we'll make sure he knows to do that here. Then he gets his after-dinner treat."

"Fine, as long as I get mine."

Laughing, she went to get their coats while he topped off her wine.

Tic, alerted by the coats, stirred from his snooze to race to Sloan, race back to Nash as he pulled out another beer, then back to Sloan. All the while yipping with joy. When Sloan opened the door, he flew out, a tail-wagging arrow from the bow.

Since they went out the back, Nash took stock.

"You could have a decent patio here."

"Mudroom first."

"Right, mudroom."

While the dog ran off his after-snooze energy, Nash wandered around the side of the house with Sloan.

"I could do about sixty-four square feet if I go for stackables for the laundry. Just enough room for that, a small counter for folding, drying rod above, cabinet below for supplies. A bench on the other side, with boot/shoe storage under and coat hooks above."

"It's a good plan. Better one is to have a carport beside it. Door there." He gestured. "You pull under out of the weather, go straight into your drop zone, and through there to the kitchen."

"I thought of that, but it means curving the driveway around to it."

"Better than tromping through the snow or the rain or whatever to get to the side door. And your driveway's crap anyway."

"It's crap anyway." She watched Tic roll around in the snow. "He gets that from Mop. He's a good dog, Nash. A sweet-natured, playful people pleaser."

"You wouldn't say that if you reached for your ball-peen hammer and found him chewing on the handle."

"Yes, I would."

She took his hand as they circled her cottage on a cold, clear, star-strewn night where the three-quarter moon sailed as white as the snow under their feet.

When he turned her, kissed her under that moon, those stars, she admitted she hadn't known how to answer his question. What was she looking for?

But in that moment, it seemed she'd found it.

# PART THREE

# LIFE

While we live, let us live.
—Medieval Latin phrase

# CHAPTER TWENTY-ONE

An early riser, Sloan started to roll out of bed before the sun tipped above the eastern peaks.

Nash reached out, pulled her back.

"Saturday morning follows Friday night."

"You know, I've noticed that."

"In life, barring emergencies, it's a good rule to stay in bed on Saturday mornings until the sun's up."

"I see your point." Especially since they were both naked. "But what if you lived in, say, Alaska, in an area where in the winter it's dark for weeks? Or alternately," she continued as his teeth scraped lightly over the side of her throat, "in the summer when it's light for weeks."

"Overthinking."

He rolled on top of her, and in the dark, found her lips with his.

Still soft and loose with sleep, she wanted that weight on her, wanted the pressure of those hard hands stirring the blood under her skin until warmth became heat. She wanted those lips, strong and sure, to seek and find all the ways to thicken her pulse and make her yearn.

Moment by moment, a touch, a taste woke her to a world of sensation. Rough stubble against her skin, firm muscles under the press of her fingers.

As those hard, calloused hands glided over her, they kindled little fires. Not to blaze, not now, not yet, but to spark and to spread as his mouth found hers.

The slow, lazy rhythm they made between them suited the quiet approach of dawn. No rush, no hurry, but time to savor, time to let arousal build like layers of thin, soft tissue.

He felt her give and give beneath him. Not a surrender, but more a meeting of minds and bodies he found impossibly sensual. In a welcoming, she gave because she wanted, and offered all he needed.

So what built between them in the quiet morning as dark lifted, as light quietly bloomed, spread into more than the physical.

As he slipped inside her, as they rose and fell together, he felt more than pleasure, more than the elemental need for release.

He felt his heart stumble. And joined with her, lost in her, didn't try to catch it.

When she lay curled against him, her head on his shoulder, her hand over his heart, he wondered what the hell he could do about it.

He'd had a plan, a carefully made plan for the life he intended to make for himself. Build a business doing work that brought him pleasure and satisfaction. Bring an old neglected house back to life, his way. He'd estimated a couple of years to fully establish the business, about a year on the house. If either or both took longer, he'd still do the work and have the place he wanted.

She hadn't been part of the plan.

So what the hell was he going to do now?

She shifted a little, let out one of those sexy purrs.

"What are you going to do now?"

For one shocked instant, he thought she'd crawled straight into his head.

"What? What?"

"What's the rest of your Saturday look like?"

"Oh." Jesus, whatever was going on inside him made him stupid. "We've got to install a new railing for a client, then take a look at another kitchen job. After that, we're going to start on the office. Needs some built-ins, but otherwise it's just paint, new lighting, cleaning up the existing trim."

"Busy." She sat up, stretched. "Me, too." Tic got up, came wagging over to her side of the bed, and got some rubs. "I want to get a workout in, then it's clean the house, do laundry before I can get into my office and do what I meant to do last night."

"What was that?"

"Write up those interviews, think about them, pick through the case files again. Then think about that, which I'll do on a hike. Maybe on Fox Tail."

"Isn't there still snow on the trails?"

"I have boots. Your dog wants to go out."

"He's Theo's dog."

"I believe he's the Littlefields' dog, of which you are one. You do that, I'll get on my workout gear and make coffee."

Since the dog continued to wag, but added some whines and a little dance, Nash got up to take care of it.

When he came back in and Tic rushed the bowls she'd already filled with food and fresh water, she stood pouring coffee.

And she wore a sleeveless black tank that showed hints of a red sports bra and tight, tiny black shorts.

"Well, okay, that might be even better than the cheerleader outfit."

"Still no pom-poms," she said, and handed him coffee. "Even a month ago, I could barely manage three burpees."

"I hate burpees."

"Everyone sane hates burpees. But I can do my twenty now."

"I'd do twenty with you, then add another five to prove my superior manliness."

She sent him a sour look over her coffee. "Oh, really?"

"Yeah, really. But there's not enough space for two in that room you've got."

"Barely space for me, but it works. You can grab something to eat if you want, and your sub's in the fridge. I know you and Theo are coming to Sunday dinner, but—"

She broke off as Tic yipped and scrambled seconds before someone knocked on the door.

"Expecting anybody?"

"No."

"Want me to hide in a closet?"

"No." She eye-rolled and laughed. "We're adults. Besides, your truck's right out there."

She crossed to the door, pointed at Tic.

"Sit."

Then she opened the door, and before the dog could leap, she did.

"Oh my God, Joel!" Laughing she wrapped around him. "Sari, look at you!"

She opened one arm to draw the female—and pregnant, Nash noted—half of the couple into the hug.

"Surprise!" Sari laughed with it. "I know it's early, but Joel wouldn't wait. *She's up*, he says. *She'll be up*."

"And I was right. Sis, you look good. You got a dog?" He bent to scrub his hands over Tic, who all but collapsed in worship.

"He's not mine. Come in, come in out of the cold. When did you get here? You couldn't have driven up from Annapolis this morning."

"Last night," Sari told her while Joel and Tic fell in love. "I was just too tired to go a step more. It's a babymoon," she added, rubbing circles on her baby bump. "We're taking a long weekend, so—"

She broke off when she finally looked around enough to see Nash.

She had full, shapely lips, and they curved into a slow smile. "Oh, well, hi there."

"Hi."

"Oh, sorry, Joel and Sari Warren, Nash Littlefield."

"Theo's brother." Joel straightened, but didn't smile. "He's marrying Drea."

"We're going to celebrate that when we have Sunday dinner at the Coopers'." As she spoke, Sari walked over, extended a hand. "It's great meeting you."

"Nice meeting you."

"Let me take your coats. Sit down! I've got coffee. You probably can't have the coffee," Sloan added as she took Sari's coat.

"I had my one sad cup already. And I have to pee again anyway."

"Right down here."

Seconds later, as Joel measured Nash, Sari clapped her hands together. "Now, this is a bathroom. And it goes with your pretty living room. Honey, that kitchen's just sad."

"I know it."

Nash stayed where he was. "You saved her life."

"She had more to do with that than me."

"You gave her the chance. I'm glad to meet you."

"All right then." Joel held out a hand, and finally smiled. "Same."

Sloan came bustling back. "For a woman who had to pee, she demanded a tour of the bathroom first. Give me your coat, Joel."

"Rules is rules. The woman won't have you tossing your coat over a chair. Has to go in a closet."

"I've noticed. I need to get mine out. I have to get going."

"Don't go off on our account."

"I've got work."

"Build stuff, right? You and your brother."

"Build, repair, tear out, whatever the client wants." He took his coat from Sloan. "We got all of that on today's schedule. Enjoy your visit." He looked at Sloan. "I'll see you Sunday. Let's go, Tic."

Then realizing his instinct to just leave reached idiotic, he turned back, kissed her.

"Sunday," he repeated, and took the dog out the door.

Joel waited a beat. "Girl, you got some 'splaining to do."

She gave him her sweetest smile. "What? That I'm a grown woman, a single woman in an adult relationship with a single man?"

Sari came out of the bathroom, looked at the two of them, glanced around. "Did Mr. Smokin' Hot leave?"

"He had work," Sloan told her.

"Well, that's a shame. That man is *fine*. You've been holding out on us, and I need details." With a wicked look to Sloan, Sari jerked her head toward Joel. "When he's not around trying to go big brother on you."

"We don't know anything about him."

"I bet Sloan does. I'm going to sit here by this beautiful fire, with my back to that ugly kitchen. Didn't you tell us that fine-looking man did some work in here?"

"That's right. The bathroom—and when I show you the second one, which is in better shape than the other was, you'll see he and Theo do good work. My father redid the fireplace, and Nash, Theo, and their helper did the rest of the living room."

She took some pity on Joel. "He's a good man, works hard and well, has a strong bond with his brother. He respects my work and me, and we enjoy each other's company."

"Does he listen when you talk?"

She smiled over at Sari. "Yes, he does."

"And in that other area we'll talk about later, does he work hard and well?"

As Joel winced, Sloan laughed. "Yes, he does."

"All right then. Joel, sit your big brother ass down for a minute. We've got some news of our own."

"What news?"

Sari clasped her hands together. "We bought a house!"

"What? When? I know you were looking, but—"

"We just couldn't find the right one. When we'd find one, it'd be just out of our range, or we'd look at one in our range and it wasn't in the right place, or needed too much work for us to take on."

Joel finally sat. "We fell for this one. In just the right place, three bedrooms like we wanted, and two and a half baths, nice kitchen, sweet backyard. Have to finish the basement sometime. But the asking? Too much of a stretch."

"We sent you a link to it a while back. Two-story colonial with a pretty front porch. I could just see myself sitting on that porch in the summer, drinking some lemonade."

"You bought it!"

"Mama Dee and my mama put their heads together, and they—"

Sari waved a hand in front of her face as tears sprang. "I get weepy just thinking about it."

"Honey, you get weepy these days if the batteries die in the remote."

"I do. I just do. They helped us with the down payment. Enough we can afford the mortgage payments. We're so grateful!" Sari pulled a tissue from the pocket of her maternity jeans.

"We'll move in next month," Joel added. "We'll be all settled when the baby comes."

"We're doing up the nursery first thing, and we'll bring our baby girl home to her own sweet room." Another tear spilled before Sari levered herself out of the chair. "Show us the rest of your house before I flood the place."

"There isn't a lot more. Second bath." With a gesture, Sloan led the way. "Second bedroom I'm using for workouts."

Sari took one look at the second bathroom. "You say the other was worse than this?"

"Considerably."

"Well then, that man doesn't just do good work. He's a remodeling genius. Tell me you're going to set him loose on that pitiful kitchen."

"In time. Exterior next, and I'm adding on a mudroom and front porch. The kitchen . . ." She shook her head as they walked back and into it. "I haven't decided exactly what I want."

"You got this little room off it. Office space." Sari gave a nod. "Good use of it. I can see why you picked it, Sloan. It's like a cozy cottage in the woods. And you know how to fix it up just right."

Joel, his eyes on the wall, moved into the room. "What's all this?"

"Something I'm working on. On my own time," she added.

"Missing persons. Three of them, in just over three months."

"Uh-oh, I see where this is going." Sari held up both hands. "I'm fine with it. Give me a drink without caffeine and I'll sit by that fire, look at baby furniture on my phone.

"I'm a police wife," she said before Sloan could apologize. "When you pick out a husband, make sure he knows he's marrying a cop."

"I've got the best police wife, or any kind of wife, there is."

Sari settled down with a ginger ale, her phone, and a trio of Oreo's.

Joel stood in Sloan's office, his hands in the pockets of his ancient jeans.

"Talk to me, sis."

She did, giving him the details while he studied the board, looked through the files. They fell easily into their old rhythm as he swigged from a Coke.

"Crazy-ass motive, so you've got crazy-ass people."

"I considered a group, like a cult, but—"

"Too many people means too many mouths that might talk, too much potential for screwups," he finished. "Could be three, but more likely two, right? Have to have two."

"One to drive, one to deal with the victim."

He'd picked up one of the kitchen chairs, squeezed it into the room. He sat, foot tapping.

"They missed some weeks in there. Has to be a reason. No reports of attempted abductions?"

"No. It could be the target wasn't available—broke pattern for some reason. Or the abductors ran into some issue. We had a bug going around, from up here, over into West Virginia, and down to Frederick County. A lot of people down with it through February."

"Yeah, yeah, we had a couple out, caught it up this way. Hard to grab up people when you've got a head full of snot. Could be it."

"Either way, they broke pattern. If they're not finished, and why would they be, they'll try again soon."

"How about before Anderson?"

Yeah, she thought, she'd missed Joel.

"I haven't found any that fit the exact pattern, but I have a couple I'm looking at. Listen, this is cutting into that babymoon. Why don't I send you what I've got on potentials before Anderson? When you've got time—and not this weekend—you can see what you think."

"You do that, and I'll do that. I promised to take my lady shopping and for a nice lunch. I'm making us a romantic dinner tonight, then we'll cuddle up with a romantic movie she can cry buckets over."

"You're a good man, Joel."

"I love that woman," he said as he rose. "And she's making me a baby girl. What do you think about Josari?"

"Are you serious?"

"Yeah, she doesn't like it either. Plus, she said our girl should have a name of her own."

"I think you married a wise woman."

"Sis, I know how to pick 'em."


Alone again, Sloan stripped the bed, gathered towels and other laundry, and made the trip to the basement. While that first Saturday chore began, she got in her delayed workout.

And wondered when she'd stop automatically assessing her system for problems.

Maybe never, she decided. And what did it matter? She had her strength and endurance back—or close to it. She felt like herself again.

As she showered off the workout, she admitted the scars bothered her. Part of that? Vanity. She accepted that. Beyond vanity lurked the memory. The moment. The shock, pain, blood, and all that followed.

If she dwelled on it, she went right back to the moment.

She'd pushed herself hip deep in cases that pulled her back into that moment. Or the moments, she thought as she dressed, where she floated above the operating table while the surgical team fought to bring her back from the dead.

Not only wouldn't that stop her, it only made her more determined.

Someone used that victory as a reason or an excuse to turn it into a tragedy. She wanted to be a part of finding them, stopping them.

As she worked on her Saturday chores, her mind shifted back and forth between the case and home renovation. The fact she kept changing her mind on details—small and large—of her kitchen design cemented her decision to put that off.

Once she'd finished her chores, she settled back into her office to take another pass through missing persons prior to Janet Anderson.

She kept coming back to the woman with the dog.

"Doesn't really fit," she muttered. "Why does it keep pulling at me?"

All the others were white; Celia Russell was Black. No parking lot involved. Add the dog. Still, an abandoned car, vanished, no trace.

She dug a little more and found an article with a statement from a neighbor.

"What the hell, get it off your brain."

She ran a search, found the neighbor's number.

Got a cheery hello when she called.

"Ms. Foster?"

"That's me!"

"Ms. Foster, I'm Sergeant Cooper with the Natural Resources Police."

"Don't that beat all! My nephew Mikey's with the NRP up in

Washington State. He just loves it. We went up for his wedding two years ago in June, and it's easy to see why. Beautiful country."

Sloan smiled to herself. This made it easy.

"I'm in Western Maryland, and I love it, too. Ms. Foster, I'm investigating some missing persons cases, and your neighbor Celia Russell's name came up. I wonder if I could ask you a few questions."

"Oh, Celia. I just don't know what to think. I swear I don't. We were friendly. Out here in the country, it's smart to be friendly with neighbors. Her husband up and left her some years back, so me and mine checked in on her now and then.

"I told the police right off there's no way Celia would've walked off like that. I think, I swear I think, somebody must've run her down when she was walking Misty—her dog? Somebody driving too fast killed her, then buried her body somewhere. I worried about her walking that sweet little dog, but Celia, she did love her walks."

"She took them every day."

"Sure did. Got herself a treadmill to use if the weather was just too bad, but she didn't care for it. 'Who wants to walk nowhere?' she'd say to me. And she wanted the fresh air, even in the dead of winter."

Sloan knew just how Celia Russell felt.

"I know y'all are calling it an abduction, but what sense is that? She wasn't rich, nobody had a thing against her."

"Could you tell me if Ms. Russell had any medical issues?"

"Like maybe she had a heart attack or stroke or something and stumbled off into the woods? No sense there either, as they searched all over and I expect that little dog would've run right back home."

"Yes, I'm sure you're right. But—"

"But since you asked, she had that heart surgery back . . . when was that? I think back last February. Yes, that's right. We kept Misty with us while she was in the hospital. Her daughter—she's a good girl—came and stayed with her at the house for a week or so after."

"She had heart surgery?"

"Had a bad valve in there, it turns out. She was looking poorly before, but they fixed her right up. To think she went through all that only to get run over by some speed demon!"

Sloan made notes, circled *surgery*, circled *February*.

"Were there any complications?"

"She was right as rain. Not that it was all easy-peasy. Took hours to fix her up, and she told me that her heart stopped while they were fixing her so they had to jolt her back."

Even as she spoke, Sloan took the photo of Celia Russell she'd printed out and tacked it to the wall. "Her heart stopped during the surgery?"

"For a minute or two. It's a miracle of God and man what doctors can do, isn't it? I take some comfort she had those good months between."

"I wonder what hospital she was in."

"WVU, in Morgantown. She said it's the best there is, and they sure took care of her. I don't suppose they'll ever find who ran her down that way."

"I know the investigators continue to look. I appreciate your time, Ms. Foster."

"She was a good woman and a good neighbor. I'm glad to help."

"And you did," Sloan murmured when she hung up. "Celia Russell, end of September. Were you the first? Maybe, maybe not. But this makes four."

She shoved at her hair, and her hand passed over the scar on her forehead before she got up to add notes to her wall.

Then she sat and began to look into October.

An hour later, she contacted O'Hara.

"I think I found two more."

When she hung up this time, she rubbed at her stiff neck. She needed to get up, get outside. Too late in the day for that hike, she decided, but a long walk would do the job.

Clear her head, let it simmer.

But first she turned back to her board. Five on there now, she thought. Young, old, Black, white, male, female.

With one thing connecting them.

Each had been given life after death.

With Theo and Robo, Nash studied the empty space of the home office, and the paint samples stuck to the wall.

"I like the gray, the middle one. It's kind of smoky."

Nodding at Theo's opinion, Nash continued to study.

"It'd look good," Robo agreed. "So would that brown. Like a Hershey bar. It's manly. Nothing wrong with that blue either. It's—what's the word?—muted like."

Nash propped the walnut wood strip beside each choice.

"No wrong choice. The built-ins we're doing work with all of these. I want to see how they all look tomorrow, morning light, early afternoon."

His desk from his home office in New York remained in storage, but it would work, too.

"Boss?"

"Hmm?"

"I was wondering. I like painting just fine, and the other work you give me. The fact is, I've never liked a job like this one. I was wondering if maybe you could teach me some more. Like how you and Theo do the built-ins you got started in your shop, and how you figure how to lay tile so it works out perfect."

"Angling for my job?" Theo gave him an elbow jab.

"Aw, come on." Smiling, Robo hunched his shoulders. "If you don't have time for it, that's okay. I just wondered."

"You come over at nine tomorrow," Nash told him. "We're finishing the first built-in. We'll show you how it's done."

"For real?" He lit up like Christmas. "I'll be here for sure."

Someone knocked on the front door. Tic raced out to welcome them.

"That can't be Drea yet. She said closer to six."

He trooped out and opened the door to Sloan.

"Hey! Come on in."

Tic blocked her entrance with wags and happy whines before he sat and held up a paw.

"Look at that. You taught him to shake." Sloan obliged him.

"You got him to sit, and once he had that—we're still working on down—shake was easy. Come on back. We're looking for opinions."

"I always have one."

He led her to the home office.

Nash turned, studied her. "How was your hike?"

"I finished too late in the day for a good one, so opted for a nice walk. This is a wonderful space. Plenty of natural light."

"It's gonna be the office," Robo told her.

"Mmm. So, built-ins flanking the big window."

"That's the plan," Nash said.

"Walnut." She gestured toward the lumber. "Nice."

"Choosing paint colors." Theo hooked his thumbs in his front pockets. "Weigh in."

"They're all good, all say something different. That chocolate brown needs to go somewhere. It's so rich. But in here, with all that walnut, I'd probably go for that middle gray."

"Score." Theo pumped his fist.

"But. I'd want to see it in different lights."

"That's what the boss said," Robo told her. "If we're finished for the day, I'll get going. I've got a date and want to clean up."

"Bowling girl?"

With a glance at Theo, Robo flushed a little. "We're getting a pizza, then going to the arcade. Skee-Ball, pinball, and all that."

"Have fun. Nine tomorrow."

"I'll be here. See you around, Sloan."

"Let's have your coat." Theo moved to help her off with it as the dog raced out to say goodbye to Robo. "How about a drink? It's five o'clock on Saturday, and we're not picking up any power tools."

"I can't stay long, but thanks. Just wanted a good walk."

"You should stay for dinner."

"Oh, I—"

"Drea's making your mom's beef stew and bringing it over about six. She had some paperwork, and we were demoing, or she'd have made it here in our high-class kitchen."

Tic pranced in with a ball, dropped it at Theo's feet.

"He wants out. Stay," he repeated. "It'll be like our little Saturday family dinner."

He tossed the ball so Tic gave wild chase, then walked out with Sloan's coat to get his own.

"Everything okay?"

"Yes, everything's fine." Not the time to tell him she'd found two more.

"I take it babymoon means you're not hanging out with your friends tonight."

"No. I'll see them tomorrow. Tonight, they've got a romantic dinner and movie planned."

"Then stay. Theo knows we're sleeping together. He beat me home, and he asked. I don't lie to him."

"No, I wouldn't want you to. It's not some secret assignation, Nash."

"Good. So stay. I'll drive you home in the morning, or you can walk, since you like walking."

"I'm so good at it now. It's a perfect night for beef stew. Got a spare toothbrush?"

"As a matter of fact."

He crossed over, pulled her in.

"This is the right time," Clara said. "And the right way. You okay back there, doll?"

"All good, babe."

"She's getting ready to close. I can see her through the window. Nine o'clock. And I'm going to time it just right. Just like we planned. You be ready."

"Always am."

"All right then. Here goes."

As Lori Preston stepped out of her empty shop, checked the door to make sure it was locked, Clara pulled the van next to her car.

And jumped out.

"Oh no! I couldn't get here sooner. Don't tell me you're closed. I need a birthday gift for tomorrow. You've got those pink crystal holders for the tea lights? I saw on your Facebook page."

"I sure do." Lori shot out a welcoming smile. "I'm happy to open up for you," she said, and turned away from her car.

Seconds later, without a peep, she was in the back of the van.

Clara pulled out, gave the tattoo parlor a quick glance, and drove out carefully.

"She doesn't open until noon tomorrow. Nobody'll even know she's gone till then. And maybe even later. How's she doing?"

"Out like a light."

"Let's keep her that way. I'm looking forward to hearing her story in the morning."

"Me, too, babe."

He'd started to look forward more to the after, but he liked the stories, too.

# CHAPTER TWENTY-TWO

Dinner wasn't as strange as Sloan imagined. After Drea brought in the stewpot, set it on the stove, she surreptitiously pointed at Sloan, herself, then made a talking signal with her hand.

*Yeah, we'll talk*, Sloan thought, then put it, and everything else, out of her mind.

Better, she decided, to just be there.

It proved easy enough. After all, she liked her sister, she liked Theo, and Nash. There were definitely feelings. And it certainly didn't hurt to take a night off from focusing on serial killers.

They sat at a folding table on folding chairs in the not-quite-finished dining room.

"Good thing we got this," Theo began. "Since we tore out the office, we figured we'd need temporary office space. Drea, this is really good."

"Right in the Mom ballpark," Sloan agreed.

"Sometime, when I don't have piles of paperwork, I'm going to cook something spectacular on that amazing and intimidating stove."

"Anytime," Nash invited. "It's a bonus to have somebody in the family who can cook."

"Sloan can cook. When she wants to." Drea's engagement ring sparkled as she sipped her wine and smiled. "You should talk her into making her Kickasserole."

At Nash's questioning look, Sloan spread her hands. "Lesser beings call it lasagna."

"The kitchen's open for Kickasserole whenever you are."

"This is like a double date."

Theo's cheerful statement had Sloan reaching for her own wine.

"We've been to a few parties and had dinner with some of Drea's friends. Good times."

"Your friends, too," Drea told him.

"Yeah, mine, too, now. But this is nice, the four of us, at home and all. We should do it again when we finish the dining room table."

Sloan grabbed the lifeline. "You're building one?"

"Restoring," Nash told her. "It's something a client had. He was going to put it on Etsy or eBay. I saved him the trouble."

"Needs some love," Theo put in. "It'll look great in here when it's fixed up. Just old-timey enough. We'll have to start hunting up things like that." He reached over for Drea's hand. "Once we find a house."

"You're looking for a house?" Sloan couldn't say why that jolted, but it did.

"Starting to." Drea sent Theo a look as dazzling as her ring. "Something we can fix up and make our own. After all, between the Fix-It Brothers and All the Rest, why not?"

"Or we could build one from the ground up if we can find the right property. Lots of options, but either way it's great knowing we'll be close to family, to work. Whatever we find, we're not thinking about it as a starter."

"A forever," Drea finished.

Looking at them, Sloan felt her heart going warm. "You'll know it when you see it."

*Like you knew each other.*

While the brothers dealt with the dishes, Drea announced she and Sloan would walk the dog. And ignoring Theo's claim he could go out on his own, she got their coats.

Five steps from the house, with Tic barking and racing, Drea said: "So?"

"So what?"

"You and Nash is so what! How long has this been going on?"

"A few weeks, I guess. Do you have a problem with it?"

"No!" She gave Sloan a sisterly shove. "But you don't even give me a hint? The first time you were with somebody you told me."

Sloan felt a wave of sweet nostalgia. "Mark Bowser. Homecoming, senior year, in the back seat of his secondhand Dodge Shadow."

She ticked a glance toward Drea. "I was seventeen."

"What difference does that make? I'm still your sister."

"You're still my sister." Sloan gave her a quick one-armed squeeze. "It just happened. And maybe I'm still processing the fact I'm sleeping with the brother of the man my sister's engaged to."

"What difference does that make?" Drea repeated. "Nash is terrific. I already love him, especially since Theo's told me Nash always, always looked out for him. Tried to protect him. You know they didn't have a happy, healthy childhood."

"Not know so much as surmised."

"Nash always took the brunt."

Sloan stopped while Tic found more spots to mark his territory. "Abuse."

"Not physical, but in every other way. Our family? They already mean the world to Theo because all he had was Nash. That silly, adorable dog? Nash gave Theo that dog because he always wanted one and could never have one.

"He's Theo's hero, so he's mine. I'm happy you're with him because of that. And because it's clear to me he's making you happy."

"Making myself happy first is—"

"Yeah, yeah, yeah." Drea just flipped both hands in the air. "But you'd already done that. You've made yourself happy. You pulled yourself out of the hole someone else put you in. You're doing work that satisfies you, and as a sergeant. You bought a house and you're making it your own—just like Theo and I intend to do."

Drea stopped, turned to face Sloan directly.

"Now you're with someone I love as a brother, I respect as a man. So yay."

"Okay." This time Sloan pressed her cheek against Drea's. "Yay."


It might have struck her strange to lie in Nash's bed while she knew her sister lay in Theo's.

When, just sleepy enough, she snuggled in, she said exactly that.

"A lot stranger if we switched that around."

It took her a minute. "Okay, yeah. They're already looking for a house. I don't know why I didn't take that next, major step in my head, because of course they are. They both want exactly the same thing. A place of their own. A place to start their life together."

"I've stopped being surprised at how often they're both not only on the same page but on the same paragraph. If they decide to go from the ground up, they'll be living here, most likely, for a while."

"They both know that. Would it bother you? Drea moving in here."

"Why would it?"

"It occurs to me you bought this place, this tucked-away place, and moved into it alone. Then Theo moved in. Now possibly—and I'm going to say very likely—Drea temporarily. That wasn't your plan."

"Plans adjust. Otherwise they're rules." Absently, hardly aware he did it, Nash ran his hand along her arm. "You had something on your mind when you walked over here tonight."

"A lot of things on my mind. I'll overthink about them later."

But what she'd pushed away came back.


She left Joel pumping gas into the truck and walked toward the mini-mart. Behind her, Joel, the truck, the pumps faded away.

The glass doors stood open, and she walked through.

Inside the bright lights she heard no sound. This time, no one stood behind the counter.

But this time, five people stood between her and the person standing in front of the counter. The five people she'd pinned to her wall.

Janet Anderson, Arthur Rigsby, Zach Tarrington, Celia Russell, and the last picture she'd put up, Wayne Carson.

They watched her, she thought, with both pity and pleading.

They spoke, first Janet, then each one in turn.

"You have to find us."

"You have to find them."

"You have to stop them."

"They'll take more."

"You're like us."

And together, they said, "You could be next."

The one at the counter turned. He had no face, but lifted a gun.

One by one, he shot them. One by one, they fell. Unable to move, Sloan felt the bullets strike her.

So she fell with them, bled with them.

Died with them.

When she dragged herself free, pressing a hand to her chest, fighting for air, Nash pushed up beside her.

"What is it?"

"I—I—nothing. Just . . . a dream."

He switched on the bedside light, then turned her toward him. Cupping her face, firmly, he studied it.

"Flashback?"

"No. No, not really."

When she started to draw back, he held on. "Then what, really?"

"Just a dream, Littlefield. I have hard ones now and then. Not as often as I did. I'm fine now."

"If you were, those eyes of yours wouldn't still look terrified. If I'm good enough to sleep with, I'm good enough for this. So tell me."

"It isn't that—" She stopped, realizing she was making it that. "The mini-mart. It's always the mini-mart, though sometimes when I go in, it changes. The woods, at night, and someone's hunting me. Or the light's so bright I can't see. But it's usually just the mini-mart. This time the counterman wasn't there, just someone standing in front of it, their back to me like that night. When I walked in, the five people missing stood there."

"Five?"

"I found two more."

"When?"

"Yesterday. I walked over here because I needed to walk, to think, to clear my head."

His thumb brushed over her cheek. "You didn't say anything about it."

"It wasn't the right time. I didn't want to bring it here with Theo so revved up that Drea was coming. I just didn't want to bring it into that."

"Okay. You saw the five of them inside the mini-mart."

"They spoke to me, each one of them. I had to find them—the missing. Had to find the ones who took then. Stop them. There'd be others. And I could be the next.

"Then the one at the counter—no face, not the one who shot me—no face. He shot each one of them. I couldn't do anything. It was like being paralyzed and I just stood there while he killed them. And then me."

She let out a breath. "I always feel it. I always feel the bullets."

Now he drew her in, gently stroked her back. "I don't think *hard*'s the right word for a nightmare like that."

"I haven't had one in a while. This was on my mind. It was planted in there, and this . . . it's what dreams do."

"I've had my share."

"Nightmares?"

"When I was a kid, so I know how real they can seem, and feel."

"It did. They do." But she could and did breathe out now, and breathe clear. "And it doesn't take a genius to figure out I conflated what happened to them with what happened to me. I felt helpless when it happened. I had barely cleared my weapon before I was down. And the missing? They didn't know what was coming for them."

"You need to fix it. You need to help stop whoever's doing this."

"Yes. I can't let it go. I don't—"

"If you'd let it go," he interrupted, "you wouldn't know there were two more."

And that settled her.

"No, I wouldn't."

"You could tell me about them."

More strange, she thought. She let herself lean on him the way she'd refused to lean on anyone other than family, or Joel.

And it didn't feel wrong, or weak.

"It's morning," she murmured. "The light's coming. I need to go home, get a shower."

"I've got showers."

"Yes, and I've seen the bathroom you're currently using. No thanks on that."

"But no offense?"

"Oh, lots of it." She kissed him first, then rolled out of bed to get her clothes.

"Wait until you see the wet room when it's done, with its steam shower."

She pulled on her pants, paused. "I'm definitely going to keep having sex with you."

"Come over here and say that."

"But not now," she said. "You've got built-ins to do and a student to teach."

"I wouldn't call him a student."

She turned to him as she finished dressing.

"I've known Robo a long time. I don't think he's ever asked someone to show him more. In any case, I'm going down, getting some coffee, then walking home because both those things will set me up. And I'll see you at dinner."

"All right."

"Maybe, after dinner if you're up for it, you could come back with me. I could tell you about Celia Russell and Wayne Carson."

"All right," he repeated.

She started out, then paused, turned back.

"It matters to me that I can tell you, and know you'll listen. At some point, there may be things you decide to tell me. I know how to listen, too."

Took the brunt, Drea said the night before. She'd never had to do that for her younger sister because there hadn't been a brunt to take.

Discipline, sure. Time-outs, groundings, restrictions. And plenty of those she felt were enormously unfair at the time. But she'd never had to stand in front of her sister and take an emotional lashing.

She wondered if he'd ever tell her what it had been like, what scars he carried.

And wanted him to, because it meant he felt able to lean on her.

She walked into the kitchen to find Tic chowing down his breakfast. He gave her a tail wag but kept chowing.

Theo, in Spider-Man flannel pants she found adorable and a faded Columbia sweatshirt, gulped coffee.

"Morning." He gestured with his mug. "You want?"

"Yes, please."

"Got you covered. Tic decided time to get up, and I guess it was, since we've got shopwork. Drea'll be down in a minute. She wanted a quick shower before she put her makeup on. Not that she needs it— the makeup. She's just beautiful."

He turned back with the coffee and a smile. "You, too. Since she made dinner, I'm taking care of breakfast. I'm making waffles."

"You're making waffles?"

"Sure."

He went to the enormous fridge and took a jumbo pack of Eggos out of the freezer. "How many do you want?"

In that moment, she tripped over the line of like and into love. Setting the coffee down, she walked over, put her arms around him.

"You're a lucky man, Theo."

"Man, do I know that."

"My sister's a lucky woman. I know that." She kissed his cheek, then the other, then stepped back. "I'll take two."

Before she went home, she ate waffles at the same folding table, then walked out to the shop to see the table, the built-ins.

And found herself pleased and impressed with the systematic organization of tools, benches, lumber, supplies.

She might have drooled, just a little, over the table with its chunky trestle base. They'd stripped it down to its natural cherrywood.

"Don't tell me you're using a stain on this."

"Why would we?" Nash countered. "Look at that grain, that color. It needs one more sanding, cleaning, then three coats of clear poly."

"Good to know, otherwise I'd have been forced to come back and steal it in the night. I have to go. Thanks for the waffles."

She turned to Nash, took his face, rose on her toes, and kissed him. "See you at dinner."

"I'm leaving in a minute, Sloan. I can drop you off."

"I need the walk. Tell Mom I'm making brownies."

"Really?"

"I'm in the mood to make brownies. Keep Tic in here so he doesn't try to follow me."

"Sloan makes awesome brownies," Drea said when she left. "And only makes them when she's in a really bad mood or a really good one. I'd say these are good-mood brownies."


Sloan walked home, and her mood rose just a little more as she caught some crocus peeking through the snow.

At home, she lit the fire, then made her good-mood brownies. While they baked, she picked up her crocheting and her first attempt at socks.

Once she'd set the brownies to cool, she checked the time. Just past ten seemed a perfectly civilized time to make calls on a Sunday.

She spoke with Carson's widow, with Russell's daughter.

She added to her notes, made more connections on her wall, and added pins to more locations.

When she'd satisfied herself she'd done all she could that day, she took a long, hot shower.

She dressed in jeans, and thinking of crocus, chose a purple sweater. Considering the idea of walking to her parents'—a little under a mile—she started to reach for boots.

The knock on the door had her leaving them to answer.

Nash stood on her stoop.

"I'll drive you over," he said. "Since I'm coming back anyway."

"Oh, fine, thanks. I just need my shoes."

When she went back to get them, he went over to the covered dish on her kitchen counter. The brownies did look awesome.

"Since your shower's better than mine—currently—I'm going to shower and change for work here tomorrow morning."

She came back out wearing gray sneakers.

"Okay." From the closet she took a black vest and a scarf with gray and black stripes. "I need to get the brownies."

"I'll get them." He picked them up, then stood for a moment looking at her. "We're going to dinner at your parents', and with your friends, so this isn't the time for you to listen."

"But?"

"But when it is, I know you will. That matters, too."

"I will. I'm going to say this because we're walking out the door. I've got a real soft spot going for you, Littlefield."

"I've got one of my own going for you, Sergeant Cooper. Let's go."

It was a hell of a thing, Nash thought, to be surrounded and not feel squeezed. To find himself so casually and sincerely welcomed into a group that had its own history.

Theo, clearly, drank it all in like water.

No, not squeezed, he decided, but more absorbed.

Conversation primarily centered on wedding talk, and baby talk. And though neither were his areas, they managed to absorb him there, too.

They zeroed in on him during an amazing meal highlighted by honey-glazed ham.

"So, you've got a bachelor party to plan." Elsie nudged another biscuit on him. "Any themes in mind?"

"I figured to go with the classics. Great quantities of alcohol, carefully selected porn, and a stripper."

At Theo's quick bark of laughter, Nash buttered the biscuit, and said, "No. Poker."

"Yeah? Cool! Nash taught me how to play poker when I was about twelve. We'd smuggle in a jumbo bag of Skittles and play for them. Christmas Eve, I was like fifteen, we had a serious marathon going, and I went all in with trip aces. I mean, who wouldn't?"

"Wiped you out," Nash remembered with satisfaction. "Full house, deuces over treys."

"You took pity on me and shared your winnings. And Skittles were major currency for us back in the day. Trouble was, the sugar high made us a little careless, and they found a couple of stray Skittles, or who was it—Maxwell did. Such a narc. And you got grounded for two weeks."

"It was worth it. We won't play for candy this time around."

"Sloan's a shark at poker," Joel put in. "We'd get a game going every couple months, and she always walked away with more than she came with. And I ain't talking Skittles."

"You have tells."

"If you'd tell me my tells, I wouldn't have them. Anyway, shark."

"Is that so?" Nash gave her a considering look. "Good thing she's not invited. But some other time, we'll have to see what you've got."

"Let me know when and where."

"Maybe when we've finished the office, Nash, we should do the game room."

"Maybe."

"Video game setup," Theo continued. "Poker table, maybe a pool table—still under consideration—and a vintage pinball. We haven't started looking for that yet."

"When you do," Dean said, "let me know. I can help you out there."

Nash turned to him. "Really?"

"Yeah, I know a guy."

"Dean knows all the guys," Elsie said with a laugh. "It's why we have a regulation shuffleboard table down in the family room."

"You have a shuffleboard table?"

"Drea's the shark there," Theo told Nash.

"It doesn't get a lot of use since the girls moved out." Dean gestured with his water glass. "We can try it out after dinner."

So he played shuffleboard in the spacious family room with a fire crackling in the hearth, with Joel and Theo competing on *Mario Kart* on the biggest screen Nash had ever seen. And one he now wanted.

Elsie and Sari cheered them on when they weren't huddled in baby and new house talk.

The dogs wrestled themselves into a nap.

Drea ended the game with yet another leaner, and her father shook his head.

"We're not bad, Nash, but you never beat Team Drea and Sloan."

"I'm a little rusty," Sloan admitted, and Drea mimed polishing her nails on her shirt.

"I've still got it."

"I should've gotten that pinball machine instead." Dean tugged on Drea's hair. "Maybe I still will, then you'll be the loser."

When her phone signaled, Sloan pulled it out of her pocket. Her expression barely changed when she read the display, but Nash saw it.

The slightest flicker in her eyes said: Trouble.

"Sorry, work."

"If that's Travis, tell him to give my girl a Sunday break."

Sloan just smiled at her father, then wandered off, out of earshot with the phone.

"Do you have to go in?" Drea asked when she came back.

"No."

"Good, because Dad wants two out of three."

"Sure. We can taunt them a second time."

"Don't Monty Python me, little girl." Dean shoved up his sleeves. "We found our rhythm."

When they won, handily, Sloan and Drea exchanged high fives.

"I'm retiring undefeated." Sloan gave her father a hug.

It took time, more hugs, insistence on taking home some leftover ham.

"Be safe." Sloan clutched Joel hard. "And send more pictures of the new house. And you." She turned to wrap around Sari. "It was so good to see you face-to-face. Wow," she added as the baby kicked. "Goal!"

"Tell me about it. And I'd tell you not to work too hard, but I'd be wasting my breath."

Nash waited until they drove away. "What was the phone call? It wasn't good news."

"No. I didn't want to say anything, bring all that positive energy down. It was Detective O'Hara. There's been another abduction."

While they drove the short distance to Sloan's, Sam wheeled Lori Preston's remains, and Clara brought the bag of lye.

Together, in the chilly dark and moaning wind, they dragged the heavy safety lid off the old, abandoned well.

"It's a shame she didn't have a story to tell." Clara took a moment to catch her breath as Sam began to toss the bags into the well. "I think this one was in denial, doll, and that might be because the story was a dark one."

The sorrow weighed on her as she helped him drop the bags down. "I got a sense of that, a sense she's one who'll be paying for her sins in this life in the next."

"Screamed and cried herself into puking."

"Trying to rid herself of the fear of the punishment coming. Reap and sow, Sam. Reap and sow." She started to lift the bag of lye from the second barrow.

"Don't you go lifting that, babe. That's man's work."

She stepped back with a sigh as he laid the bag on the lip of the well, trying to block the lye from the wind as he poured it down the hole.

Some of it flew up and away, and Clara saw it as a symbol of souls escaping the dark, or rushing into it.

"I don't think she's at peace yet, but we helped her take a step toward finding it."

Sam tossed the empty bag of lye into the well, and together they covered it again.

"God forgives," she said, "and in time God will forgive His daughter Lori Preston." She rose, stretched her back. "How about we go wash up, then have some of those cookies I made this afternoon?"

Together, always together, they wheeled the barrows away.

# CHAPTER TWENTY-THREE

It was a few days before O'Hara sent her the file on Lori Preston. She took some heart from the fact he and the other leads not only coordinated now but had cleared her to consult.

A late March blizzard dumped fourteen fresh inches, and she thought of the crocus she'd seen. Buried now, but it would show its blooms again.

She hoped the late-season storm would slow whatever plans those who stole lives had for the next.

There would be a next.

Everything Sloan read said Lori Preston had been a harmless woman. Divorced nearly a decade, she had no serious romantic relationships and maintained a civil one with her ex. They'd had two children, both now married. A son who'd moved to Atlanta for work, and a daughter who worked at a resort in the Laurel Highlands, and had given Lori her first grandchild.

A boy, now four months old.

She'd owned a small gift shop—a lot of crystals, wind chimes, candleholders, and candles—that appeared to be as much hobby as business.

Neighbors described her as a friendly, outgoing woman who'd loved to garden and putter around her house.

And when she'd puttered a few months before the birth of her grandchild, she'd started to change out a dated ceiling light for a new one.

Whether she'd been distracted or just careless, she hadn't turned off the breaker. She'd suffered an electrical shock that had stopped her heart, along with a fall off her stepladder.

Her daughter had been there, heard her fall, called nine-one-one, done CPR. And saved her.

Until now.

So another face on Sloan's wall, more pins in her map.

She worked the cases in on her own time—an hour here, two hours there—and admitted she just kept going around the same circles.

She got up at the knock on the door, and found Nash and Tic.

"I brought pizza, and the dog."

"Both are welcome." She bent down to greet the happy dog. "I see you dug out."

"Yeah. Too much for the snowblower, but your father has a plow. I think I might get one myself."

"Dad's the plow master. He loves plowing."

When she straightened with Tic leaning lovingly against her legs, Nash took a long look before he kissed her. "You need a break."

"It shows?"

"Yeah, so take one. Got a beer?"

"Sure."

She went back, got one out, and a Coke for herself as he set the pizza on the table.

"Let's try this. Tell me again what you know about Lori Preston, and what you've found out, get it out and off your mind."

"A nice woman, a good mother, a new and excited grandmother. She loved her little, barely-making-the-rent shop, and switching up the decor in her house from pieces she carried in it."

She got out plates, a treat for Tic.

"The accident made her only more determined to enjoy her life, according to her children. She'd planned to go to Atlanta to visit her son and his wife next month. She had investment income—you'd get that—so she could have her shop, live that life. No current men in her life."

She sat, grateful she could say it all to someone other than herself.

"She told her daughter she liked being single, independent, getting together with girlfriends now and then.

"Her daughter, the daughter's husband, and the baby arrived at her house about five-thirty for a visit. Planned. The shop opened noon to four on Sundays."

Though her appetite had waned again, Sloan ate a bite of pizza.

"She wasn't there, her car wasn't there. The daughter has a key, so they went in. She called her mother's phone, but it wouldn't go through. No signs she'd started on the Sunday dinner she'd planned.

"Thinking she'd gotten stuck at the shop, the son-in-law drove over. He found her car, locked, in its usual place. The shop locked. They checked with friends, with neighbors. Nobody'd heard from her or seen her since the day before. They called the cops."

Tic came over to lay under the table between them, and laid his head on her feet.

"They reacted quickly because it fit the pattern. It still does because no trace. None. They did track down a woman who'd gone into the tattoo parlor in the same shopping center about a half hour before Preston would have closed the shop. She didn't see anyone, didn't see a white van. She thinks she might have seen a black one."

"And you're thinking they might have had it painted after the last abduction."

She shrugged. "Not in any of the companies I've contacted. Witnesses aren't always reliable. Somebody swears the car was a red compact, somebody else swears it was a blue sedan."

Though she hadn't finished the first, Nash put another slice on her plate. "You can handle two. Now tell me what you think."

"I think Zach Tarrington was in that white van in the hotel lot when Rusk came out. And the people who took him knew or feared his coworker would remember it. They could've taken it out of the area to have it painted, or done it themselves. And I think . . ."

She picked up the half-finished slice.

"I should say the investigators think, and I agree, whoever's doing this most likely works in a hospital, either medical or support staff. Somebody who's found a way to access records. The missing didn't all go to the same hospital, so they've found a way. Some of the missing's accidents were reported—police reports, articles—so that's another way."

"But you're not thinking cop?"

"Can't rule it out, but again, different jurisdictions. And as far as where the abductors might be, Western Maryland, over into West Virginia, and up into Pennsylvania."

"A lot of ground to cover."

"Which helps them. If they don't kill the abductees immediately—and why would they? There's no gratification in that. They have to have a house, remote enough or secure enough to take people, hold them for however long as they do. It could be hours, days, hell, weeks. And they need a way to dispose of the bodies."

She considered as she ate.

"Digging graves in this area over the winter? No easy feat."

"Not impossible," he pointed out, "with the right equipment."

"No, not impossible. Maybe they have access to a backhoe, maybe one of them works with heavy equipment. Or a funeral home, a crematorium."

Whether she knew it or not, Nash observed, she'd started to relax a bit.

"You'd have considered those angel-of-death types who decide instead of healing to kill patients."

"They weren't patients."

"At one time they were. But they survived. Something like that—looking for follow-through? Religious fanatics against medical intervention?"

She studied him over a sip of Coke. "You've been thinking about this, too."

"I guess I have."

"Those are angles, and they're taking a look there. Lori Preston's abduction has the FBI taking an interest, and they've done or are doing a profile. I have to wait to be brought into that loop."

"Will you be?"

"I think so. They'll take a look at me."

Nash stared at her. "As a suspect? That's bullshit."

"Not entirely. I'm alive due to that medical intervention, I'm law enforcement, I live in the area. I'd look at me. I'd clear me, of course, but I'd look."

"You didn't live in the area when the first two—ones you

connected—went missing. And were barely out of the hospital when Janet Anderson got snatched."

"Yes, the first two happened before I was shot, before I moved back, but I have roots in the area, I pushed for information on Anderson, and I dug up—so to speak—the first two victims."

"Okay, you convinced me. They'd better lock you up."

That brought a smile. "They'll clear me, but they'll want to do that before they share more. Anyway, that's what I know, that's what I think, and you were right. I need a break, so tell me how the office goes."

"Nearly there. We decided to do one wall in this old barnwood we scored, so it's taking a little longer. There's enough left over. It'd look good in your office."

"My office." She turned to look toward it and those Barbie-pink walls. "Well, damn it."

"It's out in the shop if you want a look. We planed it down smooth, and it was worth the extra time. Oh, and CJ's hair is orange now."

"Sure, it's baseball season—nearly. Oriole orange."

"Huh." Because Tic got up and went to the door, Nash rose to let him out. "I guess wearing a jersey or hat isn't enough."

"Not for CJ."

"Clearly." Though he planned to stay, he got a Coke rather than another beer from her fridge. Then he sat, studied her.

"What?" Instinctively she lifted a hand to her face. "Do I look that bad?"

"You're beautiful." He spoke it as fact, not a particular compliment. "It's disconcerting sometimes. I tended toward tall brunettes."

"Really?"

"Going by that, you shouldn't be my type. And yet. I came over tonight because I missed seeing you, talking to you. We've both been busy, add better than a foot of snow. I've got no problem with alone, or I wouldn't have bought the house. No problem with busy, or I wouldn't have bought the house and started the business.

"But I missed seeing you."

The fact he'd say it, and in a tone that clearly indicated he wasn't altogether pleased by it, meant a lot to her.

So she gave him back in turn.

"I liked opening the door and seeing you there, for the same reason. And I think I make good use of alone. I'd have been glad to see you even if you hadn't brought pizza and Tic. They're the bonus."

When Tic gave one quick bark, Sloan rose to let him back in.

"We don't call them parents, Theo and I," he began, and Sloan turned back slowly. "But for clarity, I'll use the term.

"I don't know why they had us, except it's something you did, were expected to do. Have progeny and form them into doctors, lawyers, CEOs, important careers. Power careers. Put them in the right schools toward that end. Lead, guide, or push them eventually into the right marriage—not necessarily good, but right."

He paused a moment. "'Right' supersedes all. So that includes said progeny's membership in the right country club, the purchase of the right home for hosting the right people. A second home—the Hamptons, Hilton Head, maybe the tropics. All this resulting in more progeny who would continue along the same expected lines."

She sat again. "I'm sorry."

He met her look levelly, impassively. "Don't be. They made me what I am today. Theo, too. We're just not what they expected or . . . invested in. I was supposed to be the doctor. But that really wasn't going to work, and even they clued in there. So finance—the right firm, the right clients. They come from money, have money, respect money, so that was tolerable enough."

He shrugged that off. "I had a knack for it, even enjoyed it. They tolerated my summers working with Habitat, designating it as overt charity work, which is also important, at least the overt part of it. What they didn't see, and maybe I didn't for a while either, was that's what I wanted. Building.

"I did what was expected for longer than I like to admit, but you get into the habit of it. It's easier to go along, or at least give the appearance of it, than to constantly run into the wall.

"They don't like each other very much, they divorced years ago, but they still make a hell of a wall together."

"My parents make a hell of a wall together, but of a completely different kind."

"So I've noticed. They had staff to take care of us, watch us, feed us, deal with clothes. We had all the right schools, carefully curated companions, and we got trotted out when it was appropriate or advantageous. The rules were hard, fast, and not in any way negotiable. Go outside them, you paid.

"Not physically," he added quickly. "Some prized possession taken away. Not for a day, or a week. Just gone. Demoralizing lectures on how insufficient we were. They paid the staff extra to report on us if we broke some rule. Some of them did, some didn't."

"Abuse doesn't have to be physical."

"No, it doesn't. I figured that out long ago. The best parts of my life were when, for whatever reason, they weren't speaking to me. I'm in one of those now. Theo was, but they're once again to trying to push him to return to New York, back into an important law firm."

"He won't go."

"No. He's found the woman he loves, found his home, and in your family, his family. He wanted one so much."

"He had you."

"We had each other."

"Will they try to pull you back?"

"I don't think so. I think, this time, they're done with me. They can't take what's mine—and that includes Theo. With his staying here and marrying Drea, having the business with me, they'll be done with him. Whatever children Theo and Drea have won't exist for them."

"Good. They wouldn't deserve them any more than they deserved you or Theo."

"They might actually like Drea, on some level, if they got to know her, which they won't." Now he smiled. "They really wouldn't like you."

"Good," she repeated. "One thing. They didn't make you what you are. You and Theo made yourselves what you are."

She reached out for his hand. "You taught him to play poker for Skittles, then when some heartless bastard ratted you out—on freaking Christmas—you took the blame."

"Well, I'd won them fair and square."

"You gave him a dog."

Nash looked down at Tic. "Yeah, weak moment. But that's working out okay."

"He came here because he was tough enough to go after what he wanted, too. And he found it. So this, you, him, it's not because of them, Nash. It's in spite of."

Still holding his hand, she rose. "What do you say we both take a break and go sit by the fire? We can pretend to watch a movie for a while, then I'll get you naked if you do the same for me."

"That sounds like a really good idea."


Sloan gave Drea her first day off. The bride-to-be wanted to start the hunt for the perfect dress. Since the first round involved a boutique in Morgantown, Sloan slipped a possible non-wedding stop in her back pocket.

Elsie insisted on the back seat, and Drea chattered away while Sloan drove.

"I know we made the right choice with the venue. There's such a beautiful outdoor area, views of the lake and the mountains. It'll be gorgeous, just right in mid-October. And if the weather's not good, we'll move it inside. But the weather *will* be perfect."

"So say we all."

"It's the right size, too, for the number of guests we want. I mean other than Nash and some friends from New York, it's mostly our family and friends. Which is a lot, but not too many."

"Breaks my heart," Elsie murmured.

"I know, Mom, but Theo's good with it."

"We're his family now. Their family now," Elsie corrected. "It's amazing and admirable they turned into such good men with that awful, that selfish foundation. It just makes me love them more."

She shifted her attention to Sloan. "And I'm perfectly aware that you and Nash are—let me pick the easiest word—seeing each other."

"Well . . ."

"Not asking for chapter and verse. I'll only say your taste's improved. Not that there was anything wrong with Matias. That spine-less weasel."

Amused, Sloan flicked a glance in the rearview mirror. "Will it make you feel better to know he called me back in January to apologize, and to see how I was?"

"Moderately."

"But we like Nash better," Drea added.

"That's good. So do I."

"And this is a lot more fun than the last time we drove to Morgantown. Looking at wedding dresses, maybe finding your dresses, too. Did I tell you my colors?"

Sloan looked over. "I think you're about to."

"Plum and copper. I want rich colors, nothing pastel. You can pick either for your dress, Sloan. So can Leah as my attendant and Hailey for flower girl. I'm not going for everyone has to have the same style either. But I want those strong colors, beautiful flowers, and simple elegance. Not fussy, not over-the-top. And I know just the style of dress I want. Simple, sleek. No train, no veil. Forget the lace, forget the tulle. A beautiful ankle-length column and great shoes."

"Then this should be easy."

"And if I don't find it here, we'll look somewhere else."

"You'll know it when you see it," Elsie predicted as Sloan navigated Morgantown.


They had champagne while the bridal expert selected a few dresses meeting Drea's criteria.

"How lucky I am," Elsie mused, "to have daughters who want to include me in this important moment. Not obliged to include me, but want to."

"How lucky are we to have a mom who gave us love every single day. Even when we pissed her off."

Drea came out in the sleek and simple, and strapless.

"What do you think?"

"I think my daughter's going to be a beautiful bride."

She modeled it, turned this way, that way in the triple mirror.

"It's so elegant. Simply elegant," Drea said. "A definite maybe. I'm going to try on the one with three-quarter sleeves."

When Drea went back in, Elsie looked at Sloan.

Sloan said, "No. Beautiful, and she'd be beautiful in anything. But . . . too severe for her, I think. Still, it's her wedding."

"And we're here to love whatever she picks," Elsie added.

She tried on and modeled two more, and when she went back in for the next, Elsie rose. "Come with me."

She led Sloan back to a row of dresses. "This caught me when they were picking out the others."

"It's not the sleek and simple. It's a princess dress. Lace and tulle."

"I know. Maybe it's just a mom thing, wanting her baby to be a princess on her wedding day. But I don't think so, because every dress she's put on would suit you, would be gorgeous on you when you have yours."

"If you ask her, she'll try it on for you."

"That's why I'm going to ask. And whatever she picks we love it."

"Already with you there."

The attendant came out.

"She really doesn't love the last one, so I'll find a few more."

Elsie pointed to the dress. "Would you mind taking that in to her? I know it's not the style she's looking for, but ask her to indulge her mother and try it. Just for fun?"

The attendant looked at the dress, then at Elsie. Smiled. "I'll be happy to do that."

So they had another glass of champagne and waited.

Drea came out in the cuffed, off-the-shoulder dress with its full skirt, lacy bodice, and subtle white-on-ivory embroidery. The quick sparkle of sequins.

Not sleek, Sloan thought, but classic and graceful.

"Oh, I love it." Tears gathered in Drea's eyes. "I just love it. Mom!"

"Yes, yes, yes. There's my girl on her wedding day." Elsie rose quickly, hurried over to hug.

"I was so sure I wanted . . . I want this. It's not simple like I thought."

"Yes, it is." Sloan rose, made a circle with her finger so Drea turned one. "It's simply classic, simply gorgeous, and simply perfect for you. That's plenty of simple."

"I found my dress." With her hands crossed over her heart, Drea turned to the mirror again. "This is my wedding dress. I'm getting married in this dress. Let's find yours! Then I'm taking my mom and sister to lunch."

After the choices, decisions—Sloan went for the plum—the bride's first fitting, they reaped a bonus with Elsie's find of her mother-of-the-bride dress.

High on success, they had their celebration lunch. And talked weddings. Flowers, table settings, music, menu.

While her mother and sister indulged in more champagne, Sloan stuck to sparkling water. Not only was she driving, but she hoped to make one more stop.

"I need to ask a favor."

"The way I feel right now?" Drea tossed back her hair. "You could ask me for anything. Except Theo."

"I'll take him off the list of favors. I'd like to make a stop, well two. At two WVU hospitals."

"Are you all right?"

"Mom, I'm fine. It's about the missing. Two of them went to hospitals here. I just want to see if I can talk to one of their nurses, doctors, an orderly. Since we're so close."

"Of course." Elsie put a hand over Sloan's. "We'll wait in the car for you."

"Or," Drea said, "you can drop us off at the mall. I want to look at hair accessories, shoes, and I need the right underpinnings for my dress. And that way you won't feel you have to rush it."

"Thanks. Really, thanks. I'll text you when I'm done, you'll tell me where you are."

And they'd have more fun without her, Sloan thought when she dropped them off. She liked shopping, but she liked it when she knew just what she shopped for. Then anything over that equaled bonus.

She'd checked with the helpful neighbor, so knew what room Celia Russell had been in post-surgery. She made her way up and to the nurse's station and took out her badge.

"I'm Sergeant Cooper with the Natural Resources Police. I'm assisting in an investigation that involves a former patient. Not about her medical condition," Sloan added. "Celia Russell, she had surgery on a heart valve."

She gave the nurse what information she had.

"We see a lot of patients, and since you're talking about last year, I'm not sure how I can help you."

"I was hoping to speak to someone on staff who remembers her, who tended to her during her recovery."

One of the other nurses stopped by, pushed up pink-framed glasses. "Did you say Celia Russell? I remember her. Plus, the police came in not long ago to ask questions.

"You had that week off, Ally. Didn't I tell you about it?"

"No. Why did they come in about her?"

"She's missing. Has been for months now. She was a really good patient. You should remember, Ally, she showed us pictures of her little dog. She brought us in cookies after she went home. And I remember especially since I read she went missing, and then they came in to ask. They haven't found her?"

"No, we haven't found her."

"That's just awful. She brought us a big tub of chocolate chip cookies and flowers. The flowers were sweet, but those cookies were even better."

"I do remember now." Nurse Ally's brows drew together. "She was a good one. Cooperative, a pleasure, really. You told me—I forgot—Deb, when she went missing. Sorry," she said to Sloan. "It didn't ring a bell."

She glanced at the call board. "But that one does. A lot. And he's mine."

"You go ahead. I'll talk to—sorry?"

"Sergeant Cooper. I appreciate it. I wonder about visitors, or people asking about her."

"Let me think. I put my mind to that when I read about her being missing, then again when the police asked, so it's a little fresher than it might be. Her daughter—every day. Some of the people she worked with, and her neighbor. She got plenty of flowers and cards. I recall she said her neighbors were taking care of her little dog."

"You were her nurse?"

"Day nurse. But any of us would see to her if I was on break or off shift. Ah, let's see, Luke would've been on nights. Luke Renner, but no visitors once he'd come on. She was a sweetheart. Everyone on the floor liked her."

Sloan asked more questions, got a few more names before she left. And admitted the investigators would have already covered the ground.

She considered just texting her sister, but since she'd already started, she might as well finish.

She hit the next hospital ER to ask about Lori Preston.

She thought about her own trip there on Thanksgiving. The pain, the anger at herself, the depression from knowing she'd undone so much progress.

Behind her now, she reminded herself as she approached the desk.

She started the same routine at the desk when the doctor who'd treated her walked up.

"It's Corporal Cooper, right?"

"Sergeant now, Dr. Marlowe. Sloan," she added, and offered a hand.

"Well, congratulations on the promotion and your recovery. You look fit and healthy. Why are you here?"

"Actually about another patient. She was admitted after an electric shock."

Dr. Marlowe listened, nodded. Then turned to the nurse at the desk. "I'm taking five, Clara." She signaled Sloan. "I need some caffeine. Do you want something?"

"I'm good, thanks."

Marlowe fed some money into a vending machine, chose a Coke Zero. "Bad habit," she said, and drank. "I didn't treat her, Dr. Larson did. I know because I understand she's missing."

"Yes."

"I can't tell you much. I know she was admitted for observation because Dr. Larson and I talked about it the other day. You're better off talking to him. Let's see where he is."

"I appreciate it."

She guzzled more Coke Zero as they walked back to the desk. "Clara, where's Dr. Larson?"

"Exam room two. Shoveling snow. Chest pains." Clara shook her head. "Patient's seventy-two, already taking meds for high blood pressure, and should know better."

"Clara always knows. We're lucky you rotated down to ER."

"Back upstairs next week."

"Our loss. I'll take a look in exam two if you want to wait, Sloan."

"Yes, thanks."

"You sure don't look like a cop," Clara commented when Marlowe walked off.

"Off duty. But I was in the area, so thought I'd just check. I don't suppose you were on the desk when Lori Preston was admitted."

"When did you say that was?"

When Sloan told her, Clara pursed her lips. "Whew, that was some time ago. But I don't think so. You said she's missing?"

"That's right."

"Is that what you do? Look for missing people?"

"In this case."

"I sure wish you plenty of luck."

Marlowe came back. "The patient's stable, but he'll be a few more minutes. I have to get back to it."

"Thanks for the help."

"Glad to. And glad to see you looking so well. Keep it up."

"That's the plan."

Sloan walked over to sit in one of the chairs.

Clara admitted a man with a rattling cough, a woman with a sprained ankle. She input their information as Marlowe took the next patient.

And when Larson came out to speak with Sloan, she took the opportunity to do a patient search.

Dr. Marlowe knew her, had treated her, so . . .

And there she was, on Thanksgiving. Pulled pectoral muscle. Recovering from gunshot wound.

How about that?

She noted the name of the surgeon and the hospital where she'd been treated for the GSW.

Multiple GSWs.

She and Sam would do some work on that, see just who she was and why she'd come poking around after all this time.

Probably nobody and nothing, Clara assured herself. Dr. Larson wouldn't be able to tell her squat.

But it paid to do your research.

And something about the woman gave Clara a bad feeling.

# CHAPTER TWENTY-FOUR

Something about her worries me, Sam."

Clara sat with him over take-out McDonald's because she'd felt too frazzled to cook.

"What's she up to? What's some tree-hugger police doing poking into this? And she wasn't even on duty! I got her address and all off her records, and she lives over in Maryland anyway. In Heron's Rest."

"Don't you worry about her, babe." He swiped one of his fries through ketchup. "I bet she's just nosy, that's all."

Worry gnawed at her nerves like a rat on cheese.

"I don't think so, doll, I just don't. I told you how I called my friend over where Celia Russell was, and mentioned it, like in passing. And she said she'd been in there, too. Asking questions. I don't like it one little bit."

"I hate seeing you upset thisaway. You're hardly eating your Big Mac. You come on now, settle yourself. My woman needs to eat."

"Something about her." To placate him, she ate another bite. "We're going to look into her. She gets herself shot, we'll find out where and how. I got the when and how off her ER records. We need to find out more."

"We'll do that, babe, but don't you worry. She's not even really a cop, right?"

"That's the worry, doll. That's just the worry. People go missing, cops ask questions, sure. And nothing to do with us because we're careful, and doing what we're meant to do, what we've been *called* to do. So why's she poking around? There's a reason, doll. I feel it."

"Nothing for her to find out, is there? But we'll ease your worries." He patted her hand. "Then we'll keep doing what we're meant to do."

Though she didn't learn much, Sloan wrote it all out, added names to her wall. Doctors and nurses who'd dealt with the two missing.

And she'd do the same with the other hospitals. Be thorough.

Then she put it aside to make her final decision on new windows, siding, colors, the front porch, the design and position of the mudroom addition.

And damn it, the carport Nash had put in her head.

She calculated the cost. Winced.

Then reminded herself she'd be making an investment, and get the contractor's rate on the materials. Add in some free labor because even if she wanted to say no, her father wouldn't take it. He'd pitch in.

One more essential factor on the pro side of things? This was home, and home deserved the best she could give it.

After a consultation with her father, she bit the bullet and had him place the order.

"Done," she told herself. "And I won't be sorry."

Then picked up her phone when it signaled a text. From Nash.

Busy?

**Not anymore.**

Come over. I've got pulled pork, potato rolls. Your mom sent it.

**Mom's pulled pork sands? Give me ten.**

Since she'd intended to settle in wearing her sweats, she went into the bedroom, changed into jeans and a sweater. Because spring crept closer, she grabbed a vest instead of a coat, and set out.

Stopping, she turned, imagined the house with the warm blue siding, the creamy white trim, the wood porch and rails.

Add the jut of the mudroom off the side beside the open carport, and she'd have something that would make her smile whenever she drove home from work.

She decided to walk, and found herself pleased with that decision when she spotted more crocus spreading against what was slowly becoming patchy snow.

And the spears of daffodils poked through.

Swans glided over the lake, and a heron flew above them. A pretty picture over that reflection of the hills, caught in the shimmering light as it neared sunset.

When she rang the bell, a window rose on the second floor.

"It's open," Nash called out. "We're up here."

We, she decided when she walked in, didn't include Tic, as he didn't race down to greet the visitor.

Nash met her at the top of the stairs, still wearing his tool belt and Mets cap.

"Still working?"

"Just finishing up for today. Take a look."

She walked back with him to the main bedroom.

"You took out the wall! And you framed in for— Hey, CJ."

CJ and her Orioles-orange hair stood in what had been the adjoining bedroom, hands in the pockets of her carpenter pants.

"Hey back. I'll pick up what you need and start rough-in plumbing day after tomorrow. After noon, I figure."

"That'll work."

She gave him a narrow stare before pointing at his Mets cap. "You gonna keep wearing that?"

"Well—"

"You're not in New York anymore, hotshot. This here is Bird country. I'm overlooking it—for now—because you got Robo sticking to a job and liking it. Gave him a raise, too."

"He earned it."

Though CJ kept her scowl in place, the pride and pleasure showed through. "Seems like he did, so I'm overlooking it. But opening day's coming. Once the season starts, I can't be responsible for what happens to that cap."

"So noted."

"Day after tomorrow," she repeated. "Good to see you, Sloan."

"You, too."

Sloan wandered the new space. "Well, wow. Big bathroom, big closet."

"I'm still fiddling with the design, but I'm doing a coffee bar."

"A coffee bar in the closet." She spoke it reverently.

"Yeah. I'm either going to look for vintage doors leading in from the bedroom or make them. And switching the fireplace to gas in there. Maybe doing a small, interesting electric one in the bathroom."

Because a fireplace in the bathroom qualified as a long-term fantasy of hers, Sloan felt a little thrill.

"It'll be a hell of a space, especially when you add the upper porch."

"Coming up on it, and going with a glass railing system. It's all about the view."

"You're hitting all my feels, and you get top marks on vision. A hell of a space," she said again, "but I thought you were finishing the main level first."

"Changed my mind. I've lived here for nearly five months." As he looked around, Sloan knew he saw it all finished. "I want a decent bathroom."

She walked to him, rose to her toes for a kiss. "Though the size and scope of mine can't compare, I can attest it makes a difference in your day. Where's Theo and Tic?"

"At your parents'. I declined the dinner offer, but pushed Theo and the dog to accept. Your mom brought me over the pulled pork—and gave me some tips on where to look for the vintage doors."

"Elsie Cooper's tips are gold."

In an absent move that had become a habit, Nash brushed a hand over Sloan's hair.

"She mentioned pulled pork was a favorite of yours and that she'd brought plenty for two."

When Sloan smiled, he leaned down, touched his lips to her curved ones.

"I took the hint," he continued. "Your dad's making hand-cut fries. You'll have to settle for frozen."

"I don't consider that settling. Once you get the upper porch done beyond your doors to nowhere, put out some chairs, tables—and you'll want flowerpots—"

"Will I, though?"

"Yes, you will. You can tap my mom on what you'll want there. Her gardening tips are also gold. Think how nice it'll be to have morning coffee out there."

"It's a plan. And doing this now means I can start enjoying that in a few weeks instead of a few months."

She walked to the window and his view of lake and mountains, saw it with the rustic wood porch, the all but invisible rails. Maybe a couple of Adirondack chairs, a wine barrel table, add a bench, distressed, she decided, for more seating, a pair of chunky pots spilling and spiking with flowers.

"It's going to be fabulous and worth every minute of the work. I hope you'll carve out time to do some of the exterior work on my not spectacular but cozily charming place. I ordered the supplies today."

"Yeah, we'll make time. Come down, tell me about it."

She turned to look at him. "I'm getting used to telling you about things."

"That's gotten to be a two-way street."

"Want to hear about the maid-of-honor dress I picked out a few days ago?"

"Absolutely not." He took her hand. "Tell me about windows and siding over a glass of wine."

When she went down with him, she detoured from the wine and straight into the dining room.

"You finished it! The table, the room. Oh, the table's just gorgeous."

Because he'd learned preheating was an actual thing, he turned on the top oven. "Your mom sort of cooed over it. You're more a purr."

"Really? Whatever. You need more chairs, but these three are great. Not matching, but coordinating."

"Exactly what Elsie said. And since I'm not planning any dinner parties, I'm taking my time with chairs."

"Good warm wall color." She nodded in approval as she wandered the room. "Not really gray, not really green. The Federal crown molding makes it. And the big window brings in the woods. You did a hell of a job on cleaning up this old iron fireplace. It looks old and dignified instead of old and ugly."

"It took some sweat. Mostly Robo's, and for some reason, he enjoyed doing it."

"Robo's got the bug now," she murmured as she scanned the room. "You need the right art, interesting candlesticks for the table, maybe a big wooden bowl—unless you're going to do fresh flowers for the table every week."

"I am definitely not doing that."

"I thought not. But you absolutely need a buffet, a big server-type deal."

"It's in the shop. Needs refinishing."

"I want to see!"

The oven dinged.

"I'll put the fries in, then we can go out."

"Good enough. I want— Wait! Your office? Did you finish that, too?"

It added something, he realized, to have someone so genuinely enthusiastic about the changes.

It added more, he realized as well, that the someone was her.

"You know where it is. Go take a look."

After he put the fries in, set the timer on his phone, he went to find her.

"Oh, the barnwood wall. Yes, I want one. And you went with the smoky gray paint, which is just right. Your desk is big and beautiful with an important leather chair. The lights hit modern rustic without being too much of either. Built-ins, perfect, and I like the pocket for blueprints like my dad has."

"He gave me the idea. Here."

He handed her the wine.

"You need a leather sofa, offset that with a live-edge coffee table, some art, a rug—something just faded enough."

He watched her wander the space, placing finishing touches. "Dean was right."

"About?"

"You got the decor gene from Elsie."

"I guess I did, and like her, I can't help myself. You've gotten so much done. Has it really been that long since I was over here last?"

"Couple weeks, I guess. Your place tends to be more private, most of the time."

"I can't decide if it's more fun to see the progress bit by bit or to come in on a finished product. Either way, Jesus, Nash, you're making a wonderful home."

He remembered sitting in the chilly kitchen on a table of sawhorses and a door, and planning.

"It's what I wanted. I'm finding I want it more every day."

"It's good to be home, and this is yours now. I didn't know how good it was to be home until I came back to it. Let's walk out to the shop so I can envy your next piece of furniture."

The idea of Sloan Cooper worried Clara like a bad tooth. It troubled and distracted her during the day, kept her awake at night.

She read everything she could find on this constant irritation. High school track and cross-country star.

Big forking deal.

Her family owned a bunch of vacation rentals and such under the name All the Rest. She came from money then. One of those types.

She could have dismissed the woman with that background. Just some rich kid who had time to run for fun and probably hadn't spent a full day doing real work.

But she read up on the tree-hugger police, too, and they were a lot more than she'd thought. That added worry, and more yet when she found that damn name mentioned in some of their articles.

She'd worked as a kind of detective, covering the whole state. Going after poachers, sure—as if God didn't give man dominion over animals. And government cashed in with their license fees, their rules and fines.

But more than that.

She'd helped catch a man who'd killed his wife and tried to pass it off as an accident down in Assateague State Park, and busted up a meth operation—Clara did not approve of drugs—running through

Rocky Gap. Led herself a team that took down a father and sons beating up on and robbing from hikers in Deep Creek.

And it looked like she did that one the same day she got herself shot. Not by the boys and their daddy, but at some gas station store outside of Hagerstown.

She carried a gun like regular police, but that hadn't helped her.

Never in her life had Clara wished anyone dead. That was for God to decide. But she wished, and she'd prayed, that he'd take a good long look at this one. And call her home.

When Sam, reaching for her in the night, found her side of the bed empty, he went out to find her at the computer and chugging Mountain Dew.

"Babe, you need your sleep." He moved behind her to rub her shoulders, and saw she'd pulled up another search on Sloan Cooper.

"You gotta let this go, babe. It's wearing you down. She's nothing to worry about."

"It keeps pulling at me. I feel like there's a message trying to get through to me, but there's too much noise around it. I've been praying on it, and praying on it, but I can't hear it clear."

"Because you're not getting good sleep. Off your feed, too." Bending down, he kissed the top of her head. "You come on back to bed, and I'll relax you."

She reached up to close her hand over his. "I can't shake this feeling, doll. Just can't, so I have to try to follow it. I've got a knowing there's a reason she came into my ER, for treatment, and then again to ask her nosy questions. I need the reason before I can let it go."

"Babe, we haven't really done much on picking the next. You always say our mission comes first."

"I know that. I know it." Stress ran up and down her spine like fire ants. "But, Sam, what if she's part of the mission somehow? Maybe sent by the Devil himself to try to stop us from doing our work. Look at her eyes, Sam. Those are witch's eyes, I swear."

As the chill ran through her, Clara hugged herself. "And the Good Book says: 'Thou shalt not suffer a witch to live.'"

Now he sat. Rather than a chill, he felt a thrill. "You want us to kill her?"

"I'm conflicted. I'm just so torn about it all. We'd have to prove what she is first. We don't take lives, we heal. And we release the resurrected so they can go where they were meant to go."

Still hugging herself, she rose and walked to the window to look out at the dark.

So much dark in the world, she thought. Didn't she see it every day? Didn't she fight against it every day?

"I've been given this burden to carry, and I'll carry it no matter how heavy it weighs."

"Not alone, Clara. Never alone."

"You're my gift, Sam. I need to get her medical records. I think—I feel—if she's a demon, I'll find something in them to show me."

"Babe, you don't have the access down in Hagerstown. And we don't know what doctors she might've been seeing along the way."

"That's why I know—I *know* there's a reason she came into where I do have access, and came in when I was on the ER desk. She came right up and spoke to me, looked at me with those witch's eyes. Dr. Marlowe treated her in November, and I have the name of the surgeon who worked on her when she got shot. And they'd have her previous records."

A heavy burden, she thought again, but she could carry it. She would carry it.

"I can work it like I have before. Need to be careful, and I will be. The Lord helps those who help themselves. This is how we help ourselves. And if the proof isn't there? I think I can let it go. I think I can accept this was a kind of test."

"All right, babe. But what if we find proof?"

She turned to him, eyes fervent and fevered. "We send a witch back to hell."

And he felt that thrill again, hotter and stronger. "I'm with you, babe."

She let out a breath. "I swear, I feel better just knowing we're taking the steps." She smiled at him, gave a flirty rock of her shoulders. "Here we are wide awake, and me buzzed up on the Dew. And we've still got a couple hours before we have to get up and get ready for work."

As he smiled, he gave her the eyebrow wiggle. "How about I spend part of that couple hours helping you work off that buzz?"

She giggled when his hands slid under her nightgown. "Nobody does it better, doll."


It took her a few days, and a little more research. She couldn't rush it. Clara understood she had to find the right time, have all the answers to routine questions ready.

And timing meant everything.

Since she knew it best to wait until Dr. Marlowe's day off, calling on patience ranked high as well.

She dealt with patients with her usual calm and compassion. Took temperatures, blood pressures, held hands. Listened. She knew nurses, simply by their makeup, listened better than doctors.

She updated charts.

And didn't complain when a sick boy vomited on her.

She'd have brushed away the mother's tearful apologies in any case, but Clara saw it as a sign.

It gave her the opportunity to take a break to clean up, change her soiled top. Then time, just enough, to slip into an empty exam room.

Normally, if she wanted records in the system, she worked her way to them on night shift on her regular floor, when things tended to quiet down.

She didn't have to fabricate a story, make a call to another hospital—something she also took care of in private or quiet spaces.

The full medical would be in Marlowe's files.

Clara typed in the doctor's name, her ID number, all the patient information she had into the electronic health record system.

And pulled the flash drive from her pocket, bypassed into data backup.

She waited, one eye on the door—though she'd locked it—her other eye on the computer.

She saw no reason Dr. Marlowe would check the patient's file, note the access, the backup.

She'd used this system before successfully. Just as she'd used those fabricated stories to gain a transfer of patient records.

It worried her now because the woman worried her. She needed to pee; she wanted a sugary snack. Why was the transfer taking so long!

She needed a vacation, just a few days, she thought. It didn't have to be Aruba. They couldn't afford that so close to the other trip there.

But maybe a drive down to the Carolina beaches. Three or four days down there, without worry or work.

Next month, she promised herself. This time she'd surprise Sam and get them a house on the beach. Maybe with a pool or a hot tub.

Maybe both!

The idea cheered her up, cleared the headache that had started at the base of her skull.

The second the transfer finished, she snatched the flash drive out, closed down the records.

Relief flooded as she walked to the door, unlocked it. It flew open, jolting her, before she could open it herself.

On the gurney, the man was bloody and barely conscious, and the doctor already snapping orders.

Without missing a beat, Clara put on her metaphorical nurse's cap and got to work.

Since she hadn't made a decent meal for Sam in nearly a week—just too worried and distracted—Clara stopped at the grocery store on her way home.

She'd put in long hours that day, done solid work, and much of it on her feet, but a good woman took care of her good man. She picked up pork chops and potatoes—she'd make the salted ones he liked so much—butter beans she'd pan-fry like her granny's, some Parker House rolls, and add a half gallon of rocky road for dessert.

Since she'd made the stop, she picked up what she thought would do them for a week.

Then shook her head at the cost of everything. A body could work herself to the bone and barely get by!

Living off the land had been good enough for her grandparents. A cow for milking, chickens for eggs or frying up, deer and rabbit and squirrel to hunt, fish to hook out of the stream. And jars of vegetables, jams, jellies put by from their own harvest.

At times like these she wondered if nursing had taken her away from that sturdy independence.

But she'd been called to it, and had heeded the call.

The first in her line to go all the way through to college, and that was a proud thing to be.

Her daddy had worked the land, too—or under it in the mines. And that had killed him before he'd reached forty. And her mama had just faded off from the grief.

She'd had a brother, but he'd lit out and joined the army.

And that had killed him.

She had an uncle, a couple of aunts, some cousins somewhere or another. But they'd lost touch long ago.

Clara considered herself the last of her line, and based that on why she'd received another calling.

The mission.

She'd pumped at stopped hearts. She'd pushed her breath into the dead. She'd watched the paddles jerk and jolt false life back into a body.

Once she'd believed those actions a part of healing. Even miracles made by man.

But that was false pride, and that led to a fall—a fall from the only one who performed true miracles.

She listened to stories of some of those dragged back into this world. Some wept, as where they'd been, what they'd felt had been beautiful, peaceful.

And she'd seen in the eyes of those returned what she understood to be a longing for what had been stolen from them even as they embraced the world again.

For a few moments, they'd touched the eternal.

She'd been called to give them that gift again. And as her reward, their blood sustained her, gave her—and Sam—strength, clarity of vision, a purity of understanding what others couldn't.

Wouldn't.

As she drove through the hills, along the winding road, she felt a sorrow that the long winter neared its end.

For every time there is a season, this she knew. But with spring and summer came more people. Out of their winter caves like bears to roam. Some even close to the house and land where her grandmother had raised and fried up chickens.

It took more time, more care to follow the mission when the days loomed long with light and people sat outside well into the night.

But follow it they would, she promised, as she pulled up to the little house that had been in her family for three generations.

She carted in groceries, went back for more, then put them away.

While the flash drive in her pocket all but burned a hole in it, she reminded herself she had a good meal to make. Sam would be home before much longer, and they'd look at those records together.

She put the salted water on to boil, scrubbed the potatoes.

Once she got them going, she beat up eggs, dipped the pork chops in, and breaded them. Before long, she had them in a skillet, the beans in another.

She heard Sam pull up just as she put the rolls in the oven.

"Woo-wee!" He came in with a grin and a clutch of daffodils. "Something sure smells good!"

"Pork chops, salt potatoes, butter beans. I haven't made you a good dinner all week." Her heart bloomed inside her chest as she walked over, kissed him. "And you brought me flowers."

"I wanted to give you something near as pretty as you."

"Oh, Sam." She leaned against him for a minute. "You always brighten my day. I'm going to put these in water and set them on the table. Dinner's ready as soon as the rolls come out."

"I think my babe had a good day." He shrugged out of his jacket, then started to get a beer. He switched it to the bottle of apple wine she liked.

"You'd be right."

She took the flash drive out of her pocket, held it up.

"You got the records! I swear, my Clara's the smartest woman there is. What do they say?"

"I haven't read them yet. I waited for you. You'll get off your feet, have a good dinner. And after, we'll look together."

"That sounds just fine. It does me good to see that worry off your face." He handed her a glass of wine. "I'll get the table set."

"We sure make a good team, don't we, doll?"

"In every way there is."

He raved about her pork chops, and she had to admit they came out to a turn.

"Your cooking's going to make me fat," he said as he took another helping of potatoes.

"The way you work? You need the calories, so you eat up. I don't want a bag of bones."

He laughed; he ate.

When he pushed his plate away, he patted his belly. "Ain't no bag of bones around here. That was a fine meal, babe. And I tell you what. Let's just leave the dishes for now, have another glass of this wine, and see what we see in those records."

"I got rocky road."

He groaned. "For after."

"That's more than fine with me. I couldn't eat another bite, and I'm anxious to see what's on that flash drive. If we find proof, we have to figure how to deal with it."

"Burned witches, didn't they?"

"That or hanging. I think drowning, too. But getting her here's what I mean. I told you she's like real police. Carries a gun."

"Wasn't wearing one when she came in to the hospital, was she?"

"Not that I could see."

"So we take her, if we do, when she's not being police. Not carrying. We'll figure it out. We always do."

He had a way, she thought, that always settled her.

"You're right, and I'm borrowing trouble. We don't know what's what until we look."

They cleared the table, left the dishes.

After they opened the laptop, Clara stuck in the drive.

"Here we go. We'll start with the surgeon's records, work back from what he got of her history."

As they read, Sam shifted closer. "Missed her heart, but not by much."

"By enough. Had a head wound, too. No penetration there. Makes me wonder right off. People survive GSWs all the time. Even multiple. But . . ."

Frowning, she read on, then her breath caught. She reached over to grip Sam's hand.

"Look here, look!"

He leaned in a little more, then sat back. "I'll be damned—sorry. I know you don't like me saying that, but I'm just that surprised."

"She's one of them, Sam. She's one of the resurrected. That's what I felt, that's the message trying to get through. She's part of the mission, and she came to me herself."

Closing her eyes, Clara laid another hand on her heart. "We were meant to meet that way. Sam, we're meant to send her home. Whether that's Heaven or Hell, we're meant to send her home."

# CHAPTER TWENTY-FIVE

Spring popped in small ways. The honk of geese, the waddle of ducks, the glide of newly hatched cygnets guarded by Mom and Dad. Daffodils opened to trumpets even through the occasional shower of snow.

And snow melted away in rising temperatures.

Boats and kayaks joined the waterfowl on the lake along with the occasional hardy, wet-suited skiers.

Those rising temperatures brought rain as well as a shower of snow. Rain and melting snow brought the mud. Sloan assisted more than one hiker with a turned ankle or wrenched knee down a sloppy trail.

And educated more than one camper about how to stow food unless they wanted a roaming bear to pay a call.

She spotted a couple herself, as anxious to keep their distance from her as she from them.

And she watched a vixen taking a mouse back to her kits in her burrow while songbirds filled the woods with wing and calls.

She sat in Travis's office after filing her daily reports.

"How about an update on Elana?"

"I could write up her eval right now. I don't see it changing in the next few weeks."

"And what would it be?"

"She loves the work, and it shows. She listens, learns, and applies. She's excellent with people, just naturally personable. Could be a little more firm when that's needed, but that'll come. She's good at keeping it light, focusing on the educational aspect of the job. Physically, she's damn near tireless. She rarely complains, and then it's more of an observation or a joke. She works well with a team when assigned to one."

"No downside?"

"Well, she tolerates bullshit more than I would, but that's her nature. I've found her good backup when we have a dicey situation. With more experience she'll be better at it."

"Keep on the training for, let's say through the spring season. Then I'll toss another one at you."

"I'll catch them."

"Counting on it. Now tell me how it's going with the missings."

"I wish I could tell you there's been real progress. If the FBI or the law enforcement officers have made any, they're not saying. I think O'Hara would. We talk at least once a week. I have one more possible victim from last May. Female, twenty-three. Alyce—with a *y*—Otterman. She worked in a bar in Morgantown, sporadically. Had a history of just taking off, coming back, taking off again. An oxy addict, did some sex work to pay for it, has a sheet for that and for assault.

"OD'd last March, collapsed right on the street. They lost her twice, got her back. She rolled on the dealer so didn't do time, sixty days in rehab, mandatory. When she got out, she went into a halfway house—voluntarily. Two weeks after she went in, May twenty-fifth, she vanished."

"Not surprising, Sloan."

"No, but her counselor states she was doing well, sticking to it. And she took nothing with her. No clothes but what she was wearing. She left sixty dollars rolled up in her underwear. If she was going to walk, why leave sixty bucks behind?"

"You said she rolled on her dealer."

"Yeah, and I have to factor that. He was still in, but sure, he had friends who'd be willing to take care of her. Still, no trace of her? Wouldn't you want her body found? A warning against talking to the cops?"

"Or?"

"Yeah, or? She slipped, got another taste, and decided: *Fuck this, I'm out of here.* A lot of ors, Cap, but one's that she fits the victim profile. So." She shrugged. "I'm looking."

"Good, because playing devil's advocate aside, I agree with you. You're a damn good sergeant, and God knows a tenacious investigator. Just don't wear yourself too thin, Sloan."

"I won't. Give me another month, and I'll be planting flowers or sitting on my new front porch drinking my morning coffee."

"Go home, and enjoy your weekend off. I'll see you Monday morning."

"I'm ready for the weekend." She rose. "Even if I'm called in."

She hoped not.

Things were happening at her house, and she wanted in on it. She planned to scrape the damn popcorn off her bedroom ceiling, prime the walls, then paint them with the calm, soothing gray she'd picked.

Like a cloudy sky, she thought, that made you want to snuggle in and sleep.

She hoped.

And she wouldn't feel her mood plummet every day she walked in there. She'd leave the exterior work to the crew, but it was past time she got her hands on her own house.

When she started to turn into her drive, she braked. Stared.

The bumpy, potholed stretch now ran smooth and level with a thick blanket of fresh gravel.

None of which she'd arranged to have done.

As she turned, the house came into view, and she had to brake again. That level, gravel drive now curved toward what would be her carport and mudroom.

And her house sat, a sweet, pretty cottage now dressed in blue siding, her new windows gleamed, now framed in bright, clean white. The deck of the porch she'd envisioned had become reality. Even now she saw her father and cousin installing a section of railing.

And on the side, wonder of wonders, stood the posts of her carport and the framing of her much-desired mudroom.

A scatter of daffodils, buttery yellow, creamy white, danced along the edge of her currently scrubby, muddy front yard and the woods.

On the drive up, she heard the hard buzz of saws, the pop and bang of nail guns. It sounded like music.

She nosed in beside her father's truck.

As she got out, he pushed up the bill of his cap and stood grinning. "So, what do you think?"

"I can't believe it! When I left this morning, I had footers. Now I have a porch, an almost carport, and the start of the mudroom. And the siding! It looks good, right?"

"Nice choice."

"But the driveway. I didn't order that work yet."

"It's a gift. Say 'thank you.'"

"Dad." She rushed to him, hugged hard. "Thank you."

"Hey. I'm right here."

Laughing, she hugged Jonah, rubbed a hand over his beard-free face. "Thank you. You've been working on this all day?"

"Us, and the Littlefield crew." Dean gestured toward the side of the house. "After Jonah and I got the windows in the other day, we decided, hell, let's go for it."

He took a glug from his water bottle. "We juggled some scheduling, and so did Nash, so we could get this going good."

"It's going really good."

"Your mom says those azaleas we had to dig up for this should stay in the back where we put them. What you need here are the smaller ones, more to scale. She says you want the ones that bloom a few times a year."

"Yes to everything. I love it."

"You'll love it more when we finish the front door and replace this one. Should be ready to go in no time."

"And I'll have a Made-by-Cooper front door."

"On the mudroom, too. You want consistency. You've got a nice little place, baby."

"Thanks to you, and you," she said to Jonah, "and the Fix-It Brothers crew. And I guess Big Mac took care of the driveway."

"He sure did."

"I'm getting in on all this and dealing with my bedroom this weekend. I've got to go see the rest!"

She jumped off the porch, hurried around toward the sound of building. Nash set down his nail gun, and in the way of men, put his hands on his hips as he looked up to where Theo and Robo finished the last of the roof trusses.

She leaped up, legs around his waist, and added a long, loud kiss.

"Thank you! It's the best framed-out mudroom in the history of mudrooms."

"It's not bad," he said as she jumped down.

"And the siding. Oh, you put in the new door to the kitchen already!"

"Yeah, you lost that excuse for a broom closet and some wall space, but the storage here'll make up for it."

"I really didn't expect all this."

When Theo came down off the ladder, she gave him a squeeze. Then did the same to Robo.

"It's moving right along," Robo said. "It's the first time I ever helped build a whole room from the ground right up. It's fun."

"We'll put in some time tomorrow," Nash told her. "Since Dean's got an in with the inspector, he'll check out the framing, then we'll wrap it."

"I'll provide food and drinks. I can make something now. What can I make? What have I got? I have some of my mom's spaghetti sauce, I have pasta."

"I appreciate it, but Drea and I are making fajitas."

Nash turned slowly. "You're making fajitas?"

Theo gave a grin and a shrug. "I'm learning how to make fajitas. Drea worked all day, too, so dinner's a duet. But I'll take that food and drink during work hours tomorrow, Sloan."

"Got you covered."

"I got a date."

Sloan angled her head at Robo. "Same girl?"

He flushed, hunched his shoulders. "We're going to get some dinner, then there's a party. But I'll be around tomorrow for sure. I never wrapped a room before."

"I don't have a date."

Sloan looked over at Nash. "Looks like you do. Now I'm going in my new mudroom door before I go out and stand on my new front porch. Come in when you knock off."

When he did, she'd changed out of her uniform into leggings and an oversized green sweater. She had the sauce thawing in a pot, a bottle of Chianti on the counter, and stood working on a salad.

Even in that poor excuse of a kitchen, he thought, she looked just exactly right.

"I guess since you worked all day, too, this is another duet."

She glanced over. "Can you boil water?"

"I can handle that."

"That'll be your job once the sauce heats up. For now, you can pour that wine. I can't tell you how it felt when I started to turn into the driveway and saw the house. It looks happy. Before, it was it could be happy and now, it is."

He poured the wine and felt himself falling just a little deeper into whatever it was she brought to him. Contentment, he supposed, where he hadn't looked for it.

Or expected it, he realized, just as she hadn't expected to come home and see her house happy.

She moved him, he admitted. He might as well get used to it.

So he took her by the shoulders, turned her, then drew her in for a kiss that spoke of that deeper slide.

"Since this is a date, and a dinner duet of sorts, I expect sex later," he said with a smile.

"Well, you did help side my house, so it's the least I can do. And it's going to be the last night you spend in that dull bedroom."

"It's never dull when you're in it."

She toasted him, drank. "Littlefield. That's a very clever thing to say."

"Maybe, but true."

"The next time you find me not dull in the bedroom, it'll have a brand-new look. While you're wrapping the mudroom tomorrow, I'll be scraping popcorn off the ceiling. So Sunday, I'm priming the walls. If that goes smooth enough, it'll get its first coat—Decorator's White on the ceiling—the trim, too—and Cloudy Day on the walls."

"I could send Robo in to do all that."

She added thin strips of carrots to the salad bowl, then shot him a steely look. "You don't think I can handle it, Littlefield?"

"I haven't seen you not handle anything so far, Sarge. But he's quick, thorough, and damn good."

"You can take a look at my work tomorrow. I need to get my hand in, plus I need the mental health break. I don't want to think about work tomorrow, especially what I'm doing on my own time.

"I think I found another one last night. I don't want to get into the details, not now, but she fits the pattern for me."

"And we're in the first week of April. That weighs on you."

"It does. So I'm taking a break from it." She sliced some black olives for the salad, then smiled at him. "Besides, I have a date."


In the morning, she stripped off all the bedding and hauled it down to the washer. Since Nash had already helped her cart out her dresser, the nightstands, she tarped the bed, the floor, taped plastic to the walls.

She got her new garden sprayer, added a touch of fabric softener to the water. After tying a bandanna over her hair, she wet down the first section of the ceiling.

As she worked, section by section, and the softened texture fell in gloppy piles to the mud pan, she heard the dogs barking.

Crews are here, she thought, and kept wetting, waiting for the softening, scraping.

In less time than she'd estimated, and with her shoulders burning a bit, she had a popcorn-free ceiling.

She cleaned up the mess, switched the laundry—maybe for the last time in the serial killer basement—then made a pile of sandwiches.

When she walked out the kitchen door, she walked into a room with walls, a window opening, a doorway, and a ceiling going up.

"Wow, just wow! I should've made steaks instead of sandwiches!"

The dogs surrounded her as she turned in a circle.

"Come in! Take a break. I've got food and drinks. Woo!"

Since five grown men couldn't fit into her kitchen, they scattered. Standing, sitting at the table, on sawhorses in the under-construction mudroom.

Nash tugged at her bandanna. "Cute."

"Does the job. And so do I. Popcorn is no more."

Sandwich in hand, he walked out and into the bedroom. "Good job."

Behind him, Dean nodded. "That's my girl. Going to need to sand it some."

"Yeah, that's next."

She spent the rest of the day in remodeling heaven. Even teared up when she watched Dean and Jonah finish installing her new front door. Stable style, painted a rich navy with a window to let in the light.

"It's beautiful. Dad, it's just beautiful."

"Came out good." He opened and closed it. "Damn good fit."

"Of course. It's Made by Cooper."

"How's your bedroom coming?"

"Scraping didn't take as long as I thought, so I'm getting the walls primed. I'll let the ceiling dry overnight, though the texture was such crap it didn't take much to soften it."

"Man, that door's a beauty," Theo said as he walked in from the back. "I'm grabbing another Coke, Sloan."

"All you want."

"Baby, you can't stay in that bedroom tonight. You can bunk in your old room if . . ."

Sloan saw the light dawn on Dean's face, and the slight discomfort with it. And adored him.

"Yeah. Right. Fine."

"It's okay, Dean." All cheer, Theo took a swig of his Coke. "Drea's making dinner at our place for the four of us, then we're going to have a gin rummy marathon."

"Right," Dean repeated. "Elsie and I have those, too."

"Dad." On a laugh, Sloan rolled her eyes.

"Anyway. We'll get the other door in tomorrow. Time to head out," he said, and clamped a hand on his nephew's shoulder. "Just me tomorrow. This one's busy."

"We'll help you get it in. Just me and Nash. Robo's got a family thing. Taking his girlfriend."

"That's another first." Dean gave Sloan a kiss, then went out, whistling for Mop.


Because she wanted to try out Nash's kitchen—and possibly pick up some practical ideas for her own—Sloan made Sunday breakfast. She found both bacon and eggs in the enormous fridge. And some Drea additions.

Yogurt, coconut milk, arugula, spinach, Diet Pepsi, San Pellegrino.

Very Drea, Sloan thought, as were the lemons filling a glass cylinder, a vase of daffodils, and a wooden bowl of bright red apples, all artfully placed.

"Born to make a home," Sloan murmured.

Her sister could hammer a nail, but she'd much rather arrange flowers.

Sloan took out the eggs, the bacon, the butter, and because it was there, a block of cheddar. She hunted up a skillet, found it stored logically in the lower by the glorious range.

And discovered the Littlefields' cookware ran several levels above her own.

It didn't seem quite fair.

She'd beaten the eggs and started grating cheese when Nash came in.

"My contribution is bacon and eggs," she said as he headed straight for the coffee station. "I'm taking a leap and assuming since you proved you could boil water, your culinary skills include making toast."

"I can make toast. After coffee."

"I decided to make breakfast to spark ideas for my own kitchen. I know I want the spice pullout—which I'm confident Drea filled. I don't have room for a coffee station or your magnificent machine, the appliance garage, and probably not the microwave drawer. And since your pantry is actually bigger than my entire kitchen, this has been a series of frustrations and disappointments."

"Bad start to the day for you." Nash shoved a hand at his hair as he drank coffee.

"Not entirely, as I've decided to make my kitchen a study in smaller space efficiency and innovative style. When the time comes. I like a challenge."

Tic wagged his way in seconds before she heard Drea and Theo's voices. She turned the flame on under the skillet, tossed in a slice of butter. "Better get on that toast, chef."

She spent Sunday painting, and with the window open, painted to the sound of building.

After the first coat, she went into town to hit the grocery and replenish the supplies she'd depleted the day before.

She noted the car behind her most of the trip as a matter of course. An older Ford sedan, gray, West Virginia plates.

She thought no more about it, and pulled into the lot at the grocery store.

Clara drove past.

"We should've brought the van. We could take her now, babe, if we had the van."

"We're not ready for her, doll. And you saw those two trucks and the men at her house. Somebody'd likely notice pretty quick if she doesn't come back. It's enough we found where she lives, what car she's driving when she's not in that police truck. Makes it worth the trip, and using our Sunday off to take it."

"I don't like how much she's worrying you."

"Now, don't you worry about me worrying." With a little laugh, she reached over to pat his cheek. "We know she's a resurrected, and I truly believe a witch along with it. It may be she's what all our work's been leading to, doll. We'll send her where she's meant to go. We need a plan."

"I know you're right. I know you're right about it just like always. She's different. I don't just want her story, don't just want to send her back. I want to make her pay for twisting you up the way she does."

"Evil always pays in the end. This'll maybe take a little longer, that's all. We need protection against that evil, and the right way to stop her from using it against us.

"We're going to drive by the place where she works. I don't see us taking her there, but we need a look-see."

"You think of everything, babe."

"In this battle against evil, doll, a soldier has to think of everything."

"It's sure a nice day for a drive anyway." Relaxing back, he tapped his fingers on his thigh. "You can feel spring coming on. How about after the look-see, I take my woman to Cracker Barrel for lunch?"

"There you go. You think of everything, too. It's why we don't lose, Sam. It's why we were called. Together, we're like one righteous Angel of God."

She gave a contented sigh.


Nash found Sloan in the bedroom on a stepladder installing a new light fixture.

"Do you know what you're doing up there?"

"Please. I thought you'd left, then I heard you come back."

"I ran into Carl. He said he had time right now to do the rough-in electric."

Holding the glass-and-iron drum light to the ceiling, she looked down. "That's great."

"CJ's working in the plumbing tomorrow afternoon." He glanced around. "You were right about the color in here. And good job with it. If you decide to switch careers, you're hired."

"Good to know."

She finished the light, stepped down. When she started to fold the ladder, he brushed her aside. "I've got it."

"Thanks."

So she went out, flipped the breaker back on, then came in and turned on the light.

"And that's a big yes. I now have a hundred and twenty-four square feet of fresh and soothing. And like my future kitchen, smaller space innovative style. I need new shades."

"And here it comes."

"No, it doesn't. Or not much. New shades were already on the list. I won't need a new closet door now, as painting it did the trick, but I will need the new bedroom door to match the other interiors. Stick with the white duvet I have, but add some shams. Dark gray, shades and shams. Small space, keep it simple. I can crochet a throw in ombre grays."

"You can crochet a throw?"

"I have hidden skills. It'll take me forever, but I can crochet a throw. I've got some art from my apartment I haven't put up. Add a little splash, and done."

"I guess you want to haul that dresser back in."

"Yes, I do. Theo and Drea had that late-afternoon meeting with the caterer, right?"

"Yeah."

"Where's Tic?"

"At your parents' with Mop. Theo calls it, and it just makes me sad, a playdate."

She lifted her end of the dresser and grinned. "Well, they will play. Right under where I rehung the mirror."

"I figured."

They brought in the nightstands, the lamps, and since she had him, she enlisted him to help hang the art.

When he went out to check with the electrician, she remade the bed, fluffed pillows, smoothed the duvet.

And with an incredible feeling of satisfaction, stepped back to take it all in.

"I did this. By myself, for myself. Next time I feel like taking a couple days, I'll tackle the other bedroom."

More an energy color in there, she considered, since for the foreseeable future she'd use it as her gym.

She walked out, found Nash getting a Coke from her fridge.

"I'm helping myself."

"Great, help me to one, too." She stepped out, saw the rough electric in. "He finished already?"

"It's not that much. Washer, dryer, lights, a couple outlets, the split for heat. You don't have AC."

"That's why they invented windows. I'm ordering those stackables. The crap machines can stay in the serial killer basement for now."

He brought her the drink, then stood with her. And understood she saw it finished as he did.

"Got a little paint."

He rubbed some speckles off her cheek, then left his finger there another moment.

"Why don't you clean up, and I'll take you out to dinner."

She looked up at him with those wood nymph eyes. "Out? As in out?"

"Yeah, out as in. You know, where they bring you food you didn't have to cook, then you don't have to do the dishes."

"I've heard of the concept." She continued to watch him as she sipped her Coke. "Would this be another date?"

"You could call it that."

"Then I believe I will. Would this be a jeans and sweater date or more a little black dress date?"

He'd figured the first, and changed his plans.

"I wouldn't mind seeing you in a little black dress."

"Luckily, I happen to have one."

"I'll go clean myself up, and swing back to get you in about thirty."

"Make it about forty." She smiled. "Little black dress dates take longer."

"Forty then." He opened her new mudroom door.

"Nash? It's nice. Going out. It's not something I need or want very often, but it's nice."

"Next time you want nice and I don't think of it, you can do the asking."

"That's fair. See you in forty."

# CHAPTER TWENTY-SIX

For the first time in months, Nash put on a suit. He found he didn't mind it so much, especially since it reminded him he no longer had to wear one daily.

When he picked her up, looking every bit as good as he'd imagined in the little black dress and heels that must've added a solid four inches to her height, she just grinned at him.

"I knew it. I knew you'd have a selection of superior suits to fill that amazing closet you're building."

"I ditched half of them. Donated," he corrected when her mouth dropped open.

"Okay then. Good thing you kept this one." She took a leather jacket out of the coat closet. "Because you look, as Sari would say, fine in it."

Since they'd dressed for it, he took the jacket from her, helped her on with it. "You look fine yourself."

She sent him a look over her shoulder. "Yes, I do. We do. So let's get this party started."

The fact she knew just about everyone—bartender, several servers, a good chunk of other diners—didn't surprise him. She'd grown up in this little spot, after all.

Just as it hadn't surprised him just how good she looked in that little black dress.

It did surprise him, at least a little, how much they had to talk about beyond her work, his work, house plans, and paint samples.

Maybe it shouldn't have. They'd had plenty of conversations. But it seemed different sitting in a restaurant over a good bottle of wine.

"I saw your couple dozen medals at your parents'. For track."

"And cross-country. I could run. Still can. I did indoor track to keep in shape, but outdoors was it and cross-country the biggest it. Did you have a sport?"

"Tennis."

"I'd have guessed football. Got a quarterback build on you, Littlefield."

"Not on the approved list. Tennis or golf. Country club sports were acceptable activities. I went for tennis. Wasn't bad," he remembered. "Theo was better. We both went for piano—also required. I'm better there."

"You play the piano?" Those magic eyes widened. "I want to hear you play. Why don't you have a piano? You have to get a piano."

"I've got one in storage. I was going to sell it when I sold the condo. Theo talked me out of it."

"Good for Theo." She reached over to sample some of his salmon. "You've got plenty of room for one. Do you like to play?"

"Now and then." He reevaluated. "Yeah, now and then. I bought one telling myself I could play when I wanted, not when required. It worked. Do you play?"

"I play nothing. I could never sit still long enough to practice. I tried guitar awhile, during my rock-stars-are-dreamy stage." Head angled, she lifted her wine. "I guess I never moved out of that stage, but even though you can stand up and move around with a guitar, it didn't stick.

"Try some of this shrimp."

She transferred some to his plate.

"Drea was ballet girl. I liked it okay. It's athletic, physical, demanding, but—"

"Too much time indoors."

She tapped her fork in the air. "Exactly. So tennis and piano? Any other lessons and hidden talents?"

"We had to learn suitable dances. I consider myself fortunate ballet wasn't in the mix."

"Athletic," she reminded him. "Physical. But, that aside, what's a suitable dance?"

"Waltz would top the list."

She sat back, pointed at him. "You can waltz? You have to teach me. It always looks so pretty, especially in those movies where the women are in those sweeping gowns and the guys wear tuxes. Do you really have a tux?"

He had two, but just shrugged.

"I don't have a sweeping gown, but I'd get one if I knew how to waltz."

She angled her head. "What's funny?"

"Not funny so much as interesting. You're an interesting woman."

"You teach me to waltz, and I'll crochet you a throw. After I crochet mine, so it'll be a few years. But it's a good trade. Or I could do a scarf, which you'd definitely have by next fall. You can choose."

"I'll decide after I see how long it takes you to learn the waltz."

"That makes sense." She leaned toward him. "Tell me something else?"

"About what?"

"About you. We've known each other for months now, and I'm just finding out you play the piano and know how to waltz. You probably fox-trot, too, even though I don't know exactly what that is. Favorite TV show, early 2000s."

"*Alias*. We weren't allowed to watch, but Sophia would record it and let us watch it when they weren't around. Hot, kick-ass woman. Everything a young boy could want. I will forever have a crush on Jennifer Garner."

"That shows excellent taste. I wasn't a young boy, but I loved that show. And I'm sorry I keep blundering into what you had to do or couldn't."

"It's hard not to, and it's fine. And it gets less . . . important every day. I have what I want. I was happy enough in New York. I'm happier here."

"What would you do on an average evening in New York?"

"This. Dinner out. Not now and again, but most of the time. Taking clients to dinner or a dinner meeting, a date or meeting up with Theo. In Annapolis?"

"A lot of takeout or toss something together. Maybe dinner with friends, or over at Joel's if Sari took pity on us. Maybe a date. I was happy there, and I didn't really expect it, but I'm happier here. I've got what I want, too."

Because they both wanted it, they spent the night together within the soothing walls of her bedroom.

He left before her in the morning, and as she dressed for work, she dubbed her weekend—a truly off weekend—perfect. She'd put her mind and her efforts into her home, herself, and by doing so, her relationship with Nash.

She liked who he was, who he'd made himself into. The more she learned about him, the more she admired the man he'd made himself into.

If her feelings ran deeper than she'd intended, well, he was the kind of man she wanted to invest those feelings in.

And she was, beginning, middle, and end, responsible for her own feelings.

She'd come through a hard fall, a shaky start to the winter. And now with spring finally here, she had her footing, and someone she cared about who cared about her.

She had what she wanted, Sloan mused. And the weekend had only given her more.

She put on her Stetson—the straw one for the warmer season. And with it, put on the cop again.

She kept the cop on when she got home at the end of her day. Though she sat a minute or two in her car just smiling at the house. She'd put chairs on that porch, a little table, some flowerpots. She should do window boxes—just the right touch for the cottage look.

Inside, still in her jacket and hat, she ignored the kitchen and stepped through to the mudroom.

"Plumbing roughed in, thank you, CJ. Next, inspection, insulation, and drywall!"

She went back, hung up the jacket, stowed her hat, secured her weapon.

She took the Chinese takeout she'd picked up on the way home into her office. Sitting, she studied her wall, ate some noodles.

"All right. Where did I leave off?"

As Sloan ate and worked, Clara came home. She sat, took her crepe-soled shoes off her aching feet, and let out a long, deep "*Ahhhh*."

She'd been running around all day, with barely a chance to think. And thinking's what she had to do.

Maybe it was best to take another one first, before the witch. Gain some strength and insight from that.

She'd had one selected. The man had been struck by lightning and survived it. If that wasn't a sign from the Almighty, she didn't know what was.

What to do, what to do?

She took her shoes into the bedroom to put away, put on her house slippers.

She needed to make a meal for Sam. That was her sacred duty, and her sincere pleasure. Though her feet ached and her lower back with it, she went to the kitchen.

With the TV on for company, she put together a meatloaf, boiled some potatoes for mashing. Frozen peas would do fine with it, she thought, and set the timer on the meatloaf, turned the potatoes on low.

She needed just a short nap, just twenty minutes down, after this hard ten-hour day.

She lay on the bedspread, and fell instantly into a dream.

A vision.

She saw the man—his name was Terrance Brown, and brown he was, with a white mama, a Black daddy. A good-looking, well-built man of thirty. Head chef in a fancy restaurant in—it turned out—Heron's Rest.

When the storm came, it filled the sky, shook the earth. The man,

Terry they called him, went outside. He liked to take pictures, and wanted one of the lightning that pitchforked the sky.

"I didn't know it was coming for me," he told Clara. "I didn't know."

He moved away from the house, one he shared with a woman he got engaged to. Rain lashed, whipped over him, but he didn't seem to mind it. He wore nothing but the boxers he'd slept in before the storm came.

And he lifted his phone toward the sky, waiting for the next strike.

It struck with a blast like a bomb, cleaving the tree beside him.

His body shook; his hair stood straight up. The tree split in half as he fell.

Clara smelled sulfur and brimstone.

The woman in a shirt and panties—and neither did much to cover her butt cheeks—ran screaming from the house.

She ran to him, dropped down, and shouting, started pumping his chest.

"Terry! Terry! Don't leave me. I called for help, don't leave me!"

The witch stepped up beside Clara and laughed.

Clara saw her true face, those wicked eyes, the sharp, evil smile.

"Who sent the lightning, Clara? Your master or mine? Where did his soul go before they pulled it back into him? Heaven or Hellfire?"

The witch's hair, long and wild now, blew in the rise of wind, untouched by the rain.

"You think to take me on, Clara? Be prepared to pay the price."

She flicked out a hand.

Clara felt the burn, scorching, searing. And felt it even as she woke.

Panting for air, shaking so her bones seemed to rattle, she pushed up to sit on the side of the bed. She wept a little, prayed for strength.

In her heart, and that heart ached, she understood the terrible battle to come. She understood the price could be her life.

She would need that strength to continue the work. She needed courage to face what would come.

And she would need faith that if she fell, Sam would continue the mission.

In the bathroom she rinsed her face with cool water. And studied herself in the mirror.

She'd never been a pretty woman, she knew, not by society's standards. And now, with forty a few years behind her, time showed in lines and droops.

But she'd had a good husband while he'd lived, and she had a strong man now who loved her. She had a calling to heal, and the higher calling to the mission.

She'd had a good life, and had been chosen for righteous work.

If she fell doing that work, she accepted it. And she'd enter the gates of glory with her head high.

When the oven timer sounded, she walked out to finish dinner.

And when Sam came home, she greeted him with a kiss.

He wrapped around her. "Babe, some days I don't know how I'd get through if I didn't have you."

"Good thing you do. Now, you sit down, take a load off. I've got dinner ready."

"Nope, don't know what I'd do. I could sure use a beer after this one, babe."

"You know, I could, too. Why don't you get us both one while I put dinner on the table."

He opened the fridge, saw a fresh six-pack. His Clara? Best woman there ever was.

"Is that meatloaf? Clara, I swear I don't know what I did to deserve you."

"It's what you're doing. What we do together. And there's a little extra of the extra in the meatloaf tonight. We're both going to need strength and clarity, doll. We'll need all of that. I had a vision."

She told him, but not of her fear—and it was still fear—that the price would mean her life. She would spare him that, and not pit his love for her against his duty.

When she felt sure how and when they'd wage this battle, she'd leave a letter for him. She'd ask him not to grieve too long, and to lean hard on that love to help him continue their work.

"Satan's whore. I know you don't like that word, babe, but . . ."

"Truth is truth. We need to take our time here, doll. She'll be wily, there's no doubt of that. She won't be like the others. The others, they're victims of human pride."

"Because men try to be gods," Sam finished.

"With those others, we're giving them their release, sending them home. It'll be different with her."

The food soothed her, brought comfort. And she felt the strength of the resurrected blood do its work.

"I'll know when the time comes, when the word comes down and into me. But the vision? It showed me this. We're to take them both. She was there when the lightning struck the one we've chosen. He's part of this battle."

"How can we do that? Take two?"

"The way will come, doll. It will come. Until then, we watch, we wait, we prepare."

As April warmed and blossomed, Sloan welcomed the tulips, the haze of willows greening, the early pop of trillium, the graceful arch of Solomon's seal in the woods, along the banks of streams.

And as she searched for reports of missing persons, she went beyond the radius on her map.

She found nothing that fit the victim profile, and had to conclude the abductors had changed pattern.

Sickness, an accident, an arrest over something unrelated—any of those could account for the lag in time.

They could have botched an attempt that went unreported.

When she put on her uniform, she set it aside.

To add to the training, she assigned herself and Elana to boat patrol for a week.

Warmer weather brought out the locals and the spring vacationers. Kayaks, canoes, Sunfish, sloops glided silently while boat engines puttered, purred, or occasionally roared.

It felt good to cruise along, feel the air whip, the sun spread.

The swan family kept near the shoreline, where the cob rose up, big white wings flapping a warning if anyone—man or fowl—came too close. Duck families stuck together even as a head went underwater for a snack.

"It's the same out here as on a trail or any patrol."

"Education," Elana said, "assistance, advice. Always those first."

"That's right. Now for instance, those two guys at three o'clock, in the outboard? They're using walleye as bait. We're going to go over and educate them on the fact that's illegal on this lake."

"I know that's illegal, but how can you tell from here it's walleye?"

"First, the color. Olive on the dorsal side, and going more gold along the flanks, white belly. Five darker saddles."

"Okay. That tells me I need to learn more about recognizing fish."

"Do that. We're here to protect the waterways, the fish, fowl, and humans in and on them."

She cruised over to the outboard, judged the two occupants at around fifty in their fishing hats and windbreakers.

"Good morning," she called out, and idled the boat.

"Good morning, ladies! Sure is a pretty one."

Not local, Sloan concluded. New York or New Jersey from the accent. "Where y'all from?"

"We're Jersey boys," the second man called out. "Got a week down here. Sure is a pretty spot."

"We think so, too. You gentlemen may not be aware that Maryland doesn't allow the use of walleye as bait."

Their cheery went puzzled, then wary, but Sloan kept the smile on her face.

"I bet you're hoping to hook some largemouth bass. The best thing to do is head to the bait shop. Rendle's over on the east side of the lake can fix you up with some shiners or herring. My grandpa swears by shiners."

"We barely picked our spot. We haven't even caught anything yet."

"You talk to Nat at the bait shop. I bet he'll help you with that. Got your Maryland fishing licenses?"

Both of them reached for the inside pocket of their windbreakers.

"And two PFDs on board?"

The one reached under his seat in the stern.

"Good enough. Y'all reel it in now and head over to Rendle's. Tell them Sloan sent you. With shiners and Nat's advice, I'm betting you'll be cooking up some bass for dinner tonight."

"Smooth," Elana judged when the outboard putted its way east. "Nice and smooth."

"They either didn't know about the restriction or thought they could get away with it. I lean toward the first, but either way, we could've fined them. This way, they don't get pissy, they do it right, and they'll go back to New Jersey with some nice memories."

"Including the hot chicks in uniform."

"Obviously. You take the wheel awhile. We'll head over to that kayaker trying to get pictures of the swans. She gets any closer, Daddy's going to capsize her."

"I love this job!"

"It shows."

"Really?" Elana sent Sloan a long, hopeful look. "I know my eval's coming up in a week or two, and I didn't know a walleye from a shiner."

"But you will because you love this job. Let's see how you handle the kayaker."

A day on the water gave Sloan a yen for fish and chips. She considered getting an order for one, then heading home and diving into yet another search on missings.

Instead, she chose option B and texted Nash.

I'm picking up fish and chips on my way home. I can pick up two orders if you're not busy. Payment for dinner would include letting me bounce off the last couple days of basically nothing on the missing.

She sat, parked at the curb as she waited for his reply. And leaning back, eyes closed, didn't notice the car that drove slowly past, or the woman passenger who pulled down the brim of a floppy hat to hide the side of her face.

I'm never too busy when someone's bringing dinner. Don't
forget the hush puppies. Come to my place and check out
the progress.

Smiling she texted back:

I never forget hush puppies. See you inside an hour. Should I
pick up for Theo and Drea?

They're heading out in a bit for pizza and bowling with
Robo and his girl. Another first.

Thinking of the double date, Sloan hit a heart emoji as acknowl-
edgment. And had stepped onto the curb when it hit her Nash might
think she'd hearted him.

Embarrassing? she wondered. Then shook it away with a mental:
Oh well.

Inside, she placed the order, then decided to take the waiting time
with a walk. Boat duty meant she hadn't put in her usual miles on
her feet.

The town had its stone tubs full of spring mixes. Daffs and hy-
acinths, tulips, narcissus. Light jackets replaced winter parkas, and
shop windows advertised spring sales.

She considered the wind chimes in one, and promised herself she'd
come back, pick one out for her front porch. And she'd take time in
a few more weeks to go to the nursery, find just the right pots for
flowers for the porch.

Maybe more if she followed through on plans for the patio in the
back. Maybe.

As she turned, she noticed the woman across the street. Sunglasses,
floppy pink hat over brown hair. About five-four and a hundred and
fifty.

She couldn't see the face clearly, but something struck her as familiar.

Then the woman turned, took the hand of a man—about five-ten,
a hundred and sixty, Black, hair in twists.

The woman pointed to something in a shop window, and they moved closer.

The timer on Sloan's phone signaled. And thinking no more about them, she walked back to pick up her order.

"She looked right at us, babe."

"I know it. But we're protected, doll." She reached up to close a hand over the cross around her neck, and swore she felt its warmth, its light. "In that moment, we were protected. I didn't feel the burn like in the vision. I know I would have if she'd *seen* us."

But she squeezed his hand, as that turn and look had shaken her.

"We'll give it a minute," she decided. "See if she stays in or comes out. We'll stand here like we're looking at something in this shop. No, no, we're walking down to the next. We're just window-shopping."

"I don't like the look of her, babe, and that's the pure truth."

"Because we see and know what she is. It's more clear than ever. Didn't she go into the restaurant where Terrance Brown works? The signs are everywhere, doll."

"She's coming out now. Don't look around! She's got a couple take-out bags. And looking our way again, like she's trying to figure it out."

"Put your arm around my shoulders, give me a hug like you're laughing at something I said."

He obeyed, hating that he felt Clara tremble as the witch crossed the sidewalk.

"She's going to drive away, take the food home."

"We'll let her do that," Clara said. "We'll wait, give her time to get there. We'll drive by, see if anybody's waiting for her, but that's all for this trip on her. We'll come back, and get our dinner. See close up where Brown works."

She took a long breath. "Careful steps, doll. This is too important to rush."

Sloan drove past her house, but slowed enough for a quick glance. It just made her smile.

When she pulled into Nash's, she had to admit this one brought a smile, too.

They'd fixed up the porch here with new railings and wider steps. He'd replaced the old and inadequate porch lights and gone with a pair of large lantern-style lights with an oxidized copper finish.

And they'd started work on the decking of the upper porch.

He'd use the same lantern-style lights there, the same finish. And it would look fantastic.

She liked a man who knew what he was doing, who knew what to preserve, what to repair, what to replace.

And took the time and effort to do it right.

Was that part of the attraction? she thought as she parked. Sure it was. Though she hadn't expected to fall for a man with those particular attributes, she could admit she should've known better.

And she hadn't expected to fall for a man starting an entire new phase of his life. But she'd reached the point where she'd stopped denying she'd taken the fall.

Those weren't the sum of his parts, she considered, but they counted in that sum.

As she walked to the door, Theo came out of it.

"Hey!" Dressed in jeans, high-tops, a flannel shirt open over a gray tee, he jogged down to her. "That smells good." He gestured at the bags. "I told Nash you guys could join us for the fun and frivolity."

"Pizza and bowling, right?" She angled her head to study him. "Have you ever been bowling?"

"Sure." Then he laughed. "Well, once or twice. Once and a half, I guess. I'm going to get crushed. It'll be fun anyway. Door's not locked. CJ's upstairs with Nash. Wait'll you see.

"I gotta jump. Running late."

"She'll wait," Sloan told him as she moved by him, "since you're what she's waited for."

He turned at that, caught her in a hug. "Man, it's nice having a sister."

Inside, Tic bounded downstairs, sniffing the air.

"Not for you, pal." She walked back to the kitchen, stowed the foot well out of doggie reach before she bent down to greet him.

"What a good dog. Why don't you take me upstairs so I can see what's going on?"

He went with her, then raced up the steps. And stopped halfway to look back as if telling her to hurry up.

She heard the echo of voices, so walked with Tic into Nash's unfinished main bedroom and into the en suite.

He'd repurposed an old buffet for the vanity, added a more contemporary touch with new pulls on the drawers and cabinets so the matte black popped against the light natural wood. She assumed CJ had installed the two white stone vessel sinks on the long black slab that showed subtle graining of green and white.

They'd framed out and drywalled the WC, framed in the closet area.

But the star of this particular show shined in the wet room area. He'd tiled the entire area in a herringbone pattern that showed off the color variation and movement of the tile. From delicate green to deepest forest.

Now he stood on a ladder installing the second of two big, matte-black rain showerheads. She noted he wore a very new O's fielder's cap.

CJ stepped back to examine her work on the wall jets, nodded.

"You're gonna have water coming at you from everywhere."

"That's the idea."

"That big-ass tub you got comes in, we'll get that plumbed, but I'm done here today. Hey there, Sloan. You ever see anything like this?"

"I can't say I have." She looked up at Nash as he looked down at her. "Bold move, Cotton," she said, and made him laugh.

"Yeah, and we'll see if it pays off."

"Oh, I think it has. It's stunning."

"Got the idea from your shower. It's the same tile, but in green."

"This makes my shower a pretty phone booth. Good going on the floor. The white, hints of green and black."

"Heated, too," CJ told her. "The whole damn thing. Got steam in there, a speaker for music. It had a TV and fridge, hell, I'd live in it."

Nash stepped down from the ladder. "We couldn't have done it without you, CJ."

"That's God's truth. I'm grabbing a Diet Pepsi from your fancy kitchen on my way out."

"All you want. Tub and toilet coming in the end of the week."

"We'll get to them."

She stopped to rub at Tic. "You're a good job dog. You deserve a big treat."

At the word, Tic yipped, wagged, bounced. And CJ shot Nash a grin as she left with Tic rushing out with her.

"She got him to do that. And if you don't come up with the treat fast, he goes nuts."

"I'm glad you said your place. I wouldn't have wanted to miss this. I saw this"—she tapped the vanity—"in progress, and boy, did it turn out."

"Worth the effort. I've got paint samples for in here, the closet, the bedroom. You can weigh in. But right now, I'm seriously ready for a beer."

But he pulled her in first. "I'm glad you texted."

"Me, too."

She leaned into him for a moment. "What are we going to do with all the extra time once you finish the house, and they catch these serial abductors?"

"I guess we'll find out. And not 'they catch.' It's 'we.' You're a part of that."

"I feel like I've hit a wall."

"You can tell me about that. But the beer comes first."

# CHAPTER TWENTY-SEVEN

They ate at the island, a beer for Nash, a glass of Chardonnay for Sloan. The treat hadn't lessened Tic's appetite, so he made quick work of his meal before rushing outside to sniff and run.

"Let's start with this before I get rolling. When you finish the bathroom palace, the bedroom, the porch, what's next here?"

"Back to the main level, I think. Living room, library . . . sitting room, den."

"I thought you were doing a game room. Sitting room?"

"Undecided room right now. I'm switching the game room downstairs. We've got the space."

He ate a hush puppy. "Where the hell did these get a name like hush puppy?"

"It's a southern thing, Yankee. But I just call them good. And the Seabreeze makes the best in the county. I know the chef there. His fiancé and I went to high school together, and he did some work for All the Rest while he studied, well, chefing. His hush puppies are a secret family recipe, I'm told."

"The cod's nothing to complain about either."

"I was on boat duty today, and there were two guys from up your way fishing."

"New Yorkers?'

"New Jersey."

He gave her a long look. "That isn't my way."

"Sorry. They were using walleye as bait." She shook her head. "Can't do that down my way."

He couldn't imagine, just couldn't, having this conversation with anyone a year ago. And found himself delighted to have it with her.

"Did you arrest them for the walleye offense?"

"No. Just let them know where to get the right bait. Do you fish?"

"I went out deep-sea fishing with a client. An experience."

"Catch anything?"

"A wahoo. Yeah, an experience. I'm glad I did it, and don't have to do it again."

"Like bowling?"

"If I had to choose between?" He gave it two seconds thought. "I'd take the high seas."

"Me, too. Bowling's okay, and it takes skill, focus. I respect that. But you knock the pins down, then they set them up again. Again and again."

He shifted to her, ran a hand down her hair. "Are you ready now?"

"Yeah. I just wanted to move off the day, and I didn't want to dump on you the minute you moved off yours."

"If I didn't want you to dump, I'd be eating a grilled cheese sandwich solo. Tell me about the wall you've hit."

"They haven't taken anyone since Lori Preston."

"That's a bad thing because?"

"They have a pattern, and it goes back to what I've found at the end of May. The pattern didn't set until Celia Russell in September, but it's been consistent since.

"Seven people are missing that fit their victim type, and all but the first two went missing at the end of the month or within the first week at the start of the month. Not always the same day of the month, day of the week, but within that time frame. Preston edged over to the beginning of March, Tarrington start of February. The rest end of the month."

"So they changed their pattern. Couldn't it be whoever they hoped to take wasn't available? Moved, died, went on vacation?"

"Can't discount that. Which would mean they don't have a backup. They focus on only one at a time, and have gotten really damn lucky seven times. Maybe more if we haven't connected others."

She blew out a breath, stabbed at some fish.

"You like the logic of patterns."

"Well . . . yeah."

"Don't you have to consider the people doing this are lunatics? No offense to the dog."

Since the dog currently sat hopefully at the door, Nash rose, let him in. Then got out a bully stick. Tic spun in a crazed circle, then plopped down to sit before accepting it and racing off.

"That's a pattern." Sloan pointed at Nash. "Feed the dog, let the dog out, let the dog in, reward the dog."

"Or domestic routine."

"Routine, pattern, semantics." She picked up her wine, considering as she sipped. "Seven people are dead. It's not possible at this point to know how long they keep their victims alive or for what purpose, but they're not holding multiple people."

"No. I can't argue with that."

"They select them, and that has to be a process, and has to be due to the one thing all seven have in common."

"They experienced clinical death."

"Yeah. They select on that basis, which means access to medical records or nine-one-one logs, hospital admissions. It's possible they find the targets otherwise. News articles, social media posts."

"Then stalk."

She glanced at him. "Correct."

"Not only do I occasionally watch movies or series, read books, but it follows they'd have to know their targets' patterns, too." Then he shrugged. "And I confirmed that by reading up a little on serial killers."

She smiled. "Got you hooked."

"Looks like it."

At the sound of squeaking and running, Sloan looked around.

"Never," Nash said, "ever buy a ball that lights up and squeaks for a lunatic dog. Especially one who figures out how to pick it up and toss it for himself to chase."

Amused, Sloan leaned over and kissed his cheek. "You're a good dog pal."

And the sound of Tic happily entertaining himself took more of the edge off.

"Stalking phase," she continued. "Learning the victim's routine, establishing the best time and place for the grab. But in Janet Anderson's case, they couldn't have known she'd run out to the store."

"Watching her house, at that time."

"So stalking became the grab through circumstance. They had to be prepared for circumstance. They may be psychos, Nash, but they're organized and prepared. They have a place they can take them, a place, when they're done, they can dispose of the bodies. They have a purpose."

"What's the purpose?"

On a frustrated breath, she leaned back. "That's a question. If they're fanatics, and the common denominator of the victims indicates that, it may be human sacrifice."

"Well now. That's a cheery thought."

"It's the one I keep circling back to. It could be revenge over a loved one who wasn't saved—but they don't go after the medical team. Detective O'Hara tells me the task force is looking into fringe cults and groups."

"Task force? And you're not on it?"

Since she intended to stay, Sloan topped off her wine.

"No."

"And that doesn't piss you off? It pisses me off."

She toasted him, drank. "Thanks, but I'm okay with it. You've got three states involved, the feds, multiple jurisdictions, and none of the abductions happened on public land. The DNR has jurisdiction throughout the state, but including me added one more agency."

"Fuck that." Rising, he took their plates to load in the dishwasher. "You're the one who made the connection, who found the common denominator."

"You helped with that."

"Maybe that's why I'm pissed off. You handed it to them—the motive, purpose, whatever the hell you want to call it. And they exclude you?"

"O'Hara's reading me in on a consultant basis—with approval. I'm really fine with it, but boy, I appreciate the outrage on my behalf."

She propped her elbow on the counter, her chin on her fist. "It's nice to have someone in the pissed-off mode I talked myself out of."

He turned. "Why did you do that?"

"If I still worked in the Criminal Investigative Bureau, I wouldn't have. I'd have stayed pissed off, and I'd have pushed—and hard—to be included."

"What difference does that make?"

"A lot, it turns out. I made a big change in and for my life. A choice," she added. "Not the big, giant, dramatic change and choice you did, but a big one. I'm not just content with it, but happier with it than I expected to be.

"This investigation's important to me. It started with Janet Anderson because when she was taken, I felt helpless, weak, ripped out of my element. I've had the chance and the time to rebuild. She never will."

"You're in it for her."

"For her, and now the six others I've found. Initially I considered making a case to bring me on. O'Hara would back me there. So would my captain. But I realized I like working it alone, my way, my time."

She reached out a hand so he'd come back and sit.

"I like," she added, "talking it through with you. You bring a different perspective than Joel does. I like you're willing to listen and give that perspective."

"Hooked," he reminded her. "And talking serial killers is a break from tackling an unfinished basement—that's tomorrow, and not mine. Or looking at paint samples, fixtures, and finishing the built-ins for the library that will be mine."

"You've started them?"

"Barely."

"I'd love to see."

"Give it a day or two. Besides, I'm on my serial killer break."

"Okay then. Serial killers escalate, and the time between kills narrows. They crave the high like any addict. But these don't, not after those first two. They've stuck to that monthly hit—and in February and March even widened the time frame slightly. Or they've stopped. Illness, death, incarceration could account for that. Or they've reached their goal."

"But you don't think so."

"I don't think they can stop, no. Not on their own. They've succeeded. It's possible they're in law enforcement or have a connection there and feel the heat. So they're lying low awhile. But that doesn't feel right to me either. They need to do this. You don't go through all this, the time, effort, risk, and end with taking a human life unless you need it."

"But?"

"But if I'm wrong, and they've stopped, or moved on, it lowers the chances of finding them and putting them away. Anything short of that, there are seven people who'll never have justice, whose families will never know for certain what happened to them. Loved ones who will very likely cling to the hope they're still alive, will come home again. That kind of hope is another kind of death."

"So what do you do?"

"Wait, and that's horrible. Waiting for someone else to be taken, used, disposed of. Keep looking, hoping there's some detail you, and everyone else, missed."

Now she rose, wandered to those wonderful glass doors.

The sun had set and dusk had given way to night. Dark brought its comfort and quiet. The low, lyrical call of an owl just added to it.

"You've got a great horned owl nearby."

"You see an owl?" He got up to join her.

"No, I hear it. That's its call."

"The one you hear in movies when someone's lost in the woods at night?"

"Yeah, that's it. I've got a barred owl, or a pair of them. They got in a hooting match, probably with your guy out there, last night. Mates, protecting their nest."

"Mates will do that."

"Exactly. I don't think this is a cult, not in the traditional sense. It's not a group—you don't keep a violent secret with a group for nearly a year. And it could be longer. But two people? Siblings, father and son, spouses, lovers? Dedicated to this purpose and each other?"

"You're thinking mates."

"Another thing I keep circling back to. A parent and child there's a power differential, even as an adult child. And eventually that imbalance would cause issues. Siblings, yes, possible, but even with devoted siblings there's some rivalry. But mates? Spouses, lovers—if they love each other—they might establish more balance in the power structure. And sex unites."

"That's a big circle around from a hooting owl."

She let out a half laugh. "Not as big as it might seem. Your owl out there? That's the male. The female has a higher pitch. When she comes into it, they often synchronize their calls."

"They work together."

"As real mates do. Possibly they've been together for years and just found this purpose."

He could read her fairly well now, and shook his head.

"No, you think they found each other more recently. And following your line of thinking, that makes the most sense. They saw something in each other."

He turned to her, looked at her.

As he'd seen something in her weeks before they'd met as she'd pushed herself to walk along the lake.

"They saw something in each other," he repeated, "and that drew them together. Add in sex, and sure, maybe a twisted kind of love."

"It doesn't have to be twisted. They may genuinely love each other."

"That one doesn't add up for me, but fine. And through that, they found another common denominator. This purpose. It's a kind of mission, isn't it?"

"You could . . ." Her eyes narrowed. "Yeah, mission works. And if it's a mission they consider—no, believe—comes from their vision of a higher power? Fanatics again."

"These people died, and were brought back by medical intervention, so our mission is to right that wrong? Negate that human interference?"

"Along those lines, yeah."

"Wouldn't that eliminate your medical types?"

"Not necessarily. Medicine, comfort, stitching wounds, mending broken bones, treating illness. You could look at that as natural. Even transfusions, transplants because that's one human to another. But death? That's an end. It's time's up. And if they think, if they believe, man's pushed that higher power's will aside?"

It had, he thought, a kind of horrible logic.

"So possibly using their medical knowledge as a weapon, their mission is to rectify that moral wrong. And that goes back to your human sacrifice."

"It does. We're ending these lives that shouldn't continue to be lives, to honor whatever god we believe in. He or she took them, and man had no right to take them back."

"What does that tell you?"

On a half laugh, she shook her head. "You sound like my therapist. Well, Dr. Littlefield, it tells me—if this theory is correct—they're religious extremists, the sort who believe, absolutely, their god speaks to them, and they know his will. They believe what they're doing is morally just. In fact, imperative. The laws of man mean nothing when weighed against the laws of their almighty."

"Wouldn't there be a hitch in there?" he wondered. "How about the old 'Thou shalt not kill'? Stone tablets, burning bush, all that?"

"But in their view, their fractured view, they're not killing. They may enjoy it, and I tend to think they do, but it's not murder for them. They're giving back what was taken, righting a moral wrong. Whatever they do to fulfill this purpose, mission, imperative isn't merely just, it's blessed.

"This works for me. It doesn't get me over the wall, but it gives me something to push on."

"How do you push?"

"Step-by-step. And one step is to just let it cook awhile." She tapped her head. "You absolutely earned the hush puppies. How about taking a walk by the lake?"

"In the dark?"

She scrubbed at the stubble on his face.

"City boy, there's a gorgeous three-quarter moon out there. And what I can see from here, a sky full of stars. Plus, the loons are back. The waterfowl," she added at his smirk. "All you need's a jacket."

So he walked with her and the dog by the lake, and heard the loons call.

"I'd forgotten about this."

"About what?"

"That sound—the loons. I remember that sound now. I remember hearing it."

"Not in the city."

"No. We vacationed here when I was, what, about sixteen, maybe seventeen. It's one of the reasons I looked for a place here."

"You stayed in Heron's Rest?"

"Yeah. Two summer weeks Theo and I actually enjoyed. My mother's second husband liked coming here. He actually had a cabin. He liked to hunt, fish, hike, and he'd come here a few times a year with friends."

"You stayed in a cabin in Heron's Rest?"

"Oh, hell no. She'd never go for that."

He looked out over the lake with its crystal reflection of the moon, got his bearings, pointed.

"The big lake house, at about two o'clock. We stayed there."

"The Pinnacle? That's ours."

"I'm aware."

"It's the crown jewel. Three levels, two main suites, another three bedrooms and three baths, living areas with fireplaces on lower and main floors, kitchen, bar area—kitchenette and bar on lower level. Unrestricted views of the lake, views of the mountains. Decks, porches, patios. Outdoor shower and fire pit and so on."

He knew she had exceptional observation and recall skills, but . . . "You know the makeup of all the rentals?"

"Crown jewel," Sloan repeated.

"She wouldn't have otherwise."

"It's more so now than when you were sixteen or seventeen. Up-dated, remodeled."

"I can promise she won't be back. But she enjoyed boating, if I re-member. Lounging on the deck, shopping, but a week was it for her. She flew back to Connecticut, and we stayed here."

"I'm doing some math, and some memory jogging. Did you have daily housekeeping and did you bring a cook?"

"Yeah, she brought her cook—he flew back with her. Paul—the husband—he paid the extra fee for the daily housekeeping. Why?"

"Because I pitched in on housekeeping for the Pinnacle for guests that wanted daily—including fresh sheets in the main bedroom. And there was a French guy, tall, lean, about thirty-five with curly black hair, lightning-blue eyes. He gave us these amazing pastries he'd made, every afternoon. Afternoon because the guests didn't want us there until after eleven."

"Well, Jesus, that was Javier. He baked like a god."

She had to laugh. "Well, Littlefield, I made your goddamn bed. I don't remember seeing you."

"We'd have been out by the time you got there. Theo and I, in the lake, hunting up pretty girls, hiking on the trails. We even rented bikes and rode into town a few times. We didn't spend much time in the house."

"This is very strange."

"More strange because I think I saw you. I'm in the lake and look up, and there's this long-haired blonde in little shorts on the main deck, clearing up what was probably her breakfast dishes."

He looked down at her, passed his hand over her cropped hair. "What were you, fifteen?"

"Thereabouts."

"I remember you, the blonde with the ponytail and little shorts."

"And though I lost the ponytail, here we are again. You didn't try to buy the Pinnacle?"

"No. No," he repeated with some feeling. "It was a good couple weeks, but I didn't want that house. I got what I wanted."

As they walked along, he stayed quiet.

The three-quarter moon and cut-glass stars spread light, as she said. The lake breeze ran cool, but held no bite. Others walked, drawn by the water, so the murmur of voices, the occasional laugh joined the night calls.

And still strange to him, the howl of a coyote higher in the hills.

Happy with the outing, Tic stayed close, then raced ahead as they started back down the drive.

His house stood there, lights glowing, smoke curling from the chimney from the fire he'd banked before the walk.

He'd miss the fires once summer came, he realized. Yet he looked forward to the changing seasons, the changes in his home.

In himself.

"I'm not Theo."

Sloan glanced up. "Good thing, as he's engaged to my sister."

"Theo's an optimist. He always has been. Nothing could break that positive outlook of his. They sure as hell tried."

"You're not Theo, but you've got a positive outlook of your own. I said it before: nobody would have moved here from New York, bought this house, started a business from scratch without one."

"That was more going after what I wanted than outlook. I could afford it. Afford the time, the money. If I failed? Big fucking deal. I could go back to what I did before. I'm good at it."

"You may think that, but you wouldn't have."

He didn't know why he felt very nearly angry, but he felt temper scraping at him. "How do you know?"

"Because you clearly love this, and you clearly didn't love that. Being good at something doesn't mean you love it. I'm good at math, but I'd rather mow the lawn than sit down and do calculus."

It amazed him someone so insightful just couldn't get it.

"Jesus, listen. The point is I had that fail-safe, that safety net. It wasn't that big a risk."

"Again, you may think that. It's just not what I see."

"You got pieces and parts, that's all." He felt his frustration building and didn't know what the hell to do with it. "How can you understand what I came from? There's no cruelty in your background, in your family."

"No, there's not. But I live in the world. More, I'm a cop, and I see plenty of it."

"Not the same, it's not the same. That *was* my world. It was Theo's, but they never broke him."

"How much of that's because you stood in front of him so they couldn't? I'm at a loss here, Nash. Are you trying to get me to think less of you because you had lousy parents? Or worry you're going to become like them? That's just not going to happen."

"No. I'm not sure. I want you to understand . . . I came here for my own reasons. You weren't part of them."

"Okay." She slid her hands into her pockets. Those eyes of hers didn't waver but stayed steady on his. "Do you want me to take my ball and go home?"

"No." Incensed, he turned away, dragged his hands through his hair. Nothing helped clear his thoughts so he could just say them out loud. "Let's go inside. The wind's starting to kick. You must be cold."

"I'm not. I like it out here. It seems to me it's good to have plenty of air when you want to air out. You've got something you want to say, so say it. If you want to slow things down or break things off, I'd rather know it now, straight out, then have you keep circling around it."

"I'm not saying that. That's not what I want."

"Then stop pissing me off and tell me what the hell you're saying, what the hell you want."

"I didn't come here for you." He turned back. "I wasn't looking for you now any more than I was years ago when I looked up and saw you standing on the damn deck cleaning up after her.

"Why do I remember that? The girl on the deck, long blond ponytail, little red shorts, a white T-shirt. I shouldn't remember that."

"I remember all sorts of odd things."

"I saw you walking last fall, last winter, every step an effort. I couldn't get you out of my head. Then you show up at my door in that damn uniform, that damn hat, and I can't get you out of my head."

"And you want to?"

"No. I did," he admitted, "and I tried. Or I told myself I should. But no, that's not what I want. I saw you on the goddamn deck, Sloan. And I saw you walking the lake. I've been tripping over you for years without knowing it, and I don't know what the hell to do about it, about you, about this. You weren't part of the plan."

"Aren't you the one who told me plans adjust?"

"Adjusting's one thing, but you have to know what to do next. I don't know what to do next. I don't know how to handle being in love with you."

Her breath expelled in one long exhale. "Oh."

"It's another fucking first. I've been with women, cared about them, wanted them. But I never loved one. I wasn't sure I had that in me, considering. But I do, when it's you. And I don't know what to do about it."

"Well." She let out that long breath again. "Join the club. I'm president. You can be treasurer, since you're so good with money."

Baffled, frustrated, he pressed his fingers to his eyes. "I don't know what the hell that means."

"It means you weren't part of the plan. It means I'm in love with you and haven't known what to do about it. I've got a better idea now."

Slowly, he lowered his hands. Heart skipping, he stepped to her, laid his hands on her shoulders. And he felt the world that had rocked and teetered steady again.

"Want to fill me in?"

"Nash." With a tenderness that disarmed him, she cupped his face. "Take it. Just take it."

She rose on her toes to meet his mouth with hers, then felt her feet leave the ground as he lifted her up, wrapped her close, held tight.

"Just that? As simple as that?"

"It won't be, but it can be right now. I love who you are." She held on. "That's simple for right now. We're both good at figuring things out. So when we need to, we will."

"Adjusting plans along the way?"

"That sounds right to me. And I can tell you I haven't loved before either. It's downright scary."

"Good. That's good. Be scared. That way we're starting on the same level."

She smiled, kissed him again. And heard the two owls synchronize their calls.

# CHAPTER TWENTY-EIGHT

Spotty sleep and dark dreams kept Clara on edge. She caught herself stress eating, even slipping out of bed in the middle of the night to devour Ring Dings or MoonPies.

She couldn't seem to stop.

What difference did a few more pounds make if she left this life for the next? A martyr for the cause.

She told herself if called home, she'd go joyfully, but fear slithered inside her like snakes. Satan's symbol doing the work to make her doubt and fear.

So what if she ate a pint of Cherry Garcia on her break? She needed the relief.

She couldn't share her fear and doubts with Sam. His love for her, his need to protect her would overwhelm him. Then she would be responsible for turning him away from the mission, away from God's will.

If she spent time on her knees weeping and praying to have the burden lifted from her, she was human, just a woman with flaws and weaknesses.

She'd seen it herself, countless times, that desperation to live another day, even another hour no matter the pain or debilitating illness.

Some made peace with death, even embraced it. But most, she knew, denied, struggled, and cursed their fate to the last breath.

She would not allow herself to be one of the most.

So she took a day, then another and another, drawing out the time, telling herself she only took that time to prepare for the mission, and for her own acceptance.

This life, another gift, deserved appreciation and respect. She took time to savor the call of a bird, the bloom of a wildflower, the feel of Sam's hands on her body, the taste of ice cream on her tongue.

If called home—and it remained *if*—would she still know the scent of a rose, the feel of a summer breeze? Would her beloved grand-mother, her dear husband greet her, guide her through the gates and into glory?

None of the stories they'd collected fully answered those questions.

If the witch took her life, she would have those answers.

On a day Sam picked up an extra shift, she put on her good makeup, curled her hair, put on the blouse Sam had bought her in Aruba.

He said the ocean blue brought out her pretty eyes.

When she felt she looked her best, she set up the camera, and hit record.

She smiled.

"Hey, doll. Like they say in the movies, if you're watching this, I've gone to glory. I don't want you to grieve too much, but know I'm sorry, so sorry to leave you. I know we were meant to find each other for our higher purpose, but beyond that, you brought me so much happiness. And fun, too. We sure did have some fun."

She had to pause, fight off the tears.

"I loved cooking for you, and you never failed to show you appreci-ated it. You brought me the pleasures of the flesh, and made me feel, every day, like a whole woman. You gave me my first airplane ride, my first look at an ocean on that trip to Aruba.

"And so much more, Sam. So much more."

As she felt her strength rising, she took a breath.

"I'd hoped to surprise you with a trip to the Outer Banks. And that's just what I'll do if there's no need for you to see any of this. But if there is a need, if that witch disguised as a human woman ends my life, I need you to heed what I'm saying. Don't let grief hold you back. Don't let sorrow blind you to what must be done."

She shifted, leaned closer to the camera as the fire in her belly kindled again.

"You must continue the work. There are four more on the list, and you'll pray for guidance and choose the one to take first, to hear their story, then to let go. When those four are sent home, you'll find more.

"There are so many more, doll. So many who made that journey to eternal rest who were robbed of their peace, pulled back by the pride of man. Sending them back must be your life's work now. I'm counting on you."

She smiled again.

"I know I can. You've never let me down. The ones we've saved, Sam, well, they're a drop in the bucket. I know you can't save them all, like I know you'll have to find someone to help you as you helped me. I feel for certain you'll know that someone when they cross your path. It'll be meant, as you and I were meant.

"Sam, I've spent time conflicted on what we need to do next. I've fought my war on doubt and fear, and I've come to accept. And I've come to know how we'll go about taking Terrance Brown and the witch Sloan Cooper. I'm going to talk to you about that soon, and we've got more preparations to make, but I've felt the spirit come into me on this, and I know we'll prevail. If the cost of it is my life, you need to know I'm willing. Doesn't mean we'll make it easy for her, but if that's what's meant, I'm ready for my eternal reward."

She pressed a finger to her lips, kissed it, then blew it toward the camera. "I love you. I know in my heart, in my soul, that when your time comes, I'll be there to take your hand and guide you. I'll be there for your homecoming, doll."

It took her time to transfer the recording to a disk. Sam usually handled that. But she did the job, labeled it.

**For Sam with love**

She hid the disk in her underwear drawer, then put the camera and tripod away.

It settled her, she realized. She'd fix Sam a snack for when he got home. The man liked his nachos, and he'd have earned a beer.

Though tired from her own shift, and the stress and effort of the recording, she browned up some ground beef, chopped onions, jalapeños, a tomato, got out a jar of the cheese he liked.

When he walked in, she started putting it together for him.

"Whew, babe! What a day. I expected you'd turn in early and get some rest. But here you are."

He came up behind her, hugged, and she drew in his scent. Just a little sweaty after a double shift.

"I didn't want you to go to bed hungry."

"I sure appreciate it. I barely had time for two bites on my dinner break. We lost Mrs. Witner today, and damned if they didn't zap her back. That poor woman. I don't think she's for us, though, babe. Eighty-nine and fragile as glass. I expect she'll just move on in her sleep soon enough. Sweet woman. Always has a smile ready."

Clara set the plate of nachos in the microwave for a spin, and got him a beer. She poured herself a glass of apple wine because she found it more soothing.

"They oughta be horsewhipped for dragging that poor old dear back. Sit on down, doll. That's what I want to talk to you about."

"Horsewhipping?" he said with a grin.

"About half the time I wish that was the mission given to us. I know I've spent a lot more time than usual on what's to come next."

"I know it's troubled you. I wish I had a way to lift that trouble."

"I had to work through it."

She took the plate out, set it on the table with a couple of paper napkins.

"And I have. The plan's come to me. It's different than before, but it has to be."

"No way around that." He pried out a loaded nacho, said: "Mmm-mmm!"

"We'll be taking him first—and that time has to be decided careful. She'll hear about it right quick, being in the same town and all. We'll take him, bring him here, and keep him sedated."

Puzzled, Sam swigged some beer. "You don't want his story?"

"We'll get it. That's why the timing's so important, doll. We can't wait more than a day or two before going for her. We have to bring her back here, so that's more preparation."

She sipped her wine as she fought off a craving for a couple of MoonPies.

"Protection from her evil for certain, but we're going to need another hospital bed, the straps. I'm not worried about a monitor and all that for her, but we'll need more tubing."

Thoughtfully, she sipped her wine. "We don't use her blood, Sam. It's tainted. We burn it."

He nodded, ate. "Are you sure the straps'll hold her?"

"You know I don't think much of the Papists, doll, but we'll take a page from their book, get us some holy water, a crucifix, and we're going to salt a circle around her bed.

"Now, I'm hoping that's going to work, like I'm hoping we can take her when she doesn't have the gun. But if that's not how it works out . . ."

She rose, went to a kitchen drawer, and took out the Colt her father, and her grandfather before him, had used to shoot vermin.

"Clara!" Shock, and the excitement that rose with it, shined in his eyes. "Babe! You've always said no, big-time no, to using guns."

"She's not like the others, Sam, not fully a human being but at least part demon. We're sending her to Hell, and she knows it. We can't know what she might do."

And Clara had had dreams. Visions? She couldn't be sure, but in them, the witch aimed a gun at her and fired, over and over again.

"It stays here when we take Terrance Brown. But when we go for her, we take the syringe and we take this. We use whatever we need to use. This here is a Colt Single Action Army revolver. It was my grandpappy's. You're going to practice with it, and when the time comes, you'll carry it."

She set it on the table between them, and sat.

"I was going to surprise you with a trip to the beach, down in North Carolina."

"Babe!"

"But, Sam, we're going to have to take some time off real soon, a good week or more, to make sure we know where and when. He won't be different, but like I said, we have to move on her right after, so we have to know."

She lifted her wine again. "Here's how I think we'll need to do it all."

Sloan opened the door to her mother.

"Mom, you don't have to knock."

"Then next time, I won't." She moved in for a quick hug.

"Want a cold drink? I made some iced tea. It's almost warm enough to sit on the front porch. If I had chairs to sit on out there."

"That's exactly why I'm here." Elsie pulled out her phone, swiped. "I was out picking up some new pieces—new-old pieces—for one of the rentals, and saw these."

Sloan angled her head, looked at the screen and the vintage metal chair on it.

"They have two," Elsie continued, "and they just made me think of your front porch. Do you hate it?"

"I don't."

"If you really don't, maybe you want to go by and take a look. I know the rosy pink won't work, but you could paint them a deep coral, even red. They're in excellent shape and priced to sell. So I asked Deke to put a hold them. Just in case."

"Coral," Sloan murmured.

"You're more than handy enough to take care of that. And they have some nice little tables. You need small-scale. You'd want something on the other side of the porch for balance. Maybe a plant stand or a small glider or porch swing."

"I was going to look for chairs, then I didn't take the time. These would work great."

"If you're not too busy, you could come with me, drop these pieces off at Hideaway, then go back to Deke's. I've got the truck."

She hadn't finished her Saturday routine, and when she had, she'd planned to settle in her office, go over the missing investigation from the beginning.

But.

"Let me grab my purse and a jacket."

"You're doing such a good job on this house, Sloan." As she waited, Elsie looked around. "I'm so happy you found a place that makes you happy. And Drea's going to look at another house today. Drea and Theo. I'm so grateful to have both my girls close. Happy and close."

Swinging on a jacket, Sloan walked out with her.

"Tell me what's next for you."

"I think the patio." Sloan climbed in the passenger side. "Might as well finish the exterior and have the rest of the spring and summer to enjoy it. Which means . . ."

"Patio furniture." Elsie wiggled her shoulders, rubbed her hands together. "Oh, boy! Jackpot Saturday for me!"

As she pulled out, turned, a car slipped in behind them.

"A pretty little patio scaled to the house, then you've got enough yard for a birdbath, maybe a bench."

"Nash is in love with me."

Sloan didn't know why she just blurted it out that way. Maybe because it stayed nestled inside her like a secret since he'd told her.

"Yes, baby, I know."

"How do you know? He only told me a couple nights ago."

"Because I love you, too, and I've got eyes. I knew he was . . . *smitten*'s not the right word for Nash. Theo, but not Nash. I knew he was intrigued and attracted right off. And like Theo with Drea, the smitten and intrigued went deeper."

"I've got eyes. I've got really good, observant eyes, and I didn't see it."

Elsie's smile spread slow and warm. "Because you had a blind spot from being in love with him. He's a good man, and God, he suits you."

"You think?"

"I don't have to think when I know. Theo and Drea, they'll be giddy for a while, keep walking a foot above the ground. Then they'll come down and make a good life together. You and Nash have your feet planted. You're one-step-at-a-time people. Drea and Theo are leap-right-in."

She made the turn around the lake, then into the parking slab of the rental.

"It didn't give you a little *hmmm*? Drea, Theo, me, Nash?"

"It's nice and tidy, isn't it?" Elsie said, and made Sloan laugh.

By the time she got out, the trailing car had continued on. She helped Elsie carry in the new-old pieces, and carry out what her mother decided to replace.

"Now the fun begins," Elsie declared, and drove into town. "Spring's settling in. Still too soon to plant—but not for pansies. A pretty pot of pansies would look so good on your porch."

"You're going to have it decorated before I can blink."

"Well, if you get the chairs, I could help you prep them, paint them. If you buy a pot and pansies . . . I haven't spent a Saturday afternoon with my girl in ages."

"I think the chairs are a given. So paint, pot and pansies, and a Saturday afternoon with my mom it is."

"The nursery's closest."

And there, Sloan found a pot that picked up the deep blue of her door, and turned to put it in the cart with the pansies.

"Hey, Sloan. Ms. Elsie."

"Hallie." Sloan put the pansies in the cart and went in for a hug.

"Looks like y'all are doing the same as me." Hallie Reeder, tall, lithe, with a wide-brimmed hat over her fountain of curls, chose her own flat. "Spring fever's got me."

"You look great."

"I feel the same. The wedding's coming right up." She hunched her shoulders in a self-hug. "Part of me can't wait, and the other part's worried there's not enough time to get everything done. So I'm taking a day to plant flowers, and take some over to Diane."

"She sent me a picture of the baby. Justin James Blakley's adorable."

"How are they doing?" Elsie asked. "The new family."

"Mama and Daddy aren't getting a lot of sleep, but they're as happy as happy gets. I'm taking over some flowers so I have an excuse to cuddle JJ awhile. Terry tells me don't get any ideas yet," she said with a grin, "but I've already got them."

She hesitated, then loaded another flat. "Spring fever," she repeated. "And I might as well keep busy since Terry's working a double."

"I hit the Seabreeze for takeout every couple weeks," Sloan told her. "They're lucky to have him."

"That man can cook. It's so good to have you home, Sloan. It's nice to run into a friend over flowers."

"It really is."

"And you've got the best gardener in the Rest with you. I know you had a hand in the town pots, Ms. Elsie. They're just beautiful."

"There's plenty of spring fever to go around."

"And I'm going to put mine to good use. It's wonderful to see both of you. Sloan, we've got to have a serious catch-up soon."

"We'll make a point of it."

When Hallie rolled her cart away, Elsie turned to Sloan. "You really should. Have yourself a girls' night, baby."

"You're right. I haven't made time, but I will. I'll see when Diane's comfortable leaving the baby for a couple hours, and we'll do that serious catch-up all around."

When she stepped back to her cart, she saw the woman, pink floppy hat, sunglasses, browsing the garden statues. And the tall man beside her, a cap over his short twists.

"I saw them in town."

"What?" Elsie walked around a stone urn. "I can use this. Your father will groan, but I can use this."

"That couple over there. Do you see them?"

"Who?" When Elsie turned, they walked in the opposite direction.

"The woman in the pink hat, man in the red cap. I saw them in town the other day."

"Honey, people will shop around, wander about."

"Yeah, but . . . I still couldn't see her face. I'd place her if I did. I'd know where I'd seen her before if I saw her face."

Focused on the stone urn, Elsie answered absently. "They could be locals, could be on vacation. Either way, it wouldn't be strange to see them around town."

"No."

But where else? Sloan wondered. Somewhere not here.

"She saw us again," Clara murmured.

"And we're just poking around like a couple dozen other people. Don't you worry, babe."

"I won't. It's good we're getting more looks at her, too. And we know it wasn't meant for us to try for her today. We don't have the other anyway."

Clara groped for Sam's hand. "Another sign, doll. The woman who hugged her, talked to her's the woman who did CPR on Terrance Brown. The one who helped bring him back when God called him with lightning."

"I know it, babe. We found her picture on the internet. Maybe they're doing the Devil's work together. Maybe she's another witch."

"Can't say for sure, but it's another sign. Still, today's not the day."

"But soon."

"Soon, doll. Let's go on home."


Sloan spent the day with her mother and enjoyed every minute.

As the chairs dried—and coral hit that mark—Drea and Theo drove up. And Drea scrambled out.

"You have to come see the house!"

Elsie pushed back the cap she kept in her truck. "Is it *the* house."

"We really think so." Drea gripped Theo's hand when he stepped up beside her. "It needs a little work, but we wanted that. It'll be more ours that way. But we want everyone to see. We texted Dad, and he said you were over here together. We texted Nash, and he's going to meet us there. Can you come now?"

"Well, the chairs have to dry," Elsie said.

"Oh, sorry. They're great. They'll be perfect. Oh, and you have pansies. A plant stand with a pot of pansies. This is what we want, too. To do the things that make it home."

"Give us five minutes to clean this up," Sloan told her. "We'll follow you over."

Sloan gave another glance back as she climbed in the truck with her mother. She'd give the chairs, and the little table she'd painted navy, another coat. And on Sunday, at some point, she'd sit down and drink some iced tea.

"You're a good sister."

"I'll take the credit, but I want to see the house. Unless we find serious issues, which I doubt, they're going to make an offer on it."

"I doubt the serious, too. They both know what to look for. This is the first one they've looked at that excited them."

It took one look for Sloan to see why. The two-story Craftsman-style house said friendly and tucked itself into a pretty neighborhood with greening lawns, greening trees, and the rise of the hills behind.

"Can't you just imagine watching sunsets from the back deck? And you can see," Drea continued, "they updated this level. Opened it up, really updated the kitchen. I love the white cabinets, and the dreamy blue on the island."

"The basement's unfinished. We'll fix that, right, bro?"

Nash nodded absently at Theo as he wandered. "Yeah, we'll fix that."

"You'll see when we go upstairs, the main suite's good-sized. Two other bedrooms, and a full bath. The en suite in the main needs a serious update."

Dean glanced back at Drea. "We'll fix that, too. I want to take a look downstairs."

He headed off with Nash and Theo.

"There's a perfect space for an office over here. Theo said I could take that, and he'd put his downstairs. And maybe . . ."

Sloan listened with half an ear as she took her own tour, made her own judgments.

She wandered up—nice, sturdy stairs and railing, and knew immediately Drea would soon pore over paint samples. And yes, tile samples, fixtures, lighting for the en suite.

She ran up the estimated cost in her head as she toured, and knew her father and Nash would do the same.

She walked back down. "When do you settle?"

Drea's ponytail swung as she bounced. "You like it? You really like it?"

"It's you so I love it. I'll love it more when you're finished with it."

"They said if we make an offer tonight, and it's accepted, we'd settle by mid-May. We can waive a house inspection because, hello, that's happening right now. And most of the work would be done before the wedding. But I don't care if it takes longer because I just knew when we saw it."

"Like you knew the dress," Elsie said.

"Yes! I see us here, Mom. In the house, in the yard. I see—I might as well tell you we're going to start trying for a baby as soon as we say I do. We're both ready."

"Oh, honey." Elsie folded her in. "You're going to make me cry."

As she hugged back, they heard the men coming upstairs. And Sloan actually heard Drea inhale and hold her breath.

"Solid," Dean said, then held up a hand. "Not finished yet. We're going to take a look outside, then upstairs, the attic space."

"The roof's three years old," Theo began as they went out the atrium doors to the deck.

When they'd finished, Dean nodded. "Solid. Good, solid house. To do what you want downstairs, up in that bathroom, the painting you're going to end up wanting—and knowing Drea's got her mother's taste for those things? Add another fifty, and prepare for sixty."

"You didn't factor Theo's taste," Nash put in. "I'd make it sixty and prepare for seventy-five."

"You want this place?" Dean asked his daughter.

"Oh yes, I do. We do."

"Make your offer. We'll help with the down payment."

"Oh, but I can—"

Dean cut Theo off with a look. "It's what we do."

"Thank you. I . . . thank you."

"Let's do it now, Theo. Let's call and make the offer right now."

"You're buying a house," Nash said, and Theo grinned.

"We're buying a house."

"Then I'm buying dinner. Dean, Elsie, it's something to celebrate."

"It is." Elsie looked down at herself, then spread her hands. "But I'm in my Saturday run-around clothes."

"You're beautiful," he said simply. "Let's make it Ricardo's. We're probably going to be noisy."

They made plenty of noise over pizza and pasta. No one seemed to mind. In fact, Nash noted how many people dropped by the table to have a word with the Coopers. It didn't surprise him. He found himself a little surprised when more than one breezed by to greet him, greet Theo.

When Theo's phone signaled, he picked it up from the table.

"It's Reena. It's the Realtor."

Elsie pointed at him. "Don't even think about taking it outside."

"Right. Okay, here goes. Hey, Reena." He held the phone between his ear and Drea's.

It only took a look at their faces to know, so Nash gave their server the signal.

"Yeah, yeah. This is great. This is everything. We will. That's perfect. Okay. Thanks."

"Thank you!" Drea added as her eyes filled.

Theo set down the phone. "We got the house."

As he and Drea wrapped around each other, people at nearby tables clapped. The manager brought out a bottle of champagne, trailed by the server with a tray of flutes.

"Wow" was all Theo could manage. "Wow."

"Congratulations, Drea," Charlene, the manager—and one of Sloan's former running mates—popped the cork. "Congratulations, Theo. We've all been waiting for the good news. Your brother had us get a bottle chilled."

"I figured first-time homeowners can't celebrate without champagne. And," Nash added, "now I get to kick you out in a few weeks. Over to you, Dean," he said as the server poured the glasses.

"It's your champagne."

Nash shook his head. "Over to you."

"All right then." Dean took a minute, lifted his glass with one hand, took his wife's hand in the other. "A house is just a building. It's the people in it, what they bring to it and each other, that make a home. You're making a home. Here's to many happy years in your home."

"Dad." Drea wiped at tears. "You and Mom, and Sloan, too. You showed me how."

Theo looked at Nash. "I wouldn't be here without you."

"Stop."

"It's true. I wouldn't be here without you, just like Drea wouldn't be here without Dean and Elsie and Sloan. So—and it means a lot to me to be able to say this. Here's to our family."

When Elsie began to weep, Dean put an arm around her shoulders, kissed the top of her head.

"It's fine," Sloan told Theo. "She does that." She reached her glass over the table to tap it to Theo's. "To our family."

# CHAPTER TWENTY-NINE

Sloan came home from work to find both her father's and Nash's trucks in front of the house. By the time she parked, Mop and Tic had raced around from the back to greet her.

"What is this, a party?"

She heard the voices, so with the dogs walked around the house.

And found the patio she'd planned staked out, mason's lines run. Sometime while she'd dealt with an unrepentant poacher, a couple of confused hikers, a group of campers with a collapsed tent, they'd excavated, laid and leveled the gravel, added the layer of decomposed granite over it, and raked it smooth. Working together, they finished up tamping that layer down.

"Where's your work order?" Sloan demanded.

"Dads don't need no steenking work orders." Dean shoved up his cap. "You outlined your patio space with pink paint."

"Coral."

"Close enough. We're doing a dry-set. You wanted flagstone." He gestured toward the piles of stone as Nash kept tamping. "Works with the house. Jonah's handling a trail hike today, Theo and Robo, on another job. I had some time, so I dragged this guy into it."

"I'm getting a lesson," Nash said over the hard hum of the plate compactor.

"Quick study, too. We can start laying the stone tomorrow. I'm going to let the edges meander a bit. It—"

"Goes with the house," Sloan finished. "I didn't expect this."

"That's why it's called a surprise." Dean gestured to Nash. "And he needed the lesson. Looks like you got it, Nash. Let's check the level." Dean glanced back at Sloan. "Sure could use some cold drinks."

"I guess that's the least I can do."

She went in, gave the dogs biscuits before heading to the closet to stow her weapon.

After grabbing a trio of Cokes—making a mental note to pick up more—she took them outside.

Where Nash and her father laid a second stone.

"You said tomorrow."

Dean took the Coke she offered.

"And this one says how we've still got plenty of daylight, and he'd like to see how this part's done."

"Start at one end." Sloan handed Nash the second Coke. "Vary size and shape and color. A natural look. You don't want uniform for this. Level each stone. Don't want any to rock or end up tripping you."

Exaggerating the move, Dean puffed out his chest. "That's my girl teaching you."

"That's just the right gap between those two," Sloan observed. "You know, I may not fill in with gravel. I'm thinking potting soil and Irish moss or chamomile."

"See that?"

Nash nodded at Dean. "Yeah. Your dad just said that's what you should do."

"Because it goes with the house." With her Coke, she walked over to the group of flagstone, examined, considered. Then setting the Coke down, hefted one.

"This one next."

In the woods, Sam peered through field glasses.

"We're right on the time she gets home usually, babe. Giving or taking like a half hour. And yeah, she takes off the gun when she gets here."

"That's what we needed to know."

She took the glasses from him and studied Sloan and the two men with her.

"The dogs worry me some," she admitted as they ran around, sniffed the air, sniffed each other. "But we didn't see a sign of one when we came around yesterday. We don't want to deal with dogs."

"I sure don't want to hurt a dog, but they aren't little ones we can set loose miles away like we did with that woman in Hazelton. So if we have to . . ."

He looked through the glasses again. "I'm betting they go with the men. We'd've seen them in the yard yesterday or heard them in the house when we looked in."

"We don't want to deal with the men either."

"The way they're going at it, they'll have that slab of stone done. It ain't much of a space to cover."

He lowered the glasses, rubbed a hand on her arm. "You know I'm ready when you say, babe. You gotta remember we have to go back to work next week. We can't take more time off."

"You're right. We're as ready as we can be. Wednesday night. I feel that's the time to take the first. We're going to practice, doll. Practice the timing and all the rest."

She took the glasses back for one last look.

"Look at her out there. Thinking nobody sees what she is. She's going to find out different. She's going to find out different real soon."

Even, Clara thought, if ending the demon bitch's life ended her own.

As the sun set, Sloan walked over her pretty new patio. "I think the moss. The little white chamomile flowers are tempting, but I'm seeing the moss. It's just right."

She gave Dean a big hug and kiss. "Thank you. This is a wonderful surprise."

"You've got enough left to start a walkway out front. Nash knows what he's doing now."

"I'm going to keep that in mind." Turning, she wrapped round Nash, kissed him. "Thanks for learning the lesson."

"Well." Dean stuck his hands in his pockets. "I'm taking my dog and my tamper and heading home."

"I'll give you a hand loading that up."

"I've got Tic. Come on, Tic. I'll see what I can throw together for dinner because I'm starving," said Sloan.

Nash rolled the tamper around to Dean's truck, then up the ramp into the bed while Mop jumped in the cab.

Dean shut the bed door, leaned against it.

"You know, I'm aware you and my girl aren't playing gin rummy."

"Your girl is a fascinating woman."

"And nobody's fool."

"That's for damn sure."

"I don't see you as one either. So. Don't screw it up."

"You could say I'm learning a lesson on how to be a part of something."

"Son." He gave Nash a slap on the back. "That's one lesson that never ends."

Dean hopped in the truck, sent Nash a salute, and backed out of the drive.

When Nash came in through the mudroom, Tic was chowing down on his dinner.

Sloan stood at her miserable counter slicing up a chicken breast. "I'm doing a quick chicken stir-fry because starving. I'm having wine. There's one beer left. I've got it on the list for tomorrow."

He went with his heart—another lesson learned. He crossed to her, took the knife, and set it aside. Then he drew her in, letting his heart lead as he kissed her.

"I love you."

She let out a breath, then stroked a hand down the stubble on his cheek. "That's nice to hear. I love you, too."

"I'm getting used to saying it. It takes some practice."

"Practice all you want, because hearing it's never going to get old. Did something happen?"

"I fell in love with you. I'm getting used to it." He rested his forehead to hers a moment. "Okay. Let me wash up and I'll help you chop something."

On Wednesday night, Terry Brown and his crew closed and cleaned the kitchen. For a hump day, they'd been busy, and he credited his dinner special of spiced tilapia sticks for some of it.

He dearly loved to cook. He enjoyed experimenting with new recipes, new flavors and combinations. Just as he loved navigating the heat and chaos of the kitchen.

By his standards, every square inch of that kitchen had to shine clean before he walked out the door.

He felt the same about the kitchen at home, and since he did the bulk of the cooking, Hallie did the bulk of the cleaning.

And grumbled at him whenever he ended up cleaning behind her.

He couldn't help it.

While he had no desire to own or run his own restaurant, he did dream of the day he and Hallie bought a house with a real chef's kitchen.

She wanted a place with room for a garden and a little greenhouse, and he stood right with her on that.

Oh yeah, fresh herbs and veg? All about it.

They saved for it every paycheck.

But the wedding—only three weeks and three days away!—and the honeymoon in the Bahamas came first.

He wouldn't have a day off until Monday, and would do a double on Sunday, but he didn't mind.

Come May he'd have two weeks in the tropics with his lady. His bride.

His wife.

He often thought if a man got hit by lightning and lived to tell about it, and didn't live life as full as he could, that man was just stupid.

Terry Brown's mama hadn't raised a stupid child.

As he did every night, Terry went over his checklist.

"All right! Great job tonight. Boone, that Cajun sauce? Just perfect.

Margo, the raspberry chocolate mousse? Inspired. Now I'm going home to my lady."

Like most nights, several went out the back with him, some to walk home if they lived close enough, others like him to drive. They filled the night air with chatter, a little bitching, some laughs.

He let out a long sigh as he got in his car. A good night, he thought again. And Hallie would be waiting for him.

They'd go over the RSVPs that were coming in for the wedding, maybe play a little more with the seating arrangements. And after he'd peeled off his day, maybe snuggle up together and make sweet love.

He was a little tired, he couldn't deny it. But once he got home, cuddled up with Hallie? That wouldn't be a problem.

He could've driven the winding, rolling roads the six and a half miles home on autopilot. And that ten minutes or so always helped him shed the stress and excitement of a restaurant kitchen.

He'd driven half that when he saw the van, and his headlights washed over a woman looking helpless who waved her arms.

He pulled over. If his mother hadn't raised a stupid child, she hadn't raised an inconsiderate one either.

"Oh, thank you!" Clara, hands on her cheeks, walked to his car as he got out. "I can't think what happened. It just sputtered and died on me. I barely had time to pull to the shoulder. And I'm so careless on top. My phone battery's dead as a doornail."

"Could you be out of gas?"

"I don't— Oh my goodness. Maybe." She put a hand to her face again, and behind it, her eyes flicked left. "I'll check. I don't know what I'd've done if you hadn't come along."

As she stepped back, Terry heard a footfall behind him.

He turned as Sam jumped forward, and swung out. His fist struck Sam's cheek with enough force to jerk Sam's head back. As Terry moved in to strike another blow, Clara rushed in, kicked hard at the back of Terry's knee to buckle it.

Cursing, Sam jammed the syringe into Terry's neck. "Motherfucker!"

"Get him in! Get him in! I see headlights coming."

Terry struggled, weakly, but struggled enough it took them both to drag him in. Sam jumped in behind him.

"Drive, babe! Drive!"

As Sam pulled the door shut, Clara scrambled behind the wheel and punched it.

They were barely a wink of taillights when the oncoming head-lights reached Terry's car, slowed. Then stopped.

"Doll! He hit you so hard. Are you all right?"

"Yeah. Sucker punched me is what he did. He's out now. Sorry about the *motherfucker*."

"I swear I nearly said that myself, I was that scared. This is her doing, doll. I feel it. She whispered right in his ear so he knew you were coming up behind him. Gave him enough strength to hurt you."

"We'll make her sorry for it."

Boone didn't drive this way most nights, but he'd started seeing a woman who'd told him to come on over after work. Since they'd closed down a little later than usual on a weeknight, he'd lingered in the parking lot, texted her to be sure it was still on.

Her reply had given him a real boost.

**I've got the beer cold and the music low.**

Though he knew they were there, he'd checked his wallet for the two condoms he'd slipped in.

He'd driven away with the music and his mood high.

With under two miles to go, he spotted Terry's car.

"Well, shit." No way he could just drive past and leave his boss, and his friend, stranded.

He pulled behind the car, and as he got out, shouted.

"What the hell, Terry. I got a hot date waiting, and . . ."

He opened the door. He didn't see Terry, but saw the keys in the ignition, saw Terry's phone in its hands-free holder.

"What the fuck?"

Thinking maybe Terry needed a quick pit stop, he called out his name. With no response, he went back to his car for a flashlight, shined it into the trees.

"Come on, man, where are you?"

Though he knew Terry wouldn't walk off leaving his keys and phone, he shined the flashlight down the dark road.

As worry began to crawl in his belly, he got out his own phone and called Hallie.

In the dream, Sloan walked away from the gas pumps toward the mini-mart. And as she walked, dread began to spread in her belly. Overhead, a storm that hadn't been there swirled, blocking out the moon and stars and blowing a bitter cold wind.

She wanted to turn back, to drag Joel into the truck, to drive away, away from the lights of the mini-mart, out of the storm.

But she couldn't. Even as the dread spread, pinched, clawed, she couldn't stop herself from walking forward, from opening the glass door and stepping into that hard light.

The counterman radiated terror. In the dream, she heard his thoughts:

*Help me. Please, help me.*

And the man facing him turned. Raised the gun. And fired it.

As the bullets struck her, as pain tore through her, as she fell, she heard music.

She lay a moment, shocked, bleeding, watching the storm build overhead.

Tossed between two worlds, she fumbled for the phone on her nightstand.

"Yes, ah, yes. Sloan. This is Sloan."

"Sergeant Cooper, sorry to wake you. Detective O'Hara."

"Detective." With a hand pressed to her burning chest, she sat up. Beside her, Nash switched on the light on his side of the bed.

She blinked against it, fighting her way out of the dream and into the now.

"There's been another?" she asked.

"It looks that way. I can be at your place in about fifteen. I'd like to brief you in person."

"Yes, of course. Do you need directions?"

"I've got them. Fifteen."

She set the phone aside, rubbed at her eyes. "Detective O'Hara's coming here. Someone else was taken. He's . . . God, I'm slow. He said fifteen minutes. It's someone in Heron's Rest. I have to get dressed."

"I'll put coffee on, then I can head back to my place."

"You don't have to leave. If it is someone from here, word will be out tomorrow. Today," she amended, as the clock said one-fifty. "But if you want to get some sleep—"

"I'd say that's off the table for a while." He yanked on jeans. "You were dreaming. When the phone rang, I could tell you were back there."

"Yeah." She pulled on jeans of her own and decided a sweatshirt would do. "But that's over. This isn't."

"I'll make coffee."

"Thanks."

She took time to go across the hall, splash water on her face, run a brush through her hair. The eyes looking back at her in the mirror were haunted. By the dream, and by whatever was coming.

When she went out, Nash handed her coffee.

"You're afraid you know them. Whoever's missing."

"Odds are. If I don't, someone in my family probably does."

Chilled, not only because April nights ran cool, she gulped down coffee before walking over to start a fire.

"Medical records," she continued, "HIPAA. You can't just Google *Hey, who died and came back to life in Heron's Rest*."

"You did. And this is too fucking close to home."

"I won't argue with that. But those taken weren't trained, weren't aware."

Training and awareness hadn't helped her on that night in November. But, she thought, that was over. This wasn't.

She saw the wash of headlights. "That's O'Hara."

She opened the door as he got out of his car.

Stocky guy of about five-ten, boxer's build. Around fifty. As he stepped onto the porch, she wondered if the broken nose had happened in the ring or on the job.

As he stepped into the light, ruddy complexion, sharp green eyes, he held out a hand.

"Sergeant."

"Detective. It's Sloan," she added as they shook.

"Frank. Nice spot you have here." His gaze flicked past her to Nash.

"Thanks. This is Nash Littlefield."

"Okay. Fix-It Brothers. You did some work for my son and daughter-in-law."

"Jack and Grace O'Hara? Redoing a catch-all room into a nursery. Congratulations."

"Thanks. Looking forward to being a grandpa next summer. New business, right? You're not from around here."

"I am now, via New York. I can get you coffee, then step out."

O'Hara studied him another moment. "She doesn't mind you here, I don't. I'd sure take the coffee. Strong and black."

"Have a seat, Frank." Sloan gestured to a chair near the fire.

"I'll take that, too." He sat, sighed once. "Terrance Brown."

And Sloan shut her eyes.

"You know him?"

"Yes, he's head chef at the Seabreeze—seafood restaurant on Main Street. I don't know him very well. I know his girlfriend—fiancée—better. Hallie Reeder. We went to high school together. Ran track together. I've run into her a few times since I moved back."

Nash brought out the coffee, then sat down beside Sloan on the sofa. "I met him, if it matters. We did some updates to the restrooms in the restaurant a few weeks ago. He brought us out some fish tacos. Asked if he could take a couple pictures of us working."

"Sounds like what we're learning about him. Likes to cook, likes to feed people, likes to take pictures. That's how he got struck by lightning last June."

"He— I didn't know about that. I would've been in Annapolis."

"Lightning hit the tree he was standing next to."

"Side flash," Sloan said. "Not as fatal as a direct hit, but."

"Ms. Reeder saw it happen, called nine-one-one as she ran out. Did

CPR until the ambulance got there. They zapped him. He'd been gone four, maybe five minutes. No memory of the entire day, but otherwise? A lucky son of a bitch. Until tonight."

"Where did they grab him? The restaurant parking lot?"

"No, and we can figure why. They closed the kitchen up about ten—that's pretty routine midweek. The witness, that's Boone Hastings."

"I know him. I went to school with him. He started working at the Seabreeze when we were in high school."

"He and most of the kitchen crew left, with Brown. That's also routine."

"So they couldn't take him in the parking lot. They'd have studied the routine and knew that wasn't viable. Where?"

"Fox Run Road, about three miles from town, on his way home. The witness had a date out that way. He chatted up with some of the other crew for a few minutes after Brown drove off. Then texted the date. His guess is he couldn't have been more than five minutes behind Brown."

O'Hara downed some coffee. "He stopped when he saw Brown's car, figured he'd had a breakdown. But no Brown. Keys in the ignition, phone in the holder. He looked around, called out. Then he called the girlfriend. And she called the cops."

"Like Celia Russell," Sloan put in as O'Hara drank more coffee. "The side of a country road, not well traveled. A route occasionally taken. And fast," she added. "With Boone only minutes behind, they moved very fast."

"He thinks he saw taillights. He's shaken, but he's pretty sure he saw taillights when he slowed down to check out Brown's car. Son of a bitch." O'Hara muttered it, rubbed at his tired eyes.

"They had him staked out, no question. His house, the restaurant, anywhere else he went routinely. They take time," Sloan added. "They plan it out. No signs of struggle? He couldn't have fought long, not within that time frame."

"Nothing. You have to figure they staged a breakdown, van off the shoulder, one of them flagging down."

"A man who makes you fish tacos while you're changing out sinks won't drive by a breakdown." Nash held up a hand. "Sorry."

"No." O'Hara nodded. "You're not wrong. We're leaning toward a woman to do the flagging down, only her visible."

"He'd stop for someone having car trouble," Sloan agreed. "But be less alert with a lone woman than with a couple, or a man. They probably repeated the routine they used with Celia Russell. But for all of them, they'd have to make the grab fast, keep the victim from fighting back, making noise."

"People tend to shut up if you shove a gun in their face."

"But do they?" Sloan shifted to Nash. "First instinct, shout, scream, throw your hands up. Beg, bargain, even struggle. They don't have time for that.

"Janet Anderson, broad daylight," she continued. "Grocery store parking lot, the day before Thanksgiving. Store's bound to be busy with people just like her. *Shit, I don't have enough eggs. Damn it, I forgot the evaporated milk.* It has to be quick and quiet."

"We're thinking they may use a fast-acting sedative. *Oh, would you mind helping me*—and jab. Before they can react, they're in the van."

"Which brings us back to medical personnel, past, present, retired, fired, or working every damn day," Sloan finished.

"We've followed some leads that didn't pan out. The best we have is the woman in the hotel lot when Tarrington was snatched. And a van that may or may not be white.

"I've been working this since February and Tarrington. You putting the bring-back-the-dead angle gave us a pattern. But every time we think we've got something hot, it goes cold."

He polished off his coffee.

"They're not frigging masterminds, and when we get them, they're going to turn out to be loonies. But meanwhile, they've got Terry Brown."

"I think they're in West Virginia, or just this side of the border in Maryland or Pennsylvania."

O'Hara studied her. "We've got focus there. How do you figure?"

"Major hospitals in Morgantown. Some of the victims went to others, but when you see the location patterns of the majority of the grabs, they'd feed into that area."

"You should show him your wall."

O'Hara's brows quirked. "What wall?"

"The wall of my as-yet-unfinished office standing in as a case board."

"I wouldn't mind a look."

"Don't judge," she said as she rose. "There's still a lot of work to be done in the house."

"He'd be handy with that. You know what scared me most when my kids were kids? 'Some assembly required.'"

He went with Sloan to the room off the kitchen and stood, hands in pockets, studying her makeshift case board.

"You're putting in some time."

"It won't let go."

"I hear that. We got a fancier one for the task force, but this does the same thing."

Nash made them more coffee, then stayed out of the way while they talked.

"You've covered ground we've covered. From the looks of it, you covered some of it first."

"And ended up in the same place. Nothing quite solid enough."

"We've got three states involved, but they intersect right there." He circled his fingers where Maryland, Pennsylvania, and West Virginia met. "Cumberland's as far east as we've tracked them, Uniontown north, Morgantown west. But it's concentrated, like you said, here."

He tapped the hospital on the map. "They're not masterminds," he repeated. "And if they're doctors, nurses, EMTs, medical support staff—and I'm with you there—this?" He tapped the hospital again. "This is the big one. Largest staff, patient influx."

He puffed out his cheeks. "We're looking, Sloan. Nobody's rung the bell yet, but we're looking."

Shifting his weight, he looked at her. "They don't hit back-to-back, but they've struck in your hometown now. And you fit the vic profile. You watch your back. I want to hear if you get a bad feeling about anything or anyone."

"I'm watching it. There was a woman," she began as she walked out of the small room with him. "I can't claim bad feeling, but more a bothersome one. I've seen her around a couple times now, and can't give you a good description because I could never get a clear view of her face."

"What's bothersome?"

"I know I've seen her before, but I can't pin it because I can't get that clear view. Can't even give you a solid on her age. About five-four, one-fifty, white, mouse-brown hair. She's with a man. Black, mid to late thirties, about five-ten, a hundred and sixty, black and brown. Hair in short twists. Body language says they're a couple.

"I saw them last week, on Main, across from the Seabreeze, dinnertime. Then again on Saturday at the local nursery. Both times I couldn't see her face, and it felt deliberate. Floppy pink hat, sunglasses, and she turned around too fast when I looked in her direction."

"Across from the restaurant."

"Yeah, and I ran into Hallie at the nursery. I didn't see a white van either time, but it felt off." She glanced back toward her wall. "It feels more off now."

"You saw the man. Enough to work with a police artist?"

"Yeah. I think yes. We get a lot of tourists, Frank, you know that. Or people who have second homes in the area and come up for a few days here and there."

"But it felt off to you."

"It did."

"I'm going to have a police artist work with you. You on tomorrow?"

"I am."

"They'll come to you. It may be nothing, but."

Sloan nodded. "What if it isn't?"

"I'll be in touch. Thanks for the coffee."

She walked him out, then turned to Nash. "I'm probably wasting his time and manpower on this woman."

"He didn't seem to think so. You're good at this. I already knew that, but seeing you with O'Hara . . . You're sure you don't want to go back to that? The criminal investigation?"

"I still do some, and I've never worked anything like this. And this is—it's just different for me. And yes, I'm sure. What I'm doing, where I do it, at least primarily? It rings the bell for me. I wouldn't change it. I just need to see this one closed."

"You'll know, when it is, you had part of it."

"And that'll be enough. Let's try to get some sleep. We're both starting early tomorrow."

She took his hand. "How about this? I'll pick up pizza on my way home tomorrow, and we'll sit out on my new patio, eat, and drink wine."

"You don't have any chairs out there."

"Mom said she saw a couple that would work, and a table. I'm going to tell her to grab them for me. She'll love doing that, so why not let her?"

"I'm going to have the dog tomorrow night."

"He can't have any wine."

# CHAPTER THIRTY

The police artist, a woman with a rainfall of red hair and a tipped-up nose, did come to her. She waited at a trailhead, leaning against her car and sketching the greening trees and the pines.

"Sergeant Cooper? I'm Faith Loggins."

"Thanks for waiting."

"It's really not a problem at all, not on a day like this."

"Officer Sanchez." Elana shot out a hand. "I'll give you some room."

"Thanks, Elana. Why don't you see if those hikers just unloading need any help or direction?"

"I've got it."

"There's a bench over there by the rest station." Sloan pointed. "Will that work?"

"Sure will. Have you ever worked with a police artist before?"

"Not as a witness."

"I can promise, it won't hurt a bit. Why don't you give me general features as you remember. Say, the shape of the face. Round, oval, square, triangular?"

"More diamond-shaped, but squarer on the chin. Oval eyes, long-bladed nose, full lips—fuller on the bottom. Straight thick eyebrows, barely an arch."

"You're going to make this easy."

"I got a clear look the first time. The second time he wore sunglasses, wraparounds. Not quite that sharp at the cheekbones," she said as the artist worked. "A little larger eyes."

"Yours are amazing."

"Thanks. Or thank my grandmother. He wears his hair in short twists. Very neat and tidy."

As they worked, Sloan began to see the man on the page. "That's really close. Ears a little closer to the head. Lips a little . . . I want to say thicker. Really close."

"Close your eyes a minute. Just close your eyes, breathe, and take your mind off him. It must be wonderful to spend so much time outdoors on days like this. Spring's my favorite, when everything's just coming back to life."

"Wild dogwoods and redbuds blooming now. They make a picture."

"Take a look at this one now."

Sloan opened her eyes, looked at the pad. "That's him. You've got him."

"And you made it easy. Do you want to try the woman?"

"I just didn't see enough of her face. White, and the quick glimpse I'd say round face. Short mouse-brown hair, about to here." Sloan cut her hand a couple inches below her ear. "Looked curled under at the ends a bit. I can give you height, weight, what she wore both times, but not her face. But."

Sloan tapped the pad. "She was with this man. For all I know they're a couple from who-knows-where taking a vacation."

"We'll see if we can match this guy, and find out."


Clara checked on Terry Brown. They'd kept him sedated overnight, and now through the morning. Though anxious to hear his story, she thought it best to wait until they had the witch strapped in the bed beside him.

He'd see for himself the difference between good and godly and evil and dark. She considered it a gift to him before they let him go.

Sam came in. "Everything's ready, babe."

"All right. It's a long time to leave him alone, but he's well under. Even if he comes around before we get back with her, he's secure."

She laid a hand on his head. "By tonight, or the morning, he'll go to glory. I've got a strong feeling about this one, doll. He's going right into the light."

Gently, Sam rubbed his bruised jaw. "I've got a strong feeling about him, too."

Laughing, Clara went to him, rose up to kiss that jaw. "Let's give him that as a reflex. The ice packs and the Voltaren's kept the swelling down. That bruise'll fade off in no time. You're still the most handsome man I know."

He gave her butt an affectionate squeeze, but over her head sent Terry a vicious look. When the time came, he'd love every minute of cutting the bastard up.

"I'm going to go pee and get my sweater. If there's someone poking around her house today, we'll keep him quiet till there's not. But I got a feeling it's today. Today's meant for us to expose the witch and send her back to Hell."

"If you feel it's today, it's today."

"She'll burn there, Sam. I can see it so clear. She'll burn for all eternity."

They took their time with the drive. No point in getting stopped for speeding and have some nosy police asking why they had good strong rope in the back of the van, and a jumbo bag of salt.

They weren't trusting zip ties to hold her, and the salt poured around her would keep her from striking out. Duct tape to shut her witch's mouth so she couldn't say evil words.

They had another bag holding half a dozen bottles of holy water and a crucifix they'd ordered from Amazon.

Clara had packed a Bible in there, too, and had another waiting in the room where they'd hold her, dispatch her.

The Lord helped those who helped themselves, she thought as they drove. Maybe she'd be called home, but she'd use every weapon she had to stop the witch from being the one to send her.

They drove the van past the driveway of the blue house.

"See that, Clara? Nobody there. Your feelings are like gold. And I swear I've got one of my own now."

"We've got plenty of time before she usually comes, but we won't take chances. I'm going to circle back and drop you off. I'll drive around the lake while you're making your way through the woods and into the house."

"I'll text you when I'm in, give you the setup."

"Don't you forget to set your phone on vibrate. You text me again when she comes home. You give her at least five full minutes, Sam. Then you signal me when she's had time to put that gun away. And I'll signal you when I'm ready to pull in. Small house like that, you'll hear me knock on the door."

"I know what to do, babe. We've got this, just like all the other times."

"This one's different. Don't you forget that."

He patted the Colt in its holster under his shirt. "I won't, trust me."

"Never trusted anyone more." She pulled over, turned and kissed him like it was the first time. "You be careful now."

"You do the same."

He got out, hitched on the backpack like any hiker. But in his, zip ties, syringes, surgical gloves, a small crowbar as well as the trail mix Clara had made for him.

He didn't much like the woods. Looking at them, all fine, but being in them? Regardless, he'd stay true to the mission, and to Clara.

So he hiked his way back, doing his best to ignore any rustlings, until he circled to the back of the blue house.

He gave it a minute, had just started to step out when damned if a truck didn't drive up.

He hissed out a breath but hunkered down. He watched a woman haul a chair out of the back of the truck, carry it to the patio.

Damn if it wasn't the same woman the witch had been with at the flower place.

Sam could hear her humming as she walked back, carried a second chair. Old metal chairs from what he could see.

Next she carried over a table with a hole in the middle and centered in between the chairs.

"Come on, lady, what the fuck."

Idly, he fingered the gun at his side. Maybe she was another witch, like part of a coven. He could plug her from here, drag her body into the woods. He'd practiced plenty with the Colt.

He wouldn't mind doing that one bit. He wanted to see how it felt to shoot more than tin cans and bottles.

But Clara wouldn't like it, especially if the woman turned out to be human instead of a demon witch.

So he left the gun in the holster and watched.

She brought out one of those umbrellas in a kind of pink/orange color, and fit it into the hole. While his patience frayed, and his stress built, she opened it, stepped back to admire, shifted the chairs a half inch.

Then didn't she go back twice more, hauling back pots of flowers to set on the two back corners of the stone.

Another look, a walk around the patio, a nod.

He heard her say: "She'll love it. Paint them this weekend, and completely charming."

She pulled out her phone, checked the time.

"Why does everything take just a little longer than I thought?"

And finally! She walked back to the truck, got in, drove off.

He waited, made himself wait, then eased out of the woods. Nobody home, he knew that for certain or somebody would've come out.

He swung off the backpack, got out the surgical gloves, the crowbar. They'd agreed the kitchen window made the best sense. Nobody driving by would see him. He tested it first, but like the time they'd checked out the house, found it locked.

He got to work with the crowbar, and had the window open in minutes.

She'd see the marks if she looked at it from outside, but why would she?

He had to crawl in over the sink, shove the faucet out of his way. Then he eased down on the floor, took a slow look around.

He opened a door, looked down at steps, and smiled. Just like they'd figured. And he'd hole up there on those basement steps when she got home.

He texted Clara.

I'm in, babe.

**It took so long! I was worried.**

Some woman came by with chairs and stuff for the patio

they were making. I had to wait, but she's long gone. Got the basement right here like we thought.

You stay out of sight, doll. It shouldn't be more than another hour. Remember, when you hear her come in, send me a heart emoji.

And you send me one back. I got it. Love you, babe.

She acknowledged that with a kiss emoji.

He'd stay out of sight, Sam thought. But damned if he'd stay down in that basement—looked spooky—for an hour or more.

No reason not to see how a demon witch lived.

Turning, he found himself facing her office wall.

"Holy shit! Holy fucking shit!"

Sweat pearled on his forehead, slid down his spine.

She knew! She knew about all the resurrected. He hadn't remembered all those faces, but he did now as they stared back at him from the wall. And a map with pins in it marking locations, times and dates and all of it on that wall.

He wanted to tear it all down, burn it and the house with it. He promised himself they'd do just that. Get the witch, then burn it down. He wished they could burn her with it.

Maybe, maybe Clara would feel the same after she saw.

He went into the bedroom, rifled through drawers. He found earrings he thought suited Clara, and pocketed them without a thought. In his hunt, he found a hundred and twenty in cash, and pocketed that.

Waste not, want not.

In the bathroom, he found some nice-smelling soap, and took it for Clara.

So he wandered, taking what caught his eye, including a banana from the fruit bowl on the counter.

From the fridge he looked at the beer, but took a Coke instead. Keep sharp for the work to be done. Checking the time, he took the banana, the Coke, sat with them on the basement steps with the flashlight on his phone to ward off the spooky.

In town, Sloan ordered the pizza, started to text Nash she'd be home in about a half hour, but Charlene stopped by.

"Did you hear about Terry Brown?"

"Yes, and they're doing everything they can to find him."

"Do you know anything? I stayed with Hallie last night after she called me. She's worried sick."

"I wish I did. If you see her, tell her I'm doing all I can, too. She can call me anytime."

Nothing else to do or say, Sloan thought. They hadn't contacted her about the sketch. Either they hadn't found a match, or they had and hadn't told her.

She could only hope it was the latter.

She took the pizza out to the car, and as she had when she went in, looked up and down for the woman, the man.

Then texted Nash.

Home with pizza in fifteen.

Just finishing up for the day. I won't be much longer than that. Pour the wine. I can use it.

Right there with you.

And thinking of home, thinking of Terry, thinking of too many things, she drove out of town.

Terry surfaced, groggy, disoriented, more than a little sick to his stomach. For a moment he thought he'd been struck by lightning again and unable to move his arms, his legs.

Then he remembered.

He looked around the room with wide, glazed eyes. Like a hospital room, but bigger. He was propped in a hospital bed, he realized. And strapped down.

Terror had him calling out. Coughing to clear his throat, then shouting. He saw the bed beside his, like his, with straps.

"What is this place!"

He saw a single window covered with a blackout shade. Someone had left the long tubes of florescent lights on overhead.

It might have been worse if he'd woken in the dark, but he didn't see how.

"What do you want? Who are you?"

He twisted his wrists, strained. He was no weakling. He'd break the straps.

"Somebody! Somebody help me! I'm here!"

He fought the straps while his wrists, his ankles burned and bled.

When Sloan pulled up to her house, she considered contacting O'Hara, then dismissed the idea. She trusted if he had anything, he'd contact her. No point, she told herself, taking up his time when he could use it looking for Terry.

Was he still alive? God, she hoped so.

How long did they keep their victims alive? A day, a week? Longer?

Logic told her a week at most, and probably less. Holding a person by force took time, effort, attention. Food and water, unless denying both was part of it.

But for Terry, less than twenty-four hours had passed. There was room to hope.

And time, she told herself as she reached the mudroom, to put it aside for a few hours. Obsessing about it wouldn't help Terry, wouldn't comfort Hallie.

She started to unlock the door, then glanced over, let out a whoop!

She took another step forward to admire the chairs, the sweet umbrella table, the Elsie-can't-resist pots of pansies.

Different style of chairs than the porch, but the same vintage, the same feel. Maybe paint them navy, and the table coral.

She started forward, just to sit, remembered the pizza.

She'd take it in, get out the wine, spruce herself up just a little. Then she and Nash would sit on the patio, just like she'd imagined.

She unlocked the mudroom, stepped inside.

The minute she stepped into the kitchen, she knew someone had been inside her house.

She always left the faucet on the right side of the double sink. Now it hung over the left. The fruit bowl on the counter wasn't centered, and the fruit in it jumbled.

Someone had been in her house, and as she drew her weapon thought: And maybe still was.

Taking a step forward, she swung toward her office. Empty, but her laptop sat crooked on the desk.

Leading with her weapon, heart skipping beats, she swung right, then left. Listened, listened, listened, but heard nothing. Her floors creaked here and there, something she found charming. But she heard none of that.

She walked to the front closet, sucked in a breath and flung the door open. No one, but someone had been in or looked in there. The hangers had been pushed to the side, her winter uniform hat sat sideways instead of straight on, and the scarf she'd made for herself, gone.

No one broke into a house to steal a scarf.

She checked the pocket of her winter parka where she kept a twenty for emergencies.

Gone.

She shut the door, scanned the living room. No cobalt bowl she'd picked up antiquing with Sari years before. No slender green vase Drea had given her.

She'd clear the house, call it in.

She started to step back when she heard someone pull in. She expected Nash, walked to the door.

And through the window saw the dark blue van, and the woman getting out of it.

And the face clicked, a key in a lock.

Clara. The doctor—Marlowe—called her Clara. A nurse manning the ER desk at WVU hospital.

She stepped onto the porch. With the gun held to her side and just behind the door, Sloan opened it.

"Oh, I'm so glad somebody's home! I've gotten so turned around I don't know where I am."

"Is that right?"

"My sense of direction doesn't exist!" As she laughed, Clara's eyes flicked over Sloan's shoulder. Even before she heard the soft creak, she spun around.

He rushed toward her, a syringe in one hand, a gun in the other.

It happened fast, but for an instant she stood in the mini-mart, the lights too bright, a gun rising toward her, ready to fire.

This time, she fired first. As she did, the woman leaped onto her back, screaming. The man took a staggering step forward, eyes filled with the pain she knew too well. The gun rising to aim at her chest.

Sloan fired again, then twisted her body to send the woman dropping to the floor.

Screaming still, Clara crawled toward the man lying bloody and still. Sam, she called him in a voice that sounded to Sloan's ringing ears far, far away.

Training had her stepping on the gun he'd dropped.

Footsteps raced from behind, and she spun again, only to lower her gun with a shaking hand as Nash rushed in, the dog on his heels.

"Sloan! Jesus Christ. Are you hurt? Are you hurt?"

His hands flew over her even as she shook her head.

"I need—I need you to call nine-one-one. Have them contact O'Hara. I need you to . . ."

"I've got it. I've got it."

"A handkerchief, a bandanna."

Snapping at Tic to sit, Nash yanked one out along with his phone. She took it, wrapped the gun, put it inside the closet, though she wondered if Clara even remembered it.

She still knelt on the floor, still calling for Sam, as she did chest compressions with blood-soaked hands.

"Don't leave me! Sam, Sam! I thought I would pay the price, not you. Not you. Don't go!"

But he was gone, Sloan could see it. Pain didn't live in his eyes now. Nothing did.

When a wave of heat washed over her, she reached down into her gut to steady herself.

Do the job, she ordered herself. Do the next step, then the one after that.

She got her restraints, dragged Clara back far enough to secure her hands behind her back.

Clara's teeth snapped as she twisted her head, tried to bite. "Keep your hands off me, witch! He needs help."

"He's beyond help. You're a nurse, you can see that. Is Terry alive? Where is Terry Brown?"

"Burn in hell, go back to hell and burn."

As Tic whined, Nash laid a hand on his head to keep him still.

"They're coming, Sloan. What can I do?"

"In the van. Find the registration, find an address, call that in. They need to find Terry. Wait. Keep her off me."

She steeled herself again, and went to the body.

"Don't you touch him with your evil hands." As Tic leaped and growled, Clara struggled against Nash, then just sank down. She keened like an animal while Sloan pulled out Sam's wallet.

"I've got it." She rose, stepped back, and called O'Hara.

"I'm ten minutes out, ambulance is two."

"I have an address. You need to send the locals for Terry. He could still be alive." In the distance, she heard sirens. "I—the male suspect, Samuel Dunley, is down. Is dead. I shot him. I shot him. He's dead."

"You take it easy. Hold it steady. The female?"

"Secured. She's Clara—I don't know the last name. A nurse at WVU, Morgantown. I saw her there. I saw her."

"You hold on, Sergeant. You hold the scene. Understood?"

"Yes. Hurry, okay?"

"I see what you are." As tears streamed, Clara hissed out the words. "Devil's whore. You'll pay for eternity for what you've done."

Sloan crouched down. Her heart beat too fast, her ears rang, but she looked Clara in the eye. "Is Terry Brown alive?"

"This life is false. They dragged him back into it. He was called home by lightning. Man is not allowed to bring the dead to life. We send them home. Our mission is holy and blessed."

"Have you sent him home?"

"Because of you he'll be trapped in this false life, an abomination, a lie. Sam's gone to glory now, but not in his time. You had no right to decide to end his life."

"But you and Sam had a right to take mine?"

Clara bared her teeth in a snarl. "An obligation."

Sloan straightened as the ambulance pulled in. She teetered a little, but Nash held back the urge to steady her.

"I have to . . ."

"Go ahead." He put a hand on Tic's head again as the dog stood beside him. "We'll watch her."

"She'll take you to Hell with her," Clara warned as Sloan stepped onto the porch.

"I doubt that, but if she does, you can save us a couple seats."

He stood back when O'Hara and others arrived. Then stepped outside to give them room as they put up police tape.

A man in an NRP truck pulled in, leaped out. "Sloan Cooper," he snapped.

"She's fine. She's not hurt. She's inside."

"Who the hell are you?"

"Littlefield, Nash Littlefield."

"Got it. Travis Hamm. I'm Sloan's captain, and I'm family. I'm going in."

"Does the rest of her family know she's okay?"

"They wouldn't know any of this yet." Travis hesitated. "Let them know, but lead with that. She's okay, she's not hurt."

In the end, he waited outside with her family, with his brother. A unit, he'd think later, bound by sick worry and terrible relief.

When she came out, he let her parents, her sister hold her first.

"I'm fine. And Terry's going to be. They found him, and he's already at the hospital. Abrasions, lacerations from restraints, but he's going to be fine."

"Thank God for that." Elsie hugged her in again. "Are you sure they didn't hurt you?"

"Absolutely sure. And now they won't hurt anyone else."

When they brought a body bag out, Nash watched Sloan's eyes cloud, before she closed them and held her mother harder.

O'Hara brought Clara out. "Sergeant Cooper, you have the suspect's full name now. Make the arrest."

"I—"

"Charges and rights. You know the drill."

"Clara Burch."

Clara cast her eyes up, raised her voice. "I call on the Almighty to strike you down."

"I don't think he's listening. Clara Burch, you're under arrest for the assault, abductions, forced imprisonments, and murders of Alyce Otterman, Wayne Carson, Celia Russell, Janet Anderson, Arthur Rigsby, Zach Tarrington, and Lori Preston."

"We let them go. We sent them home, and all of them glory in their homecoming."

"The assault, abduction, and false imprisonment of Terrance Brown. You have the right to remain silent," she continued, and read Clara her rights.

"Your time will come, and there will be no mercy."

"Loonies," O'Hara said with a hard smile. "Did I call it? Do you want to sit in on the interview, Sergeant?"

"No. No, thanks. I've had enough."

"You change your mind, you know how to reach me. Family?"

"Yes, my family."

"You got one tough woman here, one solid cop. She saved lives today. Come on, Clara, time to go."

"In His time," Clara shouted as O'Hara marched her away. "In His time the Almighty will strike you down. He does not suffer a witch to live!"

"Yeah, yeah, yeah," O'Hara muttered, and loaded her in the back of a car.

Sloan stopped herself from rubbing a hand over the scar on her chest.

"I need to go back in for now. It's going to take a while. I'll have the next few days off. I'll come over, Mom, Dad, I'll come over tomorrow, tell you everything. Cap's here, so please don't worry."

"Why should we?" Dean countered. "You're one tough woman, one solid cop. And you're still my little girl."

He grabbed her, held her, then let her go.

"Day off all around tomorrow. I'm making pancakes. Ten o'clock."

"I'm going to take Tic." Theo glanced at his brother, sent a message without words. "We're staying at Drea's tonight. Closer to pancakes."

Drea leaned in, whispered in Sloan's ear, "Call if you need me."

As they left, Sloan turned to Nash. "It'll take a little while yet."

"I'll wait."

She shut her eyes, then held up a hand when she opened them. "I can't . . . Not yet. Just thanks."

She went back in, and he settled in to wait.

# EPILOGUE

She said nothing when she came out again, looked back at the team still processing.

"I walked over. If I'd driven . . . Well, I didn't. We'll need to take your car or walk."

"Walk. Oh God, yes, walk."

They'd gotten to the end of the drive, made the turn to his when she stopped, bent over.

"Jesus, oh Jesus. Minute."

"It's okay." He stroked her back, felt the shaking start. "Breathe, Sarge. Slow breaths."

"Trying. I need—"

"To take your time."

"I killed a man. Oh God, God, I killed a man. I didn't even hesitate. I just fired."

"And I'm thanking any god there is for that. You saved lives today, just like O'Hara said." As he spoke, quietly, he stroked her back. "You saved your own, you saved Terry's, and you saved mine."

When she just shook her head, he ran a hand over her hair. "Yeah, mine, too. I was steps away, and I wouldn't—couldn't—have stopped."

When she straightened, he put an arm around her. "Lean on me. Even tough women know how to lean."

"Oh, I'm leaning. I couldn't fall apart in front of the family."

"Why?"

"Because they were already scared. Because what happened before would've been right there for them. It was for me."

She shook so hard he wanted to just pick her up and carry her, but she took the next step.

Just as she had the first time he'd seen her on the lake path.

"He was already in the house. I knew someone was in there, or had been, the second I came in. Little things not exactly as I'd left them. Little things missing. I thought maybe kids, but . . ."

"You watched your back."

"Yeah." The next breath she drew in came easier now. "I had my gun out, clearing the house, and was about to call it in when she drove up. Blue van. A van, that was the first trigger. Then I saw her, and knew. ER nurse, I'd seen her, spoken to her when I was checking on hospitals."

Absently, she rubbed at her chest.

"Her eyes flicked from mine for just a second when I opened the door."

"You let her in."

"I was armed, and she was the link to finding Terry. That eye flick, and I swung around. He came at me, gun, syringe. I shot him. She jumped on my back, he kept coming, and I shot him again, knocked her off. And you were there."

"I saw the van, heard the shots. Christ, now I have to stop and breathe a minute."

She let a few tears come. "You can lean on me, too."

"I've been scared in my life. When I was a kid, they scared the crap out of me plenty. But I haven't been that frightened since I thought Theo drowned. You handled it."

"Part of me was sliding back and forth from the living room to the mini-mart."

"And you handled it."

"The things she said. They killed people because they decided they were meant to. And me? They had holy water and other things in that van. She'd convinced herself I was a witch, a demon sent to stop them from saving the resurrected."

Finally, they turned into his drive, walked toward the house.

"The cops who found Terry? They found labeled packets of blood. The victims' names. They drained them, Nash, but before, they demanded—they recorded—what they called their stories. What they experienced during clinical death. They had the tubing, medical equipment, restraints, and when they had what they wanted recorded, they exsanguinated them."

"Jesus Christ."

"They found a box with personal items of the victims. Like . . . keepsakes. And then?"

She pressed a hand to her belly. "Oh God, they found a well, they found bone saws, lye. It looks like they cut up the victims, dumped them in there, threw in lye."

"Tell me she's not going to do some time in an institution. Tell me she's going to prison."

"Not up to me. Either way, she'll never get out. Not with what they've found."

"Why don't we sit outside? You sit on the porch. Water or wine?"

"Oh. Can I have both?"

"I'll get you both. One thing first."

Now he pulled her in, hung on. "I need to do that leaning. I heard those shots . . . I love you."

"When you ran in, and Tic? Part of me knew it was all right. I could get through it. I felt sick, my hands were shaking, but I knew I could get through it."

"Sit." He kissed her forehead, her cheeks, her lips. "I'll be right back."

She sat, breathed in and out, listened to the birds. It wasn't like a dream this time, she thought. And if it all played back in dreams?

She'd done what she had to do.

He brought her a glass of water, a glass of wine, and one for himself.

"Can you put it away now?"

"It'll take a few days. I fired my weapon, and a man's dead. Self-defense, and there's no question of that. But there's a process. I'm fine with it. And Terry Brown will get married in a few weeks."

"That's not what I meant."

She looked at him. "Yes, it'll take time, but I can put it away. Janet Anderson, and all the rest, their families . . . It'll be horrible for them, but they'll know. And Terry? His family won't have to grieve."

"This didn't ruin the house for you?"

"No." She took a sip of wine and stared at the greening trees, the splashes of color from the redbuds. "I won't let it."

"I don't want it to, but I want you to move in here."

"Nash, I'll be fine."

"Sure, but I want you to move in here. Tonight moved that step up. I'd planned to take it when I had the library done, your office planned out."

"My office?"

He shot her a look. "Did you really think I wanted a sitting room? You can keep your place as a sanctuary when you need it, if you do. Or we finish it, and you fold it into the family business, whatever.

"It's your house, so you do what you want with it. But I'm asking you to live with me. Here."

He drank some wine. "Maybe it's not altogether fair to push you on this when you're still a little shaky, but I am anyway."

"You want to live together?"

"I want to live with you. I want you to help make this house home, for both of us. That's this step."

"It's a big one. And there are more?"

"I'm not going to take the shine off Theo, or Drea. They plan their wedding, they have their wedding. Then we can start planning ours."

"I—" She nearly bobbled the wineglass until he reached over to level it. "Excuse me?"

"That's the next step. We can look at the one after that, actually getting married, over the winter or next spring. Whatever, because we'll live here first."

He looked over at her. "I'm not asking you now. I'm just letting you know what's coming after Theo and Drea have their wedding."

"That's considerate of you."

"I'm made of considerate."

She hadn't believed she'd laugh again for days, but it bubbled right out. "So you have this planned out."

"It's something I do."

"It is. It's something I do, too. This is a really great house. Of course, if I lived in it, I'd have ideas about a lot of things yet to be done."

"That's understood."

"I've got a nice bathroom, but yours? That really weighs on your side of things. Then there's the coffee bar, and another in the closet upstairs. Really heavy weights."

"The glass rail system on the upper porch should count."

"It does. It really does."

She felt her shoulders unknot, her stomach smooth out.

"I like winter," she said. "I missed the winters up here when I lived in Annapolis. The frozen lake, the white hills. But . . ."

She got up, slid into his lap. "Since I want to get married outside, outdoors, it'll have to be spring. May, I think, or early in June."

She angled her head to meet his eyes. "Oh, I'm not saying yes now, just letting you know I will."

He ran a hand over her hair. "Considerate of you."

Smiling, she met his mouth with hers.

"And that first step?"

"I've got a few days off, so I can move in easy enough. We have to find a place for my pansies."

"Anywhere you want. I don't have to practice saying it anymore. I just have to love you."

"Just remember, hearing it never gets old. Look at us, Littlefield. This is what they call a happy ending."

"Or a beginning."

"I like that even better."

She settled her head on his shoulder.

She'd been given a second chance at life. She'd been given love and a promise of a future.

And she wouldn't waste any of it.

# ABOUT THE AUTHOR

Bruce Wilder

**Nora Roberts** is the #1 *New York Times* bestselling author of more than 240 novels, including *The Mirror, Mind Games, Inheritance, Identity*, and many more. She is also the author of the bestselling In Death series written under the pen name J. D. Robb. There are more than 500 million copies of her books in print.